SAVAGE WILD SOULS

THE SAVAGE WILDS
BOOK TWO

SEAN FLETCHER

To the resilience of the human spirit.
May it always shine in the darkest places.

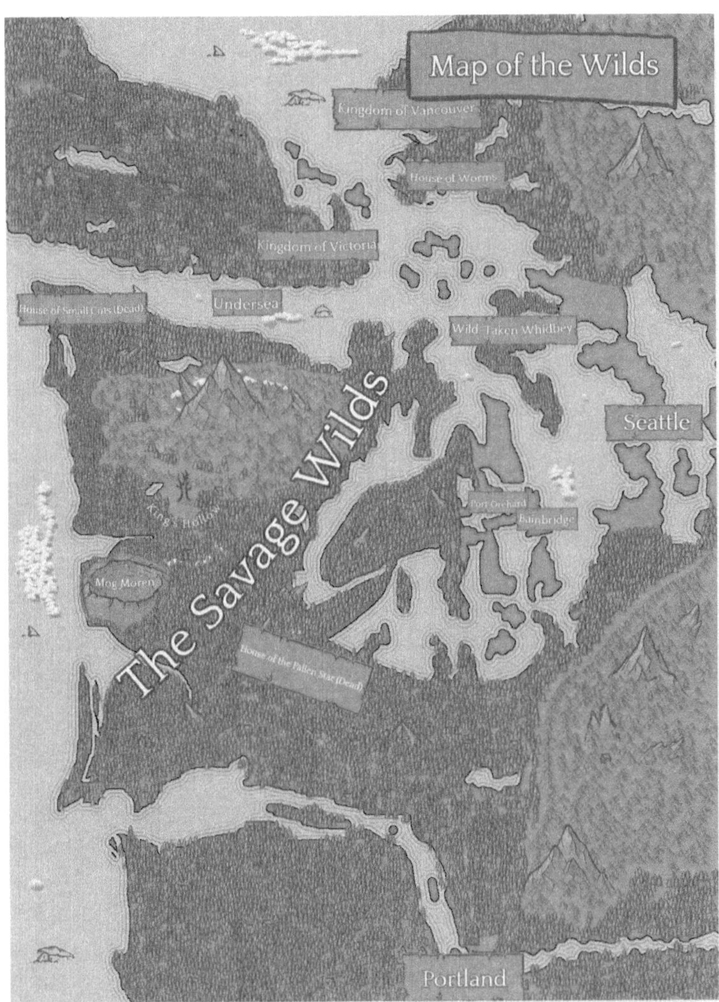

Map of the Wilds
Kingdom of Vancouver
House of Worms
Kingdom of Victoria
House of Small Ones (Dead)
Undersea
Wild-Taken Whidbey
Seattle
King's Hollow
The Savage Wilds
Port Orchard
Bainbridge
Mog Moren
House of the Fallen Star (Dead)
Portland

"Uneasy lies the head that wears the crown."

Henry IV, Shakespeare

"Power tends to corrupt, and absolute power corrupts absolutely."

Lord Acton

I was covered in grit all the time lately. Fine crystal dust between my teeth. Flecks of obsidian beneath my fingernails. Smears of coal across my skin. The filth made me feel inhuman.

Ironic, considering what I now knew.

As the guards escorted me, I smacked my lips to try to get rid of the taste of dirt. In the month—Had it been a month? Time was impossible to tell down here, and they wouldn't give me a clock—it had lingered no matter what I did. Like my last memory of Rune's bloody face screaming my name as I was dragged Below.

Sotera, Empress of Those Below, waited for me on the bridge spanning my cell and the Deep. She was smiling. That was never good.

"I hope you had a nice rest," she said. "I expect you to do better than yesterday."

When I didn't answer, her inhumanly beautiful, cruel face, composed of patches of luminous blue crystal and flesh, twisted in a frown. "You look troubled."

"No kidding?" I snapped. "I wonder why that is."

I hadn't slept well for a single night since being taken here. It was more than the hard bed they'd given me, so different than the root-made ones of the Wilds. It was the nightmares.

I squeezed my eyes shut against the onslaught of images. Night after night I'd dreamed of Father Dumas, leader of the worshippers of the Mother Tree, plunging a knife into my arm. Carving my flesh down to reveal my crystal bone. The light shining from it reflecting off his maniac, too-wide eyes.

That hadn't happened. Peyton had never left me alone with any worshippers of the Mother Tree.

Still.

I glanced at the pulpy, pale scar on the inside of my left forearm. It was only coincidence that it was in the same place Father Dumas had supposedly cut. Being down here had dragged up long-forgotten memories and conjured false ones.

It didn't matter what the nightmare showed, anyway. I knew what I was now. Or rather, I knew what other people thought I was.

One of Those Below.

Sotera's *cherished*.

"Little fox," Rune's voice taunted. "My trick."

I'd been that for him. And we'd all paid dearly for it.

"Isn't it beautiful?"

Sotera motioned for me to join her at the edge of the bridge. The city—the Deep, as they called it—spread out before us. From here, the people of the Deep were nothing but shadowy forms in the dusky light.

Just like everything else Below—the fake sunlight, grass, wood—the city resided in the uncanny valley; it appeared close to real, down to the color and texture, but still off-putting in a way that was difficult to describe. Steam rising from geothermal vents coiled around the Deep's dwellings and settled over fields of pitiful crops. In the distance, across jagged plains of crystal, was the black outline of subterranean mountains.

There wasn't a bit of real greenery in sight. Not a leaf. Not a tree. Not the sliver of a vine. Nothing living. Nothing natural.

All my life I'd been told to fear the dangerous green depths of the Wilds. Now, I feared I'd die here without seeing them one last time.

The dark chasm beneath my feet seemed to beckon me in.

"You could end it all," Sotera said. "Take one more step and hurl yourself into oblivion. It would be a far less painful death than any you'd receive from me."

Rune told me once about his time in the prison of Mog Moren. How he'd stayed alive out of pure spite so he could one day pay his captors back.

I returned Sotera's smile with one as cold as my surroundings. "I won't give you the satisfaction of knowing you drove me to do it."

If my smile was cold, Sotera's was downright frigid. "I know you won't. It's good you have some spirit left. Perhaps that will lead to better results today. Come."

I was past resisting her commands. I had the first week or so, but my lingering bruises and the threat of others getting hurt in my place made me give up.

I sped up as Sotera crossed another of the Below's many bridges in long strides.

The sun-forsaken Deep was split into three tiers, each made of slabs of obsidian, petrified wood, jade, and agate.

We snaked up treacherous stairs leading to the first tier's tight, crooked streets that bordered a steep drop off into another chasm. Sotera's presence was noted almost immediately, and soon a small crowd of Those Below flocked to us. More appeared from within cramped houses and nooks and crannies that led to the lower tiers, like worms pushing through the ground.

Sotera smiled as she cut a path through them. I tried to keep my arms tucked to my side and follow close behind, but Those Below knew by now that her arrival meant mine—Sotera's cherished.

"Stop," I bit out as one grabbed me hard enough to bruise. A hand shot through the grasping throng and pinched my cheek. I whirled. "I said—"

But the perpetrator was lost among the crowd, and more surged forward. I should have been used to this. They'd never seen anything like me. Most of them had flesh faces, but the rest of their bodies were patchworks of crystal and rock. I, entirely clothed in skin, was supposedly their purest form.

The only thing I felt like was a piece of meat.

Sotera looked amused as another grabbed me. "You don't seem to be enjoying yourself, Cherished. You should be happy. You give them so much."

"Like what, a target?" I asked. I ducked to avoid another hand. The guards stationed behind us, of course, did nothing.

"You give them something to aspire to. When we breach the surface, all of them will become as you are." She placed a gentle hand on a weeping woman's head, leaned down, and kissed the top of it. "Enjoy their adoration."

I was suffocating, like breathing lulling yarrow spore. I'd been reduced to nothing but a tool for others to gawk at while Sotera played games with purposes I didn't know and prepared to destroy my home and everything above.

I shut my eyes against another pinch and took a deep breath. I could endure. I didn't know for how much longer, but I could endure.

At last, the narrowed streets ended and the guards blocked off the last remnants of those who followed. Sotera led me down a few steps into a shallow, tiled courtyard where the latest ones chosen had been assembled.

When Sotera brought me here the first time, I'd been shocked at the state of those she'd picked. Most were old, with dust-crusted beards and wrinkles chiseled into their fleshy faces. The young were often sickly, looking as though they'd been dragged from wherever Those Below received medical help and propped up in line with the others. It seemed like a cruel punishment to be forced to endure her scrutiny, but the chosen's eyes always shone with reverence as Sotera walked before them.

"Empress," one murmured as Sotera gently placed a hand on her head before moving to the next. Soon, Sotera's palm was slick with the oil the chosen's loved ones had anointed on their heads. Strings of glittering gems had been draped around their necks and across their bodies. Sotera reached the end of the line.

"What do you think?" she asked me. "Will they be enough to work with?"

I gave a curt nod. I couldn't bear to meet the chosen's eyes.

Sotera jerked her head to her guards. "Bring them."

As the guards helped the sickly and old hobble out of the courtyard, Sotera took her place beside me once more. "I would have thought you'd have become used to it by now. Compassion is a weakness you must purge."

"Screw you," I muttered.

Sotera smiled before stepping into the street. "Rejoice," she called to the crowd. "Your loved ones have been specially selected. They will be revered above all others."

I tried to block out the grateful crying and shouts of joy. They thought their loved ones were being healed and prepared to fight for their beloved Empress. If they only knew the truth.

When the last of the chosen were taken away, we passed

through a grove of crystal oaks so detailed I could make out veins on the leaves. Below us was a lake of fire circled by a riffled shoreline, a magma river feeding into it.

I was coated in a sheen of sweat and already flagging by the time we crossed the last bridge out of the Deep. Sotera looked perfect. The enormous crystal sword she always had strapped to her belt swung easily with every step.

Normally, she left me at the crossroads, letting the guards take me to where I "practiced". This time, someone was waiting for us.

Sotera frowned as the older man waddled over, his gait stiff. "I don't recall summoning a meeting with my war council, Ulmid."

Ulmid? This must have been one of Sotera's numerous generals, the ones leading the assault on the Wilds through the sporadic and constantly shifting cracks in the earth's crust.

The crystal around Ulmid's joints had started to harden, creating fine fractures in the incandescent surface. Those Below didn't bleed, not like I did, but watery black grit leaked out. His skin-covered hands and face were wrinkled and sand-colored, coarse hair pinned with shards of nephrite those of the elite preferred.

"Empress." Ulmid gave a hasty bow. "I'm afraid this can't wait. The latest wave, the location you—*we*—determined was right, it has been... *He* has been busier—"

"Quiet!" Sotera seethed. Her eyes flickered to me, but I'd heard enough for elation to cut through the layer of numbness that seemed to have built around me like a second skin. A warmth I used to recognize as happiness rose to the surface.

He. Rune. It had to be. As the new High King of the Wilds, he was the biggest threat to Sotera's planned takeover of the above.

Ulmid could tell he'd royally screwed up. "Eternal apologies, Empress. If you'll allow me and General Abaki to try—"

"Wait for me with the others," Sotera said. "We'll discuss this later."

"I feel it may be prudent to speak of this with all possible haste—"

Sotera rested a hand on the hilt of her sword. "Do you recall what happened to the last general who failed to do as I asked? You will wait with the others."

Ulmid hurriedly rattled off another apology before stumbling away, followed by an entourage of various assistants. Sotera stared across the jagged plains of crystal that separated the Deep from the caverns and less hospitable desert. She snapped her fingers at one of the guards.

"Three, this morning."

He hesitated before bowing and hurrying off. Sotera must have caught my elated smile because she smirked. "I pray that's not hope you're feeling. Hope can just as quickly be the wings that carry you upward as the stone that drags you down. Don't *hope* this changes anything."

I couldn't resist smiling wider. "Then why do you look so pissed?"

The guard returned, riding an enormous wyrm and leading two others. I didn't know the real names of the enormous, snake-like beasts, so I stuck to calling them earth wyrms. Because their elongated bodies and slitted eyes looked like mythical wyrms and their diamond-hard scales could burrow through the earth and even crystal. Exhaustion had left me with little creative energy.

Dread curled in my stomach as Sotera mounted one. "You're coming with us?"

She took the reins and expertly brought it about. "It's time

I saw your progress in-person. Don't keep me waiting or you'll regret it."

As always, my hands were bound to the reins of my earth wyrm, as though Sotera feared I would throw myself upon one of the jagged crystals we rode past or down one of the numerous bottomless chasms.

They needn't have worried. I'd meant what I said: I wouldn't give Sotera the satisfaction of breaking me. Especially today, of all days, when she had actually come along.

Mind spinning, I kept my gaze fixed on her back as the wyrms undulated through stone and sand. She had always left me with the guards and gone to do her own thing—be it confer with her generals or whatever dozens of other tasks required of a bloodthirsty ruler intent on dominating the surface. Judging by the scant news I'd overheard from Ulmid, things weren't going her way, and she intended to see my progress and punish me if there was none.

Sotera guided us across dry lakes and around crystalline pools of seeping groundwater. In the distance was the vast underground desert, dispersed with thick columns of stone, pockmarked but strong, reaching high enough that I was sure they held up the surface itself.

The earth wyrms brought us into the maw of an expansive city, this one long abandoned after it threatened imminent collapse. More columns held up the cracking roof. Houses were carved from the walls, their doorways and windows etched with lines of glittering jade, diamonds, and blood-red opals.

Sotera waved her hand, and the lead guard directed his wyrm into the heart of the dead city. I soon lost him in the darkness of the rubble.

"Over here," another guard snapped as a couple more wyrms dragged in sleds full of the recently chosen. The guards already stationed here hauled the chosen off. They ripped away the strings of jewels from around the chosen's necks and tossed them into a growing pile.

"In line with the others," one barked.

Confused, the new arrivals joined those I hadn't worked with yesterday. These had dragged themselves up from the spots on the floor where they'd spent the night. If possible, they appeared even more sickly and forlorn. Others had noticed Sotera's arrival and were already making their way over, though moving was clearly difficult.

I avoided looking at them as the guard undid my bonds and led me to where Sotera, a few other guards, and my first victim stood. These chosen were worse than the others, their eyes having lost all their glossiness.

"Please, Cherished," my victim rasped. "It hurts so much. Heal me, *please*."

"I'm waiting," Sotera said as I hesitated. "Hurry up before I—"

"Empress."

The guard Sotera had sent farther into the city had returned. He gave the barest shake of his head. Sotera's face twisted in a snarl. She flicked her finger at me and pain, like someone squeezing my limbs hard enough to shatter, tore through my body. I resisted screaming.

"You will start," she said. "Now."

The pain slowly abated, and I stepped closer to the first man. "I'm sorry," I muttered.

I felt the magic within him the moment my hand touched his chest. Magic, much like the heart gems of the wildlings. Magic I needed to take.

Like lifting the lock of a canal, I let the magic flow into me.

Not too much, not too little. The one good thing about Sotera forcing me to do this was that I'd gotten good at it.

The man let out a weak cry, and I sharply drew my hand back. He slumped to the ground and was almost immediately dragged to his feet by two guards.

"I have enough," I said.

"I hope you're not wrong," Sotera said.

In answer, I brushed past her and plunged my hand onto a different chosen, the first of those Sotera believed had promise. There was a flash of blue light. This man cried out and then stumbled back as my power surged into him.

Then he began to grow.

His shoulders bulked with new crystal, legs and arms snapping like breaking bone as the crystallization formerly holding him immobile broke and allowed him to walk. His frame swelled immensely until he had doubled in size, a hulking behemoth of crystal and magic.

Sotera eyed this new creation hungrily. "Good. Now do the next."

"Give me a new source," I said. I gestured to the man I'd nearly killed. "He has too little now."

The guards looked at Sotera, who gave a shallow nod. Whatever her reservations, she ultimately needed me. It seemed I was the only one who could transfer their magic like this, who could create something new.

Today, that magic crackled electric beneath my skin. Maybe it was knowing that Rune was alive—that Rune was *winning*—that gave me a much-needed boost. Or maybe having Sotera here had hardened my resolve to go forward with what I'd planned for a while.

"Why are you stopping?" Sotera said.

I'd pulled magic from a new victim—leaving them limp and barely breathing, but alive—and changed the next couple chosen ones into their new forms. I'd be expected to do more and more until I was spent and Sotera had a fresh wave of crystal monstrosities. Instead, I'd been staring.

Just outside the cavern entrance pooled a smoldering lake of magma. What interested me was what lay just above that: smooth vents through which the steam rose. There were vents like that all over the Below. These likely didn't go all the way to the surface or Sotera would have been using them for her troops, but they likely came close.

"I need a recharge," I said.

Sotera returned to speaking with the nearest guard. She gestured to the columns in the far desert, merely smudges at this distance. "How many would we be able to do?"

"Possibly a half dozen, maybe more," the guard said.

"So few, even after all this time..." Sotera murmured. "It may not be enough."

The next victim gave me a terrified look as I approached him. I raised my hand, but instead of touching him, I surreptitiously looked around.

As I'd suspected, with Sotera here, the guards' attention had been diverted from watching my every move. They likely wouldn't risk leaving her side if she became threatened. In fact, I was counting on it.

A hundred meters to the vents. Then I'd have to see if they were too slick or slanted or if my magic was too weak to stop them from scalding me alive. It was a risk I was willing to take.

"If you run out of chosen today and are still unable to perform up to my expectations—"

Sotera froze when she saw my face, saw that I was unguarded, that I was already positioned to run. "Don't you dare—"

I thrust my hand toward her. Sotera leapt aside as jagged spikes of crystal shot just past her, encircling her and the nearest guards. The remaining guards reacted just as I'd hoped, closing ranks around Sotera.

"Empress—"

"Forget me and get her!" Sotera screeched.

I was already taking off toward the vents. My shambling run was pathetic, and it took me longer than it should have to get up to speed. A month without proper food or exercise had left muscles once strong protesting and lacking.

Sotera screamed again. My legs burned, but I didn't dare stop. I leapt an inlet of magma, nearly sinking my right foot in the bubbling orange. I pinwheeled over it but regained my balance.

Don't look back. Whatever you do, don't look back.

At last I reached the vent and my heart sank. The interior was totally smooth, sides slicked with steam I was sure would scald my still very human skin.

Still, Sotera had made me do nothing but practice using my magic for a majority of my unwelcome stay here. *Something* must have clicked.

I coated my hands in a fine layer of flexible crystal and then coaxed more crystal from the vent's interior to make handles. They held when I grabbed them. Better yet, they didn't burn. I could do this. I could—

I reached for the next handle. My arm slammed against the wall. It took me a full three seconds to process that Sotera's enormous sword had skewered straight through the meat of my bicep and pinned me to the rock. Close by, Sotera gave a triumphant laugh.

My scream pitched louder as the crystal coating my hands vanished with my fading strength, and extreme heat scalded my skin.

Vomit rising to my throat, I tried desperately to keep my feet on the ground and prevent severing my flesh entirely. I reached up with my good arm and tried to pull the sword free. It had stuck fast.

"Come...on..." My eyes blurred with tears, cool against my warm skin. "It can't end like this, it can't."

The sword slid free. I collapsed onto rock steaming with my spilt blood. The pain was so great I could barely move without blacking out. I had to get up. If not—

Sotera's face appeared over me, her lips twisted into a cruel smile.

"Oh, Cherished. You're going to regret doing that."

CHAPTER

TWO

They didn't even close up the wound Sotera's sword had made, but dragged me back to my cell and threw me inside. I weakly tried to cover the gash to stop the blood, but it leaked through my fingers. If Sotera wanted me alive, then she sure had a funny way of showing it.

I eventually passed out. I vaguely recalled awakening to the smell of copper and a black crust where my wound had started to dry. My consciousness was a flickering bulb ignited by bursts of pain. Fevered dreams intermingled with reality. One moment I was staring at a dull stone ceiling and the next a canopy of trees at the edge of the Wilds. Father Dumas, expression crazed, worked a knife feverishly into my forearm.

Then Rune hovered over me, smile malicious. "Is that it?" he sneered. "Is that all it takes to end you?"

I came to slowly and at last stayed there. I hadn't moved from where they'd dropped me, and sweat and dried blood ringed my body. I had to get up. If I didn't move soon, I wouldn't ever again. Delusion-Rune was right. This couldn't be my end.

I bit my tongue against the pain and set to work keeping myself alive.

One entire side of my cell was a cliff's edge overlooking the Deep, the ground a hundred feet below. I stuck my head as far over the edge as I dared to catch water dripping from above. At night—or what passed as night down here—bioluminescent glow worms squirmed from their holes in the walls. I gathered those within reach and went to work extracting their silk. I'd seen some residents of the Deep using it in their clothing, so I hoped it'd be strong enough.

That done, I forced myself to eat the remaining worms to keep up my strength and then set to stitching my wound. It'd already become itchy and angry red around the edges. I bit a piece of rock to keep from screaming as I cleaned it with hand-fuls of water, then stuffed it with excess silk, and stitched it shut as best I could with a jagged splinter of crystal.

I'd been so incredibly stupid. Sotera thought me, if not broken, then a coward, and I'd given up my element of surprise on a whim. Why? Because I'd heard Rune was alive? Because I'd had *hope*?

Like Sotera said, hope was a fragile thing.

Easy to build.

Easier to break.

<hr>

"A PERFECT FIT, don't you think, little fox?"

In my dream, Rune languidly sat on what had once been his intact throne, his long, lean body bridging the two halves. The gold and jewels, once inlaid on the arms, had been ripped free and scattered at the throne's feet.

Rune was exactly as I remembered, though his face wasn't covered in blood, nor was he screaming for me. The circlet of ivy and nightshade he'd worn when we'd met had been replaced by the gold, silver, and leafed crown of the High King, tilted at an ostentatious angle across his brow. His glass-sharp mouth was cocked in a smirk. His eyes, gold-red and intense, drank me in.

He put his feet up on one of the throne's arms. "It appears to be missing something, don't you think?"

"Me." The word sprang from my lips, unbidden. "I should be there with you."

"You should," he agreed.

Not *with him*, not like that. Venom-induced, I'd once kissed him with violent fervor, that he, just as venom-induced and passionately, returned. The emotions we'd felt had been manufactured, nothing more. Still, while in that heady state, he'd proclaimed that I would someday be his queen. He hadn't meant it. He couldn't. He'd made it clear in no uncertain terms that, once he took the throne, our deal was over and I was no longer welcome in the Wilds. I didn't even *want* to be with him again, to be under constant threat and constantly on guard against him and my own stupid feelings.

And yet.

"I'm trying to find you," I said. It felt as though my chest was crumbling inward, squeezing my lungs so hard I could barely breathe. "I'm growing tired. It's too cold down here, and I'm too weak."

Ink, dark as a moonless night, had begun leaking from Rune's eyes and the corner of his mouth. He grinned, and his teeth were stained black.

"I'm getting desperate," I pleaded.

The ink splashed across the throne and lapped against my legs. I didn't even consider running as it slowly trapped me in place.

"I already told you what desperation does." Rune leaned forward. "Do you remember?"

"It makes monsters of us all," I whispered, as the ink rose above my head and I felt nothing more.

WHAT MIGHT HAVE BEEN the fifth or sixth night without visitors, I awakened when my door was thrown open.

"No funny business," the guard growled. "We all heard what you tried to do. Play around with us and the Empress has given permission to show you just how sharp our spears are."

He leveled his at me, as though to make a literal point. I sat up, too exhausted to snap back. The guard held his glare a little longer and then drew his spear up and stepped aside.

The two attendants who'd taken care of me when I'd first arrived Below hurried in, their heads bowed. Despite being explicitly told not to speak to them more than necessary, I'd managed to get their names.

The boy with growths of colored rock along his arms and legs was Raki. He dragged a thick metal tub behind him and scurried out again.

The girl with crystal ridges jutting along her spine and tearing holes in the back of her shirt was Qell. She immediately knelt before me.

"I'm to heal you," she said in a whispery soft voice.

"Sotera's decided she wants me alive after all?" I asked.

"Our Empress would like for you to join her." Qell dipped her head in a bow. "We were told to leave no visible wounds."

Only Sotera would nearly sever my arm and then worry about it leaving an unsightly mark. At least she had some sense of humor.

As much as I didn't want to see her, refusing would only

lead to more punishment, and I wasn't too proud to admit that I was desperate for food and contact with someone, anyone, else. Also, I didn't want to get these two in trouble by saying no.

I held out my sliced arm, by far the worst of my injuries. "Do your best."

Qell held up a shard of crystal nearly the size of my hand, worn smooth and tapered to a soft point. I didn't know the exact way it worked, but supposedly it amplified the sparse magic of Those Below and promoted healing in the crystal of their bodies. For me, with my crystal bones, the effect was even more pronounced.

Qell hovered the crystal over my wound, frowning. "Did you stuff this with…silk?"

"It looks worse than it feels."

And it looked bad. The silk had soaked up the bleeding and slowed the infection, but the edges of the gash had grown puffy. Once Qell gently removed the weak stitches and stuffing, I could see the barest glow of my bone through the skin.

"Apologies, this might hurt," Qell said.

The guard pounded the base of his spear against the floor. "Keep it down," he growled. "Don't need to be jabbering while you work."

While Raki continued shuttling in soaps, towels, ointments, and more, Qell drew the crystal along my gash, closing the skin and leaving behind pale-pink, new flesh. After that, she soothed the blistered burns on my palms and fingertips, closed up other cuts, and drew the purple and black from the worst of the bruises. I was impressed. She'd never been allowed to give me this level of care. It must have been quite the occasion they were preparing me for.

"We heard you tried to escape," Qell whispered.

I'd been so lost in the bliss of soothed pain I almost didn't hear her. My eyes flicked to the guard to ensure he wasn't paying attention. "Since I'm still here, you see how well that worked out."

Qell finished with a scrape on the back of my forearm and then moved to my shoulder, leaning in close to my ear. "There are other ways up, but you can't try to escape again yet. They're watching closely."

"It has to be soon. I can't last much longer down here."

"We will help you, Raki and I. And when you leave, we would like to go with you."

She drew back and carefully returned to the biggest gash on my arm, ensuring that the fresh skin hadn't opened back up again.

My first week down here, I'd learned that Those Below had a class system based on how human they looked. At the top was me, a crystal being entirely covered in flesh. Those like Sotera, the upper echelon, who looked most like humans, held the most power. And then there were those like Qell and Raki settled near the bottom. They were reduced to servitude and barely scraping by. It was a hard life for everyone down here, but they had it harder than most.

"I don't know if up there will be any better, Qell," I said.

Her lip trembled. This close, I could see splintery cracks in the jutting crystals along her spine, spiderwebbed like when a bird hit a window. More spiderwebbing cracks above her right eye. The equivalent of a harsh bruise on human skin.

"It can't be much worse," Qell said.

"Tell me who's hurting y—"

"You done yet?" the guard said. "The seamstress is almost here."

"Nearly," Qell said, tone demure. She waited until he'd turned away again. "Do not give in just yet," she whispered fervently. "But do not say no to her demands. It will make things easier if you agree."

"Agree to *what*?"

"Your power comes from within. *Within*. You have to only call on it. Don't forget that."

"Out!"

A severe-looking woman stood in the door, wearing a dress entirely free of wrinkles over her sharp frame. Her face was perfectly sliced down the middle, half crystal, half flesh, her hands clasped primly before her. She snapped her fingers, shooting a small spray of sparks. "That means now."

Qell was on her feet in an instant, hastily bowing to her before scurrying out with Raki.

My left forearm sharply protested as I pushed to standing. When I examined it, I found there was still a small opening on the inside, almost exactly where my scar had been. If I looked closely, I could just make out my crystal bone glowing from within.

"Wait, I think she—"

I clamped my mouth shut as the woman—the seamstress, I assumed—glared at me. "Is there a problem?"

Qell had never missed one of my wounds, and she'd had plenty of time to heal me. That, and the opening was clean around the edges. Almost as though it'd been left deliberately.

I turned my forearm away from her and straightened up. "What do you want?"

The woman looked down the bridge of her nose at me. "More to work with, that's for sure. But it is as the Empress demands. Hurry up, in the bath."

I hadn't noticed Raki shuttling in water, too, but the tub sat steaming. I resisted blurting out more questions and nodded at the guard leering at me. "Not with him looking."

"I've been told to watch you," he said. "And that's exactly what I'm—"

The seamstress shut the door. More sparks scattered across the tile as she snapped at the tub. "In. We don't have time, and I have much to do. And if you think I'm too frail to be a threat, think of what I can do when I'm pinning your dress."

Dress?

But the steaming water was too tempting, and I quickly shed my filthy clothes and slipped in, trying my best to keep the still-open gash above the surface and out of sight.

The bath was heaven. The heat melted the fatigue caking my joints, and even the seamstress's violent scrubbing to remove the dirt that had become a fixture to my skin couldn't ruin the bliss. She nearly ripped my scalp, brushing out the tangled strands of my hair until it had almost returned to its sheeny black. Soon the bottom of the tub was covered in a fine layer of silt.

"Out," the seamstress ordered when she'd finished. I reluctantly obeyed.

"I won't even tell you how to behave tonight. Empress Sotera will see to that," the seamstress said. She hovered around my shivering body, covering me with towels that smelled like they'd been dipped in sweet incense.

"Can you at least tell me what I'm doing?" I asked.

"No."

She swept over to a silk-wrapped package that'd been left on my bed and unfurled a dress of deep vermillion. I gaped.

"I can't wear that."

"You can and will. Or else the guard will come in and force you into it. I'm sure he'd greatly enjoy that."

I'd never worn a dress in my life, but the prospect of wearing something not filthy quickly wore down my resolve.

The seamstress smirked as I snatched it from her, and with

some difficulty, my fingers more use to brute force than handling anything so delicate, managed to slip it on.

I understood now why Qell had been so meticulous covering my injuries. Though the hem fell past my ankles, the strapless shoulders revealed far more than I was comfortable with. It would definitely accentuate how jutting my collarbones had become since my time here.

"You are far too thin," the seamstress said, as though reading my mind. "But it will have to do. Hold your arms to your sides."

I allowed the seamstress to fit it to me and then use a little magic to dry my hair back into manageable waves, before pinning those, too. I didn't have a mirror, but I felt elegant. And, even with the unnecessary frills, I could still move freely. Function over form. That was something.

The seamstress took a step back to admire her handiwork. "You're passable," she concluded. "I personally think the Empress could do better—it is too gawdy for the likes of you—but that is not my choice. Five minutes and then they'll come for you."

She walked out. The guard's eyes bulged when he saw me before the door slammed shut and I was alone.

With no time to worry about what was coming, I wasted precious seconds admiring the actually clean fabric and my freshly scrubbed skin. It was amazing how a little comfort could bring so much joy.

At last, my attention returned to the small gash Qell left in my arm and the crystal bone beneath.

Your power comes from within.

She seemed to think I could help them, but I was nearly helpless myself. I had only a little magic, no plan of escape, and no weapon. If I at least had Sliver, the sword Xander had traded to me, and the one I had long broken and lost, then my odds might have gone up a little. The Wilds-forged metal wouldn't be terribly effective against the hardened bodies of Those Below, but it'd be something.

Yet, as I stared at the gash, the idea of gaining a weapon wouldn't leave my head. What if that was what Qell was telling me? What if I *was* the weapon? I could manipulate crystal better than any of Those Below. Crystal, just like my bone...

I hovered my hand over the cut. It was insane. But I was desperate.

Even with my magic nearly depleted, I coaxed the crystal of my arm to reach for me. It started as a dull ache and then crescendoed to sharp pain. I didn't stop. I imagined the cut in my arm as a sheath and a blade, one sharp enough to use, being drawn from within.

When I opened my eyes, part of my bone had emerged from my skin and reformed into something not unlike Sliver's hilt. My arm throbbed dully, but it was nothing compared to my elation. I had no doubt that, given time, I could conjure the rest. All this time, I had a weapon literally inside me. Granted, I didn't know the consequences of doing this, but it was something.

Deep voices and footsteps sounded outside my room, moving closer.

I hurriedly magicked my crystal blade back inside my arm and allowed the last of the slender gash to heal itself right as the door swung open.

"Follow me," the guard said.

I'D ONLY BEEN to Sotera's palace once, when I first arrived. At that time, I'd been too delirious with the effects of having my magic drained to take much of it in. Now, though, as a small contingent of guards led me beneath the stone entryway into the grand entrance hall, the sheer opulence took my breath away. The walls were made entirely of thickened, hazy crystal, like ice, glowing so bright there was no need for any other kind of light.

As I was taken down a long hallway, I could pick out shapes within: earth wyrms rearing up to engage deep-earth salamanders and cloaked in dried magma. Eyeless bats and millipedes as long as my arm. There were other creatures, too, all with sightless white eyes.

I snapped my head forward as I caught a glimpse of something that looked startingly human deeper within.

We passed through a set of contiguous arches to a pair of enormous double doors. The guards in front threw them open, and I was startled by the sudden blast of light and sound.

Dozens of Those Below, all dressed in finery, were gathered in the throne room. I could make out nobles from the highest level of the Deep, wearing nephrite around their necks, magma drippings from their ears, and strings of jewels that looked suspiciously like those that had been torn away from Sotera's chosen.

Some of Sotera's generals from her war council had collected in a loose circle—Ulmid and Abaki among them—but there were at least three more I didn't recognize. One, a woman with nicks like trophies adorning her side; another, a man so old his body had seized with age, who was forced to rock back and forth to turn with the others to look at me.

"There she is," Sotera said. Beaming, she broke through a group of nobles who'd been speaking to her. They gave me disgusted looks behind her back.

Sotera swept over and firmly took my arm. "I hope you found your time alone enlightening."

"What is all this?" I asked. "You're throwing a *party?*"

"Of course we are. They're here to celebrate."

"Celebrate what?"

The general with the nicks in her side blocked us, hand resting on a metal cudgel at her waist. "You will bow before the Empress. Or I will break your knees and make it easier for you to do so."

Sotera waved her hand. "Val does not need to bow, Tenia. This is her day, after all."

General Tenia glared at me. "Very well, Empress. Jiku claims he is tired. I will escort him home."

She supported the old man seized by crystal, and together they exited through the crowd.

Sotera threaded her cold arm through mine, and I grudgingly let her take me around the room. Servants like Raki and Qell scurried between the other partygoers, who bowed their heads as we passed. Sotera gave each of them delighted smiles. She appeared happier than I'd ever seen her. It made me nervous.

"There was a brief opening in the surface, so I invited a bit of familiarity down," Sotera said as she led me to another group. "Hopefully, they will make you feel more at ease."

"I am Lord Blis," the first man said, in a nasally voice that grated in my ears. He was slender as a sapling, with a sharp nose and honeysuckle running across his shoulders like hair.

"You're from the Wilds," I blurted out.

"How observant," Lord Blis said, mouth twisting wryly.

This couldn't be possible. No wildling with half an idea of what Sotera was trying to do would willingly align themselves with her. But Lord Blis's and the other wildlings' relaxed expressions told me they were guests as Sotera said, not prisoners.

"I see you've thrown yourself in with the enemy," I spat at Lord Blis.

"There is no *enemy*, my dear," Lord Blis said. He smiled indulgently to the two other wildlings with him—his family, or maybe other minor Lords, judging by their flashy attire. "We simply think there's opportunity to be had here."

"Rune is your High King, and as such, you owe him your allegiance. He rightfully took the throne—"

"*Took* being the operative word, and what a crude ousting it was." Lord Blis swirled his drink, the liquid sloshing against the sides of the crystal glass. "Some of us were happy with how the other Lords ran things."

I forced myself to breathe, to smile. "I see Rune hasn't completely cleaned out the filth. I'm sure he'll get to you eventually."

Lord Blis raised an eyebrow. "I had no idea you were so... loyal to him. How interesting. Should I send him your regards? He'd come down here himself, I'm sure, if he weren't so busy trying to keep his newborn kingdom from falling to pieces."

"The only way he'll come down here is as a prisoner, or in a coffin," one of the other Lords joked, and they all laughed. Lord Blis's nasally titter alone nearly broke my self-control.

I wanted to throw myself at him, to rip the smirk right off his face and strangle him with his own honeysuckle.

Sotera must have sensed me tensing up, because her grip became painful.

"We'll speak more later and come to agreement," she said to the Lords, before dragging me away.

I kept my mouth shut as Sotera led us around the outside of the room, until we were far enough removed that I could hear the swish of my dress across the floor. Every so often, someone from the party would glance at us. Some looks were filled with awe at Sotera; others, full of hate, were directed at me. It seemed not everyone thought I was as *cherished* as Sotera did.

"You're probably wondering why I'm helping you," Sotera said. "Letting you use your magic, taking you through the Deep, bringing you here."

"You and I have very different definitions of *helping*—"

Sotera squeezed my arm hard enough for the bone to ache. "You think you hide it well, but I see what you desire most; you crave power, much like I do. Look at this."

She brought us up the steps of her throne and turned me toward the party. "I'm holding court with Lords. I'm in command of generals. My armies are primed to overtake the Wilds, and soon, I will command two thrones. Those Below will never be weak again. No, *never* again.

"I have only ever known the dark and cold, steel and crystal. My mother was the same, and her mother before her. We were not supposed to look as we do now, disgusting and wretched. We were supposed to be like the wildlings, with hearts made of crystal and overflowing with power. But the Firsts who were sent to clear the way betrayed us. They conjured the Wilds and used it like a door to trap us down here. And slowly, the Below became part of us. Every generation is worse, and soon there will be nothing left of us that is *alive*."

"I'm sorry," I said. "Really. But I still can't let you take over the Wilds."

Sotera smiled. "I'm afraid you don't have a choice. In fact, you're here to *help* me do just that. That's why I've brought someone to give you purpose."

She pulled me off the steps and across the throne room, where she turned us down a broadening hallway to another enormous pair of doors.

Sotera nodded and the guards shoved them open. I stopped

when we walked inside, staring at the figure at the other end of the immense dining table.

"What are you doing here?"

King Bendeti of the Undersea turned to us, a cold smile stretching his lips. His skin was the color of a drowned man and crusted with salt. His seaweed damp hair was adorned with rainbow shells, as was his long, wavy cloak.

"Rune's human pet," Bendeti said. His eyes roved over my body, and it felt as though one of his crabs had scuttled across my skin, prickling and uninviting. "But you've since become so much more than that, haven't you?"

"What is this?" I demanded to Sotera. "Why is he here?"

"He's here for a beneficial union," Sotera said, and I tasted bile on my tongue. "You are going to marry King Bendeti."

THREE

I was forcibly seated in a chair, still grappling with what Sotera said. King Bendeti and Sotera took spots near the head of the table. Behind Bendeti was his seneschal, Melik, and a half dozen guards, their armor made of stitched lobster shells and rough coral.

Melik, his stalky eyes waving, sniffed at every plate of food as it was served. Steaks of subterranean mammal, glistening with fat and crusted with diced nuts; slices of fruit clearly deprived of any natural light, the flesh so ghostly pale I could stab my fork through and still see the tongs; fish with its flesh peeling off the bones, its sightless white eyes peering up at me.

I couldn't stomach much. The last I'd seen of King Bendeti, Rune had promised him a favor in exchange for Bendeti's knowledge of how to approach the heart tree Rune needed. Bendeti couldn't care less whether the Wilds and humans destroyed each other. However, by being here, he clearly wasn't planning on staying neutral any longer.

"You've been awfully quiet," King Bendeti said, finally turning to me. "That is my preference for all my wives, but it's strange considering how vocal and opinionated you were during our last meeting."

"I didn't realize you'd been failing so much you needed to throw yourself at his feet," I said to Sotera.

"We have a mutual understanding," Sotera said, not the least bit riled. "Both of us agree it best the Wilds and their ruler be disposed of."

"Did Bendeti also mention that he already made a deal with the High King of the Wilds?"

"I have not interfered in this conflict thus far," Bendeti said. His knife *snnked* as it cleanly cut through the fish. Blood dripped down his chin as he took a bite. "Now I want to gain what I can. I don't think there's any harm in being up front with that. You will marry me and align Those Below and the Undersea."

"I'm not one of Those Below, no matter what Sotera told you," I said. "I'm no princess or cherished—"

"Rune still owes me a debt, that is true," Bendeti interrupted. "One I plan to collect before this is over. Before then, your union to me will take place."

I more tightly gripped my blunted carving knife. "You won't be shocked to hear me refuse."

"I so hoped you would. I need a queen with a little bite, one I'll get the chance to break in. The Undersea is a much colder and darker place even than this. I need someone with spine and fortitude. We can't have you withering too quickly."

But his smile told me that I would break eventually, whether from the cold, the pressure, or his own hand. Were I to do this, I would be trading one prison for another. Likely one I'd die in.

"For now, I still have things to prep," King Bendeti went on. "You have time to change your attitude before I return."

"What if..." I tried to choose my words carefully. How best

to prod without giving too much away? "If I willingly married you, would you promise not to attack the Wilds or the human world? If we're creating fake allegiances, then I belong to both of them more than I do here."

"I'm afraid that's not possible," Sotera said before Bendeti could answer. "The terms between us have already been decided."

"Your willing acceptance would take a lot of the fun away," Bendeti said. "However, were you to make this easier, I could hold stall assault for a time, if only to get my favor from Rune."

"But not for *too* long," Sotera said. "I expect him deposed within a week after the wedding."

There was a miniscule hesitation before Bendeti nodded, but years of reading the subtleties in people told me all I needed.

"Why not kill the Wilds right now?" I asked.

"What?" Bendeti snapped.

"Go and get your favor from Rune, and then remove him yourself." I delicately put my knife down. "Why would *you* align with *her*? If you wanted to take Rune down by yourself, or use him as a puppet, why would you need…"

It clicked, and the understanding made me laugh, truly laugh, for the first time in what felt like forever.

"You can't stop Rune either," I said. "Is he threatening the Undersea, too? Have you tried to kill him? Or maybe you're *scared*—"

Bendeti's chair scraped as he rose out of it. "How dare you, insolent little—"

"I'll bet you tried to flood it, but that didn't work, either. The Wilds probably soaked it all up. You know…" I put my hand out as though testing for rain. "A couple weeks ago, there was a lot of water dripping from above. Tasted awfully salty, too. I should have guessed that was just you failing."

Bendeti's blue-ish skin purpled with rage. He looked as though he wanted to lunge across the table and drive a knife through my throat, just as much as I wanted to do the same to him.

"You will have all the time you need to work on her attitude, *after* we are aligned," Sotera said.

"And I will enjoy every moment of it," Bendeti replied. He took a long sip of water, and his drying skin once again grew flushed. "The Wilds have proven more resilient and united than we thought, even after the usurping. But yes, there is another reason we are allied. Empress Sotera has assured me that other matters will be dealt with—"

"In private," Sotera said sharply. "Matters that Val doesn't need to concern herself with. But her distaste toward you, King Bendeti, has reminded me of something."

She stood and gestured to one of the guards, who bowed and stepped out.

"We know what we need to counter the Wilds: willingness and information. Val lacks both, which is why I've brought her a friend." Her smile chilled my bones. "Call it an early wedding present, to help make this transition into your new role easier."

The guard returned, dragging Peyton along with him. I shot to my feet, but Sotera pointed a threatening finger at me. "Don't move."

Peyton wore what looked like spelunking gear, the sleeves of her jacket in tatters and her face bruised. After having not seen anyone from my old life for so long, the shock of her being here left my head spinning.

"Val, you're okay?" Peyton practically sobbed when she saw me. "When they took you, I thought... Oh, Val, I thought—"

"She's a friend of yours, is she not?" Sotera said to me.

I schooled my expression into a disinterested mask,

shoving every ounce of fear for Peyton down into a tight ball. "She's someone I thought loved me."

"And that's not the case anymore? What a shame. I thought I recognized her." Sotera tapped her chin. "Didn't she throw herself in front of my blade to save you? Well, if she means nothing to you anymore..."

Sotera raised a hand, and the guard placed a knife to Peyton's throat. She stilled, barely daring to breathe.

"I could end her," Sotera said. "Just as I ended the other humans she was trying to travel down here with. One swift, clean cut, simply say the word. I can see she hurt you, no matter how you try to hide it. Now is the time to get revenge."

King Bendeti looked between us, clearly enjoying the display. The dining hall hung heavy with silence as I met Peyton's eyes. How strange that not too long ago, with Rune pressing a knife to her neck, I would have given up everything I had to save her.

Now, however...

"Let her live." I put all my nonchalance into a shrug. "She used me to help unlock the Below. Clearly this is what she wanted for me, after all. Why spoil it for her?"

"An excellent idea," Sotera said happily. She waved to the empty chair beside me. "Give her a seat. Oh, but first."

Sotera grabbed Peyton's wrist and wrenched her to the table, slamming her hand atop it. Before I could move, Sotera drew a carving knife from one of the roasts and lopped off Peyton's pinkie.

"What are you doing?" I yelled as Peyton screamed. I hurried around the table but stopped as Sotera threw Peyton aside and leveled the bloodied knife at me.

"Don't think I've forgotten your stunt. You will not disobey me again. You will not disrupt our plans or it won't be just you who suffers. Do you understand?"

Behind her, Peyton whimpered, clutching the bleeding stump where her finger used to be. I swallowed, finally managing to pull my eyes from her. "I got it."

"Good." Sotera gave Peyton a disgusted look. "Clean her up."

Two healers appeared at Peyton's side, as though lying in wait for Sotera to finish her display. They swaddled Peyton's finger in coarse cloth, and in moments she was seated, still cradling her hand, in the chair beside me.

"Sit," Sotera ordered me, retaking her own chair and primly wiping Peyton's blood off her fingertips with a napkin. "And tell me, Peyton, what news from above?"

Peyton sat in sullen silence until Sotera pounded the table hard enough to make us jump. "I said—"

"What do you want to know?" Peyton snapped, and I couldn't help feeling a mixture of pride and fear at her insolence. "Something that all of your spies couldn't tell you?"

"Perhaps she needs another lesson," King Bendeti said. "Would you like me to administer this one? Whenever I'm away from my kingdom, I find my persuasive talents could always use a little refreshing."

"Tell me of the human world," Sotera said. "After all, it's them and their zealots I have to thank for giving us this chance at freedom. How are they faring in this war?"

Peyton stayed quiet so long I feared Sotera would take another knife to her, before saying, "The humans haven't gone to war, not officially. We're still fighting the encroaching Wilds."

"And what do they think of Those Below?"

I was surprised to see Peyton smirk. "Most of them don't believe they're real."

"Typical human arrogance." Bendeti sniffed. "They choose to ignore the jellyfish until they feel its sting."

"They will soon learn," Sotera said. She hadn't touched the rest of her food, watching Peyton and me closely. "But you've been fighting the Wilds, isn't that right? Then what of Rune? Wait... Val, what do *you* think Rune is doing?"

"How would I know?" I said.

Sotera slowly turned her fork between her fingers. "You are—were—close to him, yes? It seemed clear from the few times I mentioned his name that you have...affections for him."

Peyton looked sharply at me, while I wracked my memory for any substantial conversation I'd had with Sotera involving Rune. Had she actually discerned that from the few times she'd uttered his name around me? It wasn't possible. Surely I'd been more careful about revealing any of my feelings. And if I *had*, certainly my comments about him had been more weighted toward dislike than...affection.

But with the luxury of time and distance, I could begin to see Rune and my interactions through a clearer lens. It turned Rune's savagery and relentless grasp for power into what it truly was: a desperate attempt to keep him and those he cared for safe. The commands he gave turned from demanding into things he only asked of those few he actually trusted.

And his draw to me, and mine to him... That was nothing but two broken people seeking companionship in someone equally screwed up. That was all.

"There were no affections," I said. "We tolerated each other's presence."

"Hmm..." Sotera said, clearly not believing me. "Even still, you spent time with him, learned his ways. I'd love to hear your thoughts on what he might do."

"He's focused on holding you back, for one. The Wilds might be open now, but you can't force your way up, except in those rare times the surface opens. All he has to do is play Whack-A-Mole to keep you down."

"Whack-A-Mole?" Bendeti said.

"But he's also gathering his own forces from those who served the dead Lords," I said. "If Bendeti wasn't here, I'd guess he'd be making his own alliance with him. And Rune's gaining strength, most of all," I added. "He's High King of the Wilds, and soon I'm going to guess he'll have far more power than you."

"He's also planning to invade the human world and rip it apart," Sotera said, not looking the least bit upset.

It took everything I had not to react. "He has no reason to."

"And yet he will anyway. Am I correct?" Sotera directed the question to Peyton.

After a pause, Peyton nodded. "The Wilds have been pushing across their borders since he took the throne. We've tried fighting back, but it's stronger than ever before."

"He can't... He wouldn't..." Rune had promised me he would leave the human world alone. He'd *promised*.

"I suppose I was wrong," Sotera said to me. "You didn't know him as well as you thought."

She motioned, and a servant waiting against the wall stepped out and returned with a small tray of sweetened ice, swirled to resemble different kinds of seashells. No doubt as a pathetic way to help placate Bendeti.

Sotera selected one and directed the servant to bring the tray over to me. "I want to hear more of what's going on above—"

The servant tripped, and ice-cold dessert spattered across my chest as the entire dining room trembled. Silverware slid across the table and clattered to the floor. Glass shattered.

On instinct, I wrenched Peyton beneath the table, just as a portion of the crystal ceiling hit the floor, spraying sharpened pieces every direction. This time it was Peyton who turned me away as shards peppered us.

"What's happening?" she said breathlessly.

"No idea. An earthquake? Keep your head—"

I pulled her farther beneath the table as another chunk of the ceiling crushed the chair she'd been sitting in. After what felt like an hour, the tremors ceased, leaving only our panicked breathing and the terrified, muted shouts of partygoers from the throne room.

"I'm sorry, Val," Peyton said into my shoulder. "I'm so sorry. I had no idea what Those Below would do to you. Everything the worshippers told me made me think they'd revere you. You were Those Below's key, and their hope. They were just supposed to remove the wildlings, nothing more. Father Dumas told me to be patient, that them taking you was for the best. But I couldn't, I *couldn't*. I'm so, so—"

"None of what you just said makes any sense," I said sharply. "And all the sorrys in the world won't change what's already done."

I let go of Peyton and stuck my head out from beneath the table. The dining room walls were covered in cracks resembling the map of a bus route, so many that I feared they'd collapse at any moment. I could make out the cavernous roof of the Below through missing chunks in the palace ceiling.

Before I could entertain the idea of using the chaos to escape, Sotera's guards dragged Peyton and me out.

"Take them to the closest rooms, lock them there. Separately," Sotera snarled. Unfortunately, she appeared mostly unscathed, with only a few minor cuts and splintery cracks across her arms. Some of Bendeti's entourage were helping him to his shaky feet while Melik bounded around, incensed.

"—assured in good faith that this was a peaceful meeting," he screeched. "Only to be backstabbed by this traitorous, this conniving—"

"Silence!" Bendeti roared. Salt and dust flaked off him as he stood to his full height. "I was assured you had it under control," he hissed at Sotera.

"It *is*," Sotera said.

"You call this—" Bendeti stumbled as aftershocks rattled the room. "*This,* under control?"

"Out!" Sotera barked at her guards. "Get them out!"

The closest guard ripped me away from Peyton. I was dragged to a room down the hall where he threw me inside.

"Stay put," he said, like I was a dog. He pulled the door shut. The lock clicked.

It was a guest room. Like many of the rooms in the palace, the windows were frosted, so it was impossible to see how the earthquake affected the rest of the Deep. I recalled its tight, narrowed streets, many of them hanging dangerously close to bottomless chasms. One time, Sotera had taken me on an alternate path through the cramped conditions of the bottom layer. Down there, six or seven people had lived stuffed in a single room.

Many of them had probably died in the earthquake. Maybe hundreds. For all their belief in Sotera, I wondered if she'd thought about them yet.

A collection of rapid bootsteps passed my door. I waited until I was sure they were gone and then tested how thick the windows were. No give. The cracks within the stone walls weren't big enough for me to slip through, either. Even if I'd found an escape, Peyton being here changed everything. I couldn't just leave. I hated her. Or rather, I hated what she'd done. Still, I couldn't leave her behind to take Sotera's punishment once she found I'd escaped.

I settled on the bed, picking bits of crystal out of the ridiculous frills of my dress. Peyton's arrival was a shock, but the news of Rune was the most disturbing. He'd sworn to be better than the monsters his family and the other Lords had been.

He'd promised to never invade the human world. I'd even been so vain as to think I was one of the reasons he'd never do so. But I'd been trapped here over a month. And really, in the timeline of his entire life, could the few weeks I'd been with him have really changed his nature?

I watched the ceiling as another tremor split a fresh crack straight down the center.

Just what had Rune become?

FOUR

It was over two hours after the last tremor subsided before somebody came to fetch me.

I'd spent the time somewhat successfully drawing the crystal sword from my arm. I found—whether by magic or my biology—that the pain of the blade emerging wasn't all that bad, and the skin healed easily enough once I returned the bone to its proper shape.

I heard bootsteps and hastily sheathed the last of the sword into my arm right as the door flew open.

"Out," the guard said.

I hurried to stand, brushing off the folds of my dress as though I hadn't been up to something. "Is Peyton—the human woman—is she all right?"

"I said out. Don't make me repeat myself again."

I trusted nothing terrible had happened to her and allowed myself to be escorted from the palace and back across the bridge toward my cell. The plains of sharp crystal beneath us had fractured like glass thrown on concrete, casting iridescent light every direction. The Deep had fared as poorly as I feared. It was as though a giant had wrapped its hands around it and shook, creating deep cracks in the foundation. A few of the buildings had been crushed entirely, especially on the lower levels. I shuddered, thinking of the last moments of the poor souls trapped, likely in stuffy, hot darkness, until their lives were snuffed out.

"That was a pretty big earthquake," I said to the guard. "Haven't felt one since I came down here."

"Not your concern," the guard said gruffly. "Keep quiet."

"They happen often? Is Sotera—"

"What did I just say?"

The guard left me in my cell for what felt like an hour before the seamstress returned, trailed by a submissive Qell.

"What...?" the seamstress's nostrils flared when she saw my dress, covered in dried dessert and smears of dirt. "I hope the meeting with our Empress went better than you look. Get out of that now and hand it over."

With Qell's help, I struggled out of the dress and changed into simple, coarse clothes the seamstress had brought. She sighed as Qell bunched up the dress into a sad, dirty clump.

"This will have to be burned, I suppose. Let's go," the seamstress said to Qell.

Qell caught my eye. It was clear she needed to tell me something.

Thinking fast, I snatched up a semi-jagged piece of tile that had broken free during the tremor and, gritting my teeth, made a cut across my upper arm. Not deep enough to be serious, but enough to bleed well.

"I still need help," I said. I showed the seamstress the injury, hoping she didn't question why it looked so fresh. "Some debris hit me."

The seamstress's eyes narrowed. "Qell, take care of her.

And quick, there are other guests who need attention. I'll be with them. Don't keep me waiting."

"Of course, Mistress." Qell bowed as the seamstress stepped out. Qell hastily dropped the dress and removed the healing crystal from the rags that were her pants.

As she set to work closing up my wound, I double-checked the guard wasn't paying attention before leaning closer to her. "I have someone new who has to come with us."

Qell gave the barest nod.

"How soon can we go?"

"Just a little longer." Qell moved the crystal across the cut, stitching the seams of skin together and leaving only drying blood. "New ways have opened up because of the tremors. We'll need to chart a new path."

"We can still make it up, though, right?"

"Maybe. There might be someone above who can help us."

That surprised me. "Who?"

"You done?" the guard asked. "Wasn't that big a cut."

"Just finishing up, sir," Qell said, tone meek. When the guard turned away, Qell leaned so close I smelled earth on her breath. "Whatever happens, you must get Raki out of here. Promise me."

"I'll help you both."

"*Promise me* you will get him out."

Her fierce expression left no room for argument.

"I promise," I said.

Qell pocketed the healing crystal and pulled my sleeve back down. "We must be careful. There is something else Below. A wraith. We've heard the Empress talking to it in the palace. It is like her beast, something even her generals are scared of. If we escape, I'm afraid she will send it after us, so we must ensure it can't follow."

I only had a dozen more questions, but only then did I

notice the guard had turned back around, watching us. My skin prickled.

"Thank you for healing me, Qell," I said loudly. "We're done."

Qell gave me and the guard a rapid bow, before scurrying out. The guard's gaze followed her.

"You can close the door now," I said. "I'd prefer not having to look at you any longer than necessary."

He snickered. "A sharp tongue can be fixed with an equally sharp knife. Too bad dressing you up didn't make you any prettier."

He slammed the door, engaged the lock.

I lay back on the bed, hands beneath my head. Across the Below, the earth rumbled and groaned from more aftershocks.

I rolled over and stared at the glittering city of the Deep. At the jagged fields of crystal, orange pools of magma, and cerulean blue lakes lit with blooms of bioluminescent fish.

You were close to him, yes?

Sotera's tone had been mocking, like she already knew an answer I didn't. But if I had been close to Rune, then why couldn't I say for sure that he wouldn't hurt me?

Speculating would get me nowhere. There was only one way to know the truth: I had to escape. I had to find Rune, see for myself what he was doing.

And, if it came to it, if Rune was truly set on hurting those who didn't deserve it, all in a bid for more power, I would stop him. In whatever way I could.

"GET UP."

The gruff command had me rolling out of bed on instinct. My fists went up, every sore muscle and bone in my body protesting the sudden movement. The guard, who normally stood outside my door, loomed over me, spear gripped tightly. He smirked at my fists.

"Please. You'll hurt yourself more than me. Let's go."

The overwhelming silence made it seem incredibly early. Or maybe that was because of how I felt all the time: fatigued and overdrawn. I smacked my tongue to clear the grit from my mouth. My head swam groggily. "Where? What's going on?"

"That's for our Empress to answer."

That didn't make me feel any better.

I'd barely laced my boots before two more guards were hustling me out the door. I tried to bring all my senses on high alert. It'd been three days since the disastrous meeting with Bendeti, and all of a sudden Sotera wanted to see me? I could only guess at what new demand she might have. Perhaps she'd somehow found a way to blame me for what had happened and wanted to enact punishment. Even the simplest talks with her always had an undercurrent of savagery.

Instead of the palace, I was led to the Deep, down a steeply precarious staircase full of missing steps that hugged a sheer drop. The bottom ended at the edge of a jagged field of crystal. From the distance of my cell, they always reminded me of frozen blades of glass, spiky and sharp; in the right light, they seemed almost beautiful.

Here they were towering, their tips and edges razor sharp. Sotera stood amongst them, trailing her fingers across the smooth exterior where her face was reflected a dozen times over.

My sun-starved, sickly reflection, shoulders slumped in defeat, stood beside her, a dozen examples of how far I'd fallen. I was almost too disgusted to look.

"I wanted you to see," Sotera said. "To understand why you're doing what you are."

"I've seen crystals before," I said.

"If that's what you think they are, then you're not looking close enough."

I forced myself to peer past the smooth surface of the nearest one. Vague, formless shapes became clearer. I staggered back, swallowing a shocked cry of alarm. Jiku, the decrepit general who'd been escorted from the party early, was frozen deep within, his eyes glassy with lifelessness, hands entirely solidified, raised upward toward the Deep.

It took a moment for my mouth to work again. "He's... Is he...?"

I flattened my palm against the surface and sought out the magic Those Below carried. There was none. Not even a spark of life to draw from.

I whirled around, at last truly taking in what surrounded me. Within each crystal were more figures. Men, women, children, all of them frozen in their final pose. Most appeared in agony.

I forced my panicked breathing to steady. There were hundreds, if not thousands, here, in this one spot. This wasn't a simple crystal plain; this was a mass grave.

"Don't feel too bad for him." Sotera gestured to the old general. "He fulfilled his role and staved off longer than most what eventually takes us all. I'll be here someday too, if I'm lucky.".

I frantically rubbed the crystal dust off my hands, as though by touching it I'd become like the poor bastards trapped within. "This happens to *all* of you?"

"Every single one. The old." Sotera placed a finger on the crystal closest to her. "And now the young."

There was a newborn baby frozen within this one. I wondered if it had even gotten to draw its first breath.

"Why are you showing me this?" I asked.

"So you can understand your place," Sotera said. "And that I am not blind to my own cruelty and treatment of you. Follow me."

I pulled my eyes away from the newborn and hurried to join her on the stairs and leave the grave behind.

"Bendeti has gone back to his damp Undersea kingdom," Sotera said. "He will muse how he might take more power and plan for our alliance. What do you think of him?"

I took a moment to catch my breath. "You don't want me to answer that."

A smile quirked Sotera's lips. "I might find it entertaining. But I meant what I said, you won't give us any trouble. I know you think you're strong, but I cowed you by merely threatening to harm Peyton."

Sotera grabbed for my chin, tilting it up to her. "Until you can look those you love in the eye and end them, until you sever all ties to those who would make you weak and vulnerable, you are not strong enough to do what is necessary. You will never be free."

I shoved her hand away. I hated when she made me feel as though she actually understood how I felt. When she made *sense*.

"I, too, was married to someone I detested," Sotera said, almost wistfully. "He was a cruel and violent man."

"So you two were a perfect match."

I cringed at my stupid tongue, but Sotera merely smiled. "Naïve young fool that I was, I loved him, if such a thing was possible. He was the shining jewel who promised a better existence than the one I lived, and I believed I was his cherished just the same. I loved him until I couldn't excuse what he was anymore, or what he did to my body and mind out of the sight of everyone else.

"He honed me to a fine blade, and I thanked him for it,

right before I separated his head from his neck. I survived, and now, no one rules me. You are strong, Val, willfully so. You will survive, too, and serve your purpose."

We'd crossed the bridge to the palace. The guards at the front gate came to attention as we passed.

"I have a task for you, once you're Queen of the Undersea," Sotera said. "Once the boy king is deposed, the throne of the Wilds will be empty. Like the throne of Those Below, it requires a crown to wield its true power, but you can take it by force and rule with a crystal fist. If you do this and reign over the Wilds in my and Bendeti's stead, I will spare those you desire most." She gave me a syrupy smile. "I may even spare Rune's life, should you ask for it. He could end up being more useful alive than—"

We entered the throne room and Sotera stopped. The party guests had long since left, and the servants had cleared away all signs of them being there, save for the fractures in the floor tile and missing parts of the wall.

A lone figure, cloaked in moss, sat hunched on the steps leading to the throne.

"You are not wrong," the figure said in a voice like crackling tree bark. "Only when the thrones of the Wilds and Those Below are united can there be peace. However, you're going about it the wrong way."

"Who are you?" Sotera demanded. "Guards—"

The figure waved a hand. "Don't bother. They didn't see me enter, and they won't see me leave."

She stood, stretching to her immense height, taller even than Sotera. Her arms were willowy branches tapering to sharp, claw-like fingers and spotted with dormant flower buds. Her face was long and slender, and I realized with some shock it was a beast's skull, the white sporadically splotched with flesh. Human-like eyes stared from deep within the skull's sockets.

"Are you an emissary of the Wilds?" Sotera's hand was on her sword. "Has the unruly child king come to bargain at last?"

"I'm a warning," the creature said. "Mother Mal takes no sides."

Sotera's lips curled in a sneer. "A threat. Let's hear it, then."

"How are you faring, child?" Mother Mal said to me. "Are you enjoying her hospitality?"

"Does she know you?" Sotera said.

"I've never seen her before in my life," I said, panic growing as Sotera's expression grew suspicious. "I promise, I have no idea who she is."

"Your message," Sotera barked at Mother Mal. "Before I find other ways to get you to share it."

"Remember who your true enemy is," Mother Mal said. "Remember it now, or you will remember it before the end."

Crystal reverberated as Sotera drew her sword. "How enlightening. And I shall bring about your end right—"

I blinked and Mother Mal was gone. The air smelled like deep woods and clear nights under the stars. An oppressive gloom I hadn't noticed tinging the edges of the room drew back. As though we'd been freed from stasis, Sotera's guards burst in a moment later and spread out.

Sotera, for maybe the first time I'd ever seen, looked frightened. She walked up to her throne, checked around the back. She stared at the ceiling as though Mother Mal had somehow phased herself through solid rock and crystal. Then she walked back to me, sheathing her sword as she did.

"That's the second time you messed up, and I intend to make you pay for it."

She jabbed two fingers into my chest. The blow was an electric current, shocking white behind my eyelids, punching air from my lungs. I sank to my knees, smelling singed cloth and flesh.

"How did you bring her here?" Sotera raged. "Was it another wildling trick Rune taught you? Did you whisper to the worms or speak to the roots?"

"I—didn't—couldn't—" I gasped.

"Liar!"

Sotera paced before me. She was irate, unreasonable. She knew I couldn't have possibly contacted Mother Mal. But whomever Mother Mal was had circumnavigated the power Sotera thought she had. And that terrified her.

"I thought I'd made clear what would happen if you didn't listen to me," Sotera said, her voice dangerously low. "But time and time again you usurp me, if not with your words, then with your actions and refusal to *do what I say*."

The side doors were thrown open, and Qell and Raki were dragged in. Qell's lip was swollen twice its normal size, her right leg bent at a wrong angle as though they'd put it over a stone and smashed it. One of Raki's ears had been savagely ripped off. His blood left a wet trail on the floor.

"No," I whispered. I hadn't been careful enough. All the times I thought I'd been subverting Sotera she'd been one step ahead. "They had nothing to do with this. I coaxed them into helping me."

"Then their blood is on your hands," Sotera said.

Qell managed to raise her head. Her one eye that wasn't caked in blood met mine.

Take him. Promise me you'll take him.

Sotera grabbed Qell's hair and yanked her head back. "I'd ask for last words, had we not already cut out your traitorous tongue."

Sotera raised a hand, fingers pressed together like a sharpened knife. I closed my eyes but couldn't block out the sound of wet flesh parting as she drove her hand through Qell's chest. Raki howled. There was a dull, squishy thump as Qell's body hit the floor.

Sotera grabbed Raki's hair next and held her blood-stained hand out toward me. "There's no more collateral after him. Next will be your human—"

I pitched forward, thrown by the violent tremor that shook the palace, stronger than the one before. Earth screamed and roared as it was split apart. A deep rumbling forced me to cover my ears, and by the time the worst of the first quake subsided, the throne room looked as though it'd been bombed.

My bloody knees and palms smarted as I pushed to standing. Through the dust and broken crystal, I could just make out where Qell's limp body had been thrown onto the nearest pile of rubble, her legs crushed beneath part of a chandelier. Raki clutched her hand, crying silently.

No more. I wouldn't let Sotera kill anyone else or hold more innocent lives over my head. This was my chance. I'd take it or die.

Sotera was screaming for her guards. One of those nearby tried to stumble toward me, but I sidestepped them and slammed my hand against his chest, drawing every drop of magic from him until the pallor of his crystal dulled and he slumped dead. I used that magic to withdraw the sword from my arm. My new Sliver.

The grip was cool, the entire blade light and slightly smeared with my blood. The arm I'd drawn it from felt brittle, as though I'd bruised it against the wall, but the wound in my skin healed up almost immediately.

I found Sotera's shape through the haze.

She saw me coming a moment before I stabbed. She darted to the side, just enough to avoid Sliver's vicious point, and then stared at the sword, disbelieving.

"How—"

My next strike made contact, only a little, but the crystal blade peeled through her hardened body like flesh, in a way I'd seen no wildling steel do. Black silt, thick as human blood, seeped out.

Sotera snarled and spun out of range.

"So you do bleed," I huffed. "I'd like to see more of it."

Sotera's expression was one of unbridled loathing as she pressed her hand to the wound. "You idiot. Everything I've done, all the times I've hurt you, was to make you stronger. You could have been a queen, and now you would throw it all in my face."

Using two hands, I swung at her, but the movement was sluggish. My captivity had left me weakened and out of practice, and Sotera was a far more formidable fighter. I couldn't press the attack, much as I wanted to.

I glanced toward Raki. Beyond the pile of rubble where Qell's body lay, an enormous gash split the wall. It was big enough to slip through.

The second's hesitation cost me.

Sotera bludgeoned my side, and though I put my left arm up to block, I felt my bone shatter. Agony ripped from my wrist to elbow, shooting to the base of my neck.

"You gave up your element of surprise for a paltry attack," Sotera sneered. "You haven't learned a thing—"

She was thrown away from me as another tremor shook the palace. Cradling my throbbing arm, I kicked out toward Raki. He hadn't moved from Qell's side.

"Get up," I panted. The pain was making my head spin and the words difficult to form. "I'm sorry, but we have to go."

He sobbed harder.

"Raki, I promised her I'd get you out. Don't waste her sacrifice."

Raki at last lowered her to the floor. He wiped the gritty tears from his face.

"I have to find Peyton," I said. "Then I'm hoping you already know a way out."

"I know where," he managed. "To both."

Together we skirted the guards and made it into the maze of palace hallways. I darted left after Raki, who seemed to know exactly where to go. Around the next corner, I spotted the guard who usually stood outside my cell. The one who'd likely ratted out Qell and Raki.

"You!"

He leveled his spear, but in one clean cut I sliced off the point and drove my blade through his chest, shattering his heart into pieces.

I pulled my blade free and let his body drop. I didn't feel any better.

"Thank you," Raki said. He pointed at the door behind him. "There."

I cut through the deadbolt on the door and threw it open. Peyton was wide awake, clutching at a bedpost to steady herself.

"Val!" She looked my bloody self over. "What—"

"No questions," I said. "If you want to escape, follow me."

She followed, and for not the first time, I wondered why I'd bothered. Whether intentional or not, her actions had trapped me down here. I *should* want to leave her to whatever fate Sotera had in store, just like she had left me. But no matter how much I tried to convince myself, I couldn't do it.

Weak. Sotera was right. I was incredibly weak.

The palace was in chaos as Raki led us around the packs of guards and the worst of the destruction. He didn't hesitate at the corners and seemed to know exactly when to hang back to let packs of fleeing courtiers run past.

At last he threw open a door and led us down a darkened, narrow stairway.

"We should be going up," Peyton called, clutching a stitch in her side.

"Trust me," Raki replied.

Halfway down the stairs he turned sharply left, through a narrow split in the wall, so well blended I would have passed right by without a second glance. There were more stairs, and then we emerged at the shore of a lazuline underground lake. It smelled of clean freshwater. The tremors had cracked the ceiling and magma trickled into the center of the lake, sending steam billowing up.

"Your arm. Sword. Quickly," Raki said to me.

Sucking in a breath, I tenderly pressed Sliver's tip into my shattered forearm. With only a little pressure, it sank straight through my skin without leaving a single mark. A gasp of relief escaped my lips as some of the pain lessened. My arm was still broken and brittle, but useable.

"I had no idea you could do that," Peyton murmured.

"I'm shocked," I said. "You seemed to know so much about me already."

"Hurry." Raki pointed across the steaming lake. "Up."

I had no clue where he meant for us to escape, but I'd trust him. He'd gotten us this far.

Raki continued casting nervous glances behind us as we hurried across the smooth-worn rocks of the shore.

"We're fine," I assured him. "They won't find us down here."

Raki didn't look the least bit convinced. "Wraith," he muttered.

In the wall on the other side of the lake was a shaft similar to the one I'd tried to escape through, though thankfully far less steep and not slicked with water or burning to the touch.

We moved steadily but slow, clambering up rocky hand-holds like a ladder. Too much weight on my arm sent sharp pain deep through to my shoulder. A small hiss escaped Peyton's lips every time she reached with her injured hand. Only Raki seemed to have no trouble. He'd scamper above to the next broad ledge and wait for us. More than once he held back for us to pass, peering the way we'd come.

"Hurry," was all he said. "They are close."

"He's starting to scare me," Peyton said. "And who's he talking about?"

I didn't know. And I didn't want to admit that he was starting to scare me, too.

After what felt like an hour of constant climbing, the shaft began to level off and we reached a somewhat flat area to rest. I laid my throbbing arm over my stomach and tried to catch my breath. Peyton mopped at her soaked forehead, streaking blood from her missing finger. "Any idea where it comes out?"

"I know about as much as you," I said. The words came out more clipped than I intended, unmoored by fatigue and pain.

She frowned, eyes sad. "I know you're upset. There's nothing I can say to express how sorr—"

"Oh, would you stop!" I snapped. "I don't know what's worse, the fact that you let the worshippers of the Mother Tree use me or that you won't quit trying to shove your inane apologies down my throat."

"I wish I could explain everything to you, every bad choice I made and promise I was told."

"But you can't. And I don't want to hear it. Right now, we focus on getting out. And then, if we survive, you can give me all the lame excus—"

Grating came from beneath us, like claws on stone. I forced myself to my feet. The pain in my arm grew as I drew Sliver and held it out. "Both of you behind me. Now."

Peyton and Raki scrambled to obey. I held Sliver higher, and its faint glow reflected off glowing obsidian eyes. Two of Sotera's crystal beasts had crawled after us. They growled, mouths full of glittering teeth.

"Keep moving up," I said, voice tight. "I'll be right—"

The first beast charged. Thanks to my shattered arm, I was forced to turn my body to the opposite side to deflect the blow, knocking me into the far wall. I pushed myself off before I'd fully recovered, and not a moment too soon. Sparks flew as the beast's claws raked where I'd been. I stabbed blindly, feeling resistance as Sliver penetrated deep into the beast's crystal flesh.

It died with a satisfying whimper.

"Behind it, Val!" Peyton yelled.

The second beast leapt over the dead body of its friend, its immense weight easily pummeling me to the ground. Hot breath washed over my face as I jammed Sliver into its mouth to keep it from snapping its jaws around my throat. My left arm screamed in agony.

Just when it felt as though its weight would cause me to cleave my head off with my own sword, the beast gave a high-pitched whine and slumped off me.

I stared at its body and then scrambled to my feet, cradling my bad arm. Peyton was gawking at me.

"Did you...?" I started.

"That's an interesting sword. I see you've picked up some new tricks since we last met."

I swung around and a strong hand caught my wrist. Sliver's glow cut harsh lines over Rune's face. His teeth were barred in a villainous grin. The circlet of the High King of the Wilds—woven silver thorns, raven's feathers, jeweled berries —was ostentatiously crooked in his coarse golden hair.

"Hello, little fox," he said. "I've finally found you."

CHAPTER
FIVE

I could only stare, drinking in his every detail. The faint scar along the hollow of his neck I didn't think he'd had before. The simmering glow of his gold-red eyes, vibrant in the dark as they remained fixed on me.

Rune cocked his head. "I can see you're in awe of my majesty. I hope the reverence doesn't wear off too quickly."

I recovered some of my wits, and speech along with them. "Took you long enough."

"We can agree on that. You'll be shocked to learn I've run into some snags since we last parted. I'll tell you all about them later. The others are just above—"

I threw my good arm around him. Nothing too intimate, but a small show of how grateful I was.

"How interesting," Rune purred. The sinuous cords of muscle along his arms gradually untensed, before he cautiously returned the hug. "And I didn't even have to threaten you."

I hissed as his pressure aggravated my arm. Rune drew away, eyes narrowing as he fully took me in. Horror, then rage, flashed across his face before he shuttered both. "Marian can heal you."

"Heal them first," I said. "Petyon and one of Those Below, Raki."

"Xander!" Rune barked. A moment later, Xander—nubs of horns curling from his head, a bow wrapped in his heavily calloused fingers—appeared from the shadows above.

"Val! You—"

"Later," Rune said. "Ensure there's nothing following them. Kill whoever or whatever is."

Xander finally tore his eyes from me and hurried down into the dark. Peyton, Raki, and I followed Rune up to another flat chamber where two more figures waited in the soft glow of fluttering, caged bats.

"Our guide, Verily," Rune explained, gesturing to one of Those Below, his skin a granite gray. "He's been communicating with Raki."

"You actually made it," Marian said.

The last time I'd seen her, she'd believed I'd betrayed the wildlings and attacked me. Rune's happy reaction to finding me had been surprising enough. I didn't know if that same delight extended to Marian.

"I did," I said. "Eventually."

The scars along Marian's skin, colored like burned bark, stretched as she reached out for my arm, as though sensing exactly where the worst of my injuries were. A necklace of carved wooden totems around her neck clinked.

"It's broken," I said. "Think you could help?"

"If you didn't keep breaking it, I wouldn't need to heal it. You look terrible, by the way."

"Good to see you, too."

"Raki, Raki..." Verily said, embracing the boy. "And where is Qell?"

Raki could only shake his head, bottom lip quivering.

"Ah, well..." Verily patted his shoulder and then turned to Rune. "The Empress is a vengeful soul. We should be moving."

"In a moment," Rune said.

"But—"

"I said in a moment," Rune repeated, and I shivered at the command in his voice. "We've come this far. Any danger we encounter will be inevitable."

He glanced at me, and I knew that all he could see was my cut, bruised, and underfed frame. "And they will regret coming after us."

"I'll be all right," I said. "Verily has a point. We should— ouch!"

"Sit," Marian said. She tugged on my broken arm until I was forced to do so. Her hand glowed as she ran it over the worst of Sotera's damage. In moments, the stinging pins and needles subsided, though the sudden stabs of pain as the bone fused back together still made me hiss.

"Stop complaining," Marian said. "It's...been a while, but I obviously haven't had a chance to say anything. You know, about what happened when you came to warn us. Before Sotera took you Below—"

"Forget it," I said.

"I tried to kill you."

"Seriously, forget it. You wouldn't be the first. It wasn't even the first time *you* tried."

Her lips thinned even further, until they were nothing but a bloodless line. This obviously wasn't the response she'd hoped for. Not too long ago, I'd have been ecstatic to receive something even resembling an apology from a wildling, but now it just felt awkward. We'd both hurt so many others in so many ways I couldn't bring myself to accept what I didn't deserve.

Marian's hand reached my wrist and her magic glow faded with a small flourish. "Right. Good. Glad that's cleared up."

Rune peered into the darkness where Xander had gone. "Make sure it's healed up so it doesn't slow you down. Once we start moving, we can't stop."

I pulled my arm away from Marian and stood. I was proud that I only felt a little unsteady. "You won't have to worry about me."

Rune looked like he wanted to say something to that. Many somethings.

"I have a lot to tell you," I said. "I don't know all that's happened since I've been down here. All I know is that you can't attack the human world, no matter what they've done."

Marian scoffed. Rune's gold-red eyes snapped to mine. "It pains me to admit, but I have no idea what you're talking about," he said.

"Sotera told me—"

The near-silent scuff of leather on rock preceded Xander's return. "I can't *see* anything, but I swear there's something behind us. Like a shadow or—"

Something moved in the darkness at Xander's back.

"The wraith!" Raki gasped. "Run!"

He squirmed out of Verily's arm and scampered farther up the tunnel.

"Marian, ensure our way out is secure," Rune said. "We might need it soon." He shouldered up beside Xander and me. "Let's see about this wraith."

Marian looked ready to protest being sent away before roughly grabbing Peyton and dragging her up. Wood strained as Xander nocked an arrow and fluidly pulled it back, tip pointed at the dark.

We didn't have to wait long until the wraith appeared, clambering into the circle of our light.

"Dearest cousin Rune," Vanesi croaked, voice like grating rock. "I so hoped I'd find you."

Rune's face drained of blood. "You died," he said. "I drove a sword straight through your heart."

"You did." Vanesi paused, as though the memories of Rune slaughtering Lord Aleki and taking Portland were only now returning to her. "Yet here I am. Alive. Mostly."

Parts of her snow-pale figure had been consumed by crystal, claiming her throat and most of her left side. The flesh of her face was scoured with scars, while a glassy smooth eye replaced one of her real ones.

I could make out the faint auric glow of the heart gem deep within her chest, pulsing strongly.

"You weren't entirely dead," I guessed.

"She was. I made sure of it," Rune said through gritted teeth.

I remembered visiting the grotto after Rune's takeover, examining where the bodies had been covered by impenetrable crystal. I'd felt no magic in Aleki's corpse. Yet Vanesi's had contained a spark.

"I remained on the edge of death, insulated by the crystal," Vanesi said. "Until Sotera found me and gave me new purpose. Would you like to guess what that was?"

"Xander."

Rune had barely finished speaking before Xander released his arrow, nocked, and fired again, so fast his arm was nothing but a blur.

The first shot glanced off Vanesi's shoulder, and then she was moving. I started to bring Sliver around, but Rune deflected Vanesi's knife with his own and shoved me behind him.

"After the others!" he barked. He lashed out at Vanesi with a savage kick and then fled behind Xander and me.

"They after us?" Marian asked when we caught up with them.

"Vanesi," was all I was able to get out.

"What the hel—" Marian's eyes widened as an inhuman shriek followed us. Then she was shoving the others. "Move it!"

We didn't slow. I could still hear the scrape of Vanesi's nails on stone, her ragged breathing dogging our steps. A couple times the others stopped to heave chunks of rock behind us to cover our escape, though I doubted that slowed her down. After all, how could we hope to stop a vengeful ghost?

Eventually, the incline leveled off and the tunnel lengthened. As it did, I felt something I thought I never would again: the hum of life, tingling against my skin, calling to a deeper part of me.

"We're close," I said.

"Yes," Rune agreed. "Does this look familiar?"

We'd stepped into a cavern full of enormous crystalline trees. I recognized the path across from me—blocked by thick webs of vines—as the one Rune and I had taken to the heart tree.

I also recognized where we were, and I didn't like it.

"You came through Mog Moren," I said.

"I didn't agree to it," Marian said, casting Rune a dark look. "But it was the easiest way."

"It might have also changed since you two were here last," Xander said.

"Rune!" Vanesi's screech echoed behind us. We hurried to the other side of the cavern, and once we were all up, I helped Verily and Raki push a large stone to block the passageway behind us. Weakness tugged at my limbs, not just from my condition, but the sudden taste of lulling yarrow on my tongue. Mog Moren was full of it, using that and isolation from any Wild greenery to keep its prisoners in line.

Peyton let out a squeal of alarm.

"It's dead," Rune said. "I made sure of that."

The enormous, bark-scaled snake that had once guarded this cave lay unmoving at our feet. Venom dripped from its fangs, wearing deep grooves in the stone floor.

"Don't be so impressed," Rune said. "It was already weakened. I simply sent it to its end sooner."

Peyton seemed in a daze as our group hurried around the snake's hulking body.

"So you kept your promise?" I said to Rune.

"You'll have to be more explicit," he said. "I've made and broken so many."

"You said once that you would return and destroy Mog Moren. So, did you?"

In answer, Rune gestured before him as we stepped out of the cave.

The desolate pit of Mog Moren was in disarray. Numerous raging fires lit the ashen central columns and night sky in flickers of orange and red. The second guardian beast—this one resembling a large ape—lay dead with over a dozen arrows protruding from its flesh. Former prisoners, guards, and what I assumed were Rune's wildlings, were spread out in clumps of battle.

I spotted some of the prisoners stabbing the corpse of a guard with the very spears they'd been forced to fight each other with. Dozens more prisoners were using the chaos to flee up the narrow path sidewinding up to the lip of Mog Moren. The encircling tree line of the Wilds was beyond that. Dozens, maybe even a hundred, could escape tonight.

"Cassius!" Rune barked.

One of the prisoners broke off from the nearest group

butchering the guards. I was startled by his appearance. This wasn't the frightened boy who'd helped hide us the first time Rune and I had snuck through Mog Moren. His expression was ferocious. His arms and chest were splattered with blood.

He broke into a broad smile. "You can see it's going well. Turns out *they*," he drove his spear into the gut of the nearest fallen guard and twisted, "are not so tough after all. Perhaps instead of teaching us to fight for the Lords, they should have kept us weak."

"Gather your grandmother and those who are still alive and get out," Rune said.

"With all due respect, High King, I've waited years for this moment. I'm not leaving until I've had my fill."

"Remember what you promised me." Rune's tone was all warning. "Your freedom comes with a price."

Cassius gave a harsh laugh. "I haven't forgotten my debt, but I want all the revenge I'm owed, and I'm not leaving until I have it."

"If you keep it up, you'll die here, instead of living long enough to see it through," Marian said. "Stop wasting our time and get out."

Cassius tugged his spear free. He spun it to flick the blood off, before giving a shallow bow to both Rune and Marian. "Most of my life has been as a prisoner here. Who am I to argue with those so much more worldly than me?"

He glanced back at the few guards who were still fighting the swelling tide of prisoners. "A little more, just a little more. Then I'll join you."

Marian growled as he threw himself back into the fray. Rune didn't look all that surprised. As someone who'd endured Mog Moren, I supposed he understood all too well Cassius's desire for retribution.

Pitius, one of Rune's spies, appeared at my feet, kneeling

with a hand to her chest. The persimmons growing from her hair were dusted yellow with yarrow powder, as was her speckled green clothes. "My Lord Rune."

"Update," Rune said.

"Most of the guards are dead. Those remaining have barricaded themselves in one of the houses. Some of the prisoners refuse to leave."

"Then forget them. Get those who are still trying to escape out. Kill the guards."

"Of course." Pitius gave me a soft smile. "I'm glad our Lord has found you, Val." Then she was gone.

"Just how many do you have under your command?" Peyton said in awe.

"Enough," Marian said. "More than you pitiful humans can hope to—"

"Join those who are leaving," Rune said to Raki and Verily. "You have my protection. Xander, ensure no one gives them any trouble."

"We'll see you soon, then," Xander said to me.

Raki gave me a grateful nod before he, Xander, and Verily joined the escaping group. Rune watched one of the central pillars collapse as fire scoured its insides.

"I know what it looks like, but don't think me too noble."

"Don't worry, I wouldn't dare think that," I said.

Marian snorted. Rune gave me a wicked grin.

"After the Lords fell and I took the throne, only those guards who didn't flee their position or I hadn't yet killed remained here. The prisoners simply needed a little encouragement, and I needed access to the cave. As well as more wildings with enough desire for revenge to join me. I'm happy to say we've suffered few losses in our attempt."

"Now we need to get out, too," I said. Peyton's skin was already turning sallow with the effects of the yarrow spore, and my head swam whenever I moved too fast. Along with my already fragile state, I was near pathetically useless.

Rune gestured to the path leading to the lip of Mog Moren. "Head up. I'll follow close—"

My legs gave out. At first, I thought my body had finally failed me, but a second later another tremor followed the first. "Have you been feeling them up here, too?"

"This is new," Marian muttered. In a flash, she was racing up the winding path to the lip of Mog Moren. I could make out her slender figure peering toward the west.

"Waves!" she screamed.

My insides went cold. I hadn't considered how Bendeti would react when he found I'd escaped. Vengefully, it seemed, and Mog Moren was close to the shore.

"I didn't realize King Bendeti was so interested in the conflicts of the land," Rune said.

"It's because his soon-to-be-bride escaped," I said.

Rune cocked an eyebrow. "That will require some very detailed explanation later. You're both too slow."

He easily pulled me and a protesting Peyton to his sides. An enormous vine, half dead but stable, burst from the choked earth and lifted us out of the pit.

I steadied myself and spun to the west. My breathing hitched.

A wall of water, at least six stories high, rushed toward us from the coast, swelling with every passing second. A low roar like an approaching fighter jet shook the air. Other wildlings were abandoning all semblance of order and fleeing as fast as they could toward the tree line. All I could do was stand there, dumbfounded. There was a cruel sort of irony to escape one prison, only to be immediately crushed by the king I'd scorned.

"Get back to the human world," Rune said. "Find safety there."

I turned toward him so fast my neck smarted. "What?"

"You heard me."

I should have been overjoyed at being sent back to the human world so easily. Even without the ongoing conflict, I knew I'd be safest there, out of Sotera's and Bendeti's clutches. Out of reach of Rune's machinations.

Even still, it felt wrong to abandon them after they'd sacrificed so much. After I'd dreamed of being free for so long.

I nodded toward Bendeti's growing wave. "You can't seriously stop that, can you?"

Rune's smirk was more dangerous than I remembered, hardened and challenging. "Some things have changed since we were separated. I wouldn't have survived long among the circling snakes if my powers hadn't grown as well. Raquel, to me!"

Raquel the Beastmaster broke from fleeing masses and rushed over to us. Despite his fearful expression, his face split into a broad grin when he saw me, showing off his buck teeth and jingling the fang hanging from one ear. "You want what we talked about, Lord Rune?"

"Now, preferably," Rune agreed.

Raquel started rolling up a shirt sleeve. "He came right back to me and has been waiting ever since. It's strange. It's like he *wants* to be with you, Val."

I had no idea what he was talking about, until one of Raquel's tattoos dripped off his arm like oil. The detritus of tree branches, husks of lulling yarrow, withered vines, and dried bones drew together to form Erebus's hulky shape. Peyton backed up as Erebus bared thorned teeth.

"Take her to the human world, to safety," Rune said to him.

"I'm not leaving," I said. The wave was nearly on us, so close I could see the curl at its peak.

"I disagree," he said.

I grabbed his arm. "This won't keep me safe. Sotera's up to something, and she'll go through you to get to me. You *need* me."

"Exactly. Which is why you have to leave." His arm snaked around me.

"Don't you dare. Don't you *dare*."

I tried to hold tighter, but Rune easily threw me onto Erebus's waiting back. Peyton was placed behind me a moment later.

"Rune!" Vines curled out of Erebus's neck and secured my hands to his back. "Erebus, let me off. Rune, you stupid, arrogant bastard!"

"Don't worry," Rune said. "I found you once. I don't intend to lose you again."

My cry of rage was lost as Erebus took off. Peyton gripped my waist hard enough to ache as the desolate landscape surrounding Mog Moren blurred, soon giving way to trees before we were in the Wilds again.

It was both a literal and figurative breath of fresh air, so crisp a sob of relief escaped my lips. I'd almost forgotten how deep and vibrant colors could be; the smell of sweet fruit and clean dew; the stickiness of spider webs as we tore through them; the aliveness that radiated out of every leaf, bough, branch, from every curtain of hanging moss and every gold-eyed glint of beasts lurking in the shadows. Any fear I once had toward the Wilds was shed like an old jacket, and I felt nothing but relief.

But worry for the wildlings ate at me. I only had time to look back once—to see an enormous hand of greenery reaching from the Wilds, a lone figure at its base, to meet the rising wall of water—before the trees obscured everything.

"You *idiot*," I seethed, but my words were lost in the wind. Peyton whimpered as Erebus continued to rip through the

Wilds, sticking exclusively to the shadows. He growled at night beasts that drew too close and wove through root-lined tunnels and around towering trees. Through my streaming eyes, I could just make out the choppy water of Hood Canal approaching.

"Erebus—"

Without slowing, he burst out into the moonless night, barely grazing the tops of the waves. I tucked my head against the snarls of his back as we touched land again, and then just as quickly were back over the water.

At last, the lessening wind on my face told me we were slowing. Erebus made one final leap from the water onto an open, grassy park and came to a stop, his breath billowing in the cool night. It was early enough the park was empty. Less than half a mile away, the Space Needle poked above the skyline. We weren't in the heart of Seattle, but we were close.

"Off," Peyton groaned, smacking my back. "Need off."

My hands now unbound, I helped us both slide to the ground, and Peyton hurried to a bush. I heard her retching. Erebus growled.

"Thank you for carrying us," I said. "But you should have let me stay."

Another growl I interpreted as, *We both know that's a bad idea right now.*

But it wasn't right that I was here, either. I should be with the wildlings. If it weren't for me, Rune wouldn't even be High King. How dare he send me away, even if the move made sense.

"You can go back to him," I said to Erebus. "I might need a ride later, though."

Erebus scratched the ground with a clawed foot, shrinking from the light of the nearest lamp. Then he vanished, leaving a pile of forest debris at my feet. A cool splotch of shadow ran up my right arm and settled with a contented grumble on my shoulder.

I'm with you now, Erebus seemed to say. *Whether you like it or not.*

"Where'd that...thing go?" Peyton wiped her mouth as she emerged from behind the bushes. Her eyes darted around. "Did you send it back? Tell me you sent it back."

"You should go stay with Joshua, if he doesn't hate you, too," I said.

Peyton's shoulders fell. "You should come, too. I can talk to him. Try to explain things."

"We both know that won't work. Stay with him, or those worshippers of the Mother Tree you love so much. Maybe you can tell Father Dumas he was more right about me than he thought."

It was a risk to let her go to any of them with all the knowledge she had of Rune and Sotera. But someone from the human world had to be warned. And despite everything, I wanted her safe. She wouldn't be if she stayed around me.

"Father Dumas... The others, they want to see you," Peyton said. "You have no idea what you mean to them, Val. And to *me*. You're so much more important than you know."

I was their prize. Their *cherished*.

"I have a pretty good idea," I said. "Stay safe, Peyton. And keep that missing finger wrapped up until you get it properly looked at."

"You don't have anywhere to go," Peyton called after me.

"I'll manage," I called back as I walked away. "I always do."

CHAPTER

SIX

The realization of where I could go came to me the moment I reached Capitol Hill. I didn't like it, but I didn't like many things recently, and it wasn't as though I had much choice. I'd fled with the threadbare clothes the seamstress had given me, no shoes, and the cold was starting to sink in. The few looks I received from passersby were unkind or full of the kind of suspicion that would bring unwanted scrutiny. I had Sliver and Erebus, but he couldn't manifest with all the city lights. And I was exhausted.

Which was why, nearly an hour later, I stood at the front door of a townhouse on a quiet, sloped street, near a neighborhood market and Scandinavian café. The townhouse looked new, a far cry from the wretched apartment I lived in with Peyton. *Had* lived in with Peyton. Seemed the woman who hopefully still lived here had employers who paid her well.

I rubbed my chilled hands and then hovered my finger over the doorbell. I was taking a massive risk. I could only hope the rumors of my traitorous actions hadn't spread beyond the

70

Department of Fringe Affairs. I hoped she wouldn't stab me on sight.

I rang the bell. Then rang it again a half minute later.

From the other side of the door came the light thump of someone mushing their face against the peephole. "Who the hell is it this early?"

"A friend, I hope," I said.

It was two more long breaths before the door cracked open. Half of Gracie's suspicious, freckled face appeared, hand clutching a broom like a spear. Her eyes widened.

"Holy—*Val?*"

"Me." I held up my empty hands, trying not to shiver pathetically. "I can explain. Mostly. I need a place to crash, just for a short time."

I could almost see Gracie's mind failing to compute, but miracle upon miracles, she didn't slam the door in my face. She halfway stepped out and looked up and down the street before stepping back inside and letting out a breath. "Get in."

I did, nearly collapsing with relief the moment warmth hit me. Gracie locked the door after. "Jesus, you're not wearing anything! And your feet... Is this a relationship thing? You have to run from your boyfriend or something? Wait, didn't you used to live on Bainbridge Island..."

She waited for me to fill in the blanks.

"I need to sleep," I said. "I'll explain everything after that. I promise you're not in any danger."

I cursed my stupid mouth as Gracie's eyebrows rose. "I wasn't worried about that," she said. "Thinking I should be now."

She chewed her bottom lip, debating, and then let out a sigh. "I have a pull-out couch in the spare room. Help me set it up."

She double-checked the street once more before showing

me where to unfold the bed. I helped fit the sheets and brought pillows from the couch.

"I want answers when you wake up," Gracie said when we were done. "You understand how weird this is, right?"

"Trust me, I do. I wouldn't bother you if I had any other choice."

"That doesn't make me feel any better, you know? I gave you an invitation. I mean, I totally understand if you didn't want to be friends, but I thought you might be dead."

My eyelids were starting to droop. "Not yet."

"Not yet...right," Gracie muttered. "Go to sleep. You look ready to pass out."

The waning high of the last few hours petered out, and I practically flopped onto the bed. The springs jabbed into my side, the pillows were scratchy, and the sheets smelled so strongly of artificial lavender it almost made me wish for lulling yarrow spores.

It was the best thing I'd ever lain on, and I fell into an entirely dreamless sleep.

It was light when I awakened. My body ached and arm throbbed so badly I swore I'd rebroken it. Out the window, I caught the tawny flash of feathers in the tree overlooking a neighbor's miniscule backyard. Whatever it was fluttered away as I forced myself up and into the bathroom.

Gracie had thought ahead and left me a pile of her clothes on the counter.

Hope some of these fit was written in curly script on a sticky note atop it.

I startled when I caught my reflection in the mirror.

The seamstress had done what she could, but there was no hiding the unusually wild tangle of my cracked, dry hair. My skin was coated in yarrow spore, crystal dust, and, not surprisingly, blood—though mine or someone else's, I didn't know.

With the edgy, suspicious expression I seemed to always wear nowadays, I perfectly fit the image of something that had crawled from beneath the earth: it was a wonder Gracie had let me in at all.

Under the shower's hot water, I took my time scrubbing off the dirt and terrible memories of my time Below. Erebus growled when I tried to wash his chosen spot along my jutting collarbone.

There was another flutter of wings from outside as I stepped out and found some clothes that fit. The sleeves of the shirt billowed like a ruffled dress, the smallest jeans needing a belt to stay around my hips. Some of the muscle I'd gained from years in the Wilds still clung to my bones, but barely, giving my frame a sickly toned look. I glared at the discarded clothes from Below. They were a sad pile of filthy rags, a terrible reminder of what I'd endured, and what it'd taken from me.

I withdrew a crystal blade from my arm and furiously shredded them into pieces before stuffing them in the trash.

I didn't feel any better.

Now that I wasn't so exhausted, the worries crept in. Gracie hadn't turned me in, but she'd want answers, some of which I couldn't share. I'd have to decide just how much to tell to keep her happy while still keeping her safe.

Something shattered from the kitchen. Gracie screamed.

I rushed out and narrowly avoided cutting my bare feet on shards of a ceramic plate spread across the kitchen floor.

Gracie had backed up against the counter, gaping fearfully at Rune crouched on the center island. The skylight was open, and it seemed he'd dropped through it, clearly without alerting Gracie first.

"You're a-a—" Gracie could only sputter.

Rune glanced at me. "There you are, Val. This human's

reaction makes your lack of fear during our first meeting all the more impressive."

"You actually found me," was all I could say.

His smile was every wickedly wondrous thing the Wilds offered. "Of course. Where would I be without my trick?"

Rune speaking gave Gracie time to recover from her shock. She lunged for a kitchen knife and brandished it at him. "Wildling. Here. Val? Knows you?"

"*Put the knife down.*" I could practically taste the honeyed compulsion lacing Rune's words. "*Do it now, before you hurt yourself.*"

Gracie's limbs went slack, face smoothing to blank compliance, even while her eyes flicked fearfully between us.

"You won't compel her, Rune," I demanded. "This is her house. She's helping me."

"And if she betrays us?" he said.

"Then that's *your* fault. I went to her because I had nowhere else to go. So when we're over here, I call the shots, and I'm telling you to *let her go.*"

"Are you commanding the High King of the Wilds to do something?" Rune asked, eyebrow arched.

In my elation at seeing him again, I'd forgotten how much menace and power he could exude with a single look. How much savagery.

"I'm asking you nicely," I said. "Release her, or I'll break your hold myself. You know I can."

Rune looked as though he'd delight in seeing me try, but at last waved his hand. His compulsion on Gracie fell away, and she clutched at her chest, panting.

"You two...know each other? Of course you do, the way you talk... You've known each other for a while."

"And how does Val know *you*, human?" Rune asked.

"Gracie's an old friend," I answered.

Not exactly true. Back when I'd first started collecting heart gems from the Wilds, Gracie had been one of the rare other woman hunters, part of a pharmaceutical company researching Wild flora for medicinal purposes. She was a few years older than me and took me under her guidance like the younger sister she'd always wanted. We'd bonded over a couple near-death experiences and the older hunters' mutual dislike of us being there.

Eventually, the others' exclusion and bullying took its toll. The last I'd seen Gracie was over a year ago, when she'd put up her knives and moved into the city for corporate work. Before she left, she'd scribbled her address on the back of a crumpled receipt and made me promise to visit. I hadn't spoken a word to her since, not until my gamble last night.

I was such a terrible friend.

"Where's your broom?" I asked Gracie.

Without taking her eyes off Rune, she pointed to the closet. I found it buried beneath some branded T-shirts and dusty body armor and started sweeping up the shattered pieces of the plate she'd dropped.

"You should help," I told Rune. "This is your fault."

Rune waved a hand. The leaves of the tiny plant on Gracie's windowsill tripled in size, until they were long and thick as an elephant's trunk. They swept up all the pieces I'd missed and deposited them in the trash before curling around Rune, waiting for his next command. Gracie swallowed hard. I rolled my eyes.

"Keep showing off cheap tricks and you'll drain your magic," I said.

"Yes, I forgot how irritatingly vile and lifeless your world is," Rune said. His eyes pieced me. "Though, technically, it's not *your* world anymore, is it?"

"What—What is he talking about, Val?" Gracie managed.

Right. That. We'd need to discuss that. But later. Rune already looked pale. He wouldn't die over here, but outside the Wilds, his power was greatly diminished. He was still dangerous, though. Always dangerous, for more than one reason.

"I need a drink," Gracie muttered. She pulled a glass bottle of cold brew from the fridge, poured herself a heaping cupful, eyed the wine when she put it back, and then turned to us. "And I need answers. Now. You have no idea how much I'm risking having a wildling, a *wildling*," she muttered in disbelief, "in my freaking kitchen."

"High King of the wildlings," Rune corrected. "What you humans probably think of as your greatest enemy."

"Not helping, Rune," I said as Gracie's face paled further.

I filled Gracie in with as much as I could, trying to leave out details that might get her in bigger trouble or cause her to distrust us more than she likely already did.

Rune chimed in with a few unhelpful additions, but mostly he prepared food. He took the oranges, pears, and apples that were about to turn from Gracie's fridge and magicked them to swell with juice like sweet nectar; then he used his glass knife to cut them into manageable sizes before presenting them to us. I was surprised at the domestic action, but mostly at the thoughtfulness. I gratefully gobbled some slices down. Gracie didn't touch any of it.

"So you're saying this Sotera is the real threat," she said after I'd talked so much my voice had gone raspy. "I haven't heard anything about her, or of these Below guys."

"Those Below," I said.

"But *him*," Gracie pointed at Rune. "We're all but at total war with his kind. That's all the news ever talks about. The Wilds are taking over this, the wildlings are doing that. If they knew you could get over here so easily..."

Rune popped an orange slice into his mouth and gave her a

predatory smile. "But they won't, will they? Not unless you wish for terrible things to happen to you and yours."

"Rune doesn't want war with the humans," I said, before he could scare Gracie anymore.

"You don't?" Gracie said.

Rune busied himself with wiping off his glass knife and didn't answer.

"Right now, we're trying to figure out what Sotera's next move is and how to stop her," I said. "But during my time Below I didn't learn much. Sotera made sure of it. I've been a little out of touch. Rune knows what he knows, but I'm thinking that while we're here in the human world we might be able to find out if they've discovered something different."

"And you have an idea of how to do this?" Rune said.

"I haven't thought that far ahead," I admitted. I glared at him. "I wouldn't be here at *all* if it weren't for you."

"Yes, I'm still waiting for my thank you."

I shook my head. Gracie sipped her coffee, barely taking her eyes off Rune. She seemed to be debating something. "I've... heard some rumors that might be what you're looking for. But that's all they are, rumors. I haven't paid much attention to them because it didn't matter before, but maybe...maybe they'll help you."

"You've piqued my interest," Rune said.

"The company I work for—the department, anyway—they're on the cutting edge of integrating heart gem magic into practical application. We have hunters going into the Wilds all the time. One of them might have learned something you haven't yet..."

She trailed off as Rune's glare grew progressively darker. "Please, go on. You were just getting to the part where you used stolen heart gems."

"And you think you might be able to find out from one of them?" I coaxed Gracie.

She stared fixedly at her coffee. "Maybe. But I have to go to work first."

"What makes you think I'll let you leave?" Rune said. "You know I'm here. You could rat us out."

"And if I don't show up, they'll *definitely* know something's wrong."

"Perhaps that's a risk I'm willing to take."

"Stop teasing her, Rune," I said.

Gracie shot me a look that said, *you call* that *teasing?* But I'd grown too tired to mediate anymore. Something about being relatively safe and comfortable had my body longing for the rest it hadn't gotten in weeks.

"It'd be great if you can find out anything, Gracie," I said. "I promise I won't let Rune destroy the place while you're gone."

"I'll hold you to that," she said. I heard her muttering to herself as she went to get ready. While she did, I headed back to bed. I could feel Rune's eyes follow me until I closed the door.

Gracie had left by the time I got up. A muted silence rested over the townhouse.

I swept the apples slices that had browned into the trash and returned the other fruit into the fridge. Her dishwasher was clean, and I spent the better part of five minutes trying to figure out where everything went. These small things helped calm me. It'd been a while since I'd done anything so domestic, something that didn't feel like, if I did it wrong, there'd be disastrous consequences. Or maybe I was stalling the inevitable conversation I didn't want to have.

When I couldn't put it off any longer, I found Rune in Gracie's office. He'd coaxed the lone snake plant to sprout spiraling tendrils covering the room. I supposed it made him feel more at home. He'd sprawled on the cushy chair, feet on the desk, as though reclining in his throne.

He was already looking at me when I leaned in the doorway, his expression casually expectant, yet guarded. In the ensuing beat of silence, it finally hit me that we were the only two here, alone. True privacy was something we'd rarely experienced together, and even less rarely had it gone well.

"I'm surprised," Rune said. "You didn't seem to consider that your friend might betray us." He played with one of the snake plant's tendrils, coiling it around his finger. "It feels strange even saying that. I didn't take you for one who had friends."

"Look who's talking," I said, feeling defensive at my own deficit. "And she won't talk. I trust her."

The corner of Rune's mouth quirked, as though wondering the same thing I was in that moment: whether that same trust extended to him.

"I sent the owl after her. Should she reveal anything about us, I'll know."

I thought of the tawny flash of feathers I'd seen outside the bathroom. "So that *was* your owl I saw."

"Raquel's, but yes." One of the vines picked up a framed picture of Gracie with her arms around who I assumed were her mother and father. Rune turned it over in his hands before putting it down. "You weren't telling me the whole truth."

"Funny, I was about to say the same about you," I said. "You didn't pull a knife on Gracie or blatantly threaten to kill her in some gruesome, terrible way. You're being mostly cordial."

"Perhaps my heart has softened during your time Below."

I gave him a humorless smile. "Perhaps, but I don't think so."

"Then please, enlighten me as to what you *really* think."

Rune always had an endgame, a goal. I couldn't forget that again. "While I want to believe you came only to save me, there's something else you want."

"I really was after you. Because I need you."

There's the truth. "Of course you do. For what?"

"No."

The tendrils parted as Rune leveraged himself out of the chair. I kept my arms crossed, refusing to back away as he drew closer. "First, you'll tell *me* what it is you found," he said. "You said many interesting things as we were escaping, and I want to hear them in full now."

With surprising tenderness, he took my left arm. I suppressed a shiver as he traced the inside of it, the callouses of his fingertips coarse against my skin.

"And I recall you carrying a unique sword."

"Something I picked up Below. My new Sliver."

"So it would seem. What else did you pick up?"

"A marriage."

Rune's fingers stopped near the crook of my elbow. "Is that so?"

"According to Sotera, I'm essentially a princess of Those Below, so she decided to pull a Middle Ages and use me to assure her alliance with King Bendeti."

"The king of kelp has been busy," Rune said. "If the marriage had gone through, I wonder whether you would have been able to get the taste of fish out of your mouth, or the smell of salt from your nose."

His fingers continued moving up my arm. I didn't want them to stop. I wanted him to pull me even closer and lower his lips to mine, this time fully aware of what he was doing. I wanted to cast off all my swirling thoughts of how terribly, horribly wrong it was to want Rune like that—

"Sotera told me you were going to attack the human world," I managed.

Almost reluctantly, Rune pulled his hands away, allowing me space to breathe. "And you believed her?"

I had, almost without question. A strange dichotomy had existed within me while I was Below. I'd dreamed of getting back to the one place I'd felt safe—with Rune, the wildlings, amongst the Wilds—while simultaneously thinking Rune capable of such terrible things.

"You have to admit it wasn't the craziest idea," I said.

"No doubt Sotera wanted you to attack me on sight." Rune's smirk was teasing. "I wouldn't have minded if you had. We had such fun trying to kill each other before. Things felt a lot simpler then."

I was glad I wasn't the only one who thought that. In many ways clearly being enemies was so much easier than whatever we were now. "So you're *not* planning on attacking the human world?"

"I've entertained the thought." With a flick of his hand, thorns as long as my finger extended from the surrounding tendrils. "As High King, my magic and control over the Wilds grows every day, along with those loyal to me. The humans of Seattle are more vulnerable than they know. Should they decide to begin attacking me in earnest, taking them over swiftly would be better than fighting a war on two fronts."

"But you're not going to," I said.

"There you go again, giving commands to a king."

"Which you've been for barely a month. Rune." I brushed the thorns aside, drew as close to him as I dared. "You can't attack the human world."

"Why," Rune said softly, "do you care? You aren't even one of them."

His words felt like being drenched in glacier melt, so cold they were painful and sobering in equal measure. "Take that back."

"Admit the truth. You aren't like them. You aren't like me. You aren't even like Sotera, as much as she wants you to be. The humans have given you nothing but pain."

"It's still who I choose to be, despite what anyone, you included, says."

A tendril of his thorns had curled behind me, forcing me closer to him. With a swift flick of his hand, he severed it. It fell to the floor and immediately shriveled.

"Cut off the parts of you that aren't useful," Rune said. "Forgo your love for Peyton and all other humans you thought cared about you."

"And join the Wilds?" I said. "Join you? Love *you*?"

He blinked, clearly caught off guard.

Sever the ties to those who hold you back.

I shook my head, smiling sadly. "You're just like Sotera."

I'd meant for my barb to hurt him as much as he'd hurt me, and the flash of pain in Rune's eyes showed I'd hit the mark. I left before I had to see any more of it.

<hr>

IT WAS LATE when I emerged from my bedroom again to find Gracie putting bags of Fateez Burgers, a local chain, on the kitchen counter.

"Figured you were vegetarian, being a...you know," she said to Rune as he sniffed at the bags. "Wasn't sure what you liked, Val." She eyed my too-thin frame. "Something with a lot of meat is probably a good place to start."

I thanked her profusely and wolfed down my burger and

most of my fries fast enough to give me a stomachache. Rune nibbled on his veggie burger before giving in and taking a bite. Gracie relaxed after that, as though she'd narrowly staved off a tiger's hunger.

"I saw your owl pet, Rune," she said. "At least I assume it was yours. It hung around the office all day, even followed me to lunch. Just a tip, if you want to be subtle, barn owls are nocturnal."

"The point wasn't to be subtle," Rune said.

"I figured. Still, don't send it after me anymore."

Rune stopped mid-bite. "I don't care about your human courtesies—"

"In the *human* world, in *my* house, you will."

Rune picked at his burger in mulled silence. When he was finished, a slender root snaked through a crack in the tile and pulled his bag into the ground where I assumed it'd decompose in a matter of minutes.

"We didn't finish talking before, Val," Rune said. "You learned something else during your time Below. Something I'm not sure you're keen on sharing."

I took my time finishing the last of my shake, wondering at how obvious my tells were. Then again, Rune had always been skilled at teasing out the truth from my lies.

"Someone named Mother Mal came to visit," I said. "She told Sotera that only when the thrones of the Wilds and Those Below are united can there be peace."

Rune's brow furrowed. "I'm getting tired of not knowing the things you say. Who is that?"

"She was from the Wilds, and she wasn't Sotera's friend. I figured you'd have a better idea than me."

"The Wilds is vast and much of it still a mystery, even to its king. I can hardly be expected to know every being who resides within it. Though it sounds like she should be a counselor if she's handing out advice."

I tried to put into words what my recovering mind had pieced together the last couple of days. "Sotera wanted me to take your throne once I was King Bendeti's wife. And you were removed, of course."

Gracie's mouth fell open. "Hold up, you were going to get married to a king?"

"Involuntarily," I felt necessary to clarify. "You said you've been getting stronger after taking the throne of the High King, Rune. You didn't fully have its power until you had the crown. Sotera's throne is the same, she needs a crown for her to have all her power."

"Then perhaps we remove her crown, along with her head," Rune said.

Gracie shuddered. "Do you always talk about killing people so casually? It's seriously creepy."

Rune blinked. He'd been called many things; monstrous, savage, cruel, but "creepy" likely wasn't one of them. "It may be a necessary step," he said at last.

"We can't reach Sotera that easily, though," I said. "If we could remove her crown, then we could just remove her. Instead, we could send someone down there to find a way to destroy her throne or have you take it."

"So simple," Rune said. "I think there are a few steps you're missing and the small matter of Sotera wanting to kill me on sight. But I have one throne. What's taking another?"

"Better you do that than try taking over the human world," I pointed out.

"What?" Gracie said.

"Yes, I've been thinking about that," Rune said. "I suppose, after some more consideration, allying with the humans is a better plan."

Gracie's jaw dropped so much I could see a bit of lettuce stuck between her molars.

"You want to align with humans," I clarified. "Something that no wildling has ever done since the very beginning."

"There must be a first time for everything," Rune said. "Don't seem so shocked. I've been considering it for a time."

"And you couldn't have told me this earlier? You—" I pinched the bridge of my nose. Not only had he not planned on attacking, but he'd wanted to do the exact opposite yet let me continue thinking otherwise. "How exactly were you planning on getting them to listen?"

"I figured your stepbrother would be interested to hear me out."

"Joshua?"

"Do you have another I wasn't aware of?"

"Who's Joshua? Why would he listen?" Gracie said.

"He's a part of the Department of Fringe Affairs," Rune said. "And he's gained a surprising amount of power and leadership in a short amount of time. So much so that he's the one leading expeditionary missions into the Wilds. So much so that he might have the pull to stop them."

Suddenly, it all made sense. "And you want me to convince him to listen to you."

"That's the plan."

"And that's why..." *That's why you needed me.* Rune wouldn't have risked himself and all he'd worked for to come Below simply to free me. I had to provide something in return. It made sense, and I couldn't fault him for it, even if I wanted to.

"Why me?" I finally asked.

Rune stopped tapping his fingers on the table. "Excuse me?"

"Why'd you need me specifically? Joshua is fanatically loyal to the Department of Fringe Affairs. I'm sure he's told them how I helped you. In their eyes, I'm not some hero who valiantly tried to stop the return of the High King of the Wilds. I'm practically a terrorist."

I swirled the ketchup around with my fries. "On top of that, Joshua and I haven't been close for a while. Not nearly as close as he is with Peyton. Why didn't you use her to get to him, like you did to me?"

"It had to be you," Rune said.

"But *why?*"

His mouth turned in an obdurate frown, as though he found this line of questioning tiresome. "It just did. That's all the reason I need."

"And yet it's not enough."

Gracie watched our back and forth as one would a fencing bout. I felt out of sorts. I held allegiance to no one. And for possibly the second time since meeting Rune, I had something he needed that only I could provide. If that were the case, then I would get something out of him, too.

"I'll join you," I said, "but in return you will allow me back into the Wilds from now on, whenever I desire."

"Agreed," Rune said with surprising swiftness. "That is the least of what I'd expected to offer you. But I sense there's more to it than that."

"There's nothing else."

"Ah, there you go, lying again."

The back of my neck grew hot, like I was a child caught with my childish ideas. "Do you want my help or not?"

Rune waited, the silence building to unbearable levels.

"Sotera made me feel weak, like I was less than dirt and equally as useless," I confessed. "I never want to feel that weak again. Not to her. Not even to you. I won't go crawling back to a life where I had nothing and was nothing. I will get back at her. You can give me the chance to do so."

I also had nothing in the human world that mattered as much as getting back at those who'd nearly broken me. I didn't know *what* I was, despite telling Rune otherwise. Maybe by helping him finish this I could find out. Maybe I'd only end up getting myself killed.

"Do we have a deal or not?" I asked.

"And if I refuse?" Rune answered.

"You won't."

For once, Rune looked unsure. "I am High King of the Wilds. My word there is law. Don't forget that."

"And I'm the one who helped you become king. Don't forget *that*."

We stared at each other, until Rune nodded, smirking. "Very well."

"You wanted to speak to Joshua," I said, not willing to linger on this topic any longer. "Problem is, I have no idea how to find him."

"I might."

I startled. I'd almost forgotten Gracie was there. She shrugged as we looked at her. "It's a big *might*."

"And how would you know that?" Rune said.

"I wasn't being totally upfront before. I don't work for the pharmaceutical company anymore, Val. I do file management for a company that, uh," she glanced at Rune, "uses heart gems to create weaponry."

"What a shockingly human tendency," Rune said coldly.

"We used to outsource a lot of our designs to other major cities," Gracie went on. "But communication's been more sporadic, and shipments have been delayed. They've moved development more in-house. There's a guy working in the R&D department. He was locked up for a time, I heard, but I know the DFA has visited him a couple times. He may have a line to Joshua. I could give you his address."

There were so many potential ways for this to go disastrously wrong, so many possible dead ends. Yet still I found myself nodding along with Rune.

"It seems our way forward is clear," Rune said. "Let's meet this designer of death."

"MIND IF I JOIN?"

I scooted over to make space for Gracie on her miniscule back patio. "Of course. It's your house."

"Yeah, it is. I *almost* think Rune understands that."

I gratefully took the steaming mug of tea she handed me. Along with my borrowed hoodie, it helped stave off the nightly chill. "It takes a few times. Rune's used to making his own rules."

The tea was oversweet but with a bitter aftertaste. I stared at the sky, lost in thought. Seattle's light pollution washed out any potential to see stars. It was strangely discomforting. The thick canopy obscured most of the night sky in the Wilds, but you could always get a clear view if you wanted.

I could feel Gracie watching me as we sipped in silence.

"Problem?" I said.

"Uh, yeah, many," Gracie said. "It's just... Rune isn't what I expected a wildling to be at all. I mean, we've heard the stories. Heck, I told you plenty of them back when I still hunted. He's a jerk. And I hate what he did to my office. But he's strangely... beautiful."

She blushed into her mug. "Sorry if that's weird."

"Not all that glitters," I muttered.

"What?"

"Yes, he is. All those things. The Wilds made him into what he is."

"You spent over a month with him, didn't you?"

"And other wildlings, yes."

"But none like him," Gracie pressed.

"There are none like him."

Gracie turned to me. "You like him."

I knew exactly what she meant. "I mean, I like him well enough."

"No, you *like* him. I've seen the way you look at him. Geez, you two even argue like an old married couple. I may be a hopeless romantic, but I can tell *that*."

It was my turn to take a sip. Maybe to hide my heated cheeks. Maybe to try escaping the naked truth of her words. "I respect him and what he's done."

"And you like that respect. And power."

I did. I couldn't deny that. "What's your point?"

Gracie sighed. "I don't think I have one. We've been isolated in this Seattle bubble for so long that I'm sure there's a lot going on that I don't understand, even when it comes to wildlings. But Val..."

The wariness in her tone made me brace for her next words.

"Guys like Rune, human or not, they don't change. He may feel safe, but he's dangerous."

I recalled Rune's face, serene in sleep as we curled together on the floor of an abandoned cabin. The hitch in his voice as he spoke of those who had died for him. The rage as he killed his uncle Aleki. He was part tenderness and savagery, though not always in equal measure.

I took another sip and felt the pull of my scar where Sliver emerged from. I remembered the guard I'd driven my blade through. The light leaving the Lords' eyes as I killed them, one by one, and how, instead of being horrified, I'd only wanted more.

I remembered just how much I hurt. And how much I still wanted vengeance, no matter the cost.

"Val?" Gracie said.

"Yeah, he's dangerous." I gave her what I hoped was a reassuring smile. It probably only made her more worried. "But he and I might not be all that different after all."

CHAPTER

SEVEN

Rune and I slipped away from Gracie's house in the dead of night, when the shadows were deepest and there was no threat of dawn.

Within minutes, we were skulking through Seattle's streets, staying mostly out of sight of stumbling bar patrons and those going to their night shifts. It was impossible for Rune to summon a path for us to walk this far inland, so I took another gamble, one of many I'd taken lately, and found us a city bus.

Rune had glamoured his eyes, but they still glowed vividly. His wildling clothing didn't stand out too much in the bus's dim interior. Still, I was on edge the entire ride. Maybe because I knew what he was and what he was capable of. Maybe it was because I *didn't* know him. It seemed my time away had softened my perspective. He was Rune, but unpredictable. Dangerous. I couldn't forget that again.

The first place we checked was where Gracie told us the guy we needed to meet worked. It was well protected, surrounded by barbed wire and interspersed by guard towers and security checkpoints. It was possible to break in, even with Rune's limited magic. But I wanted to try the personal address Gracie had managed to access from the company database.

"I could get in so much trouble for this," she'd told me. "Please, *please*, don't screw it up."

Now Rune and I headed south of Capitol Hill. The neighborhood in question was gated and disturbingly close to a DFA office. Rune, light and swift as a panther, leapt to the top of the nearby wall. He offered me a hand up.

"I can do it." I needed to prove I was getting stronger. My old skills were taking a frustratingly long time to return.

Breathing ragged, I clambered up the brick and only just managed to avoid twisting my ankle when dropping to the other side.

"Elegant," Rune said.

"Shut it," I returned, taking off toward the address. "And I hope you left Gracie a gift like I asked. She's putting a lot on the line for us."

Rune easily matched my stride. "Of course I did. I guarantee she'll love it."

I suddenly regretted being too preoccupied with preparing to double check. "What'd you leave her?"

"She'll find her office plant now grows buds of jewels. And Raquel's owl will warn her should she become in danger."

I resisted groaning. "She can't do anything with *jewels*, Rune. And the owl will be spying for you, too!"

"A double-edge gift is still a gift."

"Forget it."

Rune stopped in front of a modern stately home, its yard professionally trimmed. The windows inside were dark as to be expected at this hour, but I could make out various security lights that would activate the second we moved too close.

I spotted the soft white glow of another light emanating from the backyard.

Staying deeply within the shadows, we snuck along the wall separating the two properties.

"I'll talk to him first, let him know you're here," I whispered. "Otherwise, you might scare him too easily."

Rune's malicious smile told me my decision was a sound one. "If you insist."

The soft light spilled from the open door of a workshop, professionally built and looking as though it could withstand the apocalypse. I could make out the shadow of someone moving within. There weren't any obvious cameras or security devices, but that was all the more reason they were probably here. We needed to be extra careful.

"Wait," Rune said.

He closed his eyes, and a moment later an obscuring mist cloaked the lawn. "Now go."

Using the shadows as cover, I left Rune behind and snuck close. I wiped my slicked hands on my jeans, took a deep breath, and stepped inside.

"Rylan?" I said in disbelief.

Rylan spun around. His eyes widened comically. "Are you kidding me? Val? You're still alive?"

"You know, I'm getting that reaction a lot these days."

The last I'd seen my illicit heart gem buyer, Joshua had arrested him and given me a warning to never enter the Wilds again.

Rylan's black beard was untrimmed, and his hair lay uncombed on either side of his face, thanks to the missing turban he usually wore. His fingers were absent the rings inlaid with small heart gems.

"Are you actually here?" Rylan said, still in shock.

"Unless you're hallucinating, yes. Oh, and there's someone

else." I gave him an apologetic look. "He's with me. And he'll play nice."

"That depends on how this conversation goes."

Rune was suddenly in the workshop. He'd unglamored his eyes, letting Rylan know exactly what he was. "I never thought I'd say this to a human other than Val, but I was hoping you could help me."

Rylan was quiet so long I worried we might have scared him speechless. Then he sank into a chair with an exhaled breath. "You're lucky the DFA just pulled the guards watching me 24/7."

"We were actually hoping you could get us in touch with someone in the DFA," I said. "My stepbrother, Joshua."

Rylan's expression darkened. "I'm well aware of who he is."

"What are all these?" Rune said.

He'd gone over to one of Rylan's workbenches, scattered with weapons of all kinds: assault rifles, maces, swords, even throwing stars. All of them possessed a familiar, glimmering tint around the edges.

Rune balanced the point of a knife on the tip of his finger. "All of these contain heart gem magic?"

"All but the guns," Rylan said. "Haven't figured out a way to imbue the bullets with enough magic to do serious damage. The DFA told me that the bodies of Those Below are some kind of crystalline composite, harder than anything naturally occurring."

"I can vouch for that," I said.

Rylan's jaw slackened. "You've run into them?"

"In a manner of speaking. Empress Sotera kept me prisoner for over a month."

"You've *been* there?" Rylan was suddenly on his feet. "What was it like? What were *they* like? I couldn't believe half the information the DFA were giving me, but now that you're here..."

"And how do you know these weapons work?" Rune said.

"Sometimes they brought prisoners," Rylan said. "Wildlings. I wasn't the one who tested them—"

I assumed this might come up and was already moving to step in front of Rylan.

Rune made it first.

Weapons clattered to the floor as he knocked a table aside, gripped Rylan by his neck, and slammed him against the corkboard wall.

"We need him, Rune!" I tried to wrench his arm away from Rylan, but I might as well have been pulling at a steel beam.

"I said I wasn't the one who did it!" Rylan gasped.

"But you didn't stop them," Rune seethed. His fingers whitened as he squeezed tighter. "How many have they killed for your crafts?"

"To save your kind, you'd do the same. I can see it. I—" he choked. "I don't want to do this. They're making me."

Surprise flickered in Rune's eyes. He slowly lowered Rylan, who stepped away, massaging his neck.

"You're the new High King, aren't you? Rune. I've heard the name. I'm sure it's killing you to work with humans, but I can bet I want the same thing you do: for this to stop."

Rylan nodded at me. "Val was there when I was arrested. They threw the book at me. Said I was a threat to the city and national security. Illicit dealing, tax evasion, conspiring with the enemy. Bullshit, all of it. Except for the tax evasion and dealing, of course. I was looking at thirty years, at least."

"I'll bet they came to you with a wondrous deal then," I said, catching on.

"Your stepbrother sure did," Rylan said with disgust. "I'm a salesman by trade, but I have skills working with heart gems. All I had to do was help the DFA on their little project."

He gestured to the scattered weapons. "I know technically we're supposed to be at war with the wildlings, but I have nothing against you. They never hurt anyone I knew, and collecting heart gems from beasts of the Wilds always brought good business. That's the reality, not a jab," he said when Rune bristled. "But now..."

He let out a long breath. "If I stop working on this, or make something that's not satisfactory, they'll throw me right back in prison. I'm never getting out after that. Someone as free as you, Rune, probably doesn't understand what that's like, but I'm not going back."

"You'd be surprised how much I understand," Rune said.

"Sure, great." Rylan pushed the table back into place and started replacing the scattered weapons atop it. "It's taken a while, but I think I've got something the DFA could use."

"I have a feeling that's not good," I said.

"It's really not. The thing is, the weapons for Those Below were secondary. They wanted me to work on this first."

He picked out a slate-gray scythe oozing with a sour energy that made my skin crawl. Rune took a disgusted step back.

"By the mother tree, what is that?"

"What it looks like." Rylan slowly lowered it onto the table. "It's not too powerful right now, but anything it cuts from the Wilds or grown with Wild magic won't grow back."

"I'd love to test that," Rune said with a sneer.

"You might get the chance to, soon. That's one of two things the DFA are coming to pick up."

"Why are they so fixated on destroying the Wilds?" I said, exasperated. "You have a common enemy!"

"Maybe, maybe not. You ask me, the DFA wants to fight everyone, because *that*," Rylan nodded to another blade, entirely white, with a glow around the edges, "That's for Those Below—"

Rune spun around, tense. I was already moving toward the door at the back of the shop, even before he hissed, "Someone's here."

"They're not supposed to come until tomorrow morning," Rylan said, panicked.

I didn't bother mentioning that it technically was morning, shouldered open the back door, and pulled Rune out with me.

"Erebus," Rune commanded.

"What—"

"Use Erebus to cloak us. Now!"

"Help us out here," I whispered to the shadow clotted near my collarbone.

Erebus's form leaked from beneath my sleeve, spreading like an ink drop in water. In moments, Rune and I were covered in a cold, dark veil. What little warmth the night offered was replaced by the heat of Rune's body pressed to my side. I couldn't see him, but I could sure feel him.

"Keep out of the light," I whispered.

We threaded around the stretched rectangles of light cast from the workshop's windows. A new figure stood at the open workshop door, and other figures dressed in military attire were spreading out across the lawn.

"—understand they may not be fully functioning yet, right?" Rylan said. "If I wasn't so rushed, I might have something more useable."

"It's my job to test how ready they are," a familiar voice said, and my breath caught. "But your lack of preparedness isn't what concerns me."

Joshua stepped out of the workshop, casting a shadow across the backyard. "One of your monitor alarms went off. It seems you've had visitors."

EIGHT

What terrible, horrible luck.

When Rylan had said someone from the DFA would pick up his weapons, I hadn't expected it to be the very person we needed to speak to. Except he wasn't alone. Figured that he'd be promoted high enough to command his own unit, but not so high that he was above fetching weapons of war.

Joshua spoke into his radio, "Spread out. One team sweep back here. Another start in the front and converge. Check the motion sensors, too."

Rune and I stayed out of the light, moving until we could still make out Joshua as he stepped back inside the workshop. He turned over the white, gleaming sword, the one Rylan said had been built to kill Those Below. He hadn't changed his appearance—though I supposed it'd only been a month. A DFA uniform and body armor strained against his training-earned muscles. His blond hair was cut short and combed back from a face that looked nothing like Peyton's.

"I hope whoever stopped by didn't disturb your work," Joshua said.

Rylan leaned on his workbench, forearms gripping the wood hard enough that his veins popped. "They could have, if they existed."

Joshua nodded at Rylan's neck, where a faint blush of bruises in the shape of Rune's fingers was starting to form. "I suppose non-existent ghosts did that, too?"

Rylan's hand stopped halfway to his throat, as though realizing how guilty that made him look. "Allergic reaction. Something I ate."

"Sure," Joshua continued hefting the sword, testing its weight. "I'm surprised you only have one."

"This is a new field entirely, you should be grateful for that," Rylan scoffed. He begrudgingly stepped to the side as Joshua's soldiers spread out around the workshop. "Tell them not to move anything. I have it arranged just the way I like it."

"They'll do what they need to," Joshua said. "Sorry, I interrupted while you were making excuses."

"At least I'm farther along than the others you have working on this."

"You assume. You have the other one?"

Rylan hesitated, his eyes flickering near where Rune and I crouched, before carefully lifting the scythe onto the table. There was a triumphant gleam in Joshua's eyes as he looked it over.

"And you're sure anything we cut with this won't grow back? Wilds or not?"

Rylan gestured to the confines of his workshop. "Obviously I haven't tested it out within the actual Wilds. Just the sample you've brought. But theoretically it should."

Joshua sheathed the sword and scythe and efficiently wrapped them both. "If this works, we'll be sending them to full production."

"Do you really have to use them? It doesn't seem right."

"Now's a convenient time for you to grow a conscience, after you've benefitted from all your black-market dealings," Joshua said. "It's war, of course it's not right. How we use them is up to me, not you."

One of Joshua's soldiers, a woman about his age with a perpetually suspicious expression and hand that never left her sidearm, met him at the workshop doorway. "No sign of anyone. Cameras don't show anything either."

"And there was no magical interference with the video?"

"There was some static, but it's not unusual." She leaned in closer. "I *did* warn you about giving in to his demands for 'personal space'. There are too many vulnerabilities outside normal protocol."

"Yes, yes, you've told me, Leah. Multiple times."

"And yet you always fail to listen."

Joshua looked amused. "Sometimes I think you forget who's supposed to be in command here."

"That's your fault. Sir."

Joshua swept past her to scan the yard, his eyes lingering on the blot of shadow Rune and I occupied.

"What do you think, Leah? Really?" he murmured.

"None of the private companies working on similar products would dare try to steal it from the DFA. Not when they know each weapon is marked. Other than that..." Leah's expression darkened. "We all know the risks of what we face."

Joshua grunted. "Gather the others. We're leaving."

While Leah rounded up the remaining soldiers, Joshua stuck his head back inside the workshop. "You're getting guards again. For your own safety."

"You mean because you're getting desperate," Rylan said. "I can read between the lines. The secrecy toward the public, pushing me to finish weapons without proper testing. You need these, badly. But for what, and why so fast?"

"I'd worry more about yourself." Weapon clutched close, Joshua walked right past us, heading toward the front of the house.

"I want that scythe destroyed," Rune said. "I don't care how."

"Let me talk to him first," I urged. "That's what you wanted."

"After seeing exactly what they're doing, maybe I've reconsidered."

"Let me try. We don't have to hurt him."

I could feel Rune's gaze rest heavily on me. "And if he doesn't listen, we do it my way. Rylan may be making the weapons, but you have to cut off the snake's head to stop its bite."

My tongue had gone dry. Once upon a time, I thought myself capable of doing whatever I had to in order to survive. Now I wasn't sure my resolve would hold up to allowing Rune to kill my stepbrother, no matter what Joshua was doing. "Give me a chance."

We bled into the shadows at the side of the house just as Joshua rounded the corner. I softly called his name.

He stopped, turned our direction. "And here I thought I was going crazy. Is that you, Val?"

"Of course it's me."

"Are you all right?"

The question threw me off. Both by its nature, but also that it was Joshua asking. "I am. Mostly."

"Where are you?" I held my breath as his eyes passed right over where we crouched. "Why don't you come out?"

"You know I can't. It's not safe here."

Joshua scoffed. "I know that the last time we talked it didn't end well. I was angry. But you had me so worried. I thought I'd shot you instead of that wildling bastard."

Rune shifted forward, seeming prepared to pounce.

Don't say any more, I mentally urged Joshua. *Not about him.* This conversation was already getting out of control, and I wasn't sure how long I could hold Rune back.

"Peyton came by the other night," Joshua went on. "She told me what happened, where you've been. She said you spoke with Sotera. Is that true?"

"I'm here about something else. I need you to make an alliance with the wildlings."

There was a long pause. "I can't believe you," Joshua said. "Here I am, sick with worry, trying to use all the leverage I have to ensure that you're *not* shot on sight for conspiring with wildings, and still you're working with that false king."

"You have no idea—"

"Don't tell me what I know," Joshua snapped. He took a deep breath and slowly let it out. "I don't want to fight, Val. Can I at least see you? Or is that too much to ask anymore?"

I let my silence answer.

"I can clear you of everything," Joshua said. "Things are changing so fast the DFA is willing to let past offenses go. I know people who want you on our side."

"And what about you?"

"Of course I do. You..." He let out a huffy laugh. "This is crazy. You go missing for over a month, and now you're suddenly *here* of all places and I can't even *see* you. I'm guessing it's thanks to more of that wildling magic you love so much."

"You need to align with the wildlings," I repeated. "With Rune."

"And is he here now, with you?" Joshua's fingers teased the edge of the scythe's wrapping "Did he ask you to do this?"

"Will you stop being an idiot for five seconds?" I seethed, letting my anger get the best of me. "It's just me, and *I'm* asking you to align with them. Yes, I've been Below. I've seen what Sotera can do and how desperate she is to break free."

And I'm part of the reason she's such a threat. I swallowed the words. I didn't need Joshua hating me more than he already did. "Trust me, you need an alliance with Rune."

"No," Joshua said. "We don't."

Glass slid across glass as Rune drew his knife. I reached through Erebus's shadow, nicking my finger on the blade, before I found his wrist and held tight. "Don't!"

"If he's not with us, he'll only become a greater enemy," Rune hissed.

"I won't let you, Rune. I can convince him."

"Then you'd better start."

"Val?" Joshua said. He'd moved closer. His eyes narrowed. "If it *is* Val. This could be a wildling trick. If you let me see you, then we can discus—"

"Rune will promise to keep the Wilds in check," I blurted. "You could work together to ensure—"

"I've got a request for you," Joshua said. "I know you still care about Peyton and me, just as we care about you. I know you want to keep everyone here safe, so here's how to do that: Kill Rune for us. End his threat. You know the terrible things he's done and what he'll keep doing if left unchecked."

My heartbeat thudded so loud I was sure it would draw Joshua's attention. "I've done some terrible things, too."

"With him dead, there will be peace. I promise."

"You sound just like Sotera."

"Don't you dare—" Joshua held up his hands. "We can talk more about this, but please, *please* let me see you."

"Do not," Rune murmured.

"I have to," I said. "If it'll help convince him even a little."

Against my every sense of self-preservation, against the

calming voices of reason, I shrugged away from Rune's grasp and stepped out of the shadows.

Joshua relaxed. "I don't know of any wildling magic that can make them mimic someone so exactly. It's the eyes that give it away."

"It's me," I said. "Just me."

"Not quite." Joshua looked over my shoulder. "Some king you are, hiding behind her to do your negotiating."

Erebus's cool form returned to my shoulder as the veil dropped from Rune.

"Val thought you'd be more inclined to listen to her," he said. "I see now you never had any intention of being open to reason. I'll be taking those weapons."

Joshua gave a barking laugh. "From how I hear you slaughtered the Lords and anyone standing in your way of the throne, you're one to talk of reason."

"It was necessary. Much as this is."

"Joshua, please," I said.

Joshua's hand moved to his belt. He started to draw a knife.

"*Stop.*" Joshua froze as Rune's compulsion-thick voice washed over him. *"You will put the weapons—"*

Joshua shuddered, shaking free of Rune's hold. He grinned. "Well now. Seems these weapons do more than just kill the Wilds. Not so powerful without your trickery, are you?"

Rune's eyes were wide. "What have you—"

Joshua drew his knife and lunged, managing to tear through the sleeve of Rune's shirt and nick skin.

Joshua grabbed my arm, pulled me roughly. "Did you see it?" he hissed. "What Sotera's hiding?"

My fingers itched for Sliver, but I brushed the thought away just as quick. Joshua might be power hungry and delusional, but he was still my stepbrother. "I don't know what you're talking about. You have to stop this. You have to see that the wildlings aren't your enemy!"

Joshua looked as though I'd smacked him in the face. "They really have gotten to you."

"Enough, Val." Rune flicked blood off his arm. "He's long past reason."

"Joshua?" Leah had returned. "We're all waiting—"

She saw the three of us in the middle of our standoff. Her hand flew to her radio. "Perimeter breach! Southern edge of the house!"

With a snarl, Joshua threw me away to avoid Rune's fist. Joshua had dropped Rylan's weapons in the scuffle, but now he dove for the scythe. His fingers fumbled to unwrap the covering.

The ground shook. Roots spewed from beneath my feet, wrapping around both me and Rune and carrying us above the house and to the other side of the street. More roots grew in our wake, twisting together to block Joshua and the other soldiers in pursuit.

I hit the ground hard as the roots dropped us the last few feet before shriveling up. I steadied Rune as he stumbled.

"That may not have been my wisest move," he said, voice slurred.

Joshua was slicing away at the root wall with the scythe. Everywhere it touched immediately died. He'd be through in moments.

"Hold onto me," I told Rune. He did so, and we took off at a shambling run. I cast a final look back.

Another figure had stepped out from the back of the van parked at the front of the house. It'd been years, but I easily recognized Father Dumas's bulky frame, thick beard, and tightly fitted cloth cap.

He yelled something that was lost to me and then Erebus cloaked us in shadow once more, and Rune and I escaped into the night.

CHAPTER

NINE

"This will do," Rune said. "I'll summon a path."

The fire-scarred tree at the center of a vacant park didn't look promising. I cast a look around. It'd been slow going after Rune had expended so much magic to help us escape. My anxiety had been ratcheted to eleven since, waiting for Joshua and two dozen DFA soldiers to come swooping down on us.

"Are you sure?" I said.

"Do you honestly believe we can go much farther?" Rune answered. "It has life enough left in it."

He sluggishly waved his hands. The branches didn't so much as twitch. "Give me a chance to catch my breath—"

He slumped again, nearly dragging me down with him. Lines of fatigue stretched his forehead, and his cheeks were dappled with sweat.

I double-checked that we were truly alone. "Here. Stop."

I sat, leaning my back against the tree.

"What are you doing?" Rune said.

"You need to rest, or neither of us are getting out of here. Sit." I tugged on his hand, and after some resistance, Rune slowly allowed me to pull him down. Feeling bold, I guided his head into my lap. Neither of us breathed for a moment.

"Comfortable?" I asked.

Rune stared up at me. "Are you?"

"Don't worry about me. Hurry up and get stronger."

I adjusted my position so that the bark wasn't digging into my low back. Rune didn't stop staring. "Don't make a big deal out of it," I said. "And remember, they could be right behind us."

Mercifully, he closed his eyes. His breathing deepened as he sought out what little Wild magic the park offered. The waves lapped against the shore. The wind played with my hair. Sirens rose from downtown and then faded. I hoped they weren't for us.

Eyes still closed, Rune began to hum. It was a darkly beautiful melody I didn't know. I imagined it playing during unsettling moments, times you'd lost something or mourned never having it to begin with.

"What is that from?" I asked.

Rune continued humming until the tune came to its melancholic end. "My father brought me to a summer fair, mere days before the last High King fell. There were plenty of delights for a child like me, one who'd had my share of hardship but had yet to discover tragedy. A troupe from another Wilds were performing a play. I think it was from one of our myths where a woman discovers that her child is destined to devour the world but refuses to kill them, despite everyone begging her to do so."

"I don't imagine that ends well for her."

"How astute. Yes, her child kills her and then eats everyone else. A typical wildling tragedy. They sang that melody at the end. I must have seen the play four times while I was there. I loved it. I think it's easy to romanticize terrible things that haven't happened to you yet. It is far more difficult to enjoy them once they have."

I resisted the urge to brush the silky strands of his hair through my fingers. Would he find it a comfort or disgusting? "I take it that was a happy memory."

"My father was murdered the night after the festival ended, so no," Rune said. "I suppose there's enough tragedy in my own life now that memories like that are a pleasant escape. I'd almost forgotten about it. Thank you."

"I didn't do anything."

Rune opened his eyes. He raised his hand and waved it again. This time, veins of fresh greenery wended through the cracked tree bark. What was once a small, hollow knot in the center creaked as it widened, opening to reveal an entirely pitch-black path with fronds of delicate green beckoning us in. I nearly pitched backwards into it before Rune stood and helped me up. Our hands lingered in each other's before I tugged mine free and busied myself with wiping grass from my pants.

"No being sick this time," Rune said.

I wrapped an arm around him as he swayed in place. "Funny, I was just about to say the same to you."

"I'll be fine once we get back into the Wilds."

We took a step forward, and the path swallowed us up. Vines and open flowers ushered us along. As the dark space further enclosed, I sucked in a deep breath to keep from panicking. I smelled the damp scent of pine, the slight tinge of salt, something that might have been woodsmoke.

We emerged on the other side, and I braced my legs to keep Rune standing. He sighed, face pointed to the treetops. "Better. Much better."

"We need to take a look at the cut Joshua gave you," I said.

Rune lifted his arm to show me that the cut had already healed. "You're the one we should be concerned about."

"Me?"

"It's not my stepbrother we just escaped from."

No, it was just his uncle, his resurrected cousin, pretty much his entire family that was so messed up it made mine look like saints. Maybe that was why he understood parts of me so uncomfortably well.

"I'll be fine," I said. "Which way?"

Rune pointed to where the trees thinned. He moved easier now, regaining strength with every stride. But he still didn't pull away from my side, not until we reached the edge of the trees and I sensed a disturbance in our surroundings.

"Glad to see my protective enchantments worked," Rune said, noticing my reaction. He looked over his shoulder. "It's me, Pitius."

Quick as a breath, Rune's wispy spy knelt before him. "My Lord."

"And where are the... Ah, just in time."

Half a dozen more wildlings emerged from behind the nearby trees, as though they'd transformed from them. I heard the creak of Xander's bow drawn taut. Cassius stepped forward, clutching a short sword. His eyes widened.

"It's them! Drop it, Xander!"

There was a slight pause, and then Xander leapt from above, barely stirring a leaf as he landed. His eyes looked bruised, as though the last couple days had been especially hard on him. "Made it back at last. And in one piece."

"What happened?" Cassius demanded. "Did you talk to them?"

"There will be no alliance with the humans," Rune said. "At least not today."

"Figured," Xander said, shaking his head. "I thought it was a long shot to begin with."

I prepared to intervene in case Rune harshly rebuked him, but he ignored the slight. Strange. I searched the welcome party for a missing face. "Where's Marian?"

Xander opened his mouth and then closed it again. Cassius suddenly found the scuffed dirt on his boots fascinating and wouldn't meet my eyes.

"She was lost at Mog Moren," Rune said.

A strange pain slid into my gut, like a knife being twisted. "And you didn't tell me?"

"We had more immediate concerns." Rune seemed to reconsider how that sounded. "There was nothing I could do. I'm sorry."

"Have you found her body?"

"No. It was likely drawn into the sea."

"But not for sure." I looked at the others, seeking agreement. "Not for sure, *right*? Xander, you can check, can't you? Bendeti won't expect anyone to go back there so soon—"

"Bendeti's sea still claims Mog Moren," Rune said, tone hardening. "She isn't the first we've lost. She won't be the last."

I didn't understand this, giving up so soon without a body for proof. Losing Marian mattered to *me*, of all people. It should matter to *them*.

Rune drew away from me and brushed past the wildlings. Everyone else fell in line behind him. "I need to talk with General Forcheck. She suspected an alliance with the humans wouldn't pan out. I hope she has an idea of what to do instead."

I numbly followed beside him into camp, forcibly shifting my brain to what still needed to be done without dwelling anymore on what had happened. Rune and I had met Narita

Forcheck, the General of the Killing Green, along with her grand-son, Cassius, when they were still prisoners in Mog Moren. At the time, Rune had offered her a position with him, should she ever escape. It seemed only prudent she'd end up here.

"Are there others from Mog Moren?" I asked Xander. Anything to keep my reeling mind off Marian.

"About a dozen, yes," he said. "We would have had more, but Bendeti's wave drowned the rest."

Rune's smile was hard. "King Bendeti's latest assault was exceedingly thorough. Your former betrothed must be the jealous type."

"Her what?" Cassius said, giving me a sharp look.

I muttered a curse as my body grew hot. "Don't call him that. I'd run him through if I could."

Rune's smile only grew, as if he found the thought of me doing that extremely appealing.

Their encampment was settled at the mouth of a dew-sprinkled valley, where the melt from distant snowpacks trickled into a clear lake. I tasted enchantments on my tongue. They were woven in the dwellings of raised earth and pillared trees, where sconces of bioluminescence and blue everfire were held. A frigid wind painted shivers across the lake where Raquel the beast whisperer stood at the edge, coaxing schools of fish into the shoals where other wildlings speared them to cook.

The scene looked so much like a painting that my chest ached. For all its savagery, I had almost forgotten how beau-tiful the Wilds could be. Nothing at all like Below.

But for all its beauty, the practical part of me couldn't help noticing the spot had been strategically chosen. It was surrounded on all but one side, easier to hide and funnel possible attacks into one spot. We also weren't near any ocean or sea, but away from the center of the Wilds, safe from Bendeti and Sotera's realms alike.

This felt like less of a staging ground, and more like a sanctuary of retreat.

"I'm going to speak with General Forcheck," Rune said to us. "I'll let you know what we plan to do after."

Xander hung back until all but Cassius had departed.

"Rune, did you think about what I asked?" he asked in a low voice.

"You already know my answer," Rune said. "Don't make me repeat it."

Xander's fingers whitened around his bow. "He would have expended most of his magic in that attack. He'll be weakened now! Or at the very least inattentive. It could just be me, Raquel, Cassius, maybe even Pitius. It wouldn't take more than a few days—"

Rune whirled on him. "I don't say this often, but you underestimate your importance. You're asking me to allow three of my more valuable subjects to go galivanting on a fool's errand. You want to kill yourself? Fine. But do it for *me*, under *my* orders."

I expected Xander to back down, as he always had against Rune's ferocious intensity, but Xander's stance only hardened. "If you had even the smallest inkling of what she means—"

"Don't," Rune said, voice dangerously low. "Don't go there."

Cassius put a hand on Xander's shoulder and rotated him toward the dwellings. "Get Val some warmer clothes and a weapon."

"You don't tell me what to do," Xander snapped.

Cassius gave a shallow, mocking bow, though it was obvious the formality was still new to him. "I was only suggesting you not push the matter." His eyes slid to Rune. "I might be new here, but I've learned that much."

"That's my order as well," Rune said when Xander didn't move. "Obey it."

"I do need a jacket," I said. Partly because it was true—the snow-chilled wind was running right through the clothes Gracie had lent me—partly because whatever Rune and Xander were angry about, it wouldn't be solved here. Rune had already turned to go find the general. Xander finally took off ahead of me, lips tight, back rigid.

I was unused to seeing so many wildlings in one place. At most, there had been fifty with Rune in King's Hollow, but I'd primarily traveled with groups of a few at a time.

There had to be over a hundred here. It wasn't just the young like Rune, but older ones as well. Those with missing limbs, with scarred skin the color of fresh bark and amber sap. Roots curled through the knots of their hair where they'd strung glittering insect wings. Others had beast furs draped over their shoulders, woven with jeweled berries and ravens' feathers.

On the outskirts of the dwellings, I spotted those clearly from Below, Raki and Verily among them, along with a dozen others. They looked in good shape, if not a bit uncomfortable.

"More of them escaped from Sotera than I thought," I said.

Xander grunted. "The general's been training them with the rest of us. Some don't like it. They say that if Those Below betrayed their Empress, then they'll just as easily betray Rune."

"Are these the same wildlings that switched to Rune's side the moment their Lords were killed?"

That coaxed a small smile from Xander. "Maybe. Blame it on our hypocritical nature. Wildlings or not, anyone will find arrows in their back if they betray us."

His voice had a bitter edge to it, as though he didn't feel as strongly about the threat as he once did. "Still, it's good we have them. We've lost about fifty to Sotera's soldiers. You remember Grand?"

I did. A boy with sheeny golden hair and a quick laugh, who'd helped summon Bendeti for Rune to speak with him.

"He's gone," Xander said. "Mem, Karel, Trifin, too. More than you know, I'm sure. Marian started collecting charms for each one fallen." He frowned. "Strangely sentimental of her. Did it for almost every one. At least until she…"

"I'm sorry," I said, still finding it difficult to believe. "I liked her. Even if she didn't feel the same. And I'm not giving up yet—"

"I think you should," Xander said. "It'll make it easier. At least according to Rune."

He led me to what might have been the armory, where a number of weapons had been magically sheathed into a slab of granite mountainside.

Xander gestured to the wall. "Since you broke my magnanimous gift, you'll have to pick another."

"If it helps, your gift saved my life. More than once."

"They tend to do that when used properly. Let's hope this new one has to do less lifesaving. Take your time to find one that feels right. I'll go get you a coat and food."

By the time he returned with both, I'd withdrawn Sliver from my arm and decided I was better off with it than any of the other weapons, enchanted or not. All-out combat wasn't my forte, and I'd need the stealth and subtlety Sliver provided more than anything else moving forward.

Xander raised an eyebrow as he handed me the food. "We'd, uh, heard about what you were. Like Those Below but different."

"And does that bother you?" I said.

"If it did, I wouldn't have been down there helping rescue

you. As far as I'm concerned, anyone who's not actively trying to kill us is practically an ally. May I?"

I hadn't considered what would happen if Sliver left my grasp, but thankfully it nor my arm shattered into a thousand pieces as I handed it to him. While he examined the blade and gave it a few practice swings, I hungrily finished what food he'd brought—honeyed radishes, jellied fruit, and dried jerky, all washed down with sweet, clear stream water.

Xander gave a final stab to an invisible enemy before carefully handing it back. "This is incredible. And what happens if it breaks?"

I grimaced. "Let's hope it doesn't. My arm is already brittle enough without it."

"I'll bet. That's your bone you're swinging around." He looked toward camp. "Which you probably shouldn't do here. *I* might not have a problem with what you are, but that doesn't go for everyone whose joined us. And since you're practically Rune's bodyguard, they'll be extra suspicious of you."

"Is that what I am?" I said lightly. "Rune didn't clarify."

"He can elaborate, I'm sure."

"Yes, I'm sure."

I finished sheathing Sliver. From the armory, I selected an easily concealable knife for backup and a vambrace for my left arm, woven with slender threads of silver. I put on the coat Xander offered. It was stitched with living vines that moved with me to blend into whatever foliage I concealed myself in.

"Thanks for helping me out," I said. "I guess I'd better find out what exactly my role is to Rune this time."

Xander gave what might have been his first actual smile since I'd seen him again. "Whatever the reason, I'm glad you're here. Rune's been even more insufferable since you were taken, if you can believe it. And with the assassination attempts getting worse—"

"Assassination attempts?" I said sharply. "When? How?"

"Only a couple. He's High King now, and oh-so-unpopular to some. They've tried to drown him, and then there was the attempted poisoning, of course. One of the remaining minor Lords put a bounty on his head. So Rune took his. And now that Vanesi's back?" Xander shook his head. "I don't even want to ask about that."

Probably for the best. Though we hadn't had much time to actually sit down and chit-chat, seemed there was much Rune had neglected to tell me about the dangers of his new position. I wondered if that was for his benefit, or mine.

"Val, you've..." Xander struggled with the words. "You've met with Bendeti recently. In that time, did he ever mention someone named Zuri?"

I'd already started cordoning off the terrible memories of my time Below, keeping what I hoped would be useful and what I hoped would be fuel for my rage. "Between Bendeti saying what he'd do to me once I was his wife, and how eager he was to drown the Wilds, I don't think so."

Xander was quiet for a long moment. "Remember when you asked if we did the right thing putting Rune on the throne?"

It'd been right after we'd taken King's Hollow, and Rune had started slaughtering anyone who didn't pledge their loyalty to him. I'd been horrified at what he was doing, necessary as it might have been. The question had been a moment of regrettable weakness.

"Do you still have those doubts?" Xander said.

"Rune wants to see you."

Cassius was suddenly there. He took in the new coat and vambraces I wore. "Look at that. You'd almost pass as half a wildling. Much better dress than the dust of the Below, and spore of Mog Moren, yes?"

Xander couldn't meet my eyes. He gave us both a tight nod. "Enjoy Rune's company."

"What were you two talking about?" Cassius asked when Xander had slipped away.

Loyal as Xander might be, I didn't think it wise for us to be questioning Rune's leadership. Even if Rune didn't mind, which I doubted, voicing seditious thoughts aloud could only sow unease among the other wildlings at a particularly vulnerable time. And whomever Zuri was, it seemed private to Xander alone.

"He was just glad I was back," I said.

"Hm... I'm sure he's not the only one."

He led me to Rune's chosen meeting place, given privacy by a skirt of flowering vines. I pushed my way through after Cassius to find a canopy of woven branches presiding over a smoothed oaken table.

Narita Forcheck, the General of the Killing Green, gave me an appraising look from her position at the table. The metal ringlets in her hair, partially covering a heavily wrinkled face, jingled as she waved her etched cane at me. "The Wild's celebrity returns at last. I see you haven't had your fill of near-death."

"General." I gave a small bow. "You took Rune up on his offer. I suppose that means you haven't lost your taste of battle."

"Never, child, never. Battle is in my blood. And you may simply call me Narita. Though I suppose I *am* our Lord High King's general."

"And the others will refer to you as such, even Val," Rune said, not taking his eyes off the papers strewn across table. "We need more order."

"I suppose you are right. Tell me," General Forcheck said as I joined her other side. "You have had a little time to form an impression of our lakeside encampment. What do you think of this contingent of the High King's grand army?"

Rune didn't look my way, but I could tell by the slight tilt of his head that he was listening.

"It's rough," I said. "Though it's only a part, I expected more. A lot more. I haven't seen the full extent of Sotera's or Bendeti's armies, but I imagine they'll be better trained, too. We should stick to guerilla warfare. Any all-out attack and we'll be slaughtered, just like we would have been against the Lords. In some ways, I don't think anything's changed since then."

Cassius gaped while General Forcheck cackled with delight. "More valuable than glittering jewels or a sharp blade is honest perspective, and one who can deliver it is priceless. Keep this one close," she said to Rune.

Rune finally met my eyes. "I intend to."

"Very good. Then I shall start training the next group. They are but clay, and these potter's fingers are old, but there is potential. Perhaps in a decade I can teach some of them to hurt the enemy more than themselves." With another cackle, General Forcheck hobbled out.

"I'll go check with Lothian about communication with the other contingents of the army," Cassius said. "If you're not too busy later, Lothian said he found a patch of Kebi fruit, so you should join us. Both of you."

"I will consider the invitation," Rune said. "Cassius."

Cassius paused beneath the flowering vines, waiting for Rune to go on.

"As one of the older wildlings, as one who has endured things more terrible than most, I need you to be my hand out there, guiding them. You engorged yourself on bloodshed back in Mog Moren, but now is time for more calculated killing.

Have you gotten all thoughts of petty vengeance out of your head?"

Cassius gave a barking laugh. "Have you?" he said in a mocking tone that told me that, while he'd survived the horrors of Mog Moren, the full horrors of opposing Rune were still yet unknown to him. "I don't know how you can ask that, after what you've seen."

"I ask *because* of what you've seen. You have to be better. Just as I have to be. Do you understand?"

An internal battle warred on Cassius's face. It occurred to me that, if you endured enough, your experience became your nature. Asking to discard that seemed about as hard as turning against yourself.

"This is the part where you do as I command," Rune said.

Cassius gave a short, awkward bow. "If it was anyone but you asking, I'd say no."

"Good."

Cassius left, and the full brunt of Rune's attention turned on me. His gaze was hungry. It matched my kindling feelings that refused to die, no matter how much I tried to stifle them.

"That man," Rune said, "the one you spotted as we were fleeing. It seemed like you knew him. How?"

It took me a moment to unsnarl the swirling memories of us fleeing from Joshua. I recalled a familiar bearded face shouting at me as he stepped from the back of a DFA van.

"Father Dumas. He's one of the leaders of the worshippers of the Mother Tree."

Rune turned back to the table, giving me a chance to breathe. "You have humans who partake in wildling beliefs?"

"They're not as rare as you'd think. But the worshippers are by far the biggest. They believe in one Mother Tree that created all wildlings, the heart trees, the gods and spirits, all that. Like you, I'm sure they use those beliefs for their own gain, not because they actually believe them."

Rune smirked. "You say that like it's a bad thing."

"You're both...opportunistic."

"Then we understand each other perfectly."

With everyone else gone, it felt strange to be all the way across the table from him. I moved closer. Glowing flowers and stones illuminated sheaths of curled maps and partially eaten food strewn across the wooden surface, as though Rune had spent many a late night here.

"Father Dumas has been in and out of my life since the day Peyton found me," I said.

"So that would explain why he was with your stepbrother to collect those weapons?"

That had been bothering me, too, since we'd escaped. "Maybe. So much has changed with Joshua and Peyton, even in the last few months. I guess I never really knew them as well as I thought I did."

I braced my hands on the edge of the table. "These weapons will just make things more difficult, but they won't have many. For now."

"We could find them and destroy them. Or find the one who ordered them made, and..." His silence said what he wished to do after that.

I swallowed the bile that rose at the thought of killing my stepbrother. "If it isn't Joshua, it'll be someone else. The biggest threat is Sotera, not him. It won't be long until she figures out a way to send more than a dozen soldiers at a time up. We need to take her throne or take her out."

"Which won't be easy," Rune said, surprising me. No matter how tough the situation became, he'd always met it with unflinching brutality and self-assurance. "Our weapons are ineffective against Those Below, and not everyone here is practiced in magics that can hurt them. We're holding her main force down, but if we could find a way to draw her out, make her careless, that'd be ideal."

"You've already done that," I said. "Me," I added at Rune's questioning look. "Sotera wants me. If not to marry me off for some alliance, then so she can use me for whatever she wants or make sure I can't work against her. Once word starts trickling back to her that I'm directly involved in stopping her plans, she'll focus on me. She may even try to find me herself."

"You seem to understand your importance to her perfectly."

"And what about to you?"

"Me?" Rune drew up from the map and leaned a hip against the table, fully facing me. "What is your importance to *me*?"

"I mean... What I'm saying..." The words were clumsy off my lips. "You said so earlier, but how do I know that once we finish what we have to do, you won't send me away again for my 'safety'?"

The glowing flowers washed Rune's face in clashes of warm light and shadows as deep as Erebus. "Then how about a new assurance: You get a home here. Safety. Security. As long as those last. Despite what you and others may think, I aim to bring peace. You will have a part of that, now and forevermore."

He moved closer as he spoke. So close I could reach out and touch him if I wanted.

"And you could give me all that?" I asked.

"In any way I can. In whatever way makes you happiest."

Happiness didn't matter. It came a distant last to more important needs, and seeking it was a sure way to end up the exact opposite. This was about survival.

"Since we may be negotiating with some very powerful

people in the near future, I suggest not making promises that are difficult or impossible to keep," I said.

"I don't. *You have my word, as High King of the Wilds.*"

The flowering vines trembled, as though a powerful wind had brushed through them. "I want you, with all your tricks, by my side until we reach whatever end."

As High King, his promises held power, but I still felt trepidation. What did safety and security mean anymore? What did they mean with *him?*

Coward that I was, I nodded instead of pushing for an answer. "Good. Then we finally have a deal."

Rune held out a hand. "And now we'll close it in the human way, the way you know best."

I took his warm, rough hand, knowing that once again I was making a big mistake. Only this time for an entirely different reason.

I forced a smile. "Now it's a deal."

CHAPTER

TEN

"We're ready," Xander said.

Rune took a look at those assembled, his expression sour. "Raquel, were the wolves necessary?"

The wolf pack surrounded our group, putting some of the wildlings on edge. The beasts were twice as tall as the nearest wildling, composed as much from brambles and greenery as cloud-white fur. I recognized the alpha as the one who'd faced off against Rune after we'd dragged ourselves from a raging river. The one he'd ultimately subdued.

The alpha's deep, tawny eyes locked onto me. She chuffed, as though also remembering who I was and what we'd done to her.

"General Forcheck thought bringing them was a good idea," Raquel said nervously. "She said it'd send the right message."

I'd already overheard General Forcheck pestering Rune about presentation, in a way that only she could without consequence.

"Being ruler is more than having power," she'd said. "It's how you display that power to stave off potential problems before they *become* problems. Like the viceroy butterfly, intimidation can warn off hungry predators."

And Rune would need to stave off as many potential predators as he could. He was attempting to bring all wildlings together in a way they hadn't done since the Forming. It was a deadly dance, creating alliances that held strong, instead of dissolving into murder and treachery.

Not that they wouldn't do that, either.

"How likely, would you say, is it that Sotera has already gotten to Lord Hallas?" Rune asked me.

Though the memory was already smeared like watercolor on a rainy canvas, I tried to recall the faces I'd seen during the brief turn around Sotera's throne room during my betrothal party.

"I didn't hear Lord Hallas mentioned," I finally said. "I may recognize her when I see her."

"Which may be too late." Rune sighed. "Very well."

He approached the alpha wolf. This time there was no staredown before the alpha dipped her front legs and allowed him to settle in the dip behind her shoulders. One of the wildlings brought soft scarlet fabric to drape over Rune's legs. Rune scowled.

I bit my cheek to keep from laughing. "You look uncomfortable, my Lord."

"Domesticity irks me," Rune replied, jaw tight.

"Think of General Forcheck's advice. And if that doesn't work, think of violence."

That seemed to cheer him up.

The rest of the alpha's pack chose their riders, and eventually we were surrounded by a veritable retinue of mounted wildlings. It was too early in the day for me to use Erebus, so I warily slipped onto one of the smaller wolves and we were off, the pack slicing through the trees like a strong wind.

Lord Hallas hadn't wanted to meet us in her kingdom, which I found equal parts relieving and concerning. It was a slight, but at least we'd be on mostly neutral ground. My biggest concern was the number of wildlings we had. They were armed and trained, but I would need to get back in the mindset that everything could be a potential trap.

It seemed like only minutes before the tree trunks changed to the fleshy, dirty white of enormous mushroom stems. This part of the forest held a variety of gargantuan species; those speckled with stains of bloody crimson, warning yellow, and deadly magenta. The caps of the largest ones spread above us, gills slick and filled with spores.

The wolves wove through the forest of stems and drew up short before one that had been chopped down. The house-sized mushroom cap cast shade on a small party lounging beneath. None of them rose to greet us when Rune approached.

I kept my eyes on our surroundings, hand resting on my forearm. This had to be an ambush. Surely they wouldn't show this much disrespect without a plan.

Xander hopped off his wolf and, along with Cassius and the other wildlings, spread through the stalks to cover them and take defensive positions. I guided my wolf just behind Rune. He cocked an eyebrow at the party seated below us. "I already put in effort to create such an impressive display. I'd like for it to be worthwhile."

Lord Hallas, with a snarl of poison-purple hair and the cuffs of her coat jeweled, still didn't stand. Rune gave me a surreptitious glance, and I returned with a subtle shake of my head. I didn't recognize her. It was possible Sotera hadn't gotten to her yet, but that didn't mean she wasn't dangerous.

"I rise only for the High King," Lord Hallas said.

"Then you will rise for me," Rune answered.

The gills of the mushroom above their heads opened like mouths, its flesh sharpening to glistening points, like teeth.

"You decide if you walk out of your tomb," Rune said.

Lord Hallas looked up and then back at Rune. "A trick that the more powerful of our kind could produce."

"Maybe you missed the crown on his head," I said. "One he forged directly from the heart tree of these Wilds."

The look of contempt Lord Hallas sent my way was so strong that, had it been physical, I'd have been knocked right off my wolf. "I know who you are, little girl. A meddler in affairs that aren't your own. A creature that crawled up from Below—"

"Then you know how much you don't want to piss me off," I said. "Just like you don't want to piss him off."

With an unspoken command, Rune's wolves surrounded Lord Hallas's party, baring teeth. The entire forest of mushrooms bent, waiting to enact his next command. Those with Lord Hallas looked nervous now.

"I would choose your next words carefully," Rune said.

After a long breath, Lord Hallas pushed herself to one knee, keeping her head bowed. The others mirrored her.

"Apologies, High King, Rune. You have to understand the whispered rumors and hearsay that has plagued the Wilds these last few weeks. Your ascension was so sudden I wasn't sure if it was by right of power, or by default."

"I created the default," Rune said, "since there was no one left."

"So I've heard." Lord Hallas's eyes flicked back to me. "I've heard so many *interesting* things."

"As have I," Rune said. "Like how you haven't given me your allegiance yet. I've been occupied, but I need your choice. Now. Will you pledge yourself as a Lord beneath your High King? Will you protect these Wilds under my command?"

"And if I do that, what will you give me?" Lord Hallas said.

Rune's eyes flashed dangerously. "I'll let you keep your life."

"With all due respect, High King, but if you're prepared to kill everyone who doesn't agree with you, then you'll rule over a very lonely Wilds. It's a fine balance, exuding strength enough to avoid the tragedy that befell our last High King, but not too much that you are a tyrant and meet a similar end."

"You assume that being a tyrant isn't what I want."

Lord Hallas splayed her hands. "I'm more than willing to join you. But you should know Sotera has reached out, too. If I join her, then I'll get to keep what I have and get more once it becomes available."

"You mean once she's killed me," Rune said.

"She didn't specify how, only that I would. I have no love of Those Below, but you can see that's a tempting offer."

"If you believe she's telling the truth, then you're an idiot," I said.

Lord Hallas gave me a look of contempt. "I find it strange how quickly you've come to support Rune wholeheartedly. You even seemed to have taken the role as his advisor, above even those who have more experience and loyalty. And for what?"

She sneered. "I can guess the allure of a wildlings' power and...other things might be enough. But helping while asking for nothing is more suspicious than what I'm requesting, don't you think? Perhaps you're waiting until Rune's done all the hard work before you swoop in and—"

I slid off my wolf. I didn't have to endure this anymore. In dealings with Lord Jezaline and Mordecai, the power had always been in their control. They wielded it with a heavy hand, violently snuffing out any opposition. They had been brutal, effective, and feared.

And I'd killed them.

Lord Hallas threatened everything Rune wanted, and I'd kill her too, if I had to.

"Val."

Rune's tone was a warning.

"You will await my command," he said firmly.

He couldn't command me. That wasn't part of our deal. But to make things work, to truly make things better, I'd have to endure it. At least for a time. At least until we both got what we wanted.

I curled my hands into fists. "What's your choice, Lord Hallas?"

"I still haven't heard a better offer," she said. "I'm not terribly eager to return to my shrinking kingdom and petition a High King to listen, only to have my requests ignored—"

"I have revived the Council of Loam," Rune said.

Lord Hallas couldn't hide her surprise. "The advisors to the High King?"

"The same. I offer you a spot among them. To...advise me as you see fit."

I watched Rune as Lord Hallas considered this. I had no idea he'd already started dispersing some of his power. He clearly hated it, and I didn't like this either. Lord Hallas obviously held no true allegiance to anyone but herself. But almost counterintuitively, knowing she was so clearly in it for herself and needed to be watched made things refreshingly simple.

"I accept," Lord Hallas said.

"Excellent." Rune directed the alpha to turn around. "The Council convenes in a week. I'll expect you then."

"There is one other matter," Lord Hallas said. "There's

rumor that a ghost has come back to life. Some of mine have spotted your dead cousin Vanesi's likeness moving along our border. But that can't be possible. You ensured everyone who stood in your way or had any claim to the throne was dead."

Her gaze was penetrating, as though trying to tease out just how many loose threads—or potential vulnerabilities—Rune had left open.

"It's my job to worry about those things," Rune said. "But ghost or otherwise, any who cross me will meet the same fate."

BY THE TIME we returned to the lakeside, I felt more exhausted than I should have for such a short excursion. I hadn't completely recovered from my time Below, and it infuriated and demoralized me in equal measure. Once, I believed that all I had to work with was the limitations of the human body. Now I knew I was so much more, and yet I still found myself dragging as I dismounted my wolf.

"Thank you." Among the Wilds, an excess of gratitude could be seen as weakness, so instead I stood tall and met the wolf's gold-red eyes. "You can go now."

The wolf gave an acknowledging chuff and ran off to join the rest of its pack.

Rune watched me until a wildling summoned him away, no doubt to a dozen other tasks requiring his attention.

His command to me still chaffed. I knew he was right, but after enduring Sotera for so long, any command, even a sensible one, felt like too much. Until I could figure out the weird juggle of power Rune and I were doing, I aimed to avoid him for the rest of the day. There was food to catch, armor to stitch, expeditions to recount, missives to help a girl named

Disa—a wildling with golden pollen dusting her fingertips—craft with General Forcheck's input.

I slipped into these roles with surprising ease. Despite the order the wildlings adhered to, I was the wild card. I didn't fit anywhere, was somehow both below notice and above their command, and yet could try anything.

It was late by the time I returned to my leafed hammock, and I was surprised to find Pitius waiting for me. I was more surprised to find a small pile of neatly folded human clothes, along with some very human trinkets, beside her.

"These are mine," I said in awe. There were Legos I'd been ecstatic about when Peyton had brought them from Goodwill. A Barbie doll from the same. Many of my old T-shirts, shorts, pants, and even socks and some underwear were here. I felt a twinge of embarrassment at the thought of Pitius or another wildling carrying all of these from Peyton's apartment.

"We thought you might be homesick," Pitius admitted. "We didn't do much to make you feel welcome when you first arrived. I know you don't live there anymore, but hopefully this will help ease your stay.

I picked up a couple gossip magazines and flipped through the crinkled pages. I used to pore over these for hours, wondering if I was pretty enough, smart enough, happy enough. All concerns that seemed laughably trivial now. These had been in the bottom of my dresser, tucked out of sight. Pitius really had gone through everything.

"Thank you. These are…"

Not in line with what I knew of the wildlings. If they were grateful, they would show it through wildling gifts. Candied fruit, or a new blade. Perhaps a freshly woven bed of leaves downed with feathers, or maybe simply a rare kind word. They'd expect me to adapt to their world, as I mostly had. An uncomfortable thought settled over me. It would seem my threatening display during and since Rune's coronation had not gone over as smoothly as I'd thought.

"Are you scared of me, Pitius?" I asked.

Pitius stroked at the persimmons in her hair. A nervous tic. "I'm not sure what you mean."

"All this seems..." Like penance? Appeasement? They weren't given out of gratitude, but fear. "What I did to Mordecai, Jezaline, and the others, you know I'd never do that to you, right?"

"*I* know that."

"And do the others?"

"Of course they do."

Of course they did. Which was why they were giving me this offering. While I wallowed in self-doubt at my own lack of power, others already saw me in a very different light.

"Thanks for these, Pitius," I said, tossing the magazine back on the pile. "And for the record, I have everything I need here."

Pitius's smile appeared as quickly as she usually did. "I'm glad."

I mindlessly sifted through the trinkets long after she left, feeling their texture, their shape, letting them conjure memories of a life long gone. They felt like artifacts from a completely different world, one I could never return to.

***

ONCE MOST OF the wildlings were asleep. I gathered all the things Pitius had brought: the clothes, magazines, a practice sword Joshua had bought on my tenth birthday, braided charms from elementary school, a cell phone I hadn't thrown away because it had a funny video of Joshua singing that I swore I'd watch again. All this I carried deep into the trees until I reached the base of the mountain.

There I started a fire and stoked it until it was hot enough to start feeding the pieces of my old life into it. I watched each item burn to ash and then watched the fire burn down to embers.

I wasn't that girl anymore. I also wasn't the heartless monster Rune's wildlings were afraid of.

I still wasn't sure what I was.

ELEVEN

I awakened after only a few hours' sleep to find a pair of enormous eyes hovering inches from my face. I reined in my first instinct to lash out and managed, "How did you get past the watch?"

"My mistress seeks your audience," the creature said in a raspy voice. "Please do not wake the others and follow me."

I rolled out of the hammock, bare feet cold in the grass. "What are you?"

The creature scuttled to where the everfire put him in full view; a knobby-limbed, gangly creature with a beard of moss and nails like eagle claws. At full height, he barely reached my knees. I'd never seen anything like him in the Wilds. And certainly nothing that could speak.

"I am my mistress's servant. I am Hob."

I kept my hand on my left forearm. "And who is your mistress?"

"One you know," Hob rasped. "One you've met and who takes no sides. No harm will come to either of you."

"Either of us?"

"She also seeks audience with the High King. He is on his way to her as we speak."

I was already pulling on my boots and grabbing my foliage coat. Rune would be as wary as me, but still. "Show me."

I hurried to follow Hob past rows of sleeping wildlings, fires with only embers, neatly put away practice weapons, and shaggy four-legged beasts that Those Below rode in order to move as fast as the wildlings.

"I'm taking a walk," I said to the sentry in the tree, the one who obviously hadn't seen Hob come in and didn't seem to notice him now.

The girl nodded and then returned to watching the blooms of glowing eels pattern the dark depths of the lake. Hob led me up the tributary north of the lake, until we reached a small waterfall.

"Behind it," he said.

I didn't bother hiding Sliver as I drew it. Hob's orb-like eyes widened slightly, but he didn't cower. At the very least, he would know the potential consequences of leading me into a trap.

Chilly spray coated my jacket as I followed Hob behind the waterfall.

"Now through," Hob said.

"Does this have an end, or are you leading me in circles?" I asked. I started to walk to the opening on the other side. Hob tugged on my coat.

"No. *Through*," he insisted. And then he leapt through the falling water and vanished from sight.

It was fortunate I'd seen so many impossible things during my time in the Wilds, or I might have been shocked. I fully faced the back of the waterfall, until it stilled to a surface clear as glass. On the other side was the bottom of the waterfall. Should I fall through, I'd certainly break my neck. "Hob?"

There was no answer. I gritted my teeth. Had the little goblin deserted me?

"Hob, there's no way I'm—"

"She awaits," Hob said. He gave me a solid push from behind.

A stream of curses escaped my lips as I fell through the falling water. My vision spun in spurts of churning white and glimpses of a night sky, and then I emerged in a different place. The tributary and waterfall was gone. I stood in a grove of ghost-white trees, as though I'd been blinded by a camera flash and could only see their superimposed afterimage.

Rune was already here, smirking at me.

"Seems my guess was right. That wrinkled creature said you'd met her before."

"Wrinkled!" Hob groused, appearing from behind the nearest ghostly tree. "Do not speak ill of me, especially not behind my back. All insults should be to my face, or I'll leave you wandering lost until you starve, no matter what my mistress wants."

And then he was off through the trees, leaving Rune and I no choice but to follow.

Rune nodded at Sliver. "I recommend you put that away."

"I'm not walking defenseless into a possible ambush."

Rune pretended to be hurt. "You think *I'd* do that? If this is who I think it is, had she wanted us dead, we would be. Besides." He gestured at the trees. "Do you plan on taking them all on?"

We'd been surrounded. Herds of bounding deer and elk, lumbering bears, flocks of birds, a zoo's-worth of animals matched our pace. Farther in the trees beyond them was the shadowed outline of even more terrifyingly immense creatures. I could make out the glint of their glowing eyes and hear the heavy groan of trees being toppled as they took a step.

Every single creature was as ghostly as the trees. I didn't doubt that, if they chose to attack, they would kill us just as quickly as anything physical.

"Excellent choice," Rune said as I slowly sheathed Sliver. "Let's at least see if what she has to offer is worthwhile."

"Do you know who this is?"

"Possibly."

"Is she dangerous?"

"That remains to be seen."

Not feeling at all reassured, we kept walking. The farther we went, the more the ghostly animals dispersed, until Rune and I stepped alone through an opening in a wall of tightly knitted brambles, over the fallen petals of an enormous flower, and into a woodland clearing.

"I've brought them, mistress." Hob had reappeared. He scuttled across the clearing to a tree more enormous than any I'd ever seen. The base alone was the size of Rune's camp, its trunk stretching taller than the Space Needle where its canopy blanketed miles of the impossibly dark sky.

My heart skipped as I spied an enormous snake curled around its base. Its body was nearly as big as the serpent Rune had killed in Mog Moren. It regarded us through half-lidded eyes before going back to sleep.

"Where'd you take us?" I asked Hob.

"Soon," he said. "The mistress will be here soon."

"I admire her diplomatic tactics," Rune said. "Summon us and then make us wait. It shows who's really in control."

I wasn't sure I wanted whoever summoned us to have any *more* power. So I resolved to try to find something to work to our advantage, should we need it.

Keeping the dozing snake in the corner of my eye, I approached and knelt by a pool to the left of the tree. Half of the pool was bubbling mirk, smelling like a mixture of meat gone bad and a landfill. Lustrous, fleshy orbs bobbed atop the brown. In the exact other half of the pool, as though someone had put a divider straight down the middle, the water was crystal clear. I could clearly see a scaled tail beneath the surface, flicking with agitation. I followed it around to—

I stumbled back from the edge as I realized two of the fleshy orbs were actually eyes, watching me as an alligator might watch its unsuspecting prey.

"She's very territorial. Especially now that she's laid her eggs," a familiar voice said. "And that dark half of water is deadly to mortals. Touch it but once and you're finished. It may be as natural as life itself, but not all natural things *bring* life."

I snapped my head around. "Mother Mal?"

The bark at the base of the tree had peeled back like a door, its roots rising up to form steps for her to hobble down. When I'd first seen her Below, the buds covering her arms were all closed, but now they were in full bloom, a cacophony of colors simultaneously alluring and deadly.

"Of course," Mother Mal said. "And here you are."

"Where are we?"

"Here. I already told you. But you can call it the Halfway, should you need to put a name to everything." Mother Mal turned her long, animal skull to Rune. "Even kings used to kneel before me."

"I'm not a traditionalist," Rune said. "My father used to tell me of gods who survived the Forming, but with how easily everything dies in the Wilds, I didn't believe him."

"Do you believe now?"

"There have been many times in my life I'd have begged for the intervention of gods, but now I'm not so sure. I've been High King for over a month, and only now do you show yourself?"

"I have been busy in other affairs far beyond your scope, boy."

Rune's jaw twitched. "Addressing me as Lord or High King will be sufficient. And I'd love to know what you've been busy doing. Those Below are *here*. And the Wilds have been embroiled in chaos long before I stepped in. Perhaps you should have stayed hidden and let me continue believing all those fanciful stories were just that."

Hob hissed. The snake lazily opened its eyes again, flicked its tongue.

"It is good we're having this meeting," Mother Mal said. "It is good to see the state of the Wilds after so long asleep. To measure the stock of its rulers." Her gaze, with those eyes set deep within the slender skeleton head, turned on me. "To see where things went wrong. Stop, child."

I froze mid-step. I looked down at my feet. At some point, I'd started walking toward her, though I didn't remember doing so. Mother Mal's expression had turned serious.

"I said *stop*," she commanded, but her compulsion brushed over me, as though repelled by another, deeper command from within. Thoughts flitted out of my head like hummingbirds. I couldn't remember one moment to the next.

I was nearly to Mother Mal. The pool bubbled angrily at my back. The snake had drawn its head back to strike.

Mother Mal made a hissing sound at the back of her throat, and in a flash, the snake wrapped its body around me. It squeezed and my ribs ached as my bones ground together. Its open mouth hovered over my head, ready to rip it off.

Rune drew his glass knife. Even in the Halfway, the Wilds rioted to his command. "You will stop there, Mother Mal."

"Idiot boy," she said. "Can't you even tell when someone's been cursed?"

My chest felt as though it was being ripped apart. I gasped

as a crystal leg grew from the skin of my arms, as though I was drawing Sliver, only this time, it moved on its own.

Another leg joined it and then another, a half dozen sharpened limbs struggling to tear themselves free of my body. Rune's mouth had fallen open.

"What is this?"

The snake's grip tightened as whatever was growing from me reached for Mother Mal. I thrashed my neck, trying desperately to make the pain stop. If I'd been able to cut off my arms to bring relief, I would have.

"You brought this thing to kill me, girl," Mother Mal said impassively. "How are you going to take care of it?"

Anything. I would do anything to end this agony. I could barely think straight, but I tried to free myself. "My...arm," I gasped. "Let me...use my arm."

Mother Mal gave another hissing command, and the snake loosened its hold just enough for me to pull an arm free. A whimper escaped my lips as I magicked a crystal knife. My hand shook as I tried to rest it on the closest flailing leg. Rune closed in, his own glass knife at the ready.

"Get...away..." I said through gritted teeth.

"No," Rune said. "You'll remember I'm especially apt at killing things."

"Unless you want it to attach itself to you, too, don't touch it, not even with magic," Mother Mal warned. "Or perhaps you wish to kill her? At this point, I imagine doing so would be a mercy."

Rune let out something between a snarl and a curse. "You expect me to stand aside while it—"

I swiped the nearest flailing leg, lopping it clean off. The thing's scream reverberated through my ribcage, rattled in my skull. More of its legs scraped me from the inside, shredding me raw.

I stabbed the next leg, and the next, my knife easily slicing through each. It thrashed more violently, shredding the hem of my shirt and tearing my skin down to the bone.

"Expel it for good," Mother Mal commanded. "Or let it kill you."

My strength was nearly gone. The pain was too much.

With one last effort, I sawed away at the center of the legs, parting flesh and crystal alike as blood slicked my knife. The thing's struggles weakened and then, mercifully, ceased.

The last of its severed body crawled from beneath the flaps of my skin and collapsed, dead, beside Mother Mal.

"Kaffa, feed," Mother Mal said.

I hit the ground as the snake released me and swallowed the fallen crystal creature. There was a soft sensation under my head. Rune's hand. His face hovered above me, expression so concerned I wondered if blood loss was making me hallucinate.

"You won't die on me," he said.

"That's up to her, and only her," Mother Mal said.

I sank into darkness.

<hr>

My stomach and arm stung like I'd stepped in a hornet's nest. Stinging was good. Stinging meant pain, and pain meant that I was alive.

I opened my eyes to the impossibly broad canopy and the shock-white of trees. Rune knelt nearby, his every muscle taut, as though seeking something to maim. Or barely holding himself back.

"Don't move," Mother Mal said to me. She held one of the fleshy black eggs just beneath my collarbone, where remnants of the crystal remained partly jutting from my skin. "If even a drop of this touches living flesh, you're done."

She drizzled more brown water over the jagged break of what might have been a thorax. The liquid sizzled against the crystal until there was nothing left but an angry, gaping wound.

"Did I hurt you?" I croaked.

Mother Mal sniffed. "Hardly. It will take much more than that to injure me."

"I didn't even realize what I was doing."

"How could you not?" Rune snapped. "That thing used your body like a puppet, and you still failed to see—"

"It was a clever curse," Mother Mal intervened. "I doubt Val could even tell you when Sotera cast it."

"Sotera did this?" I asked.

"She used your own magic against you, forced you to conjure a creature that held her will and desire," Rune said. "Triggered only when you met Mother Mal."

I glared at him. "How could I know that? Sotera had no clue who Mother Mal was the first time they met."

"But she suspected," Mother Mal said. "I also suspect she didn't like my message to her."

"Why?"

"To some, the truth is their greatest enemy, and Sotera's truth is more terrible than most. I was there to remind her of the consequences of what she was doing."

The bottom half of my shirt had been lifted up, and Mother Mal dripped more brown poison across a scab of crystal to the left of my belly button.

I let my head fall back. "She let me escape, knowing I'd find you. Or at the very least, she implanted the curse as insurance."

"So it would seem. She underestimated your desire to survive."

"Many have," Rune muttered. He held out a hand as Hob brought Mother Mal a handful of moss I'd seen him soak with water from the clear part of the pool. "Let me."

Hob looked at Mother Mal, who nodded. "So long as you don't get any in her mouth."

"What is it?" I said.

"From the pool of life and death," Rune said sardonically.

"If that is how you choose to see it," Mother Mal said.

Hob and Kaffa the snake drew back with her, though Kaffa's eyes stayed fixed on me. I had no doubt, should I rise up to try to kill Mother Mal again, the next thing Kaffa gobbled up wouldn't just be some scattered crystal.

Rune carefully dripped the clear water into my open gashes, and I watched with astonishment as the skin and muscle stitched themselves up. My torn arms felt usable again. Even the sluggish, fatigued feeling that'd plagued me since leaving the Below abated somewhat.

Rune still looked furious, as though he could heal my injuries purely through the force of his glare.

"You look like I actually died," I said.

"And you look like someone with no clue what takes residence inside their body."

"I'm not clairvoyant."

"No," he agreed. "Just nearly dead."

"That's nothing new."

"Strangely, that isn't comforting."

He was being particularly cagey. This *wasn't* the first time I'd nearly died, yet his reaction to this instance was different than before. Strange. Or maybe not so strange. I wasn't vain enough to believe he held anything close to love for me, much as Sotera implied it. Seeing me in the throes of death could have triggered something within him, much as it had for me when Rune nearly killed himself during his coronation. It hadn't been love then. It was the fear of losing someone who saw the truly nasty parts of me and understood. Maybe even accepted them.

Nearly losing that had made me incensed with anger as well.

I examined Rune's face as he finished thoroughly closing up my every wound: The outer lines of his hair curled across his brow and entangled in his crown. The dark slashes that were his eyebrows. The furious concentration as he focused on his sole task.

Rune's eyes flickered to me, and I forced myself to hold his gaze, even as heat rose to my cheeks.

"Yes, the crown of the High King still fits nicely," Rune said. "And as the High King, I command you to not flirt with death again."

"You need to make your commands more realistic," I said. "Especially when we're at war."

He squeezed the last of the water from the moss and withdrew his body from over mine, giving me space to sit up.

"I wonder why it is that the Empress of Those Below knew more of a wildling legend than the Wilds' own High King," Rune said.

"Perhaps you have not been paying attention," Mother Mal said. "What is it that you know of me?"

"Little," Rune admitted. "Following the Forming, most wildlings, my father and tutors included, focused on more tangible threats, rather than what could be chalked up to myths or what had slunk away into the dark folds of the trees."

Rune tossed the dried moss to the ground, where Hob picked it up to suck on. "I read every fairy tale and listened to every scholar that would tolerate me. You, Mother Mal, are—were—the tender of the Mother Tree and steward to the beasts."

"Tender. Caretaker. Impartial observer," Mother Mal said. "I do not get involved, but influence, suggest, nudge things toward the way they're supposed to be."

"And you've summoned us here. So what is it that you 'suggest' for me?" Rune said, his petulant grin returning.

"I *suggest* you start believing in whom it is you're speaking to." The edges of the clearing darkened. Kaffa barred his fangs, and the black pool bubbled. "And learn that gaining power, knowing when to exert it, and when to defer it are all very different things."

It seemed to take an age, but Rune inclined his head. "Wise words from a magnanimous woman."

And just like that our surroundings returned to peaceful normality. "Flattery will not work on me," Mother Mal said. "I didn't attend your coronation, but I heard it was quite the event. To make up for it, I will give you gifts to show my good will. Get up, child. I have something for you."

I pushed to my feet, legs still wobbly, as Mother Mal extended an arm. One of the closed flowers near her elbow unfurled. A single oval seed as big as my fingernail sat in the center.

"For you. To hold until you need it."

The Wilds had taught me that there were rarely gifts that didn't come with strings attached, but I knew better than to make her angry.

The seed stuck to my fingers the moment I touched it, as though it'd put down roots. Before I could shake it free, the entire thing vanished beneath my skin. I felt it moving up my arm, across my shoulder, and nestling somewhere in the center of my chest.

"What did you do?" I demanded.

"So you don't lose it," Mother Mal said. "I promise this gift won't try to kill anyone."

"I thought you didn't get involved."

"I offered you the seed, but it was your choice to take it. Giving you help does not guarantee you'll take the right path. That will fall to you, and you alone."

She turned to Rune. "My gift to you, High King, is a warning. Sotera has grander plans. She seeks to unite the Wilds and Those Below under her total control by forging a new crown that will allow her to turn the very Wilds against you."

"Impossible," Rune said. "She has no power here."

"There are old magics, and there are always ways to circumnavigate them. The power of the Wilds lies not in its thrones, or even its crown. It is in its ruler. In its people. The old wildlings forgot this. You, surprisingly, have not. But still, Sotera means to create a way to overpower you with this new crown, and by force. If you plan on stopping her, you must do it soon."

Rune's lips were pursed, thinking. "And do you have any idea of how to accomplish that?"

"I have offered my knowledge. The choice of what to do with it lies with you."

Rune gave another bow, this one perhaps a bit more sincere than before. "I see. I'm glad you chose to intervene for our sake."

"Don't waste my good favor. Hob will take you back."

I gave her a bow of my own, a little stiffly thanks to my still-healing body. I took a final look at the tree, trying to memorize every detail as though that would give me the answers I needed. Within the crossed roots at its base was a smooth depression, like a bed that could fit a small body. Three more beds were beside this one. An entire family, all curled beneath the enveloping branches.

Mother Mal was watching me. "It is good to tend, to pass things on to another. I have done that many times before, hoping each time they will stay. They never do, either by their choice or the choices of others. My daughter, Rhasahlyn, once resided here, as did Nieriati the Bloom Tender. Both are gone now, yet the Wilds remain. I would keep them remaining, regardless of whether gods inhabit them or not."

"We'll do what we can," I said.

Mother Mal hobbled back to the tree. Kaffa lifted one of his coils to allow her to start sinking back into the bark.

"I'm glad to be awake again," Mother Mal said. "For things are about to happen that have not happened in a long time. I'd hate to miss them."

TWELVE

Rune was contemplatively silent as Hob led us from the Halfway. I assumed discovering the legends of your childhood were real—and that they needed *your* help—could be a little unnerving.

At last, Hob brought us out the other side of the waterfall, where colors and sounds returned in full, vibrant force.

"How can we meet with Mother Mal again?" I asked.

Hob shook his head, causing his long nails to scrape on the rock. "Mother Mal always finds you, not the other way around." And then he was gone.

"I'm surprised, Val," Rune said. "Was the first meeting not exciting enough?"

"She could be a powerful ally," I said. "You see that, right?"

"I see a primal force of the Wilds that's neither friend nor foe, one who could care less about what happens to us, so long as things go exactly the way they should."

"Cynical as ever."

"Realistic as ever, you mean."

He reached out and gently tapped just below the hollow of

my throat, close to where the seed had settled. "Gifts here are seldom given without consequence. You took it, which means you accept that consequence."

I didn't pull my eyes away from his. "Trust me, I know that."

"Excellent. Then there's hope yet."

The sun was just bleeding over the horizon as we made our way down to camp. I was surprised to see that, rather than being sleepily serene, it was a flurry of frantic activity.

"What is it now?" Rune growled.

A sudden blur, and the wildling who'd been standing watch the night before landed on a knee before Rune, panting.

"My Lord Rune we—*pant*—we worried about you. We thought—"

"I was only gone a short time," Rune said, frowning. "I had business elsewhere."

Cassius was striding over, a number of wildings congregated at his back. His eyes flickered between Rune and me, as though wondering what the two of us could have possibly been doing alone.

"A warning would be nice, Ru—Lord Rune, before you decide to vanish," he said.

Rune gave an exasperated sigh. "I don't need to tell everyone when I have to leave for a couple hours."

"With all due respect, Lord Rune, you kind of do. The Mysts are already here. They took up a spot at the far tip of the lake."

"Ah, good. Keep Xander away."

Cassius gave him a look that mirrored my confusion. "Sure. Keen wanted to see Val, too."

Rune's eyes narrowed. "Why?"

"I didn't ask. I was too busy looking for you."

"I'll meet him," I said. "Right now, if he's ready."

At the tip of the lake was a particularly thick stand of trees.

As we approached, I could only just make out the two dozen figures nestled within, and even then, I suspected it was because they wanted us to see them.

Like their namesake, the Mysts wore all gray clothing that billowed off their bodies, as though sewn with clouds. Every gold-red eye was on me. I picked out who I suspected was their leader—a man with a small, irksome smile on his face—lounged on the bough of the nearest tree. His hair was a thunderhead of silver-gray, his entire body almost pellucid as a rain shower. A small crossbow was strapped to one wrist, a knife to the other.

"So this is the human," Keen said. He stretched out his long legs and dropped to the ground. Even his footsteps were mist-soft. I could see why, even amongst wildlings, Xander walked quieter than most.

"Half human," I said.

Keen chuckled. "Half, of course. I'm surprised, Rune. When you summoned us, I thought your way forward had a clear plan."

"That hasn't changed," Rune said.

"Perhaps not. But I don't know if it can be achieved with this clear liability here."

"I hold my own," I said, bristling. "And I've proven myself loyal. Which, from what I've heard, is more than I can say about you." I looked at Rune. "Why are you working with them?"

"Because he needs us, the eyes and ears of the Wilds," Keen answered. "We can traverse where others struggle to. Vanish into thin air. If needed, we can slip a knife between someone's ribs so our new High King can keep his sparkling image unmarred."

"Too late for that," I said.

"We can give him an edge," Keen said, ignoring me. "And

as a reward for our gracious service, Rune has promised to give us a little piece of the Wilds we can call our own."

"The exact terms are yet to be solidified," Rune said.

Keen brushed the words aside like an errant thought. "Still, that's the gist. No more fliting around unless we want to. We'll have a place we don't need to worry about being ruled, by the High King or anyone."

"These are his Wilds," I said. "There won't be any place like that."

"How adorable. Did you train her to say that, Rune?" Keen's smile made me want to pull his cloak over his head and smash him face-first into the nearest tree. "You don't know how the Mysts work, do you? We have survived the reigns of Mordecai and Jezaline. We can blend into every tree, every rock, every sprig. No Lord or king governs us. If they try, we disappear, and you'll never see us again."

"That might be difficult, if the Wilds themselves are looking for you," Rune said.

The trees groaned deeply, as though stretching awake after a long slumber. Some of the Mysts scrambled to safety as the ground itself formed hands of foliage and reached for them. "I've gained some power since we last met."

"Seems you have," Keen muttered. "But you still need us. This has to be a mutual agreement. And *we* don't trust *her*."

"I do," Rune said. "That should be enough."

"It's not. My Lord," Keen added. "Even the Mysts are tested constantly to ensure they remain loyal."

"If you constantly test them, then maybe it's fear that keeps them in line, not loyalty," I said. Still, it was a small price to pay if the Mysts were that useful. "I'll take your test. I don't care."

"Yet I do," Rune said. "If they can't trust who I choose to put my faith in, then perhaps I've chosen wrong."

"Are there others like them?" I asked. "Other groups who can do what they do?"

Rune pursed his lips, looking frustrated as he always did when he couldn't physically force his way out of something he didn't like. This wasn't just about proving myself to Rune or to the Mysts. In some ways, I was still trying to prove myself to *me*.

"I have nothing to hide," I said. "Their test won't hurt me to take it."

Keen shrugged, as if to say, *She agreed, this isn't on me.* "Voya," he called.

A girl appeared at his side. She opened her mouth, and I swallowed a wave of disgust as a centipede nearly as long as my arm crawled out.

Everything about it looked mean, from the scabbed texture along its lengthy, segmented trunk, to the tips of its sharp legs that dug bloody pinpricks in her arm as it skittered to the palm of her hand. Its finger-length claws clicked together, glistening with venom.

Keen seemed to be enjoying my discomfort. "This is a Magora. To most animals, it produces a hallucinogen so powerful it can run its prey to exhaustion or induce a heart attack by scaring it with things that aren't even there. To wildlings and humans, its toxin acts as strong as any compulsion, even one Rune might conjure. Not unlike the Gelvenan I believe you ran into. Enough that we can control you and tease out any secrets you might have."

The Magora arched its back as Keen stroked it. His delighted smirk said he expected me to back down and prove I was hiding something.

"Okay." I held out my hand. "But after this, I get to call on you for one favor."

"A favor isn't a light thing to ask, even if it's unbinding," Keen said. "But very well. *If* you pass."

He flicked his finger and the Magora darted up my arm. Before I could stop it, it had sunk its fangs into my neck, close to where my carotid artery was. If it pressed a millimeter deeper, if I made any sudden movement, I would bleed out in seconds.

Sluggishness almost immediately draped my body. My arms sagged at my sides. My knees wobbled. The feeling wasn't unlike being drunk, but almost as soon as it started, the sensation began to clear, as though I was rising from the depths of the ocean toward the light of the surface.

Keen watched my face intently, until he seemed assured the venom had taken effect. He began circling me. "Who sent you?"

"No one," I said. "I'm helping Rune of my own free will."

There was more to that answer than I wanted to admit, but the Magora's venom wasn't compelling me to reveal more, and it wasn't any of Keen's business.

"Did you actually kill the great Lords to help Rune ascend the throne?"

"Yes." I reached for Keen's heart gem. "Would you like to see how?"

There was a flicker of true concern in his eyes. "That won't be necessary." He gave Rune a teasing look. "You seem awfully protective of our dear Rune. Tell me what you really think of him as High King."

"He's what the Wilds need," I said. Not technically a lie.

Keen stopped circling me and leaned in to my ear. Not taking his eyes off Rune, he said, "Put your arms around me."

I didn't need to pretend to be surprised. What was he playing at?

I felt the faint tug of the Magora's compulsion urge me to

comply, but it was me who chose to play along. I locked my hands around the back of Keen's neck. He put his hands on my waist, but his eyes never left Rune.

Of course. He was watching Rune's expression, seeking any sign that I was his weakness. Rune, for his part, remained stone faced. Keen moved us around, as though we were awkward middle schoolers at our first dance. His breath tickled my ear.

"Has our High King ever danced with you? Has he ever held you like this?"

"Are you testing her loyalty, or asking if she's available?" Rune said in a bored voice.

Keen's smile was playful menace. "Tell me, Val: if you had the chance, would you kill Rune? If he moved against your precious human world, or did something you disliked, how quickly would your sense of loyalty disappear?"

I unlatched my hands from around his neck and withdrew a crystal knife from my forearm, taking pleasure in the looks of surprise on the Mysts' faces. I turned to Rune, who merely cocked an eyebrow. He waited, so stupidly exposed and trusting that I wouldn't shove the knife into him, even if Keen said but a single command.

"Do you want to hear the truth?" I said to Keen.

"Only the truth," he said.

I whirled and placed the knife against Keen's throat. "Ask me to do anything more and I'll see how many slices it takes to completely sever your head. The muscle is awful stringy." I pressed the knife harder. "I'm thinking three good cuts, but we can do another little test if you'd like."

Rune gave a barking laugh.

I gestured to the Magora. "Remove it, before I do it myself."

"Do as she asks," Keen gritted out.

The Myst, Voya, held out a hand, and the Magora detached and scuttled back into her mouth.

"Your test didn't work on me," I said. "A lot of wildling magic doesn't. If I was a spy or a traitor, I wouldn't reveal that. Now stop wasting our time."

"Keen and I will talk alone," Rune said, still trying to stifle a smirk.

I sheathed my dagger. "I'll be back later for my favor, Keen."

"I don't owe a favor," Keen grumbled.

"I upheld our part of the deal," I said. "I'll be back. Or I'm sure he," I nodded at Rune, "will question how likely you are to keep to *his* deals. And after your stunt, I promise you'd rather disappoint him than me."

<hr>

Though it hadn't fully affected me, the Magora's residual venom still made it impossible to get more than a few hours' rest, and even that was mostly tossing and turning, interrupted by brief bouts of death-like sleep. Still edgy and desperate to find some way to be useful, I helped Raquel direct his conjured beasts to hunt down the smaller prey higher up in the trees. I forced my ineloquent fingers to weave clothing out of living greenery. Eventually, I found myself sitting at the edge of a cleared field near the lake, watching General Forcheck work through the daily drills with the wildlings and Those Below.

Cassius gave me an acknowledging nod. He'd been teaching the survivors from Mog Moren fighting, strategy, even reading from human books they brought from Aleki's mansion in what used to be Portland. Many of the survivors were missing parts of fingers and ears and still others entire limbs. Most, when confronted with a weapon or thrust back into sparring had the terrified look of an animal caught in a snare.

Now finished, Cassius wiped at the thin sheen of sweat on his forehead and took a spot on the rock beside me.

"Grandmother wants you to join us tomorrow. She knows you're busy, but you've never had any formal training. She says it'll set a good example to the others."

"My stepbrother Joshua taught me to fight," I said.

"Sure, but you've never had much training from a wildling. She could teach you some new tricks."

I didn't disagree. The problem was that I was still struggling to get back the strength and skill I'd had before. I wasn't sure I wanted to share my current deficiencies with those who were supposed to look up to me, or whose respect I was still trying to earn.

Cassius must have taken my silence for disapproval. He nodded at those training. "They'll get better."

I watched one of the fighters cower from another who was swinging around a practice sword with all the grace of a blind man trying to hit a wasp. "Are you sure?"

"They survived this long. Once they understand that the punishment for failure here isn't the same as Mog Moren, they'll be fine."

Not the same, maybe, but in some ways far worse. "Fighting for Rune is still putting them in danger."

"True." Cassius waved at Xander, who was finishing teaching some of the other wildlings how to properly shoot a bow. "But, scared or not, they chose to be here. *You* chose to be here. You could have returned to the human world. You could have left all this behind. Why didn't you?"

"You really think I could run away and leave all of you here?"

Cassius frowned. "No one would have blamed you if you did."

Before I had to answer that, Xander joined us, taking up the spot on the other side of the rock. He rolled his shoulder, wincing.

"You hurt?" I asked.

He stopped. He nodded toward those he'd been teaching to shoot. "Give them another month and they might start hitting what they're aiming at," he said grimly. "As I said before, Cassius, you and General Forcheck may think this is a good idea, but it's bound to get them killed. We're not so desperate for soldiers that we'll throw bodies to be skewered by Sotera's spears or drowned beneath the sea. Send them away. Do it before they get hurt. They have no idea what they're getting into, and they won't, not until it's too late."

Cassius watched the fighters, not seeming the least bit put off by Xander's unkind words. "I didn't say it before, but I'm sorry about Marian."

Xander scoffed. "This isn't about—"

"Maybe not, but I am."

"She knew what she was getting into," Xander bit out. "Unlike them. When you lose so much, you grow numb to the grief. Don't lose that part of yourself. Don't forget how much it hurts."

His calloused fingers gouged new holes in the flaking edge of the rock. A sullenness pulled at his shoulders. I couldn't remember a moment since returning to the surface where he hadn't been angry or melancholic.

"Are you telling me not to lose my humanity?" I joked. "Might be a bit too late for me."

Xander broke into the first real smile I'd seen in a while. "Still, try your best."

Cassius leaned back on the rock. "I won't forget. But I'll be glad when this is over. Grandmother craves violence. It's the story of my family. I'm hoping I can change that. Imagine this: I could get a small, beautiful part of the Wilds all to my own. Maybe even convince Rune to make me a minor Lord," he quipped. "I could leave all this behind."

I remembered Cassius hacking Mog Moren's guards to pieces, lost in a fervor of mad bloodlust. Bits of that maniac rage still lingered within, I was sure. I didn't think leaving so traumatic a past behind was as easy as finding a place to settle, no matter how beautiful it was.

I spotted Rune leaving the tip of the lake where Keen and his Mysts were staying. Xander watched him go. He stood. "It's a nice dream. Don't get your hopes up, though."

When he'd left, Cassius jerked his head toward the training wildlings. "Help me out?"

"I would, but Pitius promised to teach me more stealth," I said.

"Ah, well. That may be more useful than fighting in the end. If everything else fails, at least you'll be able to run."

—

ONLY AFTER THE sun had begun its descent did I leave Pitius and head back to Keen. I was surprised to hear Xander's furious voice drifting through the thick trees on my approach.

"—supposed to be safe! She was your responsibility!"

"We're the Mysts, Xander, not babysitters," Keen answered, in a bored tone that made me think they'd had this conversation before. Maybe many times before. "You're the big shot now, hanging with the High King instead of us. Why don't you ask for his help—Oh, wait."

I rounded a tree in time to see Xander hit Keen, knuckles against jaw, hard enough to speckle blood on the ground. In mere seconds, gray cloaks circled them like an angry fog. I heard swords being drawn, the creaking of bows pulled taut.

"No." Keen rubbed his jaw, glaring at Xander. "As a former Myst, you get a pass, just this once. Now leave. We have nothing else to talk about."

Xander looked as though he wanted to hit him again, before turning and stomping off. Movement prickled the back of my neck, and I turned to find Voya standing there.

"I'm here to see Keen," I said.

She wordlessly led me into the center of the Mysts' encampment. Most had receded into the trees, though I had no doubt they'd spring into action the moment they were needed.

"Right, your 'favor'," Keen said when he saw me. He continued rubbing his jaw. "What makes you think I'll actually follow through?"

"You're a survivor," I said. "You didn't make it this long by forgoing promises to the wrong people."

Keen sighed, as though I'd found him out. "Fair enough. If you're going to use my bountiful gift to ask for something on Rune's behalf, don't bother. He and I already had an extensive talk about who gets what during our alliance."

"I'm here for me. What was Xander talking about?"

"Is that your favor? That I tell you?"

I didn't honor that with an answer. Keen conjured a hammock of moss between two pines and sank into it. He withdrew a small glob of purple paste from a woven pouch at his waist and dabbed a fingertip amount on his bruised chin. "Has Xander ever mentioned someone named Zuri?"

I thought for a moment. "Once."

"Surprised it was only once. He's been obsessed with her for as long as he was with us. They're lovers," he clarified, though I'd already put the pieces together. "She's from the Undersea. They met when we lived near the coast for a time. He found her washed up on the beach. She'd run away from her betrothed, and in response he'd sent a school of barracuda to bring her back. When she resisted, they attacked, commanded to tear her to pieces. There was a lot of blood. Xander helped nurse her back to health, and they fell madly in love."

"I didn't think the Undersea allowed their subjects to be with anyone from the land."

"They don't. Which is why, about a month ago, when seeking out a weakness for Rune, Bendeti kidnapped Zuri. She's not dead, at least we don't think so. She's far more valuable alive, as a bargaining chip of sorts."

It was starting to make sense. Of course Xander would be distraught about that. Enough to argue with Rune to get her back. And with the lover of one of Rune's closest confidants under his control, I had no doubt Bendeti had sent more than a couple requests to meet with Rune and attempt to get him to concede something.

Xander should know better. He had to understand that he was playing right into Bendeti's hands. But I couldn't fault him. Not after what I'd done for someone I loved.

"Xander blames us for not watching out for her," Keen said. "He blames me, mostly. As if we hadn't done everything we could to keep her safe. He's not a Myst anymore. He doesn't remember the dangers of being outside the High King's graces."

"I promise that it's just as dangerous," I said. "Especially when you have a target on your back."

Keen shrewdly watched me. "Perhaps. You think I dislike Rune. I don't. I greatly respect what he's done. But not what he's doing *now*."

"Fighting to protect the Wilds from being destroyed?"

"Look." Keen kicked to his feet out of the hammock. I let

him turn me to face the ghostly lights of the encampment across the lake. "Rune doesn't just want to protect; he wants to conquer. And his subjects? They're not soldiers, and neither are we. We're wraiths, thieves, unlucky bastards, collateral from the trite bickering of the old Houses and Lords, the same world Rune comes from. To pretend we're anything more than that is to get us killed."

"He believes that you can become something better," I insisted.

Keen's laugh was mocking. "Of course you'd think that. I forgot that you're his blade, or his right hand, or whatever fancy title they give you to describe what you are to him." His suggestive look made me want to break his nose. It was the same look he'd had when he'd commanded me to hold him. He was needling to get a rise, but like Rune, I wouldn't give him one.

I brushed his arm off. Keen laughed.

"Tell you what, I'll help you, Val, if, when the time comes, you'll help Xander. He may not be a Myst, but we were close once. In some ways, he's still my brother."

"Of course I'll help him. But not for you."

"I don't care about the reason, just that it happens."

"I'll do it, but why don't you start by telling Rune that Xander can't join us when we visit the Lords on the coast."

I'd clearly surprised him. "Why don't *you* tell him?"

Because I'd already become more involved in affairs that weren't mine. Because there were still those who saw me as the enemy, and I didn't need to worsen that by making decisions that weren't mine. "Because you've known him better and longer than me. Rune would trust that you know what's best for him. Xander's not thinking clearly, and I have a feeling things are about to get a lot worse."

Keen rubbed his jaw. "Why do I feel this is just so Xander won't get mad at *you* when he finds out?"

"Just do what you can."

"I suppose I could leave a little suggestion worming in our dear High King's ear. No guarantees he'll listen. Now is *that* your favor? As you can tell, I don't like being in debt, even if it's non-binding."

"My favor is this: I want you to find out what Sotera's next move is."

Keen scoffed. "Is that all? I can see why you and Rune work so well together; you ask the impossible with little regard to what it'll cost."

I knew exactly what I was asking. But splitting Rune's attention between rallying the more powerful wildlings and ferreting out Sotera's plans could prove disastrous. I had to concede that Keen had a point: none of us were soldiers. Our skills lay in knives and shadows, and maybe with the two of those we could stave off the worst of what was to come.

"And where do you suggest I start this impossible task?" Keen said.

"Mog Moren's flooded, so maybe south of King's Hollow," I said, hiding my relief. "That's about where the Below's city of the Deep is. There were several tremors during my time down there. Maybe go wherever you feel them."

"That's about as vague as it gets. I'll consider it."

He rubbed his jaw again, not hiding his grimace. "Now give me some peace. I've been with you and Rune only a day and I'm already regretting it."

THIRTEEN

My arms shook with fatigue. My sweaty palms made it near impossible to hold onto Sliver. The crystal sword might be able to cut through Those Below easier than any steel blade, but I had yet to fabricate any sort of proper grip, and waving it around, as tired as I was, felt like begging for a disaster.

Worse than that, I was falling behind the others.

"Again!" General Forcheck barked. "Second set."

Forearms burning, I swung Sliver around in a wide sweep, trying to will myself to remember the fighting techniques my body seemed to have forgotten. General Forcheck eyed me and then spoke something to Cassius.

"She wants us to spar," he said, coming over to me. "She thinks you're not being challenged enough."

I shot General Forcheck a dark look. "I've already embarrassed myself enough, don't you think? I'm not exactly in the best shape."

"That's why she asked."

I shook out my trembling arms. Joining the trainees had brought about everything I'd feared and more. My skills were still there, but stiff, as though covered in a fine crystal skin. Rather than encouraging the newbies, most had regarded me with a mixture of disappointment and, from the newer wildlings, outright hostility.

Still, if I wanted my revenge on Sotera as badly as I believed I did, weakness wasn't something I could afford.

I squared up with Cassius and took deep breaths to center myself. It wasn't as though I'd lost *everything* down Below. My muscles were slowly coming back, and my reflexes along with them. More than my bones, my pride had been shattered, and my confidence with it. The viciousness I'd wielded like my blade, the viciousness that kept me alive, had receded to timidity, something that would get me killed far faster.

"I'll take things slow," Cassius said.

"Don't patronize me," I answered.

He shrugged and then started off with a low swing. Much slower than I knew he was capable of, but I was secretly grateful all the same.

His sword cleaved air as I stepped to the side. Normally, I'd dart in and press the attack, but my fatigue forced me to stay defensive, giving him time to swing again. Defensive. I was all defensive, and I hated every second of it. No one survived in the Wilds long by being defensive. Eventually, you had to show teeth.

That moment came when Cassius overstepped. Instinct took over. I knocked his sword aside and drove my shoulder into his sternum, and he wheezed, dropping onto his butt. I sheathed Sliver into my arm and helped pull him to his feet. Rather than being frustrated, he was grinning.

"You seem fine to me."

"Fine won't cut it with what we're up against," I said. "But thank you."

General Forcheck had dismissed the other trainees and hobbled over to us. "Like to speak to you a moment, Val."

Curious, I followed her to where she was staying. As a respected general and one of the oldest wildlings, Rune had magicked an entirely new dwelling for her, conjuring tightly packed walls of young spruce and fir that blocked the cold. Next, he'd coaxed rows of gardenias and peonies from the soil, and made a roof of ivy that grew closed when it rained and receded during sunshine. Chimes tinkled in the branches where birds flitted about.

General Forcheck's actual belongings were sparse, though there were numerous bowls of thickened, colored liquid bubbling on one of the tables, next to delicate instruments of glass. The sweet-smelling flowers couldn't entirely mask the tang of something sour in the air, like burned rubber.

"I'm distilling my own drink," General Forcheck explained. She hobbled to where she'd bottled up some of the colored liquid, popped the cork on one, and started pouring it out into two glasses.

"Thanks, but I'm good," I said.

"You are. But you need time." She finished pouring and handed me a glass. "I don't only drink this because I've been deprived of it for so long. It will help dull the pain, which I know you have."

Despite the smell, I took a tentative sip. The liquid burned going down, but I was pleasantly surprised to find the near-constant ache in my shoulders and hips eased slightly. General Forcheck's bones popped as she took a seat in a fur-lined chair across from me. She took a long sip from a glass of her own and began rubbing an ointment on her knees that smelled strongly of mint and willow bark.

"I'm glad Rune has you," she said, surprising me. Not that I didn't see the value in my being here, only that it was rarely voiced aloud.

"I... Thank you for saying that. I'm sure Rune feels the same."

"He'd be an idiot not to. I've commanded the armies of those who reigned with iron fists, and others with weak grips. I have survived countless coups and attempted assassinations, not because I'm particularly clever or particularly skilled with a blade—though I am both—but because I stuck with what I did best and kept my nose out of the rest. At least until all that caught up with me.

"Yet in that time I'd learned that often the greatest threat of a kingdom falling is not due to enemies without, but from within."

I took another small sip, wondering where she was going with this.

"It is one thing to trust another when you have nothing," General Forcheck said. "To the starving man, even the promise of a great feast is enough to buy his friendship. It is another thing entirely to *maintain* that trust, especially after indulging in all the good things you've never had before, such as freedom. When the sun is bright and our bellies full, so quickly we forgo old promises for false ones."

"You think the wildlings are going to stop following Rune because things are going *too* well?"

"You tell me. You have eyes and ears. Could you assure me that all is going according to plan?"

Of course it wasn't. But that was just how war went, even those not fought in large scale battles but in shadows and with secrets. Surely nobody could guarantee flawless loyalty. Not even Rune. To do that would require the same kind of iron-fisted tyranny General Forcheck knew all too well.

I took another sip. The drink burned even more this time.

"It is good to have those you trust around," General Forcheck said. "Those who are fighting for more than just the comforts of home or a loved one. Those who have a purpose of their own. You can even count on those fighting for vengeance, because you may still have them even after they've gotten what they wanted."

"What about you?" I asked. "What do you gain from this? Vengeance? Power? Did Rune promise you your own kingdom when all of it's done?"

General Forcheck cackled. "Do I look like the kind of old woman content with lording over a spit of land until I croak pathetically in my sleep?"

"That's not an answer."

"I fight with the hope that my grandson won't have to, that he can live a life at peace with what he's endured, or perhaps having even been spared the worst of it."

I thought of the fervent bloodlust on Cassius's face at Mog Moren. The invisible scars Rune still carried with him. I hoped what General Forcheck fought for was possible, but I doubted it.

She finished massaging the salve into her knee and threw it aside. "If you're asking about my selfish desires, then I get to fight, to teach, to command an army. I don't care about kings and petty politics, so long as I get to smell blood and face off against an enemy cunning enough to make it interesting. Some of us..."

She leaned forward, her presence crowding me. "Some of us were *born* knowing what they were meant to do. We won't be satisfied with anything else. You hear what I'm saying? I was born to fight. It's what I am, and I'll be content with nothing less, at least until I'm dead."

She held my gaze, as though I was supposed to glean some incredible insight from her words.

"Anyone who can take down the major Lords has nothing to learn from me, except perhaps some finesse," General Forcheck said. "Your problem is not a matter of skill, but confidence."

"I don't need confidence, I need to be stronger," I said.

General Forcheck sipped her drink, thoughtful. "Perhaps. Strength is easier to maintain than to acquire. Same with trust, same with power. Never lose any of those things, if you can help it. But don't get so caught up in collecting it that you forgo everything else. Like mercy."

And what had those ever done for me, except brought me more pain? To truly be safe, I had to fight for it.

General Forcheck reached into her mottled cloak and withdrew a small metal bird with folded wings and jeweled eyes. An echo bird, used for carrying secure messages.

"From Rune," she said.

Puzzled, I took it from her. "I just saw him this morning. He couldn't have given it to me himself?"

"That's not for me to know." General Forcheck nodded at the bird. "He didn't give me the password to unlock it. I figured you'd have an idea of what it was."

This was getting stranger by the second. Strangest of all was that Rune thought I could guess the password, as though we'd exchanged secrets ahead of time. General Forcheck watched me closely.

"I expected you of all people to know," she said. "There are many things the two of you alone share."

Heat rose to my face. Again, Rune and my relationship appeared closer than it was. As much as I wanted to confide in General Forcheck about it and gain some objective advice, I bit my tongue. Whatever our relationship, it was too private. Too easily exploited.

"The password?" General Forcheck said.

The answer that first came to mind was startingly intimate. *Shockingly* intimate for Rune, but maybe...

I brought the echo bird to my lips and whispered, "Little fox."

The bird unfolded its wings and opened its mouth, whispering back into my ear in Rune's dusky voice, *"Meet me at the throne."*

"I couldn't hear, but I suspect I know what he's up to," General Forcheck said.

I slowly pocketed the echo bird, mulling the message over. "And what is your counsel on it?"

"Whether it's for the best, I can't say, but make sure he knows what he's doing. You have a clear head about these things, mostly, though you too tend to get in over it at times. Make him understand this: there are some things you can't take back."

"What makes you think he'll listen to me?"

"You're one of the few people I trust he'll listen to."

A fluttery sensation grew in my stomach, a little uncomfortable, a little pleasant. I had no reason to feel ashamed. General Forcheck, like others, could form their own opinions about what I was to Rune.

"I wouldn't keep him waiting, whatever he wants to do," General Forcheck said.

I stood, gave her a bow. "I won't. And thank you for the drink and the counsel."

General Forcheck gave a crackly laugh. "One of those is worth far more than the other. I'll let you decide which."

I SLID off Erebus's back, grateful to feel solid ground beneath my feet after a swift dusk-light ride back to King's Hollow.

"Stay close," I said. Erebus growled and melted into the underbrush. I shook out my legs and hiked toward the center of the Hollow. No birds sang. No insects chirped. It was the only place I could remember in the Wilds like that, like it was the lair of a predator. Or a tomb.

For a place that had been so important just over a month ago, I hadn't thought of the Hollow since. One look and I understood why we hadn't been back.

Sotera's attack had ripped enormous chunks of earth apart. Some of these sullied the languid blue lake, creating torn new islands among the existing. The underground passageways were snarls of shredded roots and shattered glass skylights, as though a giant had reached inside and wrenched upward.

The one good thing about being away so long was that it'd given the Wilds time to grow over all the bodies. However, I did have to watch my step for any unusual lumps.

I spied Rune next to the throne, set high above the clearing before an enormous, uprooted tree.

"What's with all the secrecy?" I said when I reached him. He was staring at the throne, and with some shock, I answered my own question.

The throne of the High King of the Wilds was wrought from polished wood, encrusted with jewels and blue crystal, not unlike that from Below. Perhaps the very same, if Sotera's claim that the wildlings were once part of Those Below was true.

The first time I saw it, I believed it to be one of the most beautiful things I'd laid eyes on. Now it was entirely ripped in two, with only a few strained vines bridging the separate halves. The blue crystal had nearly consumed all of it like a bad case of wild rot.

"I don't understand," I said. "I thought the throne gave you power. If Sotera destroyed it, then how...?"

Rune tapped the crown circling his brow. "I've been coming here in secret whenever I can, consolidating the Wilds' power into this. And into myself."

It seemed like a reasonable plan. A moving target was much more difficult to hit.

"If it's so simple, why haven't any of the other rulers done it?" I asked.

Rune turned to me, and I took him in from the light of crystal; the wan color of his cheeks, the excess weariness hanging off his frame. "The process of redirecting power from the throne to me is incredibly dangerous and taxing."

"You're killing yourself," I accused. "More than that…"

I looked at the throne, finally understanding the other problem. From what I knew of how rulers and their thrones worked, their power was always split between the ruler, the throne, and the crown. To take away one would remove a vulnerability and introduce a new one.

"If you die, there will be nothing to keep the Wilds' power in check," I guessed. "No throne to hold for the rightful ruler, not until a new one was made. That power could destroy everything, or whoever offs you could take it for themselves. There is no backup plan."

"Good thing I don't plan on dying. But if Sotera wants to rob me of my power, then she'll have to come through me directly." Rune's grin was wicked. "I'd welcome her to try."

And she would. There was no doubt about that. I could only hope that, when it happened, Rune's gambit paid off.

"What's done is done," Rune said, reading into my silence. "The throne has served its purpose. I need to destroy it, to ensure nothing else can be taken from it. To ensure that Sotera can't try to use it against me. But I can't do that with these damnable crystals blocking my magic."

Now I understood my role in all this. "Luckily Sotera *has* been teaching me some new tricks."

"One of the few good things she's done," Rune agreed.

I brushed past him and spread my palm across the points of the largest cluster of crystals. With only a little pull, I began drawing magic from them. So much magic. Not only had the crystal stifled Rune's power, but it seemed the crystals themselves had been absorbing residual magic from the throne itself.

"Is there a problem?" Rune's voice was far away. "Val?"

I drained the first cluster of crystal within moments and immediately moved to the next. My head swam like I was drunk. My feet felt like two blocks of cement as I stumbled in my haste to start on the other, nearly skewering my palm in my desperation to absorb its magic. So much power, so much wondrous power.

As though I'd gained wildling magic, roots seemed to sprout from my feet and burrow deep into the earth. I could feel the crust of the Wilds breathing. It was the skin of an enormous beast, and we were simply small irritants living upon it.

The roots burrowed deeper, and I felt lines of magic crisscrossing the Below. Down I went, until it was as though I'd reached my hand into a dark hole and brushed against something living. Something with sharp teeth and hot breath. Something exuding rage.

Hungry, its voice rumbled in my head. *So hungry. So angry.*

I sensed the moment it became aware of me. *I will devour everything. I will devour it* all. *Starting with you—*

I pulled my awareness back before it could bite.

I clumsily moved to the last cluster of crystal. My sight was filled with nothing but smeared light. I was a cup overflowing, yet still it wasn't enough. I wanted to take and take and take until—

My arm came to a jarring halt. I came back to myself to find Rune had caught my wrist.

"You've removed enough," he said. "I can do what needs to be done."

"One more," I said. My voice came out pleading. "This is incredible, like nothing I've ever felt before—"

"I said that's enough—"

"And I think you're wrong!"

I lunged for the last crystal cluster, but Rune wrenched me back with surprising strength. I hit the ground hard enough to shake loose whatever temporary craziness had taken hold. I rubbed at my eyes until the stinging went away, until the buzzing across my skin receded. I still felt drunk on what I'd taken, but at least there wasn't the mad compulsion to get more, only frustration.

"I get it," I said. "I was taking power from you, from the Wilds. You think it's supposed to be yours."

"It *is* mine," he said. "I'm High King of the Wilds. You can't handle what it takes."

I scoffed as I stumbled to my feet. It took a moment for the disorientation to pass, until I could stand without feeling like a helpless newborn fawn. "Because you said so? What if it helps me to help you?"

Rune sneered. "Look at you. Only a little and you're acting like an obstinate child demanding more sweets. Power isn't everything."

My laugh was as cruel as his smile. Perhaps I'd learned that from him, or perhaps my own cruelty was just waking up, coaxed by what I'd fed it. "That's rich, coming from you, the guy who wanted nothing *but* power. It's fine for you to take it and take it, but it isn't the same once someone else does. Face it, Rune, you just want everyone to be subservient. The only king. The only ruler."

Rune stepped up to me, and something about the magic I'd taken must have responded to the magic in him because my skin began to buzz again, in a way that wasn't entirely unpleasant.

"To rule over such a broken place isn't a privilege; it's a punishment," he said. "I'd save you from that. That power you crave so much nearly destroyed me. It may still destroy me."

"Sure, that's it," I muttered. "You still don't trust me, and I don't blame you." I put some distance between us, hoping it'd calm my beating heart. "I've done as you asked. Now you can finish doing exactly what you want."

Without taking his eyes off me, Rune half turned and raised his hand. The wood beneath our feet shredded apart, its fibrous strips retwining themselves into giant hands that began ripping the now-crystal-free throne apart piece by piece. Bursts of rapidly growing flowers split apart the gold, while thousands of insects swarmed from the dirt and chewed away what remained.

"Won't you even look at it?" I said. "This is what you wanted for so long."

"I can't," Rune said, a small hitch in his voice. "I want to, but I can't."

I felt a twinge of sympathy. Rune told me once that taking the throne had been the dream that kept him alive through Mog Moren and all the terrible things that had happened since. But ever since acquiring that dream, it seemed he'd discovered it wasn't like how he imagined. Not at all.

When the throne was nothing but dust and shreds of wood, Rune moved his destruction to the hollow tree behind him. The giant hands clamped either side and began crumpling it inward. A faint scream rose above the creaking wood.

"Did you hear that?" I asked.

"What?" Rune said.

Another faint scream, and this time I knew I wasn't imagining it.

"Rune, stop!" I pulled his arm down, and the destruction halted. "I thought... Stay here."

Drawing Sliver, I ducked beneath the low ceiling of the semi-crushed tree. The carved-out rooms of the hollowed interior had served as Rune's living space and planning area before the Lords had driven him out. I avoided the worst of the splintered walls and made my way toward where Rune's room had been.

There was someone inside among the sawdust, lying on the floor after having clearly been cast out of what remained of Rune's bed. I lifted Sliver higher.

"Who are—"

I gasped as Marian pushed herself to her elbows and looked up at me. She gave a resigned, throaty laugh as Rune joined me. "Look who it is. I thought you might make it back here eventually."

FOURTEEN

I sheathed Sliver and immediately knelt to help her. I wasn't sure where to start. The lower half of one of her legs was twisted almost entirely around. The ankle was missing and the fleshy stump that remained was difficult to look at. Her entire body was covered in a thin sheen of feverish sweat.

I decided to start with the worst of the leg and close up the festering cuts. "This is going to hurt."

Marian gestured to her missing ankle. "Gee, a bit too late for that, don't you think?"

She was aware enough to smart back. That was promising.

I went to work. I couldn't remove the blood, but as my paltry healing magic made it through the minor gashes and scrapes, Marian's pained hissing gradually softened to even, shallow breaths. Rune hovered over us, his looming presence growing more distracting by the second.

"I thought you were dead," he said. "Why didn't you call out for me through the Wilds or send a messenger instead of hiding here? I would have found you sooner."

"Are you done?" Marian asked me.

I wasn't sure moving her was the best idea, but she needed healing from someone who actually knew what they were doing. "Help me, Rune."

Rune didn't look like he wanted to. Then he knelt and easily scooped Marian up, carrying her back outside the torn tree.

Marian gaped at the ripped apart throne. "Why did you do that?"

"You don't answer my questions, so you don't get my answers," Rune said.

"That throne meant *everything* to you."

Rune stopped abruptly, dropping Marian into a chair of woven vines that had sprouted up beneath her. "Not everything. Not anymore. Show Val your leg." To me, he said, "Seal up the wound the best you can."

"Val doesn't need to see it," Marian snapped. "I'm way better at healing than her. If I could have done anything, I would ha—"

She hissed as I pulled the stump of her lower leg into my lap and started to gently prod at the blackened, ragged flesh. Marian was right, this was beyond anything I or even she could do. Even the wildlings' accelerated healing hadn't saved her. It smelled of infection, too. Judging by how many minor wounds I'd already attended to, she'd been too injured or delirious with pain to even take basic care of herself.

I pushed more healing magic into it but continued hitting resistance. She'd been without treatment so long the remaining bone had already fixed into its new, twisted position.

"How did this happen?" I asked.

"Bendeti's damn wave, of course," Marian grumbled. "I was trying to get some of the prisoners out of Mog Moren. Should have left them. They obviously wanted to die there. By the time I got out, it was too late to get behind Rune's protection. And then the wave hit, and I…"

She paused, as though her memory of what happened after was just as tumultuous as the wave. "I awakened in the Wilds' canopy. This," she gestured disgustedly to her injured leg, "was already missing. Made it hell getting down to the forest floor."

"I've done all I can," I said.

"Let me," Rune said.

Marian weakly tried to pull her leg away as he knelt. "I don't need—"

Rune's severe look silenced her. "You may want to look away."

He murmured something under his breath. Marian tensed as dozens more insects scuttled up from the ground and swarmed across the blackened stump of her ankle. In moments, the infected parts of her leg were impossible to see beneath writhing antennae, jointed legs, and shiny abdomens. Marian whimpered and squeezed my hand so tight I lost circulation.

Rune murmured again, and the insects dispersed, leaving Marian's leg with clean, ragged flesh. Rune waved his hand and sinuous white roots rose from the ground and began attaching themselves to the stump of where her ankle had been, until a fibrous prosthetic had replaced it.

"Get up, Marian," Rune said.

Marian remained on the ground, panting, staring at her new ankle as though she couldn't believe it. "I'm fine right here."

"You need to get up."

"I said I'm fine."

"Get—"

"That's why I didn't try to find you again," she snapped. "Because I knew you'd do this."

"Fix your leg?" I said, incredulous.

"He didn't *fix* it."

Marian savagely pushed off me and, after a few attempts, managed to stand unsteadily on her feet. She took a couple wobbly steps and dropped to a knee. A small sob escaped her lips. "Even if the bone was healed, I'll never be able to do what I could before. I'm useless now. I can't run. And I definitely won't be able to fight."

She looked up at both of us, daring us to disagree. "I knew that from the moment I woke up. So before you could cast me aside, I thought better to do it myself. So no, I didn't call for you to come save me, *my High King*. I wanted to save you the trouble of doing it in front of everyone else."

Rune looked as though she'd punched him in the face. "I... realize that my past actions have made you feel as though I would let you go the moment you lost your usefulness," he said after a pause. "I can only tell you that you're wrong."

"Did you even look for me?" Marian said.

"Whenever I could for three days after, until I lost hope. I tore the trees aside, uprooted the loam, coaxed flocks of birds to be my eyes. I even sank briefly beneath the waves in what was left of Mog Moren. Bendeti's attack must have carried you farther than I thought."

He'd done all that? Why hadn't he told me when I'd asked? It would have saved me a few extra days of thinking terribly of him.

"Now get up," Rune repeated. "I need you."

Marian didn't move.

"Marian?" I said softly. "Come back with us. Please."

"Come back or I *will* leave you behind," Rune said sharply. He sneered at our surroundings. "If you stay, I'll even carry you back to where my room used to be. Then you can die pining over this husk of a place when you should have let it go. We're done here. All of us."

He stalked away. I stood and offered Marian my hand. She ignored it and, gritting her teeth, managed to get to her feet.

"Don't you dare make me feel like I'm holding you back." She limped toward the path Rune had summoned at the edge of the Hollow.

I followed her, unable to hide my smile.

FIFTEEN

Marian didn't speak a word to anyone when we returned to the lakeside. She walked past the shocked faces, ignored the questions and shouts of greeting, found an open bed, and lay down, back facing everyone.

Rune went the other way without a word.

The next couple days were lost in a swirl of more drills, scouting with Pitius, and meetings with Rune, Xander, and General Forcheck about our next move. The second meeting, Xander was late coming in, and I knew he'd been at Marian's bedside, trying once again to coax her to speak to him.

I'd tried once already and learned that any questions, especially about how she was doing, would only earn a caustic silence or one-word, venomous response. Other wildlings left her ripened fruits and baubles of jewelry. The former, she let rot. The latter, she cast into the trees where they dangled, twinkling, like gemstone mobiles.

"Sotera hasn't made any move since we freed Val," Rune said at our latest session. "It's making me nervous."

"Unless you plan on sending wildlings down there, then we'll have to wait for her," General Forcheck said.

"I notice Keen hasn't been around," Xander said sullenly. "You haven't shared what he's been up to."

"I'll share when I have something," Rune said.

Keen hadn't checked in with me, either. That could mean he hadn't found anything, or he'd run into trouble he couldn't get out of. Neither option was particularly heartening.

Rune pulled out a new map from beneath the piles of others. "Regardless, we need to start thinking about moving position—"

The curtain of flowers parted, and Marian limped in. Her face was drawn from lack of sleep, cheeks stained light with moisture as though she'd recently been crying. On the way over she must have grabbed a haphazardly broken branch to use as a cane. She limped to the other side of the table, not meeting any of our eyes.

Without looking up from his notes, Rune waved a hand and Marian's cane sprouted a smooth, sheeny outer layer, and extended to a height that fit her. Its handle scooped into something that didn't bend her wrist at such an extreme angle, and delicate flowers wrapped around its length.

Marian opened her mouth, possibly to yell at him, before grumbling to herself. She brushed some of the flowers off and leaned against the table.

"You were saying, General," Rune said, as though nothing had happened.

The moment the meeting was over, Marian left before any of us could approach her.

"I'll talk to her again," Xander said.

"Leave her," Rune said. "She's chosen isolation as her way of recovery. Give her time and soon she'll share all the venomous words she's been holding back, just as before."

"She's had her warrior's spirit broken," General Forcheck said seriously. "More damaging than anything that could be done to her body. She may never be the same. You have to prepare for that reality, my High King."

Rune clenched his teeth. He shoved aside the flower curtain to leave and came to an abrupt halt. "Who are you?"

I stepped out after him to find a sapling-slender wildling waiting for us. He wore oddly formal attire, with gold bracelets around his wrists and delicate lines of refined amber trimming his jacket. He dropped to a knee. "My High King, the Council of Loam has assembled and now requests an audience."

"Their first meeting and already eager to waste our time," Rune said. "Well, let's get this over with."

"Apologies, High King." The wildling's voice was a panicked squeak. "They only want the, uh, girl. The human, I mean. And General Forcheck, of course, since she's on the Council."

Rune gave me a look that was hard to read. "Is that so? Seems you've caught their eye, Val."

"Not for anything good, I'm sure," I said. A knot of unease coiled in my gut. What on earth could the Council want with me and not their own High King? I had a few suspicions, none of them encouraging.

The formally dressed wildling made a few other hasty bows to Rune before leading General Forcheck and me to a pre-summoned path. We stepped out onto what had once been a human street, the asphalt nothing but gritty chunks nearly lost under a thick layer of greenery. On either side of the road jutted small cliffs perched with human buildings that had been repurposed by wildlings. At the end of the street loomed what looked like a colosseum, archways circling the exterior.

"Any idea why they want to talk with me?" I asked General Forcheck once our guide was out of earshot.

The numerous lines of her face furrowed in thought. "A few. None you likely haven't come up with yourself. I do know this: don't upset the Council. Already, in such a short time, you've begun to garner some legend. Among some who know the specifics of how Rune's throne was taken, and how you act now as Rune's blade, you're respected and feared. But if they're anything like the Council of Loam from the Wilds I came from, they have something more powerful than legend backing them: hubris. They cannot directly oppose the High King, but they could make your life very difficult."

General Forcheck held up her cane to stop me. "You know the laws of the deep Wilds and murdering Lords. Now we enter something even more dangerous: the realm of politics. Hold your temper. Speak little, if you have to speak at all. Words are knives, and if used poorly, they will use them to kill you."

With her warning ringing in my ears, we stepped into an expansive inner auditorium, sunlight streaming through the holes trees had created in the ceiling. My nose filled with the overpowering, sickly sweet scent of lilies.

Five figures lingered around a table that had once been the trunk of an enormous tree. One of them, Verily, the man from Below who'd been with Rune when they'd found me, gave me a wane smile. He was wringing his hands nervously.

"You already know Verily," General Forcheck said as we approached. "What about the others?"

I knew them. Or knew *of* them, what little I'd gleaned from brief talks with Xander. There was General Forcheck and Verily. Lord Hallas, of course, with the overwhelming scent of lilies emanating off her, and an irksome smile on her face.

Across from them was Lord Ryndin. Roots snaked beneath his wood-toned skin, puckering the flesh like he was perpetually on the verge of losing his temper.

Beside him was the traveling scholar Yava. A literal bird nested in his snarl of hair. His face was smooth and clean shaven, making it nearly impossible to tell how old he actually was.

The last was Erena. Rune had told me she was a former historian from the long dead House of Worms, and she looked the part; her skin was covered in a mucus-like coating, face sprouting with writhing black leeches.

She was giving me a look of such disdain that for a moment I almost turned around and marched right back out.

"*This* is who Rune's chosen to be his advisors?" I said out of the corner of my mouth.

"This is all who's left," General Forcheck answered. "Remember, manners."

I ignored Erena's look of disgust, bolstered myself, and took a spot on the empty side of the table.

"You seem displeased, Val," Lord Hallas said. "Do you find the Council lacking something?"

Hold your temper. There were a couple ways to play this game, and neither I was very good at. I could be blunt and open, hoping that the Council would drop all pretense of false civility and tell me what I needed to know. Or I could go for flattery, possibly my worst skill.

"I was just surprised by the composition of its members," I said.

"As were we," Lord Ryndin said, roots squirming beneath his skin as he spoke. "In the past, this Council was composed of a number of ministers from the Undersea and various Houses. But they're not here. Obviously."

"Rune has done away with them," Erena hissed. "As he's done away with almost everything else, tradition included."

"From what I've heard, it was well deserved," I said, and General Forcheck let out a sigh. Erena barred her teeth and leaned over the table, as though she might lunge across to strangle me.

Yava let out a long breath. "A cycle, death and rebirth. Once this Council, too, was gone. Yet here we are again."

Lords Hallas and Ryndin looked at the scholar with disgust. That was at least somewhat encouraging. For as much wariness as I had for the Council, they in turn held wariness against each other, too.

"Why am I here?" I asked.

"You're here to ensure that the bloodline of the High King remains clean," Lord Ryndin said.

I stared at him. "Excuse me?"

"Perhaps a bit of history, so she has a clue what you're talking about," General Forcheck said. When no one answered, she stabbed her cane at Yava. "You. Scholar. Make yourself useful."

"The power of the Wilds lies within the power of its High King, the throne, and the crown," Yava said in a dreamy voice. "The proper bloodline forges the crown. The proper crown wills the throne to accept its new ruler, and all the Wilds rejoice. We know this."

And yet I wondered if *they* knew how recently that had all changed. If they knew Rune had destroyed his throne, they might be more willing to move directly against him, since it would be just him to remove and the crown to take. They could cut of the head of the snake in one fell swoop.

Rune might have formed this Council and given them trust, but the bitterness and rivalries of the wildling Houses still remained, I was sure. No doubt there were some here who were still loyal to the old Lords.

Coming here was a mistake.

"And how does one get the proper bloodline?" Yava went on. "It resides in the strength of the wildlings who compose it.

The more the bloodline is…" He stared into the air, as though the word he was looking for would come drifting from the sky.

"Dirtied," Erena said, staring right at me.

"Compromised," Yava amended, "the more the power of the Wilds is diminished."

"Some would say it already is," Lord Hallas said in a low voice. "Our new High King is the bastard son of a minor Lord. It's only luck he had a straight line to the throne."

"A rightful line, all the same," General Forcheck growled, pounding her cane on the floor. "You'd do best to remember that, or my blade will help carve it into your memory."

Lord Hallas looked scandalized. Lord Ryndin was smirking, as though he enjoyed watching others get put in their place.

"What was that about holding your temper?" I muttered.

General Forcheck grunted.

"So you see," Yava went on, as though the conversation had not continued on without him, "we worry about the bloodline, not just to keep it pure, but to keep us safe. The stronger the blood, the stronger the ruler. And a High King without power is no High King at all."

"That is what happened to the last High King," Lord Ryndin said. "He had his vices and his trysts, but he branched too far from the main tree. His family grew so filthy his subjects sensed weakness. As was right, they removed that weakness before any true harm could be done."

I wondered if Rune would see the murdering of an entire royal family, along with his father, as *right*.

"We've noticed how close you and Rune are," Lord Hallas said. "We've also noticed you've been spending a lot of time alone with him. Traveling together. Speaking of things that he doesn't discuss with us nor his own trusted wildlings."

I let out a sharp laugh, overcome by this ridiculousness. "Let me get this straight: your first meeting, and your great concern is who Rune spends his time with? No wonder they disbanded the Council. Clearly they're incredibly useful if they spend time worrying over gossip instead of figuring out how to keep the Wilds safe from *actual* threats."

"Keeping it safe is exactly what we're trying to do," Lord Ryndin said.

"I have to agree with Val on this," General Forcheck said, frowning. "You have enemies on all sides and a severe lack of wildling support or preparedness to combat them. There are other ways to be spending this Council."

"We've decided this is our first order of business, and most pressing matter," Lord Hallas said smugly. "In order to win this war, Rune's focus must be unwavering. He doesn't need any... distractions."

"Deny that anything is going on between you and Rune," Erena hissed. "Say it. I want to hear it out of your filthy human mouth."

I was struck dumb. Not just because of the sheer fury building within me at their clear disdain and insinuations, but because the words they wanted to hear wouldn't come easily to my lips.

The curtain obscuring the distressing thoughts I'd had about Rune had been ripped back, forcing me to examine them. Rune had never said anything about wanting me as more than his blade, his trick. Maybe because I'd never shown any interest first, and for all his bouts of cruelty and savagery, when it came to my feelings, perhaps he held them in respect.

That couldn't be right. *I* couldn't be right. Rune had never shown any interest because there was none, simple as that. I couldn't act on my own traitorous feelings. Doing so would only hurt us. I'd spent a lifetime running from anything that might cause me harm. Why bother changing that now? Especially when any relationship we had could be weaponized by people like this?

"There's nothing happening between us," I said. "There never was."

"And it will remain that way," Lord Ryndin said. "Rune would do well to learn from the mistakes of rulers past. But as an extra precaution, avoid being alone with him, and stay away all together unless absolutely necessary."

I gripped the edge of the table to keep my hands from shaking. "You petty—"

"Val protects Rune, in ways no wildling can," General Forcheck interrupted, saving me from saying something I'd surely regret. "I for one wouldn't leave our High King unguarded."

"A High King should have the power to defend themselves against all threats," Lord Hallas said. "If they cannot, then nature will take its natural course."

Erena was giving me a triumphant look, the leeches on her face writhing with delight. "The moment Rune gets more involved with you, mongrel, that's the moment the Council will pull its support and cease to be. Or maybe..."

Her smile grew. "We are here to advise Rune toward the Wilds' best interests. Should you displease us, that may include suggesting he follow through with conquering the human world. We know how you love them so."

"Rune won't do that," I said. "I made him promise."

"Those are as easily broken as they are made," Lord Ryndin said. "I think you overestimate your sway over him." He waved a dismissive hand. "This conversation is at an end. That's all we have for you."

"Leave," General Forcheck muttered. "Before you do something rash."

I didn't want to do something rash. I wanted to do something terribly violent. How dare they think they could waltz in here and order me around, pretend like they had a clue what Rune and I had gone through. There was nothing happening between us.

If that's true, then why am I so upset?

"We told you to leave," Erena snapped.

With great effort, I unclenched my hands from the table and walked out. Lord Hallas's sickly sweet scent followed, nearly making me choke.

CHAPTER
SIXTEEN

Those Rune had chosen were assembled around the edge of the lake by mid-morning. I double-checked my backup knife was looped at my belt and the vambrace firmly lashed to my forearm. I'd raided some of the stockpiled infirmary supplies to supplement my lackluster healing magic and carried what I remembered Tris using on a felt pouch around my waist: grubber's root, eclipse flower, herb bloom, and something new called frost flower that grew deep in the subterranean tunnels farther inland. I could feel the chill of its petals through the pouch's fabric.

Along with Marian and me, there were thirty of Rune's wildlings ready to leave.

"He's asking me to go out of pity," Marian had spat when Rune came by to tell her she was coming along. She continued methodically running a whetstone over the edge of her blade. "The only way I'm killing anything is if I trip over this stupid foot with my knife pointed in the right direction."

"Does that mean you're staying here?" I'd asked.

"Are you crazy? Of course not."

I'd smiled, but only when she wasn't looking. She'd been holding a knife, after all.

"About time," Marian muttered next to me, as Rune emerged from the planning area and approached us. With the tip of her cane, she scratched at the spot on her leg where her flesh and the prosthetic merged. "You think he makes us wait for dramatic effect?"

"Please," I said. "When has Rune ever done anything dramatic?"

"In case you weren't aware," Rune announced, "we're heading to Lord Blis's estate, at the edge of the mire lands."

There was some murmuring and some exclamations of surprise. I'd been similarly surprised, but only just so. Following his ascension, Rune had been surprisingly lax about demanding subservience from the remaining minor Lords. If he could get them to pledge loyalty out of *actual* loyalty, then all the better. But after Mother Mal's warning, Rune had made it a priority to start sealing off points of potential weakness, through whatever means possible.

Rune gestured to me when the talk had died down. The Council of Loam's warning reverberated in my ears before I savagely shut it out. Their will be damned. "I've been told Lord Blis has already chosen a side, and it isn't ours," Rune said. "We're here to give him another option."

I didn't need to guess what the two options would be. Every other wildling was fully armed and armored. Rune wasn't taking any chances.

"We're there only to visit. To start. Lord Blis's choice will decide what happens next."

Rune's gaze snapped to Xander, who'd walked up, still securing his bow to his back. "I don't remember asking you to join us."

Xander looked around, as though Rune couldn't possibly be talking to him. "I always come along."

"Not this time."

Xander chuckled, though it quickly faded. "You're joking."

"Not if I can help it."

There was a long silence. Rune's stern expression didn't so much as twitch. Though he hadn't said it, I suspected he knew I'd been the one behind Keen's request to exclude Xander. I still couldn't tell whether he agreed with me, but I was grateful he was following through.

Xander's mouth hung open. "You can't—"

"General Forcheck will be assuming command while I'm gone," Rune continued. "She'll tell you what needs to be done. The rest of you, with me."

"You can't be serious," Xander sputtered. A few of the other wildlings were starting to stare. "You need me!"

"Don't make a scene, Xander," Marian said. "We're all adapting."

"*Adapting*? You can barely walk!" Xander snarled.

Marian looked as though he'd kicked her cane out from under her. Xander pointed a bow-thickened finger at Rune. "I've been with you from the very start—"

"Then you know better than to question my choice," Rune said, voice soft with warning. "I've determined I don't need you on this excursion, and that's final."

It was difficult to watch Xander as his expression cycled between hurt, then betrayal, then anger. I stepped between him and Rune before things could get too bad.

"Enough, Xander. It isn't like Rune hasn't asked you to stay behind before," I muttered.

"This is different, I know it is. He doesn't trust me!" I side-stepped to cut him off as he tried to brush past me. "He thinks I'm too unstable."

"And you're proving him right!"

"So we risk our lives getting those you care about to safety, but not our own loved ones," Xander said. "You tout victory at any cost, Rune, but we've all sacrificed a lot to make sure you get everything you want and nothing of ours!"

Everything Rune wanted? He wanted nothing but the throne and now to secure it from Sotera. Xander couldn't possibly think there was anything selfish in that.

Xander shook me off. He backed up with a mocking laugh. "You know, Val asked once if we'd made the right choice helping you get the throne."

"Xander!" I said warningly.

"She doubted you'd make a good ruler. Now I'm starting to doubt, too."

I felt Rune's anger coat the Wilds. Everyone backed up as the trees themselves seemed to growl. Trunks bent, vines twisted, branches wended together until our surroundings had transformed into an enormous, snarling face, every inch of it exuding deadly intent.

Rune gave Xander a cold smile. "Thank you for making your feelings clear. Now I must leave your tantrum behind and keep making my Wilds safe, whether you think me *right* to do so or not."

The snarling trees morphed into a path, and Rune walked through. Marian ushered me after him, and then my world was spinning, the path heaving me to the other side where I landed unsteadily behind Rune. It took me a moment to reorient.

"Yes, I asked him that," I said, scrambling to justify myself. "I had my doubts, but I don't have them anymore."

"Be on guard," Rune said. "I don't expect Lord Blis's reaction to be welcome, or else he would have sided with me already."

His tone was cold and detached, much like it'd been when we'd first met. I felt its venom like an icy chill.

"I understand," I said. Later, I wanted the chance to explain myself. In removing Xander, I'd hoped to make things better. Seemed I'd only made them worse.

As we made our way across one of the narrow strips of solid ground between the bog, an estate of stone, dark-green moss, and glittering glass rose from the low edge of the mire lands. The surrounding trees were bleached milk white as though the color had been sucked from them. Biting flies as big as a needle's tips and just as sharp swarmed thickly in the air.

"Split off," Rune said as we neared the mansion's front door. As though they'd practiced this, half his wildlings moved quickly around the outside, crouching low to keep out of sight.

"They're already watching," Marian said. She pointed to an upstairs window. Curtains fell back into place as whomever was there quickly stepped out of view. "They're prepared for us. Rune, are you sure—"

"I think I've had enough questioning of my commands for one day, don't you?" Rune said.

The front door swung open before Rune reached it. A wildling servant dressed in green finery bowed deeply. "Our High King Rune. Lord Blis welcomes you to his humble home."

"Unless he's learned how to turn himself invisible, I don't see him doing the welcoming," Rune said pleasantly. "I suppose I should be happy he's acknowledged me at all. I plan on remedying that."

The wildling bowed even deeper and stepped to one side. "Of course. Please, come inside."

I entered first, fingers staying close to where I could quickly draw Sliver.

"My master awaits you in the dining hall," the wildling

said. He led us that way, moving with a slight limp as though his legs were stiff.

Rune made a motion with his hand when the wildling's back was turned, and another half of those with us spread out into the rest of the estate.

"Stay close," Marian muttered, and Rune gave a faint nod.

We were led down deserted hallways, past an empty ballroom and a shaft leading into the darkness of what I assumed was a basement. More than once, I caught Rune's eyebrow twitching at our guide's slow pace.

"Even I could walk faster," Marian mumbled. "Is he purposefully taking the long route?"

"Are you hurt?" I asked the servant.

"It is nothing," he assured us. "I've had problems with my joints for a while."

"I wonder, has Lord Blis reconsidered joining me?" Rune said.

"That's not for me to say. But I hope his answer is favorable for you."

At last we reached a pair of double doors, inlaid with what I assumed was Lord Blis's crest, the flowing lines burning softly with bioluminescence. With a surprising amount of strength for one so slender, the servant began tugging the doors open. One of his sleeves rode up, exposing the skin between his gloves and elbow.

Crystal skin.

"Trap—" was all I managed before the doors were entirely open.

Inside, a dozen of Those Below, all armed, surrounded a table circled with high-backed chairs. Luella—Rune's cousin who was supposed to be safely in Portland—and her daughter, Olette, sat in two of them. Their arms had been secured in place with crystal, their mouths gagged with the same, forcing them to sit tightly upright. Luella's eyes were full of tears.

"I'm afraid Lord Blis is permanently indisposed, dearest cousin Rune."

Vanesi lounged at the head of the table, her feet up, twirling a slender needle between her fingers. A bloodied body, its upper half out of sight, was strewn beneath her.

"And now the last survivors of the House of the Fallen Star are together again," Vanesi said. "After all, what's a family reunion without family?"

CHAPTER

SEVENTEEN

Vanesi looked satisfied with herself, as though she'd known every move that would bring Rune to her. And perhaps she did. From Rune's description of how she'd tortured him—acidic berry juice in his eyes, thorns lodged beneath his fingernails— she excelled at knowing exactly how to hurt him best.

"You may be High King, but your habits don't change," Vanesi said. She pointed the tip of the needle she held toward the immobilized Luella and Olette. "You kept your weaknesses exposed."

"And you didn't stay rotting in the dirt, where you belonged," I said.

Rune appeared immobilized with fear. He hadn't spoken about our earlier encounter with Vanesi, not even once, and I could see now it was because he couldn't bear to. Facing her again had brought one of the nightmares of his past back to life.

"Rune," I hissed. "What do you want us to do?"

"Spread out!" Marian ordered when Rune didn't answer.

The other wildlings dispersed. I moved closer to Rune. He

needed to snap out of it. Between splitting our forces and the ineffectiveness of wildling weapons against Those Below, this fight would be short if we didn't have the strength of our High King. I needed to stall.

"What false promises did Sotera feed you when she brought you back?" I asked. "Dominion over part of the Wilds? All the poor victims you could ever want to torture?"

Vanesi stood, dragging her fingers across the wood as she circled the table. "She promised me nothing but endless servitude. But if she allowed me to request anything, all I'd ask for is the chance to kill Rune."

Rune blinked. Shifted his feet. It seemed the threat of death had temporarily stirred him back to the present. "How original. But a little unfair. I killed you first."

Vanesi's laugh was grating and coarse, as though her vocal cords were already partially crystalized. "I could respect your wonderful brutality when you slaughtered most of Aleki's family. I even respected you killing me. It took years, but you finally grew a backbone. But you couldn't even do that properly. You could have saved me *this*."

The half of her face that wasn't solid crystal twisted into a sneer. She traced her nails across Luella's hand. "Now I'm that bitch's dog, cursed to do her biding with some small hope she'll let me die and free me from this agony."

Vanesi swept up a table knife and plunged it at her own heart. It stopped an inch from touching her. Vanesi struggled to push the knife closer before throwing it back onto the table. "I'm not even free to do that. I'm not *me*."

"Then allow me to help you," Rune said. In his eyes was the same cold calculation I'd come to rely on. "I could do the job right this time."

"Tempting, but no. I've been given a chance, you see. And a job."

She drew the needle up and gently pricked Luella's neck. Luella seized. Small bubbles leaked from the corners of the crystal gagging her mouth, and the veins in her face turned purple.

"I'll bet even your human pet knows this one," Vanesi said. "Night blush. Slow acting, but incredibly painful. She won't die for at least a few minutes. I used it for years on some of the more expendable of Aleki's servants. It took a few tries, but eventually I figured out the proper dose that ensured they didn't die so quickly."

"We can counteract it, but it has to be soon," I muttered.

"I'm aware," Rune said. "She wants us to panic. Wants me to make a mistake."

"I'm actually doing you a favor, Rune." As Luella continued to seize, Vanesi circled behind Olette, stroking her cheek. "I know exactly who Aleki sired with his own daughter. With Luella dead, this girl is the final familial threat to your throne."

Olette went incredibly still as Vanesi rested the tip of the needle on her throat. We were out of time. Luella might have minutes before the night blush killed her, but a child would die much sooner.

"Rune?" Marian whispered. "Your command?"

Rune said nothing. For one horrible moment, I thought that what Luella had feared most had come true: that Rune thought them a threat and would let them die, if only to secure his rule and ensure the wildlings didn't prefer someone else with legitimate claim to the throne.

"What will you do, Rune?" Vanesi purred. "How far are you willing—"

A crossbow bolt shattered the window at our back and narrowly missed Vanesi, who had flung herself to the side. Within moments, the wildlings that had split to secure the rest of the mansion surrounded the upper mezzanine. Some moved down toward us.

"End them," Rune ordered, and chaos erupted.

In the ensuing confusion, Vanesi darted toward Olette, poisoned needle held aloft. There was no way I could reach her in time. But at the last moment, snarls of thorns dripping with golden sap burst from the ground and cut her off. The arrangement of flowers on the table came alive to obscure Luella and Olette in a cloak of petals.

"Always with your tricks!" Vanesi screeched.

"I've got more than that," I heard Rune reply, obscured by petals and thorns. "Come a little closer and I'll show you."

Even with the quick shift in numbers, the soldiers of Those Below had rallied, forming a hasty perimeter around Vanesi that would be difficult to break through.

A soldier lunged at me, far faster than anticipated, and it was only by instinct that I was able to avoid getting my arm cleaved off. Erebus growled and my shoulder smarted as I hit the ground and rolled. I came up swinging Sliver, knocking aside the point of the guard's sword, diverting it moments before it gutted me. But now I was on one knee, at a severe disadvantage. He reared back to club me, perhaps to shatter my blade and arm in one go.

Ice crawled up his front, seizing his arms in place. He roared and stumbled away, trying to break free.

"You're still too slow, Val!" Marian snapped, cutting off her ice. "You can't use being human as an excuse anymore."

Another soldier attacked her exposed side. Marian's save brought me enough respite to orient myself, and I slid past her and slammed my free hand against the soldier's heart. With a single enormous pull, he slumped, dull and lifeless, to the floor, his magic entirely gone.

"Now we're even," I said. "Worry about yourself, and I'll worry about me."

Marian smirked. "Fine. Get to Rune before he gets himself killed."

She limped away, sword aloft, to help the other wildlings deal with the largest cluster of Vanesi's soldiers. I'd have to trust Rune could handle himself for a little longer. Luella and Olette needed my help first.

The sharp thorns interlocked even tighter as I approached the threaded cage surrounding them.

"It's me," I said. The brambles extended a single thorny tendril. I allowed it to prick my finger and bright-red blood welled up. The thorns receded just enough for me to tenderly thread through them.

Luella's eyes were closed, face so purple I was afraid she was already dead.

"She'll be fine," I tried to assure Olette. I melted the crystal bindings on both of them and gently lowered Luella to the floor. I sifted through my dusty knowledge of night bloom. I hadn't had much experience with it, since it was only common far deeper in the Wilds than I used to travel. If ingested, vomiting could be induced to counteract it. But since it was in Luella's bloodstream...

"I need you to be brave for me, Olette," I said. "Can you do that?"

Olette wordlessly nodded. I rummaged through the pouch at my waist for grubber's root and pierced it with my knife so that green liquid oozed out. Next, I manipulated shards of the fallen crystal into a slender needle of my own and then slathered the grubber's root on the tip. I infused as much healing magic into it as I could and then pierced one of the bulging purple veins at Luella's neck. I had no idea how long the grubber's root would take to cleanse her blood. I had no idea if it would even work, or if I was trying to heal a dead woman.

I scooted over. "Take my place, Olette," I directed. "Hold the needle in the wound. Don't move it."

Olette obeyed without question, not even flinching as her mother's blood soaked the edges of her dress.

"Perfect," I said. "Just like that, don't move it. I'll be right back."

I picked up Sliver and stood to find Rune. He and Vanesi were facing off in the center of the fighting, as though knowing no one would dare interrupt them. A bleeding cut scored Rune's forehead, while part of Vanesi's side beneath her torn shirt had been shattered.

Rune nodded to her wound. "A shame. Normally that'd bleed more."

I vaulted the dining table to join Rune, my sword raised toward Vanesi. Her eyes flickered from my sword to me. "Did I mention Sotera gave me a message?"

"Demands?" Rune said. "This should be good."

"Sotera says to return the girl. I'm sure I can have my fun before I deliver her, so long as she remains in one piece and isn't too scarred for Bendeti. If you do that, Rune the boy king, kill the human priest and lay down your weapons, Sotera will entertain the possibility of stopping her attack before she razes everything to the ground."

Vanesi motioned to her remaining soldiers, still holding Rune's wildlings at bay. "These few are just a taste. More are coming through every day, and soon there'll be enough that even you won't be able to stop them, not with all the power of the Wilds at your command."

Rune smirked. "Had she been half as strong as she threatens, Sotera wouldn't ask for anything. She knows what my answer will be. What it will *always* be. If Sotera wants to see the extent of my hospitality, she should come herself."

It was Vanesi's turn to smile. "I was so hoping you'd say that. Now I can tell her you refused, and I had no choice but to kill you."

Crystal spikes flew from her hand, one piercing Rune's side as he barely spun away. Within seconds, Vanesi closed the distance between them. Rune stabbed with his glass knife, but it shattered against Vanesi's ribs, the pieces of the blade tinkling as they hit the ground. Vanesi sank her fist into Rune's stomach, punching the air from his lungs, before she skirted out of reach of his next strike.

"I'll admit, there are some advantages to this body." Vanesi flicked her fingers and more crystalline spikes fanned between them. Rune couldn't move out of the way fast enough as she cast them, and he cried out as a couple pierced his side.

One of Vanesi's soldiers cut me off as I tried to dart in. I ducked their sword and shouldered them back into the rest of the fight. I reached Rune's side as he tried to staunch the blood leaking through his fingers.

"Stay back," he said through gritted teeth. "She's mine."

Vanesi lunged, a maniacal glint in her eye. Rune shoved me to the side before she collided with him, and together they rolled into a wall of earth Rune had tried to summon. Vanesi came out on top, pinning Rune's arms to the ground.

"Even as High King, you're still weak, helpless little Rune," Vanesi purred. "I'm almost doing you a favor, ending you like this."

Rune tried to throw her off, but Vanesi drove crystal shards through his wrists, spraying blood. Rune screamed. Vanesi raised more crystal, prepared to sink them into his neck.

I reached them only a moment before. Vanesi leapt off with a snarl as I swiped at her with Sliver.

"You still need a savior!" Vanesi seethed. "A useless High King who can't fight his own battles!"

"All the worse for you I can't," Rune panted.

He pulled at one arm until, with a wet squelch, it was free of the crystal pinning it. He yanked his other arm free and made it to one knee. Blood ran rivulets off the tips of his fingers.

"Don't kill her," Rune said to me. "I need to make sure I do it right this time."

I raised Sliver higher. "Why don't we *both* kill her? Double the chances."

Rune touched the ground. The tile beneath Vanesi's feet split, and marsh water bubbled up. Vanesi slipped backward and Rune lunged, stabbing with a knife I hadn't seen him draw. This time it was Vanesi's turn to scream. She cast Rune away and clutched at her crystalline side where an enormous chunk was missing.

"Impossible," she hissed. "Where did you... How could you...?"

Rune held up the knife. Its edge glowed with a familiar magic, and with a start I recognized it as one from Rylan's workshop. "Tell Sotera that if she decides to pay me a visit, I'll be ready with ways she can't hope to fight against."

He made no move toward Vanesi as she backed up.

"Rune, we can't—" I moved to go after Vanesi right as she thrust her hand behind her. The wall at the far end of the dining room collapsed, leaving a perfect opening for escape. And that was exactly what she and her remaining soldiers did, scampering out into the marsh like scattering rabbits.

Panting, I sidestepped the fallen and remnants of Rune's thorns and rushed to the hole. Vanesi and the soldiers had already vanished, leaving nothing but soggy, empty ground and the mournful call of distant birdsong.

I clenched Sliver hard enough that my knuckles ached. "You *idiot*!"

I stomped over to where Rune had sunk back to the ground. "Why would you let her go?"

Rune continued brushing at flecks of crystal growing from his skin until they broke off for good, leaving jagged, bleeding wounds that stained patterns on his shirt. His gaze was unfocused. I'd seen him despondent like this once before, in Mog Moren, when the weight of his past had threatened to crush him. "Vanesi was... She nearly..."

I bit back several curses and knelt beside him. "I know. But you're not a child anymore," I murmured. "You fought back. You don't have to repeat the same story where she gets away without consequence."

Rune rubbed his face, leaving thin smears of blood. "I need to check the others."

I reached for one of the larger crystals still sticking from his skin. "Let me remove those. You need to check yourself, first, or else they'll soon be talking to a corpse."

Rune ripped the last of the crystal out, spraying more blood messily across the tile where it mixed with marsh water. He sucked in another heaving breath and stood to survey the results of the battle. Heedless, reckless idiot.

I sighed and stood along with him. "If you die from blood loss, I get to be the first one to tell you I told you so."

"If my demise came so easily, I'd *want* to die," he replied with a grin that was far too pale for my liking.

I looked at the hole Vanesi had escaped through. "You've created a problem. They weren't ours to use, but now Vanesi knows about the weapons. Soon, Sotera will too, and she'll try to prepare for them."

Rune sheathed the knife back inside his cloak. "Exactly.

She'll think twice about attacking me again anytime soon, thinking I have access to weapons that can even the playing field."

We needed Sotera confident and reckless, not cautious, but Rune had already swept toward the wildlings. Thickened tendrils of thorns brushed the bodies of Those Below aside while enormous petals became litters that held the few wounded and dead wildlings for the others to carry away.

Still upset, I sheathed Sliver. Marian had drawn Luella onto her lap, and I hurried over to check her condition.

"She'll be fine, eventually," Marian assured an anxious Olette hovering beside her. But when she looked at me, I saw doubt. "That was good thinking on the grubber's root. Would be better if we had some vine viper venom to counteract it."

"I'll go ask one of the others where I can find it," I said, standing.

"I already did." Marian jerked her head toward the hole in the wall. "I heard Vanesi say she wanted Rune to kill a human priest. You know what in the green hell she's talking about?"

That could be a number of people in a number of human religions. However, there was only one religion she'd likely care about. But why would the Empress of Those Below know of any worshippers of the Mother Tree? More importantly, why would she want them dead?

Feeling as though I was missing a vital piece of a much larger puzzle, I shook my head. "I'm not sure what she wanted. But I intend to find out."

I CHECKED on Luella over the next couple days, between coordinating Rune's next move and helping bury the dead. We let the Wilds consume the bodies of Those Below, but Marian insisted burying the wildlings by hand. I avoided looking at their faces as we covered them with dirt. Seconds after finishing, white corpse flowers grew over top of the graves. The scent was so sweet I felt sick.

I wasn't surprised that Rune came to help, and none of the others were either. He remained stone-faced throughout the burials. He didn't say a eulogy. He didn't comfort anyone crying. He didn't even acknowledge Marian threading more pieces of carved wood around her necklace, one for each wildling we'd lost. Rune had confided to me once that after you'd lost so much, you became numb to it, but still I felt myself wishing he would show that there was some part of him that mourned.

For the rest of the time, I joined Cassius and others in searching the surrounding areas for more crevasses. If Vanesi had been able to find a place to slip beneath the earth, I had no doubt she'd head straight back to Sotera, whether compelled by her magic or out of spite. That didn't mean I wanted to make it easier for her to get back.

I closed up the couple openings we found, until the spiky crystal tips barred anyone but the smallest insect from getting through. It was difficult to ignore the other wildlings' looks of suspicion as I did so. Some of them whispered about me when they thought I wasn't listening. Others did so when they knew I was.

"What are you looking at?" Cassius snapped at one of the girls who was giving me a glare akin to driving a knife into my back. "Go check for more crevasses."

After a disgruntled sniff, she joined the others as they spread out to search.

"Thanks," I said. "I don't blame them. Those Below—those like me—killed their friends."

"You're not like them," he insisted fiercely, and I felt a great swell of gratitude toward him. Mog Moren, for all it had done to him, hadn't taken his kindness.

It was late when we finished up and returned to the marsh. Erebus had only grown more restless since being unable to join the fight against Vanesi, so I split off into the nearest glade and let him run free. I told myself that we'd done all we could, that Vanesi nor anyone else would get the drop on us. But they already had once. I suspected, no matter what we did, they would again.

I was flagging with exhaustion when I reached the mansion. A bone-deep tiredness had latched onto me since the Below and never left. Only fighting and dancing along the edge of death seemed to alleviate it, though I knew neither of those things were good for my long-term survival.

A few of the wildlings I'd gone out with were gathered in the kitchen, murmuring in low, sleepy voices. Some of them abruptly stopped talking when I came in, watching me with narrowed, suspicious eyes. I ignored them and grabbed some thick slices of cured meat, scallions, radicchio, and pickled duck eggs they'd pulled up from Lord Blis's cellar. I'd barely sat and dug in before Idwal, the second of Rune's spies, appeared at my elbow. He was built for being unnoticed, slight and similarly soft spoken like Pitius, as though shaped from a wisp of smoke. The only thing remotely remarkable about his appearance were his slightly protruding ears.

"Have you spoken to Rune yet?" he said, voice breathy.

"No, why?"

"He just seemed..." Idwal considered his next words, and I got the impression he wasn't used to thinking of ways to talk about Rune behind his back. "Weird? Off? The others have noticed it, too."

I took a surreptitious look around the kitchen. Any of us

would be "off" after just fighting with Those Below. But Rune normally kept what he was truly feeling close to the chest. If others had begun to notice, then it must have been noticeable indeed.

"I'll check on him," I said.

Idwal nodded, relieved, and I suspected I was the only one he'd asked to do such a thing. Because Rune trusted me. And I *should* check up to see how he was doing, as someone close to him. Ensuring the High King was emotionally sound was part of protecting him. Simply another aspect of my job, nothing more.

Before that, I returned to my room to change to clothes that smelled less marshy and grab a tonic General Forcheck had handed out to ward off fatigue.

I knew I wasn't alone the moment I entered. Staying near the door, I scanned until I found the shadowy outline of a figure in a chair near the bed.

"It's me, Val," Luella rasped. "I wish to speak privately."

I checked no one had heard us from the landing and closed the door behind me. I found the two hanging jars of fireflies on either side of the bed and gently shook them until warm, flickering light filled the room. Luella winced, as though she'd been sitting in the dark for a long time.

"I didn't know you were out of the infirmary," I said.

"No one does. I'd prefer it stay that way."

I frowned. Her skin still held an unhealthy paleness, making the receded purple veins on her cheeks and forehead stand out all the more. I suspected she was sitting because she had to, not only because she was waiting for me.

When my eyes had adjusted to the light, I was surprised to see Olette sound asleep in my bed, tucked beneath the covers.

"I've drugged her," Luella said. "She won't wake for a few

hours yet, and I wanted her to be with you, someone she knows and trusts, when she did."

"I don't understand. What's going on?"

Luella stroked Olette's hair off her forehead. "Rune has asked me to leave and to take Olette with me. However, I'm calling on the promise you made to me, to find her a safe place when the time came. My journey will be hard, and until I reach my destination, I want her watched over."

Only now did I empathize with Keen's dislike of unbinding promises. I'd made mine to Luella when I didn't know better and was more concerned with staying alive long enough to see it through than actually seeing it called on.

"How could Rune throw you out like that?"

"Don't you know? I always suspected you understood him better even than other wildlings."

I was getting a little tired of others stating that I knew so much more than I believed I did. It made me feel stupid. "I can't take Olette."

"You must. You prom—"

"She won't be safe here, Luella. Think about it. You really want to keep her here, with the ones who just got attacked? Things are tenuous at best, you know that."

"You *have* to protect her," Luella insisted. "You're the only one I trust to do so."

Having Olette around would just make me vulnerable, the opposite of what I needed. I huffed out a laugh. "Then you must be seriously desperate. I don't have anywhere she can be safe, Luella. There are far more powerful people than Vanesi who want Rune—want both of us—dead."

"You'll find a place," Luella said. "Somewhere she can be happy and free for a time, until she's able to join me."

"And where are you going?"

Luella looked wistfully out the window at the moon-shadowed marsh and the dark invitation of the trees. "I'll go to another Wilds. You know there are others, don't you? Just as I know there are other great human cities. Perhaps in those Wilds they have learned to live together in a way these Wilds have not. At the very least, maybe there are unwanteds and outcasts like me, who are free of the power struggles and the politics. Wouldn't that be nice? It sounds like a dream."

It sounded implausible. But my viewpoint was skewed from all I'd ever known here. I had to believe a peace and security like that existed, otherwise why was I fighting to make that a possibility?

Luella leaned over to give Olette a kiss on her cheek. "Though I was barely conscious, I saw the way you tended to Rune after you ran off Vanesi."

I didn't know what she wanted me to say to that. It was my job? I needed him alive if I was to survive?

"Something to consider, if you haven't," Luella said. "You're aligned with Rune's goals. In some ways, I think you're integral to them. But sometimes becoming the most important piece creates the very vulnerabilities you're trying to prevent."

"I don't know what you're talking about," I lied.

Luella gave me a knowing smile. "I'm sure the realization of what you mean to each other is more terrifying than anything you've ever faced. It's only natural you'd avoid it."

I was nothing more than a tool, a trick, to Rune, and he was nothing more than the means to an end for me. How many times had I repeated that? Yet the words felt hollow now.

"Don't wait too late," Luella said. "If being away from him is best, then that's what you have to do. Even if it's only for yourself."

"Thanks for the advice. I'll walk you out."

But I didn't feel any better as I led her swiftly around back of the mansion, where a wooly beast made more of leaves than fur waited, saddled with supplies. My stomach still churned as she threw up her hood and whispered, "Take care of her."

Don't wait too late, Luella had said.

I wouldn't. I couldn't. But maybe I already had.

EIGHTEEN

I went back inside and climbed to the top floor to find Rune.

He'd taken up residence at the farthest end of the farthest hall, picked for its obvious isolation.

I found him in the adjoining sitting area. He'd lit the fireplace and filled the room with the scent of pinecone and cinnamon. The remains of his scant dinner sat on the table. He held a flute of the drink Lord Blis had kept stored in his cellar, thick like syrup and more potent than anything we had in the human world.

After I stepped in, neither of us spoke for a minute, waiting, I think, for the other to break the silence.

"Despite what happened," I said, "I don't think sending Luella away was best for her safety."

"It's curious to hear you talk about her safety, when you clearly think being near me is the worst possible thing for her," Rune said.

I scrunched my nose. "What are you talking about?"

Rune's expression was remote. "You thought me a monster. Again. I saw it in your face when Vanesi poisoned Luella. You thought I'd let them die, the same way you thought I'd let them die with Aleki. For all that's happened since then, it seems some things haven't changed."

It occurred to me only then that the aloof, detached way Rune had been acting toward me the last couple days was *because* of me and not his usual callous indifference. Stranger still, I realized how much that hurt.

"It was only for a moment, but yes, I thought you'd let her kill them," I admitted. Old habits died hard, and distrust of Rune, it seemed, died harder than most. "I was wrong."

"Was that an apology? How so unlike you." Rune twirled his glass, smirking. There was no dark stain of his lips on the rim, as though he'd poured it with the intention of numbing out but couldn't bring himself to even take a sip. "That isn't the only time you misjudged me. You also weren't sure of my place as High King, apparently."

I raised my chin. "If we're going to lay out faults, then I won't be the only one taking the blame. You told me once you weren't going to be a benevolent king, and you'd proven it over and over again. That was all I knew of you, so what was I supposed to think? That once you took the throne, rainbows would crisscross the sky and all would be right with the world?"

"I suppose that was asking too much. But maybe I hoped for a little more faith in me. Belief that I'd be better than the monsters we'd usurped."

"Of course I think that."

"Apparently not."

The depth of hurt in his voice shocked me. Not just hurt, but betrayal. Just how wide had he let me see his true self, in a way he'd never done with anyone else? And how badly had I trampled over that trust?

"You are a good—" I started.

"Don't."

Glass smashed as Rune stood. Red stained the carpet at his feet. For a moment, his expression was furious and fearful in equal measure, before smoothing to the unreadable mask he wore so well and so often. "Don't lie to me, you of all people."

I threw up my hands. "I'm not lying, Rune. You are…"

Confounding? Aggravating? An enigma? "I didn't have a problem with you gaining the throne through bloodshed. I spilled my fair share, and if I'm being honest, I'd do so again, without hesitation."

"My blade and my trick," he murmured.

"Now to keep things under control you have to make tough sacrifices to get what you want. I *get* that. But…if you sacrifice everything, even if it's for the greater good, what's left to fight for?"

He sneered. "You expect me to say love? Family? Those are dreams for people who are not me. My reward is blood, and power, and dissatisfaction, no matter what highs or lows I attain. I fight so that others can experience the joys I'll never have."

It sounded as lonely an existence as when I'd first met him, and one he was even more resigned to than before.

"There's more to it than that," I said. "There has to be. When I first came to know you, I thought you were…"

Rune straightened up, as though bracing for my answer. "Cruel? Callous?"

"A monster," I confessed.

He seemed equally surprised to hear me say aloud what we were both thinking. "And now?"

"In some ways you still are, we both are, at least to others. We've become what we had to in order to survive. But even after all that, I still believe we deserve some happiness. I *have* to believe that."

"Then you'll keep being disappointed. Happiness is for the deluded and the stupid."

I stared at him. "Fine. If you're going to stand here and lie to me, then we have nothing else to talk about."

Rune didn't look away from the fire, jaw tight.

"I thought you were stronger than this," I said. "In fact, I was counting on it."

Rune's eyes closed, squeezed tightly shut as though to block me out. I turned to go. What point was there in me staying? It was like talking to a man who'd already accepted his death.

I'd only taken a single step before his firm hand gripped my arm.

"I..."

Rune drew back, as though touching me burned him. "You want to know my greatest secret?" he said, voice barely above a whisper. "You saw a taste of it before, but very well, Val, I'll reveal it just for you.

"I am scared. All the time. Scared of losing the ones I care about. Of being unable to stop bad things from happening. Of being too weak and having everything I've worked and fought for get torn down in an instant. And when I get scared, I do the only thing I know to: I lash out. It isn't right, and it isn't kind, but it's how I've learned to cope.

"But from the moment we killed the Lords and I took the throne, I became scared for a different reason. That this might actually *work*. This insane, pinprick dream of a helpless child who had nothing else to hold on to. And if it did work, then what? Things would change, and change, I've found, even change for the better, is the most terrifying thing of all."

I waited for him to go on, as though he hadn't shared more in the last minute than all I'd been able to glean a dozen times before.

"Yes, I hesitated with Luella and Olette," Rune said. "Like so many others, I thought them better off dead and at peace than alive and constantly pawns at another's mercy. Because that's all they'll ever be if they're around me. I'm not good for anyone, and especially not for them."

"But you didn't let them die," I pointed out.

"And maybe I'll regret that. Or maybe they will. But in the meantime, I did the only thing I could think of and sent them away. They'll be safe far away from me."

It wasn't worth telling Rune about Olette. Not yet. "They might be in more danger now. Sotera knows they're a weakness, and without your protection, she could get to them easier."

"Sotera's sole focus will now be on me and these new weapons she thinks I have. And since I hesitated to save Luella, Vanesi may even tell her I have no problem letting my family die. Sotera may even respect that."

Sever the ties to those who hold you back. Sotera's voice echoed mockingly through my head.

"She really might," I agreed.

If it had been his plan to reveal the magicked dagger simply to turn Sotera's entire attention to him, to shift her mindset from waging all-out war to considering a truce, then the idea had been stupid and brilliant in equal measure.

"Still, sending Luella and Olette away won't solve your problem," I said.

"Oh?" Rune's arrogant smile told me I was wrong, but that he'd play along. "And why is that?"

"Because there will always be others you worry about. You'll have to send them all away. Starting with me."

Rune's smirk tightened. "I don't need to worry about you."

"But you still do, don't you?"

Rune blinked slow, the only sign I'd thrown him off.

"You're either underestimating your ability to survive or reading too far into my actions."

It was easy to tell he was lying. His words danced around the truth as he would an enemy's blade.

And try as I might, my traitorous tongue couldn't call him out. How could I, when *I* couldn't even put into words how I felt? Loathing Rune was safe. Respecting him was understandable. Liking him was okay.

But beyond that?

As I stared into his gold-red eyes, I realized I'd already begun moving beyond that and hadn't even realized when it happened.

"Send me away, too," I said. "I hate following your commands. Sometimes I want vengeance more than I want to do what's right. I'm a distraction."

"I said that I would keep you close, and I intend to."

"Even if I hurt you?"

It was a wonder to watch the corners of his lips turn up. "We're so good at hurting each other. It'd be a shame to stop now."

"Send me away, Rune. Say the words and I'll obey them."

Now his eyebrows slashed down in annoyance. "I already tried. I told you never to return to the Wilds, that you wouldn't find welcome here if you did. I even gave you an out, and yet here you are."

"Send me away again, then. It should be easy."

I hadn't realized I'd stepped closer to him, only stopping when Rune put his hands on my hips. My face rested just below the glass-sharp line of his mouth. This close, I could see strands of his coarse hair curling around the thorns of his circlet. What would it feel like to prick my fingers on them, to sink my fingers into his hair?

"I..." Rune swallowed, seemed to have difficulty finding the words. "There are things I need that I can't do without you, my weapon, at my side."

"And there always will be." My voice had dipped low to match his. "It will never end. But you can let me go, and I will be one less problem for you to deal with."

My stomach was a swarm of fluttering mayflies. My skin felt hot from the fire, and certainly Rune's touch as it lingered on my hips. The smell of spiced drink made my head fuzzy, as did Rune's scent, the tint of absinthe, and earth, and thunderclouds before a storm.

"Tell me to leave," I said. "Make this safer for both of us."

We weren't drugged anymore, not as we had been in another marsh just like this. Back then, I'd welcomed his touch, his kisses. Would I welcome them just as eagerly if we were to—

Looking as though he was drawing a knife from his neck, Rune pulled his hands from me. He stepped away, as though space equaled safety.

"You don't know what you're asking of me. Remember that."

I exhaled as he swept out of the room, leaving me with the crackling fire and an assurance that Sotera had been wrong. It wasn't severing ties with those we loved that made us strong. It was continuing to love even after losing so much.

Even if that meant pain. Even if that meant death.

NINETEEN

Olette was a serious child. She didn't cry when she awoke to find her mother missing, or even ask where she'd gone. She sat and listened with wide, somber eyes as I explained that I was going to take care of her for a little while, at least until I found someone who could do it better. Literally anyone who could do it better.

When I was done, I'd awkwardly patted her leg and told her that if she needed to talk to me about anything, she could. Olette had considered this and then perched herself by the window and stared outside, leaving me to puzzle over what to make of her. From the stories Peyton had told me of my childhood, I'd been similarly silent and serious, too. I wondered if she'd been equally worried and doubting that she was capable of keeping me alive.

Thinking of her still hurt.

The next day, after a misty rain came and went, I took Olette out into the safer parts of the marsh to play. Only, Olette didn't play. She didn't complain. She didn't want. She barely slept or ate, and I didn't know if that was normal for a young wildling.

"She spooks me," Cassius grumbled.

"She's a kid, Cassius," I said. "And stop moving so much."

I knelt and helped him and Marian weave the defensive charms into the ground. Once or twice Marian looked back at Olette and then returned to the charm, expression unreadable.

"Sorry, but being a kid doesn't make her less creepy," Cassius said. "I mean... Look at her."

Olette was where she'd been from the moment I brought her out: crouched at the edge of a murky pool, dress bunched around her ankles, staring unblinking into the water. She hadn't so much as twitched.

"Like I said, spooky," Cassius said.

"Enough, Cassius," Marian snapped. "If you'd gone through what she has, you'd be *spooky*, too. Hell, you still are."

Cassius smirked but looked properly chastised. "Fair enough."

Crass as it was, Cassius's assessment of Olette highlighted my very real problem. I was at a loss as to how to take care of her. Making the promise I had to Luella hadn't seemed monumental at the time, but unless we found Olette somewhere relatively safe, I feared for her wellbeing.

Cassius and Marian connected the last threads of the charm, and I released my hold on it. I stood to stretch the stiff muscles in my back.

"Olette, we need to get something to eat."

Olette didn't move.

"Come on, I know you're hungry." I went and peered over her shoulder. "You make a friend down there?"

Olette pointed. Beneath the water's surface, ink-black eels with glistening bodies as thick as my arm coiled in the murky black. One came close enough to strike, giving me a clear look at its inch-long fangs.

I snatched Olette away from the water's edge. "I think that's enough playing out here for today."

"I'll look after her, if you're busy," Marian said.

I lowered Olette to the ground. "You?"

Marian frowned. Though I didn't think it possible, I was pretty sure I'd hurt her.

"Sorry, that came out wrong," I said.

"There were lots of kids in Mog Moren," Marian said. "You couldn't get away from them. I had a little sister, too."

My mouth hung open for a beat as I considered how to answer without insulting her again. "I didn't know that."

"Me neither," Cassius said.

Marian rolled her eyes. "Because I didn't tell anyone. I lived six good years with her before my House exiled me from my home and sent me to Mog Moren."

"What did you do to deserve that?" Cassius said.

"*I*," Marian said proudly, "was too difficult. I didn't conform, didn't listen, didn't want to take part in my tiny House's petty politics. I didn't want to simper to guests or marry whomever they told me. I didn't want to kill."

She smirked at the ground. "Now killing's the thing I'm best at. But my sister, my poor, sweet little sister, was as perfectly moldable as they could ever want. So they got rid of me and made her their first born. She's dead now. At least, I've never found her body, and I doubt they would have let her live. My House was always one of the weaker ones—nothing like the House of Small Cuts or House of Worms—and they were one of the first to fall during the Sundering."

"I'm sorry," I said.

"I'm not," Marian replied. "I only wish two things: That my sister had lived, and that I could have been there to see the

House fall. Maybe even to drive the final knife into my parents' chests myself."

Olette was looking up at Marian with eyes so wide that—had they not been a simmering gold-red—they'd resemble the full moon on a clear night.

Marian knelt beside her. "Forget I said all that stupid stuff, Olette. What do you say, want to hang out with me? I can teach you how to properly hold a knife. You may not think so, but it's a pretty useful skill."

"Why don't you start with something more her age?" Cassius said.

Marian looked confused. "Knives *are* for girls her age."

"Then maybe something younger than that."

"Oh yeah? Like what?"

Hands on his hips, Cassius looked around the marsh and then to the trees. "Do you know how to gather moths, Olette? We're running low, and Pitius was telling me she wished to weave a cloak from their wings."

Olette slowly nodded.

"Moths," Marian scoffed under her breath. "Very well. And then I will braid your hair with twine of spider's silk. We can't have it getting in your eyes once you start using your knife."

Cassius sighed with a shake of his head. Marian took Olette's hand, and they and Cassius went to find a suitable swarm of moths. I trusted Marian. Cassius, too. Having them watch Olette would give me much-needed time to figure out what to do about her. As sure as I was that her being with me was bad, I was equally sure she couldn't stay. Rune might have had the right idea after all; the only way to keep someone truly safe was far away from me.

My eyes traveled back to the pool Olette had crouched beside, to the churned black mud and wyrm-like eels just beneath the surface.

I might have already found my answer.

For the next three nights, after I'd helped write correspondence to the wildlings at the lakeside, drilled myself so my skills wouldn't dull, and coaxed Olette to sleep, I went deep into the trees to a waterfall that shimmered like a mirror. A couple times, when the reflection stilled enough, I tried walking through, but only found myself on the other side and soaking wet.

If I had a different kind of magic—a wildling kind of magic—I was confident I could cross on my own and find myself where I wanted to go. But I didn't want to impose more than I was already going to. I needed Mother Mal in a good mood so that maybe she'd listen to what I had to say.

Each time I went, I brought freshly picked musk mallow, their scent strong; honeycomb wrapped in waxy leaves; and thick slices of eel flesh. Erebus would check on me each night before continuing to roam his territory. I'd sit at the waterfall until I nodded off, and when I awoke with the dawn's light, I'd leave the food on a rock beside the river and head back.

The fourth night, Hob waited for me.

"Mother Mal doesn't like being called on," he rasped.

"I have a favor to ask," I said.

Hob's lips puckered sourly. "She likes doing favors even less."

I suspected he'd been the one taking my offered food, so I held out what I'd brought for that night. With great reluctance, Hob snatched it from my hands and bit into the honeycomb, leaf and all. Honey dripped down his wrinkly cheeks into his beard.

"Be here at the same time tomorrow night," he relented.

"Someone will be with me," I said. "Someone new."

The next night, with a sleepy Olette in tow, I led us back to where Hob was waiting. He scratched his wrinkled cheek agitatedly. "Mother Mal won't like her."

I hoped he was wrong. In fact, I was counting on it.

No animals escorted us as we traveled with Hob back to the Halfway's clearing of ghost-white trees. When we arrived, Mother Mal was already sitting among the snarl of roots outside the enormous center tree. Kaffa the wyrm hovered around her shoulders, tongue flicking.

"I see you bribed my messenger," Mother Mal said.

"Apologies, mistress." Hob gave a hasty bow, though he didn't let go of my gifts.

"I am the one doing the summoning," Mother Mal said. "Who is the child?"

"Go play," I told Olette gently. "I'll call you over when we're ready."

Mother Mal watched Olette as she wordlessly approached the pool and knelt at its edge. I held my breath until, after a long moment, a watery face poked above the surface. The creature blew a bubble. It hovered in front of Olette, reflecting her face, before bursting. Olette giggled, actually giggled. The creature gave a gentle splash of contentment and blew another bubble.

"Xin has never taken to anyone," Mother Mal said, astonished.

I'd had four nights to mull over exactly what information I needed from Mother Mal, but now that I was here, I found it difficult to put my thoughts into words.

"How true are the wildling legends?" I asked. "I need to know if the stories of the Mother Tree are real."

Mother Mal waved Kaffa away, and he curled around Olette and Xin, watching the pair wordlessly converse.

"I sit here before you, and you dare ask something so ignorant?" she said. "Are you blind, or do you mean to anger me?"

"I meant no disrespect," I said. "Call it curiosity."

This didn't seem to satisfy her, but she wasn't calling on a swarm of locust to devour my flesh or casting me out with flowers sprouting from my ears. I took that as a good sign.

"How true any belief is depends on how much others believe in them," Mother Mal said.

I curbed my frustration. "That's not an answer. I know you're not supposed to get directly involved—"

"And yet here you are, and I, old fool that I am, am allowing you to stay."

"Nieriti, Rhasahlyn, Mishari, the Mother Tree, are they real?" I demanded.

"What has happened?"

It occurred to me that Mother Mal could very well already know everything—omniscient as she seemed to be. But allowing me to share showed a certain amount of trust. Or it was a test of how well I lied.

"Sotera wants a human priest dead. The only priest that makes sense would be from the worshippers of the Mother Tree. I can't figure out *why* unless she thought him a threat. But how would someone like that be a threat to *her*?"

Mother Mal leaned forward. "How could the leader of a religion be dangerous? Influence over the weak, the cultivation of false belief, zealously, corruption. There are many plausible reasons."

"But none of those are the right one," I pressed.

It was difficult to hold Mother Mal's gaze. She didn't have the gold-red eyes of a wildling, but neither were they comfortable to meet. Her eyes were filled with eons, fathomless doorways that, if I stepped through, I was sure I'd be lost in forever.

"I know many things," Mother Mal said. "But I can't know

the hearts of everyone. You wish to believe there's meaning in what she asked, just as there are those who desperately wish to believe that every terrible thing has a reason."

That was frustratingly vague and useless, which I suspected was Mother Mal's goal. Like the faerie stories I'd grown up reading, she dealt in small lies and half-truths. I suspected whatever answers she might have would only be revealed to me later, possibly when it was too late.

"Can't you tell me anything else?" I begged.

"Has your High King progressed in stopping Sotera?" Mother Mal said. "What about the Undersea? The humans? I hear they are all closing in like a wolf circling its prey."

I was suddenly bone tired. "No. We haven't made any progress."

"Yet you come to me asking about things that are far beyond your understanding. It is the ignorance of the young to meddle in things they can't possibly grasp."

"And it's the ignorance of the ancient for believing the young are unable to do it," I snapped.

Mother Mal bristled, and I realized I might have made a grave mistake. Then the mouth of her long skull parted a couple inches, revealing rows of teeth in what might have been her version of a smile.

"Have you considered that the solution to staving off all your enemies is not more peace, but savagery?"

"We tried that. We can't keep fighting forever."

"*Rune* tried that. And he must continue to do so. But perhaps your place would be better served on a throne of your own. You would be one of the blades instead of the hilt."

Mother Mal appeared amused while I scrambled to form words. "I'm not taking Rune's place."

"Who said anything about taking Rune's?"

Sotera had told me that once I was Bendeti's wife, once

she'd removed Rune, that I would take the throne of the wildlings. I'd been too disgusted by the thought of marrying Bendeti that I hadn't fully considered what she was saying. Becoming any sort of queen was absurd. I was a girl from Seattle, created Below, yes, but neither of those things gave me the qualifications to rule.

Rune didn't have the qualifications either, a small voice reminded me. *He had to take it.*

And that had nearly destroyed him. It still might.

"I'm no ruler," I said.

"You're not," Mother Mal agreed. "But you could be. Who is the child?"

I relaxed a little, relieved to be changing the subject. "She needs to stay somewhere safe. With someone who can look after her properly. She's in too much danger with what we have to do."

Mother Mal looked heavily at me. "I am not a depository for lost souls."

"But you have experience. You raised Nieriati and her siblings. But of course, that's only what I *believe*."

"And because of them, I have had my fill of cultivating children. They tend to grow up and become nothing like you intended." She waved a hand. "Take the girl and go."

Mother Mal turned away, though the long snout of her bony face remained tilted, watching us.

I didn't leave my spot, hoping that I'd somehow guessed the heart of her nature. Even as a spirit, a god, whatever she was, she was a mother first and foremost. I prayed she hadn't forgotten that part of herself.

"I know you are still there. And you are beginning to test the generous ends of my patience," Mother Mal said. She looked at Olette. "The child hasn't spoken a word."

"That's just who she is," I said.

"Hmph. She may be loud in other ways." Mother Mal brushed light fingers over one of the depressions in the tree's roots, where the smallest of bodies might perfectly fit.

"How long has it been since you've had someone to call your own?" I asked.

Mother Mal sighed, her shoulders slumping as though releasing a secret. "Ages and ages still. There is very little to live for, when not living for another. Very well. She will be safe here. But..." She held up a finger. "Only for now. There will come a time when not even I will be able to protect her."

It was a risk. It always would be. But whatever small dangers Olette faced here had to be better than what I could provide. "I understand."

"Do you?" Mother Mal gestured to Olette. "Come to me, child."

I knelt beside Olette as she stood and brushed her skirts off. "I'd like to leave you with Mother Mal. She's kind and she'll take care of you. You'll get to play with your friends. Is that okay? Would you like that?"

Kaffa vibrated like he was purring as Olette stroked his scales. From the water, Xin watched her, waiting.

"I won't force you," I said. "You can always come back with me."

"I want to stay here," Olette said softly. "With them."

"I'm glad to hear that. I'll return to visit. I promise."

Clutching the front of her dress, Olette approached Mother Mal, who directed her to sit against her legs. Using her long, sharp-nailed fingers, Mother Mal began tenderly teasing out the knots of Olette's hair. "That's twice you've played me for a sentimental old fool," she said to me. "You're lucky I don't mind it."

"I have one more favor to ask," I said. "But not from you."

Xin barred her teeth at me as I knelt again at the edge of

the pool. Moving slow, I unwrapped a slab of smoked eel skin, its scent so potent it made my eyes water. Even though the smell could classify it as a weapon of war, Raquel had assured me that many creatures loved it.

"Move closer, if you want her mouth to be the last thing you ever see," Mother Mal said.

"I need one of your eggs," I said to Xin.

Mother Mal scoffed and Xin hissed, curling her tail protectively around the glassy orbs in the clear side of the pool.

"Not one of those. A dead one." I nodded to the other side of the pool and the black orbs with wrinkled, fleshy shells.

"To touch those is death," Mother Mal said. "Be very sure you know what you're doing."

I hoped I did. So many things were happening so quickly that I found myself doing increasingly desperate, stupid things just to keep up.

"I only need one," I said to Xin. "I won't take it without permission."

Xin looked between me and the dead eggs, as wary as a starving dog who wanted to hold onto the first food they'd found in weeks.

Then she reached up and gently took the eel skin between her teeth and dragged it below. A moment later, her tail pushed one of the dark, dead eggs onto the shore. To my surprise, she breathed an air bubble from her nose and a small orb of the clear water joined the black egg. I expected it to be absorbed immediately into the ground, but it held its solid shape.

"Thank you," I said.

In lieu of any Ziploc, I wrapped them both in the same waxy, waterproof leaf I'd used for the honeycomb and tucked them carefully away into my jacket. "And thank you," I said to Mother Mal. "I'll be back for Olette once things are safer or her mother contacts us, but hopefully she'll bring you some happiness in the meantime."

Olette had already curled up in the depression at the base of the tree, looking more serene than I'd ever seen her.

"After so many years, I forget that occasionally I can be wrong," Mother Mal said. "I hope whatever your plot is, it works. Else others may suffer as a result. I trust you can find your way back alone."

I cast Olette a final look before I left, clutching the dark egg and watery orb close. I tried to ignore the fear of their poison sinking straight into my heart.

I STEPPED out of the waterfall and found Rune waiting in the shadows of the nearby trees. A jittery energy filled me, equal parts elation and nervousness. Whether by circumstance or me subconsciously taking the Council of Loam's demands to heart, we hadn't been alone since the night in the study. I found it laughable that, after saying so much to one another then, it was impossibly difficult for me to come up with anything to say now.

I settled on, "Hope you didn't have to wait long."

"You weren't gone long," he answered. He'd dressed in a loose fur poncho over a jacket of poison green, one of his older ones that didn't have so many slim gashes in the fabric, remnants where blades had tried to pierce him. "I didn't know you enjoyed such late-night walks."

I mulled over how much to share without adding more to his already full plate. "I left Olette with Mother Mal."

"The child?" Rune turned the words over on his lips, as though trying them out.

"*Olette*," I insisted. "I didn't think you'd like it. But she'll be safer there, for now."

I started back toward the mansion. Rune kept a slow pace at my side, not seeming in any rush to return to the others just yet.

"And you truly believe this Mother Mal can protect her?"

I gave him a side-eyed glance. "You tell me, Rune. She's part of your legend. I trust her not to hurt her, so that's something. And she won't give me a straight answer, but I suspect she's way more powerful than she lets on."

"Powerful enough that, were she to become an ally, she might be able to turn the tide against Those Below and the Undersea?"

His words came out a bit thick and unwieldy. I examined his face in the glowing light of moon lilies overhead, looking for any ruddiness on his cheeks. "Have you been drinking?"

"No, of course not."

"Don't act so surprised. You seemed to want to the other night."

He smiled at me, in a way that was wrong in how kind it almost seemed. "I'm not drunk, I'm *tired*, Val. Everywhere we turn there is another enemy at our throat. Every decision we make only seems to make things worse."

"It's always been that way," I said. "Hopefully not forever."

"Sometimes I wonder..." Rune sighed and stopped, and I stopped with him. He rubbed his mist-slicked cheeks. "I can't face sleep tonight. Remind me again of how to get to Mother Mal. I may go speak to her. Convince her to help us in ways you couldn't."

We stood in the depression of a game trail full of hoof-worn plants, along the outer ring of where Marian, Cassius, and I had cast protective enchantments. I was grateful for the tingle on my skin, a sign the protections still held strong. "I don't think Mother Mal is in the habit of directly taking any side."

"Still, I would speak to her." Rune looked deep into the Wilds directly opposite the glittering lights of the mansion. "Maybe she will even give me insight into what I should do next."

"You know what to do. It's being brave enough to follow through with it that's the problem."

"I'm always brave."

I gave him an indulgent smile. "Of course you are. Which is why you know what we have to do next.

"Oh?" Rune appeared amused. "And what is that? I seem to double-guess myself so much these days I've forgotten."

I stepped across the game trail and motioned for him. "Seems you're so tired your memory's going. Let's head back and we'll talk about it. Just you and me."

"Perhaps another time."

"Rune, step over to me."

Rune looked at my outstretched hand, at where my finger-tips just brushed against the barrier of the protective enchant-ments. He licked his lips. They looked strangely dry.

"There is much I have to do—"

"Step over to me, Rune. Now."

He stepped back instead. "I'd better not—"

"Erebus!" I barked.

Rune tried to spring away from me, but a fully corporeal Erebus, whom I'd sensed had returned, blocked his way. Rune snarled, trying to slip around him.

I lunged across the enchantment and grabbed his arm. My fingers sank into mushy flesh, as though I tried to hold on to Silly Putty. I pulled him toward me, but to my horror his skin ripped away entirely. I gaped at a torn piece in my hand until it bubbled and fizzed like sea spray hitting the shore. In moments I cupped nothing but foam.

Erebus howled. The thing that was not Rune had slipped past him. I could make out a nimble shape—pale, long legs; body slender as kelp; skin glistening wet—darting through the trees. More of its flesh dripped off its body like wax, turning to foam where it hit the ground. The smell of salt hung heavy in the air.

"Go after him," I ordered Erebus, and like a flicker of shadow, he was gone. I paced the edge of the enchantment, debating furiously whether I should follow the false-Rune. I imagined a creature like that could disguise themselves as anyone, and I wouldn't know until it was too late.

With a frustrated growl, I spun and took off back toward the estate. I'd recognized the trick eventually, but by the time I had, it'd been too late. I'd told them so much already.

Just what had I done?

CHAPTER

TWENTY

My boots were soaked with marsh water by the time I burst through the mansion's front door and hurried, soaking the carpets, up to Rune's room. I didn't let myself give into the fear gnawing at my chest. Didn't entertain the thought that, if the creature had been able to imitate Rune down to his every intricate detail, what if that meant the real Rune…

My taut muscles sagged with relief as I burst into the planning room and saw him. He gave me a quizzical look, one eyebrow cocked, his gaze roving up and down my body.

"Did you enjoy a pleasant swim? Perhaps you thought the smell invigorating enough to share with the rest of us."

"You're okay," I gasped.

"And you're distraught," he said, his amusement growing. "Which makes me believe you thought I was in trouble."

"What happened?" Marian said.

Only then did I realize we weren't alone. Marian and a few of the older wildlings were gathered around a table in the center of the room. Some appeared disheveled as though they'd been dragged out of bed.

"A spy from the Undersea was here," I said. "They know where we are."

To my surprise, nobody else appeared shocked.

Rune held up an echo bird. "We were just leaving anyway. Those at the lakeside have encountered some issues. Make the preparations," Rune commanded the others. "We depart within the hour. Val, you stay here."

"You weren't assigned to scout tonight, Val," Marian said after the others had left. "Where were you?"

I tried to come up with a plausible excuse that wouldn't give away more than necessary. I'd already done that enough tonight. "Out," I finally said.

"Out…" she repeated deadpan. "Supposedly with Rune, which nobody else seemed surprised by. Which tells me you two have been 'out' together before."

Neither Rune nor I finished her thought.

"Olette's gone," Marian went on. "I assumed she was with you, Val."

"Wait, you went to check on her?"

"I always check on her. Children tend to have nightmares, especially when they're sleeping in a house where terrible things have happened to them."

My cheeks heated with shame. I'd been so incredibly selfish I hadn't even thought of that. "She's safe."

"What does that—"

"Later, Marian. I promise she's safe."

Marian looked between Rune and me. "Is there something you—both of you—need to tell me? Maybe about the real reason you've been sneaking off alone?"

My face heated further at the insinuation. Rune's cocked eyebrow climbed higher. "Do you feel it's something you should know?" he said.

"Do *you*? You two are being so secretive. I get that you don't feel the same as I feel—felt—about you, Rune, but that doesn't mean you can't trust me."

"Of course I trust you. That's why you'll trust me to share another time."

Marian stared at him, waiting, perhaps, for him to capitulate and tell her everything. When he didn't, she sighed.

"Can't blame anyone but myself, I suppose. I wanted out. I should have expected the result. You okay?" she said to me. "The spy didn't hurt you?"

"I'm fine, thanks," I answered, touched. At least, I was physically fine. But the feel of Rune's foam flesh tearing under my fingers had left me more distraught than I cared to admit.

"You thought I was dead," Rune said after Marian limped out. Across his face was the smug, Rune-like smile no creature could entirely mimic. "You burst in more flustered than I've ever seen. It was a welcome surprise. I didn't think anything could shake you."

"They used me, and idiot that I was, I fell for it," I said. "They knew I'd talk to you, that I'd be comfortable enough to tell you anything."

The spy had exploited our relationship, something that ashamed me more than I cared to admit. How obvious were Rune and my...interactions that even King Bendeti knew how to manipulate it to his own ends?

"Some of the wildlings at lakeside are dead," Rune said, tone sobering. "Ambushed while on patrol by humans, one of them using magic weapons. Your stepbrother is likely leading them. We have a couple days to return and prepare before we have to move again."

I swallowed the apology that crawled up my throat. Joshua's choices weren't mine. And sympathies wouldn't help anyone.

The echo bird danced between Rune's slender fingers.

"Keen of the Mysts has been in touch. He tells me that some of the other minor Lords I have yet to sway have either defected to the Undersea, Sotera, or left the Wilds completely. The ones who have fled I couldn't care less about. But the rest..."

I could see he believed their betrayal was his fault. And why wouldn't he think that? He could reason that if he was a good leader, then surely they'd stay. That if he did everything right, those who had long ago made up their minds would change it.

Why wouldn't he blame himself when Xander questioned him and Marian wanted no more part in his war? Why wouldn't he, after learning that I'd doubted him, too?

"You can't worry about them," I said firmly. "They're against you now, so they're enemies, simple as that."

"Simple as that," Rune repeated in a low murmur. "Things used to be simple as that. Me against the guards of Mog Moren. My wildlings against the Lords. It's strange how fast all of that can change. I should alert the Council of Loam."

"If they haven't learned of the other Lord's betrayal yet, then I think you should hold off. For now."

Rune gave me a narrow-eyed evaluation. "And you feel this way because...?"

"Some on the Council are minor Lords. They might be emboldened by the defection or have allies who have defected."

Rune tutted. "Not trusting my own advisors. That isn't a good start to my new way of ruling."

Maybe not. But where did trust begin, and where did it end? Who started it first, and how often could you have it broken before deciding you were an idiot?

"But I understand your concern," Rune said. "And I suppose you're right." There was an intensity in his gaze, a sharp edge to his smile when he focused on me. "Which is why you must stay close."

"Thanks, but you don't need to worry about protecting me."

"With blood and blade, you are the last person who needs protection from anything. This is for me."

For your safety, your peace of mind, or something more? I wanted to ask.

But, coward that I was, I only nodded.

TENSION LACED the air when we arrived back at lakeside. The first thing Rune did was visit the mounds of dirt that were the dead. He didn't stay long. They were dead, and the enchantments keeping us hidden would only do that for so long. Especially with how fervent Joshua had been about taking Rune down.

I stuck close to Rune as he caught up with General Forcheck, as he checked in with the sentries, as he mulled over what to do next, occasionally asking my input. All the while, I felt useless. My brush with Bendeti's spy had reminded me there was still very much a wider problem out there, waiting. I wanted to lash out. I wanted to draw blood. Yet it was impossible to tell who to strike. If I was Rune's blade, I felt sheathed.

"I should go with Pitius and Idwal," I said to Rune as we double-checked the perimeter for the fourth time. "Maybe I could find out where the humans will attack next."

"No," was Rune's distracted reply. "I need you here."

Doing what? Mulling over nothing? How strange it was that we seemed to switch places; Rune the contemplative planner, hesitant to shed blood, and me more than willing to seek out a fight. I wanted to get things under control. To make sure that whatever had hurt the wildlings couldn't do so again. With each passing hour, my frustration grew and I began to understand, just a little, how Xander must feel.

Thankfully, I finally found an excuse to tear myself away from Rune's side and join Marian at a small hollow where we kept most of our intel. She needed help poring over maps of the area, trying to find a new place we could set up encampment. We didn't have the luxury of GPS, so I'd gotten used to delicately sifting through reams of crackling parchment and dried beast coats stained with scribbles of berry juice. My eyes had become more attuned to picking out small marks denoting hidden paths and secluded sanctuaries.

We had just started narrowing down our choices when General Forcheck swung by to give her input.

"We don't need such a large area this time," she said. "Some from the other parts of Rune's army have fled. Word has gotten out about those new weapons the humans are using. Cowards, all. I say we should hunt down those who abandoned their High King and put them at the forefront of the next battle."

Marian stared more furiously at her map, fingers creasing the edges. "I like to think those who left had their reasons."

General Forcheck noticed Marian's hands whitening. "Perhaps. I suppose I don't know the whole story. In the grand scheme, they are just a few deserters." She gave me a terrifying smile I was sure was the last thing some of her enemies saw. "The noose is tightening, and that's when the wolf bites hardest."

"Except when the wolf has lost some of its teeth," Marian said.

General Forcheck grunted in agreement as she left. Marian caught me staring at the freshly carved charms strung around her neck, tokens to remember the recently dead. She tucked them beneath her shirt. "Have you seen Xander?"

"Not since we came back," I said.

Marian frowned. "Me either. He was supposed to check in."

"He'll turn up. General Forcheck probably gave him something to do."

Marian turned back to the maps with a huff. We continued searching for another secluded place, one that was still close enough to the center of the Wilds that Rune could counterattack when we found a way to do it. Her glare rested on Keen as he passed by, speaking intently with Rune.

"Has Keen done something?" I said, almost feeling sorry for him.

"He's part of the Mysts. What he's done that would upset me is likely a very long list."

Moments later, I caught her staring again. "Marian?"

She startled. "What?"

I nodded at my outstretched hand. "I wanted to see the map you were looking at."

She practically threw it at me. "It's nothing."

"What isn't? I only wanted the map. Or are you talking about you and..."

The force of her glare turned on me like a punch to the throat. "I know what you're thinking, and you should stop."

"You just seem to be a bit distracted. And I've noticed you and Keen talking."

"On strategy, yes. Nothing more. I'm done with guys who will sacrifice everything and everyone for their own goals. I want someone simpler."

"Grandmother told me to give you these," Cassius said, dropping a couple more maps on the table. He pushed one over to Marian, his fingers slightly brushing hers. "I suggest starting with this one."

"Sure, we'll handle it," Marian said brusquely. She cleared her throat. "Uh, thanks, Cassius."

Cassius stood there, a soft, almost goofy smile on his face.

"Yes, thanks, Cassius," I repeated. "We've got it from here."

As though coming out of a trance, Cassius nodded and hurried off.

"Someone simpler, like Cassius?" I asked. I almost immediately wished I could shove the words back in my mouth. "That came out wrong, sorry. I'm not saying he's simple."

"You," Marian said, "have the amazing ability to insert yourself in the last possible place you're wanted. Just so you know, it's not the worst thing in the world, desiring simple things. And I like him. That doesn't mean I have to love him or confide everything in him. Surely you get that."

I did. Far more than I was comfortable admitting.

"As long as you're happy. That's all I care about," I said.

"Don't be stupid. My chance at happiness died long ago. Best I can do now is contentment. I suppose that doesn't sound too bad either."

Perhaps it wasn't so bad, not asking for more than you were owed or more than you believed you deserved. Rune also seemed to think he didn't deserve happiness, only punishment for what he'd done. He was necessary, but not adored.

That also wouldn't be so bad either, I supposed: to be needed rather than loved.

"Val?"

It was my turn to startle from my thoughts. Marian was holding one of the rolled-up maps. "I asked you to bring this to Rune, show him what we found."

"For what little chance he might actually take our suggestions," I said.

Marian smirked. "He'll listen to you."

I tried to ignore that. "You don't want to give it to him?"

She practically shoved the map into my hands and then busied herself with straightening up the others. "I think it's best if you do. We have a good thing going, he and I, but... It's best if I'm not distracting him."

"I'm sorry things didn't work out between you and Rune," I said. "And I mean that."

Marian braced against the table with a loud sigh, hanging her head. "What have I become, that I'm getting sympathy from a human?"

"Half human," I corrected. "Maybe thirty percent?"

"Whatever. I don't hate you for it, in case you were wondering. Not anymore. I would have been bad for him."

"And you think I'm not?"

She gave me a long look. "I'm not sure yet. I think you could both hurt each other spectacularly. It could all tear apart in an instant, but everything's tearing apart, it seems, so what's there to lose? Anyway." She rifled unnecessarily through the maps. "If you see Xander, tell him I want to talk with him."

With an uncomfortable churning in my gut, I gathered the maps and headed to Rune's planning area. I could already hear the low, fierce undertone of arguing voices before I even reached the curtain of flowers surrounding it. The angrier voice was clearly Xander's.

"If I had been with you at Lord Blis's estate—"

"Then you wouldn't have been any more useful than you were here," Rune said sharply. "If not for you, the humans would have killed more."

The flower curtain between us twitched like an agitated cat's tail, making it difficult to push through.

"I'm tired of you questioning my every decision," Rune said. "Of not having you back me like you once did."

"I still have your back," Xander murmured.

"Yes. Only now I have to worry about you going behind it to undermine my command. And sometimes.... Sometimes I wonder if I have to worry about you sticking a knife into it."

Xander gave a distressed scoff. "Don't say that. Never say that."

"Can you blame me?" Rune's voice held a sneer. I was reminded, with some shame, of the way he sounded when he accused me of doubting him. *All I asked was that you believed me better than the monsters we usurped.* "Ever since Zuri—"

"Don't," Xander bit out. "She has nothing to do with this."

"But she has everything to do with *you*!" The flower curtain rioted, and I was nearly shoved away as Rune's magic spurned outwards. "I thought I could trust you to see this to the end."

"You can," Xander said.

"And yet I find myself fighting with you more than our enemies. I need to find allies right now, not instigate another battle we're not ready for."

"If you would just *talk* to Bendeti, maybe we can fix this! You don't have to give up anything; just ask him to release her."

"You're not stupid, so don't act like it," Rune said. "He wouldn't take her except to use her against you and by extension against me. If I submit to him—if I give in to *your* request —where does it end? We've all lost someone. Mothers, brothers, wives, husbands, lovers. We all have our petty revenges and grievances that would demand my action."

"Petty?" Xander's laugh was harsh. "When Sotera took Val, that was all you could focus on. You barely ate or slept. I've seen the way you treat her. We all have. And some think you're weak for it, for caring so much about a human. But I never did. I still helped you get her out, and now you—"

"I would stop," Rune said. "While you still can."

There was a long silence. Then the flower curtains parted

as Xander forced his way out. I caught Rune's eye before spinning around and hurrying after Xander. I knew all too well that desperation led to poor choices, and to him, there was only one choice that made sense.

"You can't go after Bendeti," I said.

"So now you're telling me what I can't do, too?" Xander snarled. "You two are incredible, really, you know that?"

"Did you learn to breathe underwater? I'm pretty sure that's necessary to reach the *Undersea*."

"There are magics," Xander said. "There are ways."

"He'll kill you," I emphasized. "You're playing to his every advantage."

We were attracting attention as we reached the sleeping area. Other wildlings pretended not to listen, while cocking their ears toward us. Marian limped over, eyes narrowing on Xander.

"What's happened? Where are you going?"

Xander grabbed his bow, quiver, and then stuffed a few other belongings into a large pouch. Just enough supplies to get him to the Undersea, likely. Either he anticipated foraging once he'd found his love or didn't expect to make it that far.

"Xander." I grabbed his arm, but he easily shrugged me off.

"It might seem childish and stupid to you," he said. "But Zuri is the last bit of my old life. The last bit of anything good before...this, all this. I can't leave her there to suffer just because she got involved with me."

"And what about us?" Marian said. "What about those who need you *here*?"

Xander continued grabbing his things.

"I know things are tough." Marian sounded on the verge of tears. "But we've gotten through worse. We'll get through this. You can't leave now. We *need* you."

Xander slung his pack over his shoulder and stood. He

wavered, seemingly on the precipice of a monumental choice. A moment away from stepping off the edge or moving back.

"Xander, please..."

"Don't let Rune get you all killed," he said. "I'm not sure if it's worth that anymore."

It was a long time after the Wilds swallowed him up before Marian turned from where he'd gone. The moon hung bright and full, its light shimmering off the silent tears streaking her face before she hid them from view.

TWENTY-ONE

"I believe you've overstepped your bounds."

Mother Mal was waiting for us as we entered the forest clearing of the Halfway. I was happy to see Olette at her side, half her face peeking out from behind Mother Mal's cloak. Olette gave me a shy smile.

Rune swept his hand past Marian to Hob, who was munching sheepishly on some honeycomb I'd gifted him. "If you have a problem with our arrival, you need to take it up with your attendant."

Mother Mal's bony gaze cowed Hob, though he didn't stop eating. "I will. I also don't recall requesting someone new to join me."

"I insisted," Marian said.

She had. After I'd received the message from Luella, Marian had appeared, demanding I tell her where Olette had gone. There was no placating her. Xander's leaving had opened some raw, fresh wound that wouldn't be satisfied with anything other than seeing Olette and seeing what we'd been up to.

Rune had agreed, with little coaxing. With one of his most

trusted friends now gone, it seemed the remainder of that trust would fall on her.

With great difficulty, Marian bowed. "I am Marian of the Wilds, usurper of Lords, yarrow-spawn of Mog Moren, subject of the High King."

Mother Mal's gaze traveled across her, from her fierce expression to the bone-white part of her missing leg. She seemed almost impressed. "And what business does the High King have with me now? If you're looking for more answers, then you should have talked to her." One gnarled finger pointed at me. "I have given all I mean to."

I held up a small echo bird. "We have a message from Olette's mother."

Though impossible, I swore Mother Mal's bony face softened. "Very well. Go, child, go and see what your birth mother has to say."

Olette delightedly stole from around her cloak and took the bird I handed to her. "She didn't give us the password," I said.

Olette didn't seem to care. She crouched at the edge of the pool, where Xin's face was just poking above the surface, waiting for her. Olette whispered something to the echo bird and held it up to her ear.

"You shouldn't be here," Mother Mal said to Marian. "These matters don't concern you."

"Then you shouldn't have made it so damn easy to get in," Marian said. "You're lucky we used Hob as a courtesy."

"And why *are* you here?"

"For Olette, not you. Anything you tell my High King I trust he'll tell me eventually, so you can chatter away all you want." As though to prove how little she cared, Marian limped over to Olette, hovering just far enough away to respect her space.

"A spy from the Undersea found out about you, Mother

Mal," I admitted, though not elaborating on *how*. "We came to make sure Olette—and you—were all right."

"Everything will happen as it's meant to be," Mother Mal said. "I would worry more about the claws closing around your throat."

"What a helpful anecdote," Rune said pleasantly. "Care to elaborate?"

Mother Mal remained silent, and I was saved from prodding her for more by Olette coming back over to us, Marian in tow. Olette tucked the echo bird back into my hand.

"Is everything all right?" I asked.

Marian waited to see if Olette would answer herself before saying, "Luella found other wildlings, in the Wilds humans once called Yellowstone."

"Then Olette can go and be safe there," Rune said.

"Luella doesn't want her. Not yet." Marian scowled at the echo bird, and the ever-nagging worry I'd had since Luella left took center stage again. Luella loved Olette, but fool that she was, believed her daughter safer among the High King and all his strife than with her own mother.

"I was afraid of this," Rune said, and I didn't miss the glance thrown my way. "If I had to guess, she'll never want Olette back again."

"She's her child!" Marian seethed. "You don't just dump your kid like that. Does she have *any* idea how many of us would kill to keep someone they love—" She looked furious that she'd let that slip. "I'll take her," she said to Mother Mal. "Let me take her."

"You'll be busy with me," Rune said immediately.

"Not for much longer," Marian said. "I told you I'd take her wherever I ended up. I'll give her a home and will never leave her."

"We'll discuss this later."

"There's nothing to discuss. Well?" Marian demanded, not taking her eyes off Mother Mal. "Will you let her come with me?"

"That's not entirely up to me," Mother Mal said.

Marian's leg trembled as she knelt to Olette's level. "I can't replace your mom," Marian said softly. "But I can make sure nobody ever leaves you again. I'll do everything I can to make us hap—make us content. You'll get to eat sugared fruit, drink nectar, and dance under the moonlight whenever you'd like. I'll string glittering jewels above your bed and sing you to sleep every night with a different lullaby. I don't know many, but I could learn."

"The more you bribe, the less a true choice it is," Mother Mal warned.

"Do you want that, Olette?" Marian said, undeterred. "Do you want to come with me?"

Olette shrank farther behind Mother Mal's cloak.

"I promise I'll give you all that." Marian's voice cracked. "I'll give you so much love you won't know what to do with it."

Olette turned and ran beneath the roots of the tree, where Kaffa curled to follow. Marian looked ready to follow after her. "Olette—"

"Enough. Give her a chance to decide," Mother Mal said. "Come back at another time."

"We plan to," Rune said. "But when Val and I return, it will be alone."

<hr>

MARIAN LAGGED behind on the walk back. I suspected part of it was due to her leg, but most of it was so she wouldn't have to talk with Rune.

I glanced back in time to see her take a swig from a clear

bottle. Likely a tonic from General Forcheck to help dull the pain of her injury. I'd seen Marian drinking it with increasing frequently. I made a note to tell General Forcheck to give her less but then scratched the idea. More and more I found myself trying to control others, maybe in some inane attempt to prevent what I knew was coming. But Marian, like Xander, would make her own choices. I could only make mine and leave hers to her, as painful as that was.

The wind through the trees sounded like flutes. In the distance, a fox or some other small creature screamed, and Rune slowed. He looked frustrated. Maybe sad.

"I can't lose Marian, no matter what she wants," he said. "I trust very few around me, and there are few I trust as much as her."

"That choice may not be up to you," I said.

"She made me a vow. Xander made a vow. From the very beginning, they knew what joining me meant. And now… Promise me something, Val."

Rune was looking at me, eyes shockingly vivid in the twilight. "Promise me that you… That you won't—"

I'd been extra vigilant following the disastrous last time I'd left Mother Mal. So much so that I sensed the attack the same moment Rune did.

He leaned back, as though stretching after a long night's sleep. There was a *snnk*, and something thin zipped past where his neck would have been and embedded itself, quivering, in the tree beside me.

I stared at the dart for much longer than I should have, trying to make sense of it. The fins were gold slivers, trimmed with soft, downy feathers to help its flight. The tip was dipped in something purple and shiny. Venom, no doubt.

The ones who shot it came out of the trees like phantoms, two in the branches above us, two more on either side of the trunk, trying to hem us in. Their faces were covered with pale white masks with only eye slits. Their clothing was rough-hewn, sleeves pulled back just a little to reveal their crystal arms.

Even with the masks, I could tell they were surprised Rune wasn't alone. They really must have expected him to be, otherwise Sotera wouldn't have only sent four to take down the High King of the Wilds.

"Having a nice evening stroll, High King?" one of them called, taunting.

"Admittedly, it was a little uneventful," Rune said. "Are you here to remedy that?"

Two of the assailants raised their arms. Small crossbows with more venomed darts were attached to their wrists. Rune and I split apart, the darts brushing air across my skin as they shot just over my head. Marian was yelling something, clumsily tripping in her attempt to reach us.

"A shame you aren't alone," one of the assailants called. "Now they have to die as well."

I tried to return to Rune as the assailants closed him in, rapidly firing their crossbows to stop him before he could use his magic. Rune knocked each dart aside with a tree branch mirroring his movements. One of the assailants tried to block my way, and I nearly lost a hand to his blade as I skirted around him.

"Focus on yourself," Rune snarled at me. He ducked beneath one of their knives. "You can't fight with me if you're dead!"

"The great High King," one of the assailants taunted. "We were afraid of you, did you know that? All the stories we've heard were like nightmares to our ears. But you've let your heart become soft and your power along with it. Where is the strength we've heard so much about?"

Rune gave them a smile so cruel I almost wanted to warn them. "A demonstration, then, just for you."

Rune swiped with his knife, driving the nearest assailants back. One of them tripped, and for a moment, I thought he'd lost his footing on a root.

"What the—"

His leg hadn't just caught a root, it had been partially sucked into the tree itself, as though the bark had turned to quicksand. "What is this?" He wrenched at his knee, eyes widening in fear when the leg didn't so much as budge. "Kill him! Kill him before he—"

Rune squeezed his hand into a fist.

The trunk of the tree split like a gaping mouth, revealing nothing but darkness within. Fringes of bark closed around the screaming man's lower half and closed. Bone cracked, followed by a high-pitched scream, long and loud. The skin of his arms swelled and split like an exploding water balloon.

By the time the trunk opened again to swallow the rest of him, he wasn't screaming anymore. And when the tree returned to what it had been, there was nothing of the man but blood dribbling down its trunk, like a baby having just burped up milk.

"Now do you understand the mistake you've made?" Rune said.

The other three assailants tried to run. One ducked as knives of ice shot just over his head. Marian leaned heavily on her cane, frost-covered hand extended in front of her.

"Don't stare at me," she snapped. "Get them!"

She shot another bout of ice, forcing the closest assailant to dodge and giving me space to dart in close. Sliver was in my hand before I realized I'd drawn it, and I slid the point of the blade easily into his exposed side. The blow forced the air out of his punctured lung so fast I felt his warm breath on the back of my neck. He crumpled to the ground, dead.

Rune had already dispatched the second assailant. He looked to the canopy. "The last one—"

I scooped up a handful of dirt and took off before he'd finished, using the dirt to magic crystal handles along the nearest trunk and clambering to give chase. A highway of sprawling sturdy branches spread out before me. Rune's last attacker was making his way skillfully across them, barely hesitating when he leapt from one tree to the next. It was strange how easily someone from the Below could move through the Wilds. But as I pursued them, using crystal on the bottom of my feet to bind me to the bark, I realized that perhaps it wasn't the craziest thing.

The man saw me closing in and spat a curse. I threw myself to the side as a couple more darts pierced the leaves beside me.

"You weren't supposed to be with him," he snarled. "You were supposed to stay away!"

"It seems you didn't do your homework," I returned, panting. "I stick around him for this exact reason."

The assailant tried to cut right, dipping toward a snarl of thicket that would make it a hundred times more difficult to follow. If he managed to slither his way inside there, I'd lose him.

I summoned a crystal spike and hurled it at his retreating back. He must have sensed it coming because at the last second he rotated his body and let it slide past.

Exactly what I'd hoped for.

Forcing him to dodge had slowed his momentum enough that I was easily able to close the distance between us. He cried out as I knocked us both to the ground. My stomach lurched from the force of the landing. My head spun, but I was lucid enough to draw Sliver again.

The assailant was already trying to stumble to his feet, but I tackled him again, using my knees to pin his arms as I brought Sliver's blade beneath his chin.

"Keep that one alive."

Rune was beside me. Marian joined a few seconds later, panting, shirt slick with sweat. She caught me looking at her.

"Don't you dare ask if I'm okay. Eyes on him, idiot."

Rune knelt beside the assailant, who continued thrashing until I pressed Sliver's blade closer and he stilled.

"Sotera has been quiet," Rune said. "I was beginning to feel forgotten. I'm going to ask what she's been up to, and you're going to give me the correct answer."

"Try it," the assailant snarled. "See what happens."

Rune smiled. "I intend to. Now, why don't we start with—"

I readjusted my legs, and my knees nearly slipped as the top half of the assailant's forearm came off entirely. What I thought had been the skin of Those Below was nothing but thin crystal vambraces and, beneath, the sapling green hue of a wildling.

"I don't get it," I said, shocked. "Why would you disguise yourself as one of them?"

"An excellent question," Rune said. "Answer her," he said to the assailant.

The man coughed. His mouth opened, wider and wider, his eyes bulging, until his jaw cracked as it popped free from its socket. I leapt up with a cry of alarm as a flower stem as thick as my arm burst from the back of his throat and forced its way out, unfurling its bloodied petals as it grew. Leaves spewed from his ears. Roots pushed through the skin of his arms, covering him so completely that within moments there was almost no flesh visible.

"Rune!" I said.

"For once, that wasn't me," he said, equally shaken.

"There's your answer," Marian said. "Even if they failed, whomever sent them wanted to ensure you never suspected what they really were. They would rot without Rune ever figuring out that it wasn't Sotera."

The roots continued to squirm over the wildling's body like a nest of worms. The exhilaration of the chase was slowly being replaced with frustration. With this wildling's death, we had no way to figure out who'd truly been behind this.

And then I noticed the smell, so thick it made my nose itch. So overpowering I couldn't believe I hadn't noticed it before.

I stood, head spinning.

Why had there only been four sent to take on the High King of the Wilds? They had prepared—from the venom that would ensure Rune's quick end, to their disguises—yet they hadn't considered Rune would be guarded. That meant they'd been sure, or assured, that the High King would be alone. That the High King had been *ordered* to be without the protection of one whom might give them trouble.

"What is it, Val?" Rune asked. "What are you thinking?"

The nauseatingly sweet scent of the flower stoked my fury. "I want you to assemble the Council of Loam."

RUNE, General Forcheck, and I stepped into the Council auditorium less than an hour later, sidestepping waterfalls trickling from the holes in the ceiling. All five other Council members were already assembled around the table. Rune had demanded an emergency meeting, and despite the members' insistence that they knew better than him, they also knew better than to dismiss a command from their High King.

Rune suspected what I did, but he didn't know what I was going to do. I felt stupid. Betrayed. I'd been tricked by the spy from Bendeti and truly believed that Rune could convince the other Lords to give him a chance. And now the Council, the one who was supposed to be on Rune's side, the one I should have opposed from the very start, had moved against him. This was what I got for being kind.

When would I learn?

"Is there a reason we've been assembled with little warning?" Lord Rynen said haughtily. "I don't recall an event requiring our input."

"Why did *she* return?" Erena snarled at me, the leeches on her face writhing. "We didn't summon her."

Verily was looking at the floor, and Yava hummed a soft tune, staring at the light glinting off the waterfalls. All I could focus on was Lord Hallas. She looked at me as though she knew a secret just the two of us shared. "I distinctly remember telling you, girl, to stay away from the High King. Yet here you are, his faithful pet, trailing in his wake. Perhaps an appropriate punishment for disobeying us is in order."

My vision turned red as lily scent filled the air. Lord Hallas straightened as I stormed toward her. Her hand went to the short sword on her waist. "What's this? Does the mongrel have an issue with righteous discipline—"

I held out a hand toward her heart gem. Lord Hallas backed up, snarling. "Don't you dare come any closer, witch—"

With fury sharpening my focus, I pulled with my magic harder than ever before. Lord Hallas seized. She coughed blood. Then she collapsed onto the table with an ominous thud, dead. The front of her coat bled in the shape of her heart gem, as though I'd reached into her chest and tore it out.

Erena screeched. Lord Rynen drew his sword. "What is the meaning of this! Rune, what has your...your beast done?"

Rune looked at me as though he'd never seen me before.

"You knew it, didn't you," I said. "You knew she sent those assassins."

"Assassins?" Verily said quietly.

"How strange, from within, from without," Yava hummed. "And now forever gone. Fly away little bird, fly away." His gaze turned lucid. "I'm afraid this Council is at an end. I will continue my travels, wondering at how spectacularly you failed, my High King."

He drifted out.

"If you think we're going to stand for this, then you're wrong," Erena snarled. She gestured to Lord Hallas's body and then spat at Rune's feet. "Destruction and damnation on the House of the Fallen Star. Rotten before, and rotten until the end."

General Forcheck half drew her sword. "If you wish to join Lord Hallas, by all means, continue insulting your High King's family line. You were chosen for the Council to *give* counsel, not to air past personal grievances."

Erena backed up, fear in her eyes. "Like crows to carrion, bloodthirsty, all of you. Sotera may be the enemy of the Wilds, but I'm sure she doesn't do this! You are finished."

She swept out after Yava.

"We warned you what would happen if you crossed us," Lord Rynen said. "Now you have no one. The Council of Loam and our support is ended just as soon as it began."

He slowly retreated, still wary. "I would have followed you, High King Rune. But until you take care of *that*," he jerked his head at me, "until you figure out what it means to rule the Wilds and retain the power you so desperately covet, you'll be on your own."

"Then not much has changed," Rune said coldly.

"As you say." Lord Rynen gave a final bow and then stepped out.

General Forcheck limped over to Lord Hallas's body. She poked it a couple times with her cane. "She sent assassins, you say?"

"Four of them, with venomed darts and dressed to look like Those Below," Rune said, still looking a bit stunned.

"That's incredibly crude and ineffective. No wonder she only stayed a minor Lord and never challenged Mordecai and Jezaline. Apparently couldn't defend herself worth a damn, either." General Forcheck gave me an appraising look. "Though against what you can do, I'm not sure that's possible."

"What Val did was incredibly stupid," Rune said.

The embers of my anger were stoked again. "I just *saved* you."

"In the worst way possible," he snapped. "The Council was designed to complement my rule, and in less than a month, one of them has already been put to death with no investigation into their wrongdoings, and no trial. That can't be the way I rule, not if I want things to be different."

I could only stare at him. "Yes, because the Council of Loam worked out so well for the past High King. You knew it was her, as much as I did. So you'd do what? Come here and give her a slap on the wrist while you brought together evidence? And in the meantime, she would have continued plotting against you. *They* don't care about ruling properly. *They* only care about getting their revenge and seeing themselves with more power."

"And that's why they're not High King!" Rune said. "Because they don't have those restraints!"

"I want a better way as much as you do, but those ideals are going to get you killed! If not by your own Council, then Sotera. Where's the Rune that would never allow a single slight against him, that would do *anything* to protect what he had?"

Rune straightened up, his expression darkening. "Do you truly want him back?"

Of course I didn't. Rune's savagery had always been a problem for me, one I'd slowly come to accept as a necessary evil. When had I taken over that role for him?

Rune filled my silence. "It was clear from my reaction that you undermined my authority. So not only do I not have a Council, but the survivors will think I'm weak. You've made things worse than ever."

When put in such stark terms, he was right. I'd acted almost without thought, something I prided myself on never doing. In hunting through the Wilds or working with Rune, there was no room for stupid mistakes. Now I'd made a colossal one, and I had no idea why.

"General Forcheck, send Idwal and Pitius to make sure the other Council members—the former Council members—get back to their territories," Rune said.

Then he left before I could muster up an explanation for my actions, an explanation I didn't have. General Forcheck gave me a look that bordered on disappointment.

"I only wanted to protect him," I said lamely.

"Sure you did," she said. "And you *did*. But every choice, even if it's the right one, has consequences."

Those stinking lilies Lord Hallas loved so much had already begun overgrowing her body. Thankfully, their petals draped over her face so I didn't have to see the horrified expression etched there in death. "What should I have done instead?"

General Forcheck leaned on her cane with a sigh. "Truthfully? I don't know. There are parasites in every host. The moment I discovered Lord Hallas's treachery, I imagine I would have done the same as you. But I suppose that's why I'm not High King, either, and now have Rune's dilemma."

"I won't let him die," I said fiercely. "I'll do anything to stop others who couldn't care less about him or these Wilds."

"Remember my words: don't get so caught up in collecting power that you forgo mercy," General Forcheck warned. "Maybe these Wilds can't be fixed, but Rune has to try. I don't think he has any other choice. If he does nothing, they remain as terrible as they've always been, and if he fights to make things better, then he surely risks his life. There's no other way around that."

There had to be a third option, a line between savagery and naïve contentment. Maybe I'd started to draw it. There was Rune on one side, the High King trying to be different than his predecessors. And me, his blade, on the other, doing the dirty work in the shadows. Bloodying my hands to maintain his righteous image others felt more comfortable following. Could I do that, even if Rune hated me for it? Moreover, had I already started?

"What do you think will happen because of...of me?" I asked.

"We'll just have to weather the storm and see," General Forcheck answered.

I didn't feel the least bit better. I didn't deserve to.

I could hear Rune and Marian speaking beneath the arches as I left the auditorium.

"—useless I was," Marian whispered fervently. "*That's* what I'm talking about. You rely on me like you used to and look where that almost got you! No, never again."

"Marian—"

"Your silver tongue won't convince me this time. A week. That's all. You can help me, or not. I don't care."

Rune watched her as she limped off. His expression mirrored how I felt, like the world was unraveling at the seams.

TWENTY-TWO

I knew what I had to do. The realization was a terrible, gnawing certainty I couldn't escape. Either it would work or it would fail spectacularly. And Rune, if he knew, would surely try to stop me.

So I wouldn't tell him.

Stepping lightly thanks to my training with Pitius, I snuck around the camp, gathering all I needed. There was no telling how long I would be away. The most unlikely scenario was that it would only be for a night. If things went well—or terribly, depending on one's perspective—I wouldn't be coming back for a while, if ever again.

I tucked the last bit of food into the side of my pack and zipped it up. The last thing I needed was a dress, something I hadn't realized would be so difficult to find.

There was rarely, if ever, time for parties or celebrations among the wildlings, especially now. The only thing that halfway resembled a dress I knew were the single-piece shifts the girls who worked gathering food wore. While they slept on,

I found a girl about my size and smuggled her mostly clean shift along with the rest of my things.

The surrounding sentries were too focused on spotting anyone trying to come in rather than out, so with my plunder safety tucked away, I skirted them and headed deep into the trees.

"Erebus," I whispered. "Come to me."

The leaves stirred as they caught my words, and the wind spirited them away, hopefully to wherever he was. While I waited, I tried convincing myself that I wasn't stupid; that in fact I was being wholly, uncharacteristically selfless.

In some ways, Rune was too proud to acknowledge when he needed help. Convincing him to even request an alliance from Joshua rather than kill him had been as difficult as any fight. And as snake venom filled Rune's veins while we were in Mog Moren, I swore he was prepared to die rather than ask me to save him.

We didn't have the luxury of his pride anymore. Not now that I'd royally screwed up and disbanded any help the Council of Loam might have been willing to offer. Rune needed Xander and every single ally he had left. He needed pressure off him. Hopefully what I was doing would accomplish both.

A smear of darkness richer than the rest peeled off from my elongated shadow. Undergrowth rustled and Erebus's jumbled, hulky form of thistle, branch, and discarded foliage appeared. He growled in greeting.

"I need you to take me to the coast," I said. I unfurled a map, one that Rune and General Forcheck had been using to discuss possible places the Undersea might invade. I tapped one of the marked locations closest to us. "Here."

Erebus gave another growl, this one of question. I didn't look away from the sheen of his obsidian eyes. "I need you to do that for me. Please."

I waited, breath held, while Erebus debated. I hadn't pestered Raquel on the specifics of whether Erebus choosing me meant I had the power to make him obey. It didn't matter if I controlled him, as long as he helped, and as long as he left after. I wouldn't force him to potentially die alongside me.

Erebus lowered a hulking shoulder. Exhaling a sigh of relief, I tenderly clawed over the bramble of his legs, buttoned the front of my coat, and gripped the root reins just behind his neck.

"Go," I breathed.

I didn't need to direct him. I don't think I could have, fast as he was going. The breath was stolen from my lungs within seconds of him taking off. My eyes streamed with tears as the air carried them away. I hunkered down close to the sweet scent of mint leaf along his back and made sure that, no matter what, I didn't let go.

After minutes that felt like hours, Erebus slowed. He growled. *We're here*, he seemed to say.

I slid off his back and took in the sound of crashing waves and the smell of salt. The beach was rockier than I'd hoped, but I spied a promising tide pool close by. Just down the shore, seals with slick silver and gold coats had cast themselves onto the rocks, watching me with beady black eyes. Soon-to-be witnesses to my foolhardiness.

"You can go," I said to Erebus. "Thank you."

Instead of vanishing, Erebus merely sank deeper into the trees' shadows. I could tell there was no point trying to make him change his mind. Besides, I was nervous, and him being here helped.

I dropped my backpack on the rocks and pulled out the thin shift dress before stripping off my old clothes. The cold air on my skin made me shiver. Other than the smell of salt, my frigid surroundings reminded me of the Below and the many nights I spent curled beneath a ratty blanket, teeth chattering against the cold.

Breathe, I thought as more horrible memories rose unbidden in my mind. *You are here. You are free. For now.*

For now, yes. If things went right, I'd be trading my freedom for a prison equally bitter.

The dress I'd stolen couldn't hope to match the luxury of the one Sotera had forced me to wear the first time I'd met with Bendeti, but hopefully it'd be enough. I slipped it on, then used a small vial of dew gathered at midnight to make my lips glisten, and smeared petals of blood rose to give my cheeks a faint blush. I intertwined jeweled shells scoured from the shoreline into my hair, making sure every one of them glittered in the moonlight.

My fingers felt as dexterous as hot dogs while I worked. I was no good at this. I was a creature built for combat—all sharp edges and cutting words—not comfort and desire. I had never tried to weaponize my looks, but I would now. And I imagined, if used right against Bendeti, allure could be as sharp as any blade.

Lastly, I strapped my sheathed knife around my leg. It made me feel a little less helpless, at least. I stuffed my old clothes away and quickly went to work on the second part of my plan, refusing to give myself time to double-guess. In the Wilds, I gathered incensed root, cut so that it leaked its over-powering scent—holly branches and salmon berry—and, out of spite, a single leaf of night blush. Not concentrated enough to kill, but if Bendeti was involved with Vanesi, too, he'd know I remembered.

I lashed all this together. I couldn't cast everfire, but I could add one more ingredient that should draw him up.

The tide pool was formed like a large audience chamber, with smooth arched rock enclosing three sides and a dark drop off at the ocean's edge. The water reached halfway up my calves. My mobility wouldn't be great, but it was close enough to entice him, and I couldn't risk meeting any deeper.

For my final ingredient, I cut my forearm deep enough to bleed well. I dribbled the blood over my offering and then dropped the entire thing into the deep.

Lastly, I used a little of my magic—being sure to save some —to craft a crystal throne, one befitting a future queen. I settled in it, feet still in the surf, to wait.

So much waiting. So much time to reconsider and understand how poor of a choice I was making.

An hour passed. Two. A bar of pink settled on the horizon. My feet had long gone numb, and my ears were filled with the endless crashing of waves against rock.

I'd miscalculated. Or overestimated my importance to Sotera and Bendeti. I had fought their plans every step of the way, so of course he wouldn't be keen to meet now.

Then I saw four shark fins slicing through the water toward me, two on either side flanking a center fin.

King Bendeti rode his Orca chariot to the lip of the tide pool where he stepped off, his short, stalk-eyed seneschal Melik at his side. Bendeti gave me a long smile, as a barracuda might give to wounded prey.

"Welcome, King Bendeti," I said, inclining my head. "Welcome back to the Wilds."

"What a lovely welcome it is," King Bendeti said. "And what a terrible mistake you've made."

TWENTY-THREE

Bendeti gestured to the half-dozen lobster-armored guards he'd brought. "Bring her to me."

They surged toward me. Without lifting a hand from the arm of my throne, I coaxed spiked crystal from beneath the water to cut them off, presenting them with a deadly path forward. I returned Bendeti's cold smile, trying to exude the grace and power of a ruler, trying to convince him that picking me was the right choice.

"I didn't bring any refreshments, I'm afraid," I said. "But if you're really hungry, keep approaching and get your fill."

"Impertinence!" Melik squawked. I'd forgotten how grating his voice was.

"I'm here to talk first," I said. "We can get to the other matters later."

"Leave her. For now." Bendeti waved his hand again, and Melik, with great reluctance, threw himself beneath the waves. He returned a moment later with a coral-covered chair, crowned with spiral-top shells and pearls inlaid at the seams. Bendeti settled himself neatly into it, peering at me through the points of my spiked wall. "I would enjoy clearing the air, my once-betrothed. Especially without the Empress of dust and stone hovering over us."

I frowned. "That was a bit rude. I thought you were allies."

"Allies, not friends. She claws her way toward a prize that isn't rightfully hers. Even Rune, as much as I detest the brat, more deserves his place in the Wilds." King Bendeti took a goblet filled with seawater Melik offered and swirled it. "But she does have things I want. You, for instance."

"Not anymore. I'm nobody's pawn, and especially not Sotera's."

Bendeti smiled against the lip of the goblet. "So you think. What is it you wished to accomplish here? Surely you understand I won't be letting you go, not when you so willingly come to me."

"I have a request."

"This meeting is very one-sided. But I'm patient and magnanimous."

He was neither of those things, but I'd let him believe it. "I want to see a member of your kingdom, the one named Zuri. I want to make sure she's alive."

Bendeti's expression was all delight, and I couldn't help feeling I'd played right into his hands.

"I told you, Melik," he said. "I knew it would pay to prepare her. Go fetch her."

"As your Lord commands." Melik bowed and, with a watery plop, sank into the deep. He emerged far sooner than I expected, tugging whom I assumed was Zuri on the end of chains magicked to resist rust. Melik secured one end of the chains to Bendeti's chair. Zuri shivered as he stroked her cheek and then rested a hand on her back. "As you can see, she's completely unharmed."

I stood and approached the spiked wall. Some of the iridescent scales along Zuri's shoulders had been ripped away. A short, mermaid-like tail stuck out from her lower back, shivering in a way that radiated up to her webbed ears. Her seashell blue eyes were dulled with malnourishment, and they looked at me, a stranger, with complete desperation. As though whatever I could do to her couldn't possibly be worse than what she'd already endured.

"Are you all right?" I asked Zuri.

"As good as she can be," King Bendeti answered. "I've done as you've asked. What do you have to offer me?"

I pretended to continue examining Zuri while trying to get the jumbled mess of my hastily concocted plan straight. "Rune still owes you a favor."

"That he does. Unfortunately, he's not been very forthcoming in fulfilling that."

"Then I'll do it for him."

I stood taller to try to make myself feel more in control than I actually was. "I will marry you, on the condition that you absolve Rune of the favor he owes, stop conspiring with his enemies, and let Zuri go."

King Bendeti looked amused at my proclamation. "It seems I get nothing."

"You get me."

"Which I already have. If not from Sotera, then Rune. You jumped ahead. My favor from him was that he hand you over to me."

Water sloshed as I took a startled step back. "He wouldn't do that. He doesn't have the right."

"Neither did Sotera." Bendeti's smile was cruel. "She was prepared to give you away to secure her own goals. Can you honestly say Rune wouldn't do the same if it meant helping protect all he's fought for?"

Rune would never. Bendeti was playing mind games, that was all. Making me forget my reason for coming here.

"You think you have power over me," Bendeti went on. "But you do not. You wave your sword around and summon some crystal. But the sea dissolves all, and even the Wilds tremble beneath the power of the waves."

"Will you take me as your queen or not?" I demanded, barely keeping my voice from shaking. "Will you forgo your alliance with Those Below and make one of the Wilds?"

"And what of Mother Mal?"

Of course his spy would have handed that information over to him by now. I'd guessed that, yet still it was a struggle to force a shrug. "What about her? She's a senile, old wildling who gives bad advice. Are you saying you're afraid of her?"

"What is her treachery? What weapon has Rune found, and how does he plan to use it against me?"

"He hasn't found any weapons—"

"The wounds Sotera found in the one called Vanesi say otherwise. Has he been talking with the humans? How long after we came to an agreement would it take for Rune to stab me in the back?"

My thin plan was being washed away like sand under a tidal wave. "Will you accept me as your queen or—"

"I will not." Bendeti stood, casting his goblet into the depths. "Since you won't answer, let me tell you what *I* know. You're desperate. You have no intention of marrying me, or if you did it would only be to murder me and take my throne. Perhaps Sotera asked you to do that. Perhaps you thought of it yourself."

Melik's stalky eyes leered at me. The water around my feet suddenly felt impossibly heavy, as though Bendeti had commanded it to hold me in place.

"Or maybe you thought to kill me here," Bendeti went on.

"You're never truly defenseless. But unfortunately for you, I anticipated that treachery, too."

More of Bendeti's guards appeared on the shore behind me, cutting off my escape. The next second, the crystal spikes I'd summoned collapsed. I'd been so focused on Bendeti that I hadn't seen the hundreds of nearly transparent crabs gnawing away at the base.

"You're not Sotera's Princess of Glass, nor will you be my Queen of Waves," Bendeti said. "You're coming to the Undersea as a prisoner. You're more valuable that way. Take her—"

I withdrew the dark, dead egg Xin had given me and smashed it into the water between us, where it began to spread like spilled ink. Just a small stain at first, but rapidly growing until I was sure the entirety of the pool would be covered. Bendeti laughed.

"Perhaps if we were underwater that might have obscured your escape. But your trickery won't save you here—"

The first of his guards touched the ink. He shuddered, armor clacking, before collapsing face down in the shallows. Bendeti stopped laughing.

I drew my knife from its sheath and sprang around everyone as they moved in a panic. A guard tried to block my path, but his spear was too cumbersome and I was already too close. I sank my knife into the soft part of his neck and kept moving. A couple guards failed to escape the spreading poison in time and collapsed, dead.

"Protect your king, you idiots! Pile your bodies to stop the spread—" Melik's screeching voice grated my ears, before he too fell mercifully silent.

"You deceitful bitch!"

I ducked, and Bendeti's corral-encrusted sword whipped

just over my head. Sea water splashed my tongue and stung my eyes. "What dark deal have you made?"

Sliver was already in my hand by the time I darted around him and reached Zuri. Her eyes were wide with fear. "Hurry!"

Not daring to look at how close the poison was, I severed the manacles around her wrists, helped her to standing. "Stay close to me," I said.

Most of Bendeti's guards lay lifeless in the shallows. Bendeti himself stood atop Melik's corpse just above the water. The loathing in his expression told me that whatever I'd done to his subjects, he'd do to me ten times worse.

Zuri clenched my arm so much it hurt. "The poison is nearly touching us!"

Like I didn't already know that. Praying to the gods of the Wilds and humans alike, I took the second orb of clear water Xin had gifted me and smashed that at our feet.

Moments before touching us, the inky poison diverted, circling our feet but not moving any closer. When I took a step, the circle remained intact and the water cleared before me.

"We have to get out of the water," I told Zuri.

"I will tear the Wilds and the Below in two for what you've done," Bendeti seethed as I passed. "There will be no place you can run, no hole deep enough you can crawl into."

Bendeti's guards still waited on shore as we waded closer. I worked to keep hold of Sliver and Zuri.

"What will you do?" Zuri whispered.

"Just stay close. I'll figure it out." I hoped.

Zuri clutched me tighter. Her gaze flicked between Sliver and the spears Bendeti's guards held. "I don't mean to doubt you, but their weapons are *much* bigger—"

There was a splash in the black water in front of us, followed by blooming warmth at my side. Bendeti was smiling triumphantly when I looked back at him.

Zuri sagged against me. An enormous gash in her side, where Bendeti's thrown sword must have cleaved, spilled blood into the clear water at our feet.

"Hold them when they get there," Bendeti said to his guards. He moved his hands, and to my horror, a clear path of water dispelled the thinning poison between him and the shore. "I will deal with both of them personally."

The water seemed to push against me as I sloppily picked up my feet, spilling more of Zuri's blood in the process. Semi-solid ground was just ahead. If I could just make it...

My boots sank into the sand as I lugged Zuri free from the tide pool. I hastily raised Sliver as the guards closed in. Even at full strength, it'd be difficult to take on all six. At such a severe disadvantage I'd be lucky to down one before Bendeti reached me.

Suddenly, the guard nearest the Wilds vanished with barely a scream. From within the trees, I heard the crunch of teeth through armor and the guttural choke of a throat being ripped out. Erebus growled. The other guards looked frantically around, buying me enough time to drop Zuri and slide Sliver between the crustacean shell of the nearest one. I sliced at another, but by now they'd figured out to stay away from the shadows the Wilds cast and quickly surrounded me. Bendeti was panting with delight as he emerged onto the shore.

"Blade. Now," he demanded.

I stabbed at the nearest guard. Missed. I clearly missed. And yet they stiffened as though Sliver had run straight through their heart and then slumped over, dead.

Rune stood in his place, expression full of such fury that it made my stomach knot. Marian and a dozen other armed wildlings stood at his back.

"King Bendeti," Rune said. "I guess you got your meeting

with me after all. Now I have to ask what you're doing on the shore of my Wilds. I hope you have a good answer."

Bendeti didn't seem the least bit frightened at being caught ashore. If anything, he seemed...happy.

"I knew meeting with your human pet would draw you out," he said. "You're nothing if not predictable, Rune."

"High King Rune, thanks to you. Now I'm here. And now I'll ask you to leave. Unless you still believe to call upon that favor I owe, though you and I both know I never had any intention of honoring it."

"I mean to take much more than that," Bendeti said. "If only you had been the malleable puppet you were supposed to be."

The deeper waters just behind Bendeti started to churn, as though a school of fish was being corralled against the surface.

Marian saw the danger at the same time I did. "Everybody get back!"

An enormous splash cut her off. Two slick, long-neck heads shot up from beneath the waves, serpents of the yawing depths that only months ago I wouldn't have believed existed.

I could have stood without any problem within the slits of their orbed eyes. Blade-like fins ran down their narrow heads, shelled scales interlocking into an impenetrable defense. Their nostrils flared, drinking in our scent.

"*Kill*," Bendeti commanded, pointing at Rune.

I was running to reach Rune, stupidly thinking that somehow my paltry sword and I could do anything against these monstrosities.

Brave idiot that Rune was, he stoically faced down the pair of jaws dropping toward him. I saw his lips move and felt a word of power in a language I couldn't hope to understand tremble through me.

A beast of the Wilds erupted from the trees. It was so enormous it had no discernable shape, as though the land itself had gotten to its feet and lumbered to do its King's bidding. It blotted out the moon and sent a tremor through the ground with every single step.

The beast caught the first serpent in its mouth and, with a violent twist, snapped its neck. Purple blood beaded the sand at my feet.

The second serpent changed direction to this new threat and within moments had encircled it, squeezing so tightly that if the beast had lungs they surely would have burst. The Wild beast scratched to tear it off, casting seashells like hail. The pair of them went tumbling onto the shore and then splashed into the waves, snarling.

Rune gripped my arm and hauled me toward the trees. "Now we run. Unless you were enjoying his company."

Still shocked at his appearance, still shocked at all that was happening, I could only manage, "I've overstayed my welcome."

"So it would seem."

Rune stumbled in the sand as his beast took another blow. And then we were all fleeing deep into the Wilds as the earth rumbled and Bendeti howled with rage.

CHAPTER

TWENTY-FOUR

We didn't go far enough inland for me to feel safe from either Bendeti's serpents or the angry churn of the sea should he decide to try drowning us all again.

But by the time we entered the large subterranean chamber beneath a hill covered in boughs of pine, I could tell we wouldn't be going any farther for a while. Rune had been wavering while we walked the path. And as the other wildlings dispersed to their illuminated cubbies within the jewel-covered walls, or to the low-hanging vines that made up a second floor, he stumbled once more.

Marian caught him, whispered something fierce into his ear that I could only make out part of, "—overdid it. Again."

"That's not possible." Rune's words came out a little weak; though every time a wildling approached, he straightened up, shrugged her off. "I'm perfectly fine."

"Of course you are," Marian said dryly. "Now lean on me for support again, Your Majesty."

A corner of the hill had been taken over by a colossal

flower. Rune approached, and one side of its petals, colored like blood-stained snow, peeled open to let him in.

"A moment's rest, for all of us," Rune said. I could feel his piercing glare, even from across the room. "Then we will talk."

As the petals closed, I half-carried Zuri to a makeshift bed and laid her down. Her skin was damp with sweat, which I hoped didn't precede the onset of infection. Her eyelids fluttered as she fought to stay conscious.

"This'll ease the pain." A wildling handed me a small pitcher plant with molasses-like liquid inside. I dribbled a little into Zuri's mouth and her breathing evened as she fell into sleep. There was commotion nearby. Wildlings parted as Xander, face flushed as though he'd sprinted here, pushed his way through.

"You got her!"

He knelt beside the bed, petting Zuri's salt-crusted arm. Tears gathered at the corners of his eyes. "I can't believe... I thought she was lost to me forever."

"And I thought you left," I said.

"Rune caught up to me," Xander said, a note of bitterness in his voice. "Cut me off from going to Bendeti myself, moments before he learned you had."

I remembered the fury in Rune's eyes as the petals had closed after him and shuddered. If he was still angry now, how furious must he have been when he learned I'd left him? "How did he know where I'd gone?"

Xander shrugged. "I suppose you two think alike."

I was grateful he was too fixated on Zuri to see my frown.

Xander turned as Marian approached. "She's still bleeding, can you heal—"

Marian's slap echoed through the hill. Xander reeled back, cheek stinging red.

"That's the least of what you deserve," Marian spat.

"Because of you, Val nearly killed herself rescuing Zuri. Because of Val, Rune had to show his vulnerability. All because you couldn't *bear* to be without your dear sweet love."

Xander touched his cheek as though she'd drawn blood. "If Rune had gone after her earlier, then—"

I caught Marian's hand as she drew back for another strike. "Going after Bendeti was my choice," I said. "I had my reasons, and getting Zuri was a bonus. You want to blame anyone, blame me."

"Don't worry, I'm already doing that plenty," Marian snarled.

I was sure. "Berate me later. Right now, Zuri needs help."

Marian ripped her wrist out of my hand. She knelt and got to work closing the worst of Zuri's injury. Bendeti's sword had cleaved the flesh deep, and whatever magic he'd charmed it with had left barnacles encrusted along the edges of the opening, worsening the bleeding.

"I hope you at least made Bendeti squirm," Marian said.

I recalled the fear on Bendeti's face as his soldiers and seneschal died around him. The unbridled loathing he directed toward me, the girl he thought once to control, the one who had dealt him such a terrible blow.

"A little," I admitted. To Xander, I said, "Don't forget what we did for you. Rune needs you to help him, not run away."

Xander nodded mutely, fingertips still resting against his stinging cheek. I hoped Marian's anger and having his beloved here had driven the point home. I hoped. Much like my actions against the Council, I had to believe that what I'd done wasn't as disastrous as it felt. Our dysfunctional little family was back together, but hopefully less fractured than before.

Maybe what you did was wrong, a traitorous voice in my head whispered. *Maybe letting Xander go would have been easier. That way, at least he'd be safe during the downfall.*

"I'm going to check on Rune," I said to silence it.

"You may want to wait," Marian said. "He's exhausted and furious. Especially at you."

I bet. But the longer I put off talking to him, the larger the conversation would loom in my mind, and the more it'd seem I was hiding. Better to face him now while I had a little righteous anger of my own.

I dropped my knife and backpack off in an opening in the wall and scrubbed my hands clean until I'd gotten rid of all the blood from Zuri and Bendeti's soldiers. I found a private spot to strip off the dress and changed back into my regular clothes.

As I approached Rune's room, a single petal curled open, as though expecting me. My heart thudded as I stepped inside, and when it closed behind me, I tried to ignore how I felt: Trapped. Skittery. Nervous. I drew myself up. I had done what was necessary. This didn't just involve Rune. It involved me as well, and I had tried to deal with it in the best way I knew how.

Rune sat across from his bed in a chair of petals molded to his body, watching me. There were only few hovering fireflies overhead. They reflected off his glowing eyes, making them feel as though they were searing into me even more.

"Come to make excuses?" he said.

I stepped away from the door. I wouldn't cower, not in front of him. "Never."

"Good. I'm not in the mood to hear them. Imagine how I felt when I sought you out, only to discover that you were gone. Did you consider, for even a moment, what went through my mind—"

He bit his words off, composed himself. "I thought we'd moved past you running off and doing your own thing without telling me."

"We agreed that I don't need your permission," I said. "I'm your ally, not your soldier. This wasn't about you."

"And yet I got involved. Again." His presence filled the room as he leaned forward, but I found myself drawn rather than repelled. A moth fluttering closer to a flame. "This is about trust."

"You trust me."

"But you don't trust *me*. I don't blame you. I've given many little reason to, you least of all. But still I thought, still I'd *hoped*..."

"You needed Xander," I said. "I needed to take care of Bendeti."

"And if you'd *trusted* me, you'd have found that I was working on a plan to deal with both. Though I have to say your method was far more effective. I do hope you struck a little fear into his soggy heart."

I was temporarily lost for words. He'd kept quiet while Xander had beseeched him for help, while other wildlings had begged him to save their loved ones. He hadn't given them false hope that he could save anyone, meanwhile he'd been planning to rescue all he could?

"You were?" I managed.

Rune seemed pleased that he'd startled me. "Are you shocked?"

Very. I'd often—for good reason—thought him callous and uncaring. I'd almost forgotten that I wasn't the only one who'd changed in the month we'd been apart.

Rune used my silence to unfold himself from the petal and stand. "Your lack of trust is not what bothers me, though. I don't know the extent of what you meant to do, but I can guess that, had the first part of your plan gone through, you'd be on your way to the palace of the Undersea to prepare to be Bendeti's bride. You'd have married him to get what you wanted, wouldn't you?"

"Bendeti wasn't going to marry me. I was going to be his prisoner."

"All's the pity to him. He missed the chance to have a blade as a wife, someone to cut him as easily as she cut her enemies."

"Is that what you think I do to you?" I whispered.

"Don't you?"

I lifted my chin as he drew nearer. "I don't need to defend my choices. My plan would have worked."

"Maybe," Rune's voice was soft. "And yet it made me see clearly, probably more clearly than ever before, just what I've done. The Wilds and my family have forged me into a cruel leader, Val. I am not kind. I find it difficult to trust. I'm not sure I remember how, and I have extended that flaw to you and those closest to me. But I want to be better."

My throat had closed so much I could barely get the words out. My heart thundered in my ears. "Why?"

"Why?" His tone was laced with anger, though somehow I knew it wasn't directed at me. "Because though I've gotten what I wanted through fear and subjugation, that, it seems, is not enough. I still lash out. My closest friends are willing or trying to leave me. I make promises that all the power in the Wilds can't help me keep. I am walking on a knife's edge.

"And you... It would seem you still detest or fear me so much that you would marry an enemy rather than trust me enough to see things through—"

I didn't remember closing the space between us, only that my lips were suddenly on his, hungry and greedy. This was no poison-induced kiss, and yet I felt more out of control than I ever had when poison ran through my veins. I had no excuses. Nothing I could say to deny why I was doing this, other than it was what I wanted.

Rune had seized with surprise the moment my lips touched his, and for one horrible moment, I thought I'd misread everything, that all his furtive looks I'd assumed had been filled with craving had only been my fantasy.

Then his mouth took mine, and he was deepening the kiss, consuming me. He scooped me up, and I felt the plush press of the petal wall on my back as he shoved me against it. He turned me, moved me, so easily, as though I weighed nothing, as though I was something delicate to be cherished, something he had to restrain himself not to break.

I gasped as his lips pressed against my neck, trailing kisses to the base of my throat. He moved me again to get another angle, but it was my turn and I resisted, my lips on him, my hands on him. Rune resisted my touch at first, but I persisted. I showed him how to surrender, that it was okay to give up, and at last he relented, letting me draw my lips over his bare collarbone where his shirt slipped down and then back to his lip, his gorgeous lips. Our teeth clacked together with the force of our mouths meeting one another. He pressed me back more firmly against the petal wall. His kisses were all taking, but I was okay to give.

His hands went up the back of my shirt. His warm fingers left streaks of fire across my ribs, my spine, moving to my hips. I pressed my hands against his chest, right above his heart gem, trying to draw every kiss from him—and then draw more. Power. Magic. My hands were alive with it, dancing on the tips of my fingers.

Rune gave a gasp, not of pleasure, but of pain.

"No!" I cried.

My butt hit the ground as Rune dropped me and stepped back, clutching his heart. My own heart felt as though a knife had gone straight through it. I scrambled up, reaching toward him before drawing back, realizing that my hands were what had hurt him.

"I didn't mean to—I forgot that I—we can't—"

"And yet we could, and yet we have," Rune said.

There was need behind the pain in his eyes. "Say the word and I'll stop. Tell me this is craziness, and I'll believe you."

"Of course it is! I nearly killed you, Rune!"

He rubbed at his chest, devilish grin returning. It was a grin that brokered a challenge. "It'll take more than that. You'll notice I have a thing for death. Bringing it. Avoiding it. Flirting with it."

My next protest was cut off by Rune's mouth. I kissed him back but fought to keep my hands off him, clutching tightly at the wall. I had to control myself. *Must* control myself.

But there was no control, and we were soon tangled in each other again, arms wrapping one another. Only this time it was Rune pulling away, giving a little gasp of ecstatic agony as he did. My palms were glowing.

Neither of us moved, our faces inches apart, drinking each other in. I wondered if he felt as I did: now that the itch had been scratched, did it feel inflamed or tempered? Like me, he was probably thinking about the consequences of what we'd done.

My voice was barely a whisper. "Are you all right?"

"Of course I'm—" Rune swallowed, reconsidered. "I am... *terrified*."

"That makes two of us."

"Yes... No. No." Rune drew back, and it was like pulling the stitches on a wound that hadn't yet fully closed. He straightened his clothes, smoothed the hair beneath his crown where my fingers had run through.

My face hot, I straightened my own clothes, though I couldn't look at him. I felt as though both of us had revealed a deep, shameful secret, and now that it was out, we couldn't stand to face it anymore.

"Val," Rune started.

"This doesn't change anything," I said before he could start making excuses. I didn't need to hear him say aloud what I already knew: we were inextricably wrong for each other in every way. I couldn't bear it if he did. "This was only some temporary insanity. Right?" My voice cracked. "*Right?*"

The question came out pleading, begging for him to agree. Rune's expression fell, before retracting to the cold detachment I knew. Comfortable. Safe. "I…"

"It's best this way," I said. "For both of us."

I hated how much I wanted to touch him as he stepped closer. "You…" He swallowed. "You're right; it's what's best. You can't like me, Val. And you certainly can't love me. I will only break your fragile human heart."

Each word was a punch in the gut. It was the pain I needed to hear, to remind me just how wrong this was.

Even still, as the petal opened to let me out, I couldn't resist throwing back, "It's not human. And it's tougher than you know."

CHAPTER
TWENTY-FIVE

The next few days passed in dreaded anticipation. Worse than mites crawling on my skin. Worse than walking on thorn-pierced, bare feet.

That terrible anticipation grew every time I heard a rumble in the ground and panicked, thinking it was Sotera, or a flock of birds took flight in the distance and I feared seeing Bendeti's next wave crashing over the Wilds' magic and drowning us. That anticipation grew the worst every time a conversation with Rune diverted from the familiar topics of battle and preparation and uncomfortable silence, filled with too many unspoken things, lingered.

You'd marry an enemy just to escape me?

Wrong. He'd gotten it all wrong. Both of us had. And both of us had too little time and too much pride to address it.

To keep my traitorous thoughts busy, I helped the wildlings pack up the lakeside camp. We moved to one farther south across the Salish Sea, close to where the city of Port Angeles used to be. While others set up new living spaces and cast protective enchantments, a few of us scoured the overgrown streets and the strip of land jutting from the coast where a naval base had once been. We searched through rusted carcasses of beached ferries and picked wild grapes in what had at one time been a vineyard, the wine in their cellars long ago raided by other opportunists.

The new camp was off the ground in trees whose bark flared at the middle like umbrellas to give us platforms, with planks of wood set atop thickened strands of spider's silk bridging between them.

Two days after we arrived, I dropped to the forest floor to get some water and gather eclipse flowers for those still wounded. Near the river, I stumbled across Rune speaking to an unnaturally dark cluster of trees. Whatever was hidden inside the interlocked branches turned its attention to me. My hair stood on end. My heart thudded a panicked rhythm, so fast I thought it would burst with fear.

Then Rune said something to it in a commanding tone. The darkness slowly receded, taking the oppressive pressure along with it.

"We won't be found here," he said, as though he'd known I was there the entire time. "Not for a little while, at least."

All I could do was nod. Rune's lips parted. His face, impossibly, softened.

Then his expression snapped shut again. Guarded. Cold. "Self-loathing doesn't look good on you," he said. "You're morose and sulking, rather than assured in your talents. You blame yourself for all that's happened recently."

"Not all," I said, ignoring how he managed to turn what should be a compliment into an insult. "But most."

"We never spoke about what happened before like we meant to. We were..."

"Distracted?" I offered.

There was a shine in Rune's eyes that even he couldn't

hide, though he seemed a little embarrassed by it. "I was a bit harsh on you before. I understand now what you meant to do with Bendeti. It wasn't your fault."

"I had some blame." Then before I could keep my tongue in check, I said, "But thanks for your magnanimous pardon."

Rune's smirk was all knives. We had both retreated safely back into our prickly shells. All was right.

With barely a goodbye, he left me to internally berate myself for the rest of the day. How difficult was it to speak to one another without aggression? Why did every conversation turn into a game to slip past the other's defenses?

To let off some frustration, I found a spot at the edge of the river where I could be alone and drew Sliver. I worked through sword sequences General Forcheck had been teaching me, my only audience small Nauplins that hovered in the cattails on the other side of the moving water. They had slick, porous skin speckled like leopards' spots, with eyes coated in a filmy lens and needled teeth. I kept my distance and more than once feigned a lunge in their direction. They were skittish, and I knew they'd only attack if they had numbers and felt they could easily take me down. I almost wanted them to try. It'd let off some more stress.

With every stab, I tried to drive away the feel of Rune's lips on mine, and with every parry, I went over again and again why thinking about him was a terrible idea.

The problem was, the more I tried to convince myself how bad an idea it was, the more it seemed I was convinced it was right.

Dark painted the canopy when Marian found me.

"Zuri pulled through. She can speak and says she has something we should know. Figured you'd want to listen in."

I splashed river water on my face, sheathed Sliver, and followed her to the third level of the treetop encampment, to a height that made me dizzy if I stood too close to the edge. I was more grateful than Marian knew about being invited. Not just for new information, but because she'd apparently forgiven me enough for what had happened with Bendeti.

Zuri lay in a chute bed cushioned with petals and trimmed with sandwort. Sunstone embedded in the bark walls cast an even sicklier pallor over her face. Worse was Xander's, drawn and tight like he hadn't slept a moment since she'd returned. He was seated in a corner beside Rune and had intertwined his calloused fingers so tightly they were white.

General Forcheck was there, too. She gave me a toothy grin. "Methinks you found a number of things to fight tonight."

"The others are here, Zuri," Rune said. "Tell us what you know."

A carafe of seawater sat beside Zuri's bed, and she sipped it to remoisten her skin. When she spoke, her voice still came out raspy. "I wasn't allowed out of the cage they kept me in. Sometimes Bendeti would visit me. Sometimes he came just to look, to gloat, I think. Sometimes he'd ask me things. About Rune. About the human—"

"Val," Marian said sharply. "She has a name."

"Val, yes." Zuri licked her dry lips, leaving a fine layer of salt behind. "He wanted to know all about her, especially after returning from the Below. I didn't know anything. I *never* knew anything, but Bendeti didn't care. He'd hurt me when he didn't like the answers I gave him. He'd hurt me just for fun."

Xander made to grab her hand, but Rune's look stopped him. "I'm assuming Bendeti let something important slip."

"Not him, the guards watching me," Zuri said. "They hated me for being with a wildling. They thought me little more than an animal. After Bendeti stopped visiting, they didn't pay much attention to me. There are soft currents that run past my cage, and they carried their words, even if they whispered. They were especially excited the day after Sotera visited."

"Sotera went to the Undersea?" I asked. "After I escaped?"

"Yes. I believe it was after. Bendeti broke off their alliance."

Rune and I shared a look. Not too surprising, since Sotera had been the one to instigate the alliance in the first place. "Because she didn't have me," I guessed.

"No. One of the guards was there when they spoke, as part of her assigned escort. Before she arrived, they caught one of Sotera's spies in Bendeti's kingdom."

"Hardly a reason to end an alliance," General Forcheck said. "It's only natural for allies to keep eyes on each other."

"This spy was trying to steal something," Zuri said. "A piece of Bendeti's crown."

There was a long silence.

"What game is Sotera playing?" General Forcheck said. "Stealing crowns?"

"*Part* of a crown?" Marian said, and Zuri nodded.

"Perhaps a token?" Xander said. "Something she could point to and say, 'I could end you at any moment'? Intimidation could make him want to keep her as a friend rather than an enemy."

"Don't be stupid," Marian said. "Of the two responses to intimidation, cowering or retribution, we all know which one Bendeti would pick. Threatening him would only make Sotera's life harder."

"You two have been awfully quiet," General Forcheck said to Rune and me.

I was thinking of what Mother Mal had warned Rune about. She'd told us from the start that Sotera had been creating a way to control the Wilds, something that supplanted even Rune's power as High King. But Mother Mal had said nothing about needing parts of *other* rulers' crowns to make her plan a reality.

"Zuri, did they say anything about Sotera forging a new crown?" I said.

"Why would she need to do that?" Xander said bitterly. "She's already Empress."

"Only of Those Below, and only for now," Rune said.

"I didn't hear anything like that," Zuri said. She clutched at the tufts of the sandwort, her face fearful. "What could she possibly do with that?"

"She's trying to trap the Undersea, too," I said, and Rune nodded.

"General Forcheck," Rune said. "You know more about the old magics than any of us. Is it possible that a crown forged with a piece of other rulers' crowns could subvert their power?"

"Sounds like you already know the answer, my High King," General Forcheck said. "Someone far older and wiser than me has been giving you that knowledge, I wager."

It was both better and worse news than I'd hoped. It seemed not only was Sotera's plan possible, but she'd been active in trying to see it through. On the other hand, there was no way she could get a piece of Rune's crown without him knowing. And since we hadn't seen much of Sotera or her soldiers lately, it didn't seem likely she'd slipped past us.

Xander had gone gravely white, as though Zuri had died and we were all circling her corpse. "Bendeti could drown Sotera. Why hasn't he?"

"Those Below are stronger than we know," Rune said. "And though she failed one of her plans, the hydra has more than one head. General Forcheck."

"Right." General Forcheck's knees cracked as she stood. "I'll take a small contingent to the Wilds' most vulnerable spots. I suggest you keep some on the coast. Bendeti won't soon forget your slight."

"I imagine not," Rune said wryly. "Seems we're doomed to be buried or drowned. Personally, I wish they'd stop taking their time about it."

His eyes moved to the door. "You're back."

Keen wandered inside. His eyes grazed Zuri. "And so is she. You've been busy since I've been away."

"And what were you doing, exactly?" Rune said.

Keen nodded to me. "That's for her to hear, since it was her request."

"I'll be right back," I said, hastily getting to my feet. It was impossible to ignore Rune's questioning gaze as I hurried after Keen.

Beneath the light of the everfire, I noticed his eyes had dark bags beneath them. There were smudges of dirt across his cheeks he hadn't bothered wiping off, and unless I was imagining it, was he leaning on one leg more heavily than the other?

"I take it you found your way Below?" I asked.

"More than that," Keen said, not sounding the least bit happy about it. "I upheld your request, and then some. If I'd known... But I suppose I should also thank you. So the Mysts could be ready, too."

I wasn't liking the sound of this. "Ready for what?"

"It's easier if I show you. Bring your weapons. Meet me on the forest floor in five minutes. Don't," he met my eyes, "tell anyone other than Rune. There's no sense in starting a panic. Not until we know what to do."

I hated being kept waiting, but I agreed and Keen leapt into the darkness below.

"That sounded ominous."

Rune's voice made my skin prickle. He lounged in the shadows behind me, his gold-red eyes shining. The moment night had fallen, gently glowing leaves had started fluttering down from above, briefly illuminating him as they passed.

I was gawking. Like a preteen with their first crush. "Keen seemed to think it's bad news," I finally said, shaking from my stupor.

"That's just news," Rune said.

"I'm going to find out just how bad. You should come, too."

"If you'd like."

"You're High King. It doesn't matter what I like; it's what's best."

Rune's lips thinned to a capricious line, and I began to entertain the possibility that I wasn't the only one who wasn't sure where we stood. I tried to remind myself that *he* was the one who stopped, no matter that it was at my insistence. If he could keep a leveled head about what we'd done. I could too.

Wood creaked as I shifted my feet. "Rune..."

He pushed off the tree. Glowing leaves outlined his shoulders. "Yes, little fox?"

We've got this out of our system, right? We can keep these callous feelings between us, just as we've always done?

"Meet us below in five," I said and then brushed past him.

I repeated what Keen had asked Rune to do, still not entirely believing it. "You want him to take us back to the human world?"

"Just north of Seattle," Keen said. "There's still some greenery there that Rune's path can lead us to. The Mysts had to do it without fancy magic, so surely he can."

"They're more alert than ever. I'm assuming you have a reason."

"Or else I'd never go there if I could help it, yes."

If Rune had a problem with this, he didn't show it but closed his eyes and began to weave his magic. It took longer than usual, but eventually a path twisted before us. We walked through to the other side and emerged among an ugly, barely alive smattering of trees in the median of an empty highway.

"Sometimes I'm envious of you," Keen said to Rune. "You've saved my legs from hurting quite so much. Quickly. It's not far from here."

We darted across the highway, though we needn't have

worried about being seen. Only people who had refused to move into the city and carved a harsh existence on the edges lived out here. Or runners not under the protection of the governmental convoys making trips for supplies from other cities. Both existences were surefire ways to a shortened lifespan.

Keen led us to what used to be a town but now acted as a barrier the Wilds hadn't yet managed to breach. Seedlings were stuck in growth stains on brick. Roofs had trees punched through them.

I saw the blue glow in the center of the road before I saw the crystal lining the opening.

"I didn't know Sotera had made it this far over," I said in disbelief. "I wonder if the DFA know it yet."

"If they don't, they will soon," Keen said. "Trust me."

I didn't like the sound of that.

Rune summoned root chutes for us to slide down past sharpened crystal and below. I went first, digging my hands into the sides to slow my descent, until even Rune's power diminished beneath the scab of the earth and the roots shriveled up. We got to our feet and continued clambering down steep shelves of rock. The air grew colder. I started picking out faint noises apart from creatures burrowing through the walls or the viscous flow of magma.

I dropped through a hole at the bottom and instinctively pressed my back against the rock wall to keep away from the sudden narrow ledge I'd landed on.

"Hope you're not afraid of heights," Keen said, landing beside me with a smirk.

I squeezed my eyes shut until my breathing didn't come in such tight gasps. "Thanks for the warning."

"Do you recognize where we are?" Rune said.

It took me another moment to get over my vertigo before I

could peer down the hundreds of feet between where we stood and the ground. I realized I *did* know where we were.

"I trained near here." I pointed to the dozens of immense stone columns lined up across a vast underground desert. "The city where Sotera had me use magic is out of sight, but it's not far."

"They look unstable," Rune said. "Was she having you fix them?"

"No. She was forcing me to make soldiers."

Keen had gone pale. He pointed at the nearest column. "I'm assuming that's your handiwork, then?"

I squinted. "I can't tell from this distance."

Keen produced a folded leaf from his sleeve and dabbed a drop of sticky liquid onto the tip of his finger. "Put this in your eye. It won't hurt, and it wears off quickly."

The liquid did sting a little, but when I'd blinked away the blurriness, the columns looked much closer, as though I were viewing them through a telescope.

Figures were lined up at the base of the nearest one. I refocused on the structure of the column itself. It took me a moment to realize that the slender, crystalline offshoots I was seeing sticking out from the sandstone-colored rock were actually bulky arms and legs. Dozens of Those Below had been fused together, like ants stuck in honey, around the column's base.

As I watched, a line of bulkier Those Below moved forward. The one in front was forced to touch the columns. I couldn't hear his scream from here, but I could imagine the anguish as his arm melted like wax and he bled in among the twitching crystalline mass. The next hapless victim tried to back away, but the guards prodded him forward.

"Those are the people Sotera had me work on," I gasped. "The ones she wanted me to make into soldiers."

"And have we actually *seen* any of these monstrous soldiers above?" Rune said.

We hadn't, at least none of the behemoth beings my magic had helped create. I'd assumed Sotera had been gathering them together to form her main army, yet there were so many here I couldn't imagine she'd have any left to fight with.

"I'm guessing those columns continue that way?" Keen pointed to the left, where our ledge ended out of sight. I knew from my time down here the columns did continue that way, for quite a distance.

My eyes drifted up. We hadn't come straight down, but at an angle. If I remembered correctly, the direction the columns went followed the line of the highway straight into Seattle.

Pieces were coming together in my head, and I didn't like the picture they were forming.

"What Sotera's doing doesn't look good," Keen said. "I thought maybe she was using their bodies to fortify the columns."

"She could have just had me do that," I said distantly. "I could have bolstered them directly."

"A better question is, what happens to Those Below you put your magic into, Val?" Rune said.

It took me a moment to retreat from my swirling thoughts. "They grow bigger, bulkier. I basically juice them up so much that, as long as the magic still runs through them, they're ten times stronger."

"And what if they don't survive the process?"

That had happened a couple times, back when Sotera had first ordered me to start. With little experience regulating my magic, I'd pumped too much into my poor victims. One had choked to death, his throat bulking so much it'd crushed his windpipe.

The other had overloaded.

The ensuing explosion and violently cast shards of crystal had injured two guards and half a dozen other prisoners. I'd wound up with deep cuts and lay awake all night, crying as I mentally replayed what I'd done.

"Only you can create those things," Rune said slowly. "But could Sotera release the magic within them?"

It was becoming difficult to think over the terrible possibilities hitting me. She could. I was sure that was within her power.

And with that realization, I understood at last.

"She's doing it again," I said, turning in panic to Rune. "Just like how she collapsed the ground beneath King's Hollow. She's going to destroy the columns."

"And take down Seattle," Rune finished. He appeared stunned. Even for him, someone who had seen and caused his share of violence, the sheer scale of what Sotera had planned seemed almost incomprehensible. The DFA likely had no clue, or they'd be doing something. If nobody was warned, thousands would die. Hundreds of thousands. It would be genocide.

"I have no idea how long until she's done," Keen said grimly. "My guess? Days, maybe. She could use the threat of collapse as a bargaining chip, but..."

"She won't," I said. "This is too much prep just for show."

"Could she do this to the Wilds?" Rune said to me. "Is there somewhere else she could collapse?"

It was difficult to fight through my panic. *Focus, Val.* Focus and adapt. "Possibly. She may not even need to. Once the surface is collapsed, she'll be able to move her soldiers up unimpeded, all while taking out anyone who might oppose her. Including you."

Rune glared down at the steadily moving line of magic-created soldiers. At another catastrophe I'd inadvertently helped create.

"Back up," he said. "Now."

THE FRESH AIR of the surface didn't make me feel better. An iron band with a ticking clock had wrapped around my chest the moment I'd realized what Sotera meant to do, and now it was tightening every second.

I leaned against one of the dead trees, lost in a daze of terrible understanding. This was partly my doing. If Sotera went through with destroying Seattle, and from there the Wilds, I wouldn't be blameless, no matter that I'd been a victim myself.

Still, I didn't have the luxury of pitiful regret. I had to make penance.

I forced myself to focus on the moment; there was still air in my lungs, tight as they were, and strength in my muscles. I wasn't rotting in the ground yet.

"We have to tell Joshua," I said the moment Rune emerged, with Keen close behind.

"The human cutting his way through the Wilds?" Keen scoffed. "Yes, I've heard who's leading that little party. They may be small, but they carry foul magic that poisons everything. Even the Mysts won't go near the northeast Wilds now. Why would you ever want to talk with him?"

Rune was silent, waiting, perhaps, for me to explain.

"He has pull," I said, not willing to get into the specifics of my connection with Joshua. "It's easier to go to him rather than someone in the heart of Seattle. He *has* to believe me."

"Yes, because the last meeting between you two went *so*

well," Rune said. "I can understand why you'd want to try again."

What happened before didn't matter. Not Joshua and my broken relationship, nor the animosity that had festered between us since the moment he'd caught me working with Rune. All of it paled in the face of what we were dealing with. I needed to convince Joshua of that, no matter what.

"I don't know why you're asking me," Rune said. "You'll go speak to him regardless of what I say."

"I want your help," I said.

Conflict raged behind Rune's eyes, one I understood; should he take another chance to make an alliance, as flimsy as it might be, or leave the humans to their fate and remove one more threat?

He was taking so long to answer that it allowed a traitorous thought to enter my head: perhaps he wasn't just deliberating what helping Joshua would mean to the humans. Perhaps he was considering what it would mean to *me*.

"Fine," he said at last. "We'll warn him."

I let out a breath. "Okay, good—"

"But let me be clear," Rune went on, and I stepped away from the tree's branches as the ends sharpened into something that could pierce flesh. "I don't care if he's your stepbrother. Familial bonds mean nothing if they use them against you. If he tries anything, if he's a threat, I *will* kill him. And you won't stop me."

"I know," I said, my conscience unbearably heavy already. "Trust me, I know."

***

I'd rarely seen Rune truly frustrated, but the amount of time it took us to reach Joshua wore his patience thin. Even with the powers of the High King of the Wilds, Joshua must have learned some tricks of his own to keep hidden.

The contingent of DFA soldiers had holed up in a consumed town the greenery had allowed to retain some semblance of its original shape. Keeping to the edges, Rune and I skirted a group of soldiers clustered around a warming strip beneath a strung-up tarp. Dead beasts rotted in a pile beside them, fleshy holes carved into their chests where their heart gems should have been. There were empty packets of MREs cast thoughtlessly aside. Rune's nose curled at them as we slipped past.

I couldn't see any of the magicked weapons Rylan had created or the heart gems I knew DFA soldiers wore. Though their magic was weaker than any wildlings', if we were caught, even we would have trouble.

"Erebus isn't with me," I muttered. "I can't sneak up to him. We'll have to somehow get Joshua alone."

"And say what, exactly?" Rune said. "Appealing to your shared past won't work. At this point, if he thinks it will help him win, he'll have no problem killing you."

It seemed in the time it'd taken us to leave Keen and find our way here, Rune had started reconsidering his choice. "I still don't believe that," I said.

Rune barred his teeth. "And here I thought you had enough smarts to survive."

I scowled at him.

"Harsh truths seem to be the only thing that will make you understand how stupid this is," Rune added.

Both of us sank into the undergrowth as a pair of DFA soldiers walked past, rifles slung across their backs.

"What would you do instead?" I whispered. "And don't say you'd leave all of them to die. It might only be for your benefit, but even you wouldn't let Sotera kill an entire city's worth of people."

Rune said nothing.

"That's what I thought. We'll just have to be smart about this."

"Too late for that," Rune muttered.

Being extra cautious to avoid discarded bits of crinkly plastic and fallen branches, we snuck around the rest of the soldiers. Rune parted an impenetrable snarl of holly, and we slipped through a narrow alleyway between what had once been two stores. I scanned for a building Joshua might have picked as his base of operations.

Rune pointed. "That looks like a meeting place. You humans sure like your gaudiness."

Said the guy whose former throne contained rubies and lumps of gold. But he was right, the Wilds-eaten courthouse looked like the perfect place to coordinate local operations.

We made our way to where the petals of an enormous blossom had long ago shattered through the first-floor window. That same blossom lay withered and dead across the windowsill, its stalk severed. There was no touch of new greenery growing in its place—no seedlings or dusting of moss.

Rune knelt and pressed the tips of his fingers to where it seemed a scythe had sliced right through. His fist trembled.

"I can't feel any life in the earth. It's not dormant. It's entirely dead. What they've done..."

"We have to talk with him first," I said, knowing exactly the conclusion his anger would bring him to. "Get them to leave and focus on evacuation."

"And if he doesn't? What then, Val?"

Then we'd be in real trouble. One magicked weapon was bad enough, but there would be more. There'd always be more.

"You have to trust me like I should have trusted you," I said.

"Yes, we must do the very thing we're most terrible at." He looked down at my hand, which I hadn't realized I'd put on his arm. With a huff, he silently vaulted over the windowsill and inside.

I followed, the spongy soil silencing my landing. In the quiet of our surroundings, I picked out voices just down the hall. Joshua had cleared out one of the larger courtrooms, at least as much as possible. The floor was still littered with fallen logs from a tree that had long ago toppled the left wall. Damp, leafy ferns dripped moisture from the ceiling onto piles of dead foliage, behind which Joshua stood talking with two other soldiers.

I held up a hand to stop Rune. "Let's wait for them to—"

"*Leave*," Rune commanded, voice thick with magic.

The two soldiers straightened up, as though someone had stuck a cattle prod in their spine. They turned about and walked right past us, expressions blank.

"You have your audience," Rune said. "Don't waste it."

I hated when he used compulsion. I hated that it worked so well.

Joshua was striding after them. "I said stop! Where are you—"

Rune and I stepped in front of him. Joshua froze. Then he drew his gun.

I held up a hand. "No, Joshua—"

But Rune had already moved a moment before Joshua fired, his bullets chipping away at the wall behind where Rune once stood.

"I'm not in your human world this time," Rune said with a sneer. "You won't hit me again."

Before Joshua could fire again, I darted in close, knocking the gun out of his hand and kicking it under a log.

"Stop this, both of you. Joshua, we need to—"

Joshua's body was already glowing with the magic of a heart gem he'd attached the back of his hand. A powerful one, by the looks of it. The heart gem of a wildling.

Rune noticed it, too, and if I wasn't sure he wanted to kill Joshua before, his murderous expression left no doubt.

"Try to compel me, I dare you," Joshua taunted. He cast a fireball at Rune who easily stepped aside. "You've been slithering around letting others fight for you, oh great High King. It's time you faced me yourself."

I raised my hand, and with a tug on the earth, drew up a spiked wall of crystal between them. Joshua's jaw dropped as he looked at me. Maybe Peyton hadn't told him about what I truly was yet. Maybe she had, and he hadn't believed it until now.

"Rune, bar the door and windows," I said. "Others will have heard the gunshots. We need a little more time."

Rune didn't move.

"You promised," I reminded him. "Give me a chance."

Without taking his eyes off Joshua, Rune gave a jerky nod. In seconds, thick vines crisscrossed over the door we'd entered. Small trees grew in front of the windows, their branches obscuring anyone from looking in.

"You command him now?" Joshua spat. "What is this, Val?"

"Whatever you think of me, I'm still your stepsister, and I still care about you," I said. "I came to warn you."

Joshua jerked his head at Rune. "You think you'll scare me into forging an alliance with him, like you tried to last time?"

"I'm here to warn you about everybody *but* him. No tricks, no lies. All of Seattle is in danger."

Joshua blinked slow, as though trying to puzzle out how

this could be a trick. "We've secured it. No wildling or any force from the Undersea is getting in."

"I mean from Sotera, Empress of Those Below. She's going to destroy everything. You have to get everyone out of the city."

"Hurry this up, Val." Rune appeared concerned. His summoned branches were swaying back and forth, as though testing to air. "Something's not right."

"Sotera? The Below? I think you're lying," Joshua said to me. "You want to clear out Seattle, weaken our defenses. Where will we go, did you think of that? The Wilds, where your boyfriend here will slaughter them?"

"He won't," I said, bristling.

Joshua laughed. "Really? Make him promise he won't harm anyone. As if a promise from him is worth anything. But you can't, can you? You think I'm the bad guy, but he hates us just as much as we hate him."

I wanted to tear out my hair and scream like a madwoman. Curse Joshua and his stubbornness that made him unwilling or unable to see problems beyond his narrow little world.

"Did you ever stop to think that we don't have to keep hating each other and doing the same things that *clearly* haven't worked in the past?" I spat.

It was almost comical watching Joshua's face purple with rage. "Save your self-righteous speeches. The wildlings have encroached on what's ours for years. They've killed those who trusted me."

I tried to come up with some response, but Joshua wasn't finished, "*You've* helped them do that, Val. That trick you pulled, using the DFA as a distraction against the Lords? That got people hurt. And Rune's subjects, they've hurt my people, too. One of them, she'll never walk again. And each time I visit her, I have to look her in the eye and know that. How do you think she'd feel if I suddenly started working with the creatures who did that to her?"

I thought back to the soldier I'd seen Joshua speaking to at Rylan's house. The one that, unless I was mistaken, he seemed to have close familiarity with. "Was it Leah?" I asked softly.

"How do you know her name?" Joshua snapped. "It doesn't—" His voice broke. "It doesn't matter who it is."

Maybe not to him, but it did to me. I was ashamed to admit that recently I'd stopped seeing Joshua as someone who had a life and goals and maybe even loves that were entirely separate from mine. He'd simply become someone else who was against me.

"I'm sorry, Joshua. I'm sorry for anyone who's gotten hurt—"

"And yet here you are, begging for the other side."

"Val." Rune's voice was filled with warning. "We're finished here."

"Sotera is going to destroy the foundations beneath Seattle and collapse the city, Joshua," I said. "She means to take all of it down in one go. Rune and I have both seen it. We risked coming here to tell you. Believe us or don't, but I wanted you to know."

Joshua was shaking his head. "That's not possible. She wouldn't do that."

"Why? Because you think she has no reason to fight humans?"

"No, because she—"

My body froze, as though I'd been encased in a layer of crystal. It was difficult to breathe, never mind blink.

"Because I don't attack my allies," Sotera said.

Rune might have barred the doors and windows, but we'd missed the small crevasse in the corner. Sotera emerged from it like a spider who'd caught some particularly delicious prey in her web. She gave Rune a mocking bow.

"Your Majesty. I don't believe we've had the pleasure of officially meeting yet. I've heard *so* many things about you."

"I've been busy," Rune said. For his part, he didn't look surprised in the slightest to see her here. "Perhaps you under-stand why?"

Sotera smiled. "Oh, I do."

Attack her, I wanted to scream, *Now, before she does anything else.*

I could barely move my jaw. My innate magic was wearing away her hold, but her power over me was stronger than I'd realized.

"Is it true, Empress Sotera?" Joshua asked. "Are there pillars beneath Seattle?"

"There are. As there have always been," Sotera said. "But I'm not capable of collapsing them as she says. Only Val has that power."

Joshua looked sharply at me. "*She* can destroy them?"

Sotera gestured to the crystal spikes separating him and Rune. "Perhaps you missed the demonstration of her talents? She's already taken steps to destabilize Seattle's supports. *I* would never do that, even if I could. If I had to guess, she knew you and I were aligned and wanted to ensure it didn't stay that way by lying about an imminent attack on Seattle. After all, what better way to ensure the Wilds' survival than to make its enemies distrust each other?"

"Yes, that's so unlike Sotera," Rune said pleasantly. "She would never create an alliance for her own gain, just to destroy it as soon as she got what she wanted. As someone who's done just that, you have my grim admiration."

I could move my neck. Sotera's hold was diminishing

quickly, even as her eye twitched with the effort to control me. Her hand started drifting to the sword at her side.

Watch her! I tried to yell at Joshua. *Behind you!*

"If what you're saying is true, then you wouldn't mind having some of my people going Below to double-check," Joshua said.

The first flicker of annoyance crossed Sotera's face. "I said I'd deliver you Rune dead or alive, and here he is, and here he'll stay. Your traitorous stepsister, too, though she's mine to keep. I gave you so much, and all I want is a little trust in return."

"Which you'll get," Joshua said. "After I check."

"You believe her, after all she's done against her own kind?"

"I thought you said she was of the Below." Joshua looked at me. "And no, I don't trust her. That's why I want to check."

Sotera's hand rested on the hilt of her sword. "Very well, I'll give you a tour of our home. *After* I remove the High King of the Wilds. He's exerted his rule for too long."

I needed more time. More magic. More—

"I thought it didn't matter if I was in power," Rune said. "Not if you had that new crown you're so desperately crafting."

For the first time, Sotera looked surprised.

Rune smiled mockingly. "But I suppose you didn't get all the pieces you needed. Bendeti was quite upset about what you did. He took his anger out on us. I'll admit, non-violent diplomacy has never been my strength, but I'm not nearly so bad as you."

"It doesn't matter what Bendeti wants," Sotera said, and there was a feral ferocity in her eyes. "And after I get my crown, perhaps I should keep you alive as a pet, or maybe a reminder of your own hubris. How much more satisfying would it be to have you watch everything and everyone you loved die?"

Rune removed his crown and held it out to her. "Take a piece. Craft your new crown and try to use it. Let's see how well that works out for you."

Sotera looked tempted to snatch it from his fingers. Then she returned his mocking smile. "I don't need it. Not anymore."

At last her hold on me broke. "Down, Joshua!" I barked.

Sliver was already drawn, pointed straight at Sotera. I shoved Joshua aside and lunged away as Sotera cleaved where my stomach had been.

"You're not the biggest problem," Sotera said. She swung her sword, and slender darts of crystal sprayed out and tried to pin me against the wall. Then she was running toward Rune, crystal forming beneath her feet with every step.

Rune raised his hand. I waited for roots to explode from the ground, for a beast to burst in to defend him, for the Wilds to rise and protect its master.

Instead, blood sprayed as Sotera's sword came down. Rune lurched back, stunned, clutching his bleeding arm.

Sotera crowed with delight. "Having trouble, High King?" She tapped the left side of her chest. "What is your puny heart gem compared to the power that courses through my entire body? This close, I can block any tricks you might conjure. You're nothing without your magic to help you."

Rune attempted to coax the trees to do his bidding, tried conjuring thorns to wrap around Sotera, up until the moment she brought her sword down. Rune scrambled over a log to escape, and the blade cleaved it entirely in two. Sotera laughed.

I hurdled what used to be a table, trying to draw closer to her before she swung again. Rune was lithe and dangerous, even without his magic, but Sotera was no unprepared, unskilled assassin. Eventually, his luck would run out.

"Stay still, Rune," Sotera taunted as lines of crystal chased in his wake. "I don't mean to kill you, not anymore. Merely pin you like an insect so that you understand just who it is you're dealing with."

"You're trying so hard to gain my attention," Rune snarled. He flipped out of the way of her next attack. Sweaty hair plastered his face. He was avoiding, but against her relentless onslaught, it wouldn't be long before he made a mistake. "It's pathetic, really."

I aimed Sliver at Sotera's exposed side. She saw me coming, swinging around faster than I thought possible.

"And *you*. You will return with me, in one piece, or many."

Air brushed my skin as I narrowly avoided getting my chest sliced open. My steps faltered as her magic gripped me and then fell away. Sotera's eyes narrowed.

"Not this time," I growled.

I lunged. My fingers brushed her shoulder, barely a touch, but enough that she flinched as I drew power from her.

Sotera's hand went for my throat. "Don't you dare—"

I rolled beneath another table and directed my newly acquired magic at the nearest window. Bark and fibrous debris exploded every direction as I punched a way through.

"Now, Rune!" I barked.

I brought Sliver up just in time to deflect Sotera's next blow, allowing it to push me toward the window. I surged over the sill after Rune, passing DFA soldiers surrounding the place, feeling Sotera's looming presence rapidly gaining on us. If she could block Rune's magic before he could summon a path...

The ferns ahead of me knotted together in an architrave, the center of it twisting until it led somewhere else. The thick scent of loam wafted from the other side.

Rune swung around. One arm wrapped around me while his other started to close the path behind us as we fell through.

The last thing I saw of the other side was Sotera. She'd

stopped, a smile on her face, like she delighted in seeing us run.

Then it felt as though a hook had snagged my intestines and yanked hard. My ears popped, and then we were spit out the other side.

CHAPTER

TWENTY-SEVEN

I remained half-attentive and fighting exhaustion as Rune finished giving instructions to Pitius and Marian. It was impressive how through it all he didn't slouch and he didn't wince. In the presence of others, he always did an impeccable job of hiding any weakness.

Upon returning, Rune had summoned the two wildlings to the comfort of his current room. Though *comfort* would be the wrong word. It was sparse, with only a bed, a couple weapons, and clothes neatly folded atop a chair alongside the latest discards from patching him up. Again. Bloodied leaves, thickly smelling tonics, fine-tipped needles for sewing flesh. All of these were becoming the trimmings of a High King who narrowly avoided death on the regular.

When Rune dismissed them, Pitius vanished as softly as a flutter of a bird's wings. Marian gave me a look torn between concern and annoyance. Probably that we'd gone off to talk to Joshua without informing her.

"Sotera let us get away," I said to Rune when she, too, had

312

left and I could no longer hold my thoughts. "Why would she do that?"

"You have a strange definition of 'letting us get away'," Rune said. He raised his arm to show me the deep cut Sotera had made across his bicep. Upon returning, he'd applied a sloppy dressing of ointment and stitches of dried root shavings and decided to let his wildling healing take over. I itched to redo it. I itched to touch him more than that, but that was only the insanity talking.

"Still, it felt as though she held back," I said. "She changed her mind about wanting you dead."

"Because she thinks we're caught," Rune said. "Because she isn't worried that we're a threat anymore."

"She's not wrong," I said. "We're running out of options."

Rune drew himself up, though I didn't miss his wince. "Many have thought similarly, and they're in the ground now. Sotera's overextended herself. She might think she's safe aligning with your stepbrother, but it could be the perfect time to kill her or sneak Below and destroy her throne."

"I don't think that will be enough," I said. "Simply destroying your throne wouldn't stop *you* anymore."

"I know." Rune scowled. "Sotera's cunning enough, and ambitious enough, that she may not have left a vulnerability like that so easily open." Rune picked at his stitches, scowling. "You saw what she did against me. Or rather what I *couldn't* do against her. But you..."

But me. Always me. His blade. His trick. I'd resisted her control. I could do it again, I was sure, and quicker the next time. I could be the one to slide Sliver into her throat. Perhaps I should have been revolted at the thought, but all I felt was anticipation.

"If we can get in the right position, I'll do it," I said.

Rune smirked. "And I have no doubt you'll enjoy every—Yes?"

Xander was in the doorway. The tense way he and Rune stood across from each other told me there was still plenty left unspoken between them, plenty left still to heal.

"I heard Val's voice," Xander said. "I didn't know you were in here, too, Rune."

"I'm sure it's baffling, finding me in my own room," Rune said.

Xander's eyes flicked between us. Rune was in his own room, yes, and here I was, too. Alone with him.

I coughed to cover my embarrassment. "Did you need me for something, Xander?"

"I had something I wanted to... But it can wait." Xander held up a gathering of leaves and ointments. "I'm going to check up on Zuri. Marian said she doesn't heal as fast as we do."

Rune frowned at his back as he left. "We'll convene later," he said to me. "See where we stand. See where we can hit that'll hurt Sotera the most."

It seemed she was already ahead of us in that respect. "Thank you for not killing Joshua," I said. "I know you had every right after what he's done, especially now that he's aligned with Sotera. But... Thanks."

"I wasn't doing it for his sake," Rune said. "However, you're welcome."

I sighed as I stood. My muscles were stiff, and I felt filthy. I needed a bath, bad. And judging by the room's smell, that even the minted ointment couldn't mask, I wasn't the only one.

"You should clean yourself up," I told Rune. "There's blood on your shirt."

He looked at the sleeve as though just noticing the stiff,

dark stain covering his wound. In one fluid move, he peeled the shirt off.

To my credit, I didn't give him the shocked reaction he was undoubtedly looking for. I almost managed to keep my gaze off his chest, where corded lines of muscle intertwined with old and new scars alike.

I met Rune's eyes. His expression was questioning. Teasing. He knew *exactly* what he was doing. Embarrassment heated my entire body.

"I'm cleaning myself up, too," I muttered, storming out. Rune's sharp laugh chased after.

He's an ass. A complete, unapologetic ass.

That was nothing new. But what was he playing at? *He'd* made it clear this thing between us wouldn't work. And I'd agreed. And yet he kept testing the limits of my resolve. I shouldn't let it bother me. I *didn't* let it bother me.

I was fantastic at lying to myself.

I angrily grabbed a change of clothes and mossed towel and descended to the forest floor. Here I could be alone with only my thoughts to bother me. Normally that was a blessing, but at the moment they weren't in a kind mood. I felt entirely justified in not being willing to leave Seattle to Sotera's plans, but my insistence on always reaching out to Joshua had nearly gotten us caught twice. It'd gotten Rune hurt, badly, as many times as that, which made his restraint at not killing Joshua all the more astounding.

I wasn't doing it for his sake.

I didn't know where my loyalty lay anymore. With humanity, as one of Those Below, among the wildlings. Not being certain could get people hurt, or worse. In some ways it already had.

"Scram," I snapped at the Nauplins. With small chirps of fright, they skittered into the rustling cattails.

Confident that they wouldn't bother me, I slipped off my clothes and forced myself to sink to my chin in the frigid pool. With a bar of mint and mock orange flower soap, I scrubbed off the coating of blood, dirt, and sweat that were my constant companions, feeling as though I were trying to scrub away all my past mistakes.

When the pool became too cold to endure, I got out, dried off, slipped the fresh clothes on, and pulled my foliaged jacket over my shoulders. The walk back was unnervingly quiet.

"There you are."

Xander appeared as flustered to find me out here as he had in Rune's room.

"I thought you were going to see Zuri," I said.

"I was—I am, but... I needed to see you first. To tell you something."

Between the refreshing bath and events of the day, I could feel my limbs coaxing me up to bed. "Could it wait until tomorrow?"

Xander caught my arm. "Val," he said softly. "You need to hear this. I need to know, did Sotera say anything about finishing the crown she was working on? The one she means to use to control both the Undersea and the Wilds?"

Between the fight and the escape, the details were fuzzy. "She mentioned it, yes. But she can't complete it, not without part of Rune's crown."

Xander jumped when Marian appeared, cane in hand. Since her leg wouldn't allow her to easily get up to the canopy, she'd been living in a warmly pleasant room concealed behind a false rock nearby.

She scrutinized both of us. "I feel like I'm crashing a party."

"What did you want to say to me, Xander?" I asked.

Xander's lips had thinned, as though he were seriously regretting opening his mouth.

"You thought to share something with Val before me?" Marian said coldly. "Really?"

"I wasn't sure how you'd react," he said.

Marian clenched her cane tighter. "That's never stopped you before. Shouldn't matter now."

I'd seen animals caught in traps. How they struggled. How their eyes went wide when they saw the hunter coming to finish them off. Xander had that look.

Marian huffed. "Seriously, Xander—"

"I helped Sotera," Xander said, and whatever thoughts I had vanished like ash in the wind. "She was forming this crown—the same one she mentioned to Val, I'm sure. I didn't know what it was at the time. She was still allied with the Undersea then, and she said that if I helped her, she would petition Bendeti to free Zuri. More than that, she wouldn't attack Rune and the other wildlings."

I'd once believed Sotera could never have finished her crown without help. I'd been right. I wished I wasn't.

"You didn't," Marian said, the undercurrent of a growl in her voice. "You weren't that stupid."

"Believe me, I know how badly I messed up a hundred times over," Xander said bitterly. "When I first spoke to her, Sotera wasn't sure what she needed to finish the crown, but the pieces had to be something powerful of the Wilds. Something with meaning. I went back to King's Hollow and managed to take a shard of the broken throne to her. That didn't work."

Fury like magma coursed through me. It was a good thing Marian didn't have her weapon on her, or I was certain she would have stabbed him.

"Do you..." I tried to keep each word even, but still they emerged sharp as biting wolves. "Do you have *any* idea what she wanted that crown for?"

"Not then," Xander said. "I swear."

"What else could it have been for, Xander? I mean, really, what possible reason could she want a crown made partly of the Wilds?"

Xander grimaced like I'd punched him in the gut. "She told me she only wanted to leave the Below. She seemed...scared. Desperate."

"Because Rune was *beating* her," I nearly shouted. "She was running out of options."

"Maybe. It didn't seem like she was scared of him, though. But..." Xander tore at his hair. "It didn't matter, anyway. After using part of the throne didn't work, she decided she wanted a piece of Rune's crown. I couldn't do it." He pulled down the collar of his shirt to show a puffy, purpled scar running from the base of his neck across his collarbone. "She tried to kill me. Nearly did, too—"

Marian's slap scared a nearby flock of grouse into flight. Xander stumbled back, the blow coloring his cheek.

"I wish you had died," Marian seethed. "It would have been better for all of us. You were supposed to protect Rune. That was what you swore to do when you left the Mysts. Do you remember that?"

"Of course."

"Of *course*. You remembered and abided by it. That is until your little...little...*whore* of a girlfriend—"

"Marian!" I said.

"—got involved, and all your promises rotted away. It only lasted until you *really* had something to lose. *Think* what would have happened if Sotera had ever had you followed. If she'd captured you and ripped secrets from that stupid head of yours. You could have gotten us all killed. Maybe you still have."

"I've already thought of all that, and I know how wrong it was."

"I—" A sob choked Marian's words. "Not you, Xander. I trusted you, just as much as Rune. Maybe more."

Xander looked as though she'd driven a knife straight through his heart gem. "I'm not sorry for why I did it. Just that I did, and that I hurt you."

I gave a semi-mad cackle. "How *noble*. That makes your betrayal all better."

"I'm trying to make things right," Xander pressed. "That's why I wanted to know how close she was to finishing the crown, or if she'd given it up all together."

"And if she was? What would you do, run off again and try to kill her yourself? I nearly gave myself away to Bendeti to keep you by Rune's side."

"I never asked for you to do that," Xander said, jaw tight. "And I don't know what I'd do, only stop her however I could." Xander had shrunk away from Marian and me and now tried to straighten up again. "I have no right to ask this, but you can't tell Rune about what I've done."

"We won't, because you will," Marian said. "Before you can do any more damage."

"I will, I promise, but not yet. Not when Zuri's in such a vulnerable state."

Marian looked shocked. "You think—Rune would never punish her for what you did—"

"Wouldn't he? Remember Aleki? Remember what he nearly did to Olette because of him?"

Rune had changed since then. He was trying to be better. I didn't know whether that would be enough to protect Zuri, but at the moment I was the one Xander needed to worry about.

"I have a better idea." I grabbed Xander's arm and dragged him away from camp. "I'll handle this," I called back to Marian.

"Good," she answered. "Otherwise, I might kill him."

"You have to believe that I didn't want to help her," Xander said.

"I honestly don't care," I replied. I was furious at him, furious at myself. Though what I'd done against Bendeti had been spurred mostly by desperation and vengeance, it'd been in no small part in the hopes that Xander stayed. Now he'd thrown that away. He'd endangered all of us.

We walked until I found where the Mysts were camped, in a secluded grove of young pine, away from the rest of Rune's forces.

"Keen!" I bellowed.

Mist-gray cloaks appeared from thin air. Keen stepped out from within their shroud a moment later. "Xander knows better than to call on me again, but by the looks of things, he didn't come willingly. I'm guessing this isn't a social visit."

"When are you leaving?" I asked.

His gaze grew suspicious. "Not soon enough for you, apparently. Why?"

"Because you made me promise once, that when the time came, I'd protect Xander." I turned to Xander. "Take Zuri and go with them."

"What?" Keen said, as though this were a joke.

"I can't," Xander said. "Whatever you think of me, I love Rune like a brother. I wish to protect Zuri, but I have to see this to the end in whatever way I can. Perhaps Zuri can go with them, to be *protected* this time," he shot at Keen, "and I'll follow when everything is done."

"I think you've already done enough," I said. "Whatever help you have left to offer won't be around Rune."

"I know I've destroyed it, but you have to trust me on this. Please."

I gave a harsh laugh. Xander didn't look anguished

anymore, but irked. "I've known Rune longer than you," he said. "I've bled and killed for him. I've helped him get his throne, and yes, I've had my doubts, and yes I screwed up, but I'm trying to make amends. I'm trying to make this better."

"You can do that by leaving."

"Not when there's still work to be done. Do you know why I came to tell you first, Val, instead of Marian? Because I thought you'd understand better than anyone."

I scoffed. "Why would you think that?"

"Did you so quickly forget that not that long ago you hated Rune? Enough to try killing him, multiple times." Xander's eyes hardened. "Every moment I left you alone with him, I extended trust I didn't feel, and every time the two of you were off together, I wondered if he would return or we'd find him overgrown with corpse flowers and a knife in his heart gem.

"I could have put arrows in your back at any time, but I trusted you, someone who wanted nothing more than to be free of him. I'm asking you to show me that same trust."

I tried telling myself that my initial loathing toward Rune wasn't the same as outright betrayal, that I hadn't endangered all of us as Xander had. But...he had a point. Not only that, I had done worse than Xander by actively working against Rune. I had only been in it for myself.

"You'll still have to tell him what you've done," I said at last.

"Eventually," Xander said. "And I'll accept whatever punishment he doles out. Even if that's..." His throat bobbed as he swallowed. "But not until the worst has passed. Rune needs to focus on other things. He needs his allies now more than ever."

"Not sure what's going on," Keen said, "but if you're going with us, Xander, now's the time. It might be best to leave these Wilds all together."

"Why?" I asked.

Keen laughed. "You mean besides the all-out war that's only going to grow worse? You forget that there is a much larger world out there. My ears have been pricked for whispers from other Wilds. Their Lords are taking notice of what's been happening. When this conflict ends and the corpse of these Wilds is barely cold, they'll swoop in to feast and clear out whomever the survivor is."

I filed that potentially catastrophic information away for later. "Have you told Rune?"

"And General Forcheck, yes. For what little can be done about it." Keen looked at Xander. "I'll only extend this invitation once more: you and Zuri can join us."

"We'll stay here, for better or worse," Xander said. "But thanks. I'll be seeing you."

"You probably won't, if you keep getting involved. But who am I to stop you. Val." Keen gave a bow so low the mist-laden ferns brushed his face. "Until the unlikely day we meet again, I will only recall your ferocious hospitality of knives and threats."

It was quiet on our walk back, my thoughts more turbulent than Bendeti's tidal wave. Every potential way to get the upper hand against Sotera, or Bendeti, or even Joshua was met with nothing but dead ends. I was exhausted. I wanted to consult with Rune or General Forcheck but wasn't sure what to say. I even stupidly longed for the Council of Loam, if only to have someone else to make the decisions, no matter how traitorous those decisions might be.

I let out a frustrated growl. "It doesn't matter what Sotera does next, be it a crown or an army. She's going down either way."

I caught Xander smiling. "That sounds exactly like something Rune would say."

I felt warm at that, though I shouldn't have. I let out a long breath. "Thank you for trusting me before. I'll try to extend the same to you, for now. But Xander, if I think you're doing anything else—"

"I know," he said. "I'll try to not give you a reason to put a sword through my gut."

"Please don't."

I felt drained by the time we returned to the treetop camp. Xander said he was finally going to tend to Zuri, and we split apart on the second level.

"Xander?" I called after him.

He turned, perhaps looking a little apprehensive at what I might say. As though even he, too, had come to believe I was the violent beast some of the other wildlings thought me to be.

"Don't make me regret this," I said.

Marian intercepted me on the way to my room. The red of her gold-red eyes was lit with rage, her hands clenching the fabric just above where the lower half of her leg used to be.

"I know you're mad at Xander—" I started.

"I'm not just mad at him. Not anymore."

I blinked. "Are you blaming me for this?"

"I'm blaming all of you!" Marian exploded, and a few nearby wildlings jumped. I managed to move her around the other side of the tree where we could speak in private. Marian pushed me off.

"You're mad at...us," I clarified.

"You, and Xander, and Rune, and Keen, and... And..." She threw up her arms, as though that summarized all her grievances. "I would have followed Rune to the end to make the Wilds a better place. But this isn't what I signed up for."

"You knew that things wouldn't be easy."

"Oh, that's rich, coming from someone who only joined halfway through. What have you sacrificed?"

Everything, I wanted to shoot back. My family. My home. My place among humans that I thought I was part of.

But saying that to Marian while she leaned on her missing leg, after she'd endured horrors I could never imagine, after her closest friend had betrayed her, the words felt hollow.

"And you, Val, you're just as selfish as Xander."

I bristled. Being called out by Xander was about the limit of verbal abuse I was willing to take tonight. "I wasn't the one who tried helping Sotera."

Marian waved a hand, clearly disgusted. "No, you just tried to help yourself. I thought when we started this that Rune would do what he needed to in order to finish things. I helped as much as I could, but I've been dragged back and kept here. For what? To watch my family rip apart at the seams? I don't want any part of it. I want a quiet place; I want someone to love. But you, in that selfish way of yours, wouldn't keep Olette, even after Luella asked you to watch her."

I blinked stupidly at her. "Is *that* what this is about? You know as well as I do that if she stayed with us—"

"It's not because you thought she'd be safer," Marian said. "You didn't keep Olette because it was best for *you*. Rune won't let me leave until things are done—even though I'm as useless as a broken blade—because it was best for *him*. And now Xander did what he did because it saved who he wanted…"

Her throat seemed to close up. "You might pretend you're fighting for the Wilds, but all of this is about *you* and what *you* get out of it. Everyone wants something for them."

"And if that's true," I said, "is that really so bad?"

"I guess not, since you're not the ones getting hurt the most." Marian laughed, shaking her head. "And I'm the worst out of all of you, thinking that after all I've done I could live a somewhat normal life. That's the biggest joke of all."

Her words spent, she sagged, exhausted. "I'm so done with everyone right now."

I tried to think of something to yell back at her, to make her understand that she was wrong. But all I could do was watch her limp away before making my own slow, sore climb up to my room.

Sleep wouldn't come. Marian's words swarmed in my head like hornets. The most frustrating part of all was that every barbed quip I could have thrown at her, every clever response, decided only then, long after they were needed, to make an appearance.

I wasn't helping Rune only for myself, or solely for him. I was doing this for the other wildlings. For the human world, too. I *couldn't* have liabilities like Olette around. I *needed* power to keep them all safe. And if that required being selfish, then that wasn't so bad.

Was it?

With a soft growl, I turned over and punched my pillow. What was truly selfish was keeping Xander's betrayal to myself. That meant I was just as guilty as he was. I claimed it was to protect Rune, but in doing so, I was only protecting myself.

All these swirling thoughts eventually put me to sleep.

I awakened what felt like minutes later to a pair of bright, orb-like eyes hovering over me.

"Hob!" I gasped. He scuttled off me as I sat up. "What are you doing?"

"Mother Mal," he squeaked, distressed. "The child. They're both in danger!"

TWENTY-EIGHT

It took two minutes for me to alert Rune. It took another three for Rune to give Marian instructions to "Prep the others for anything." Three more still for Rune, me, and a few other armed wildlings to descend to the forest floor and start following Hob.

Minutes that felt like hours.

Minutes that might make us too late.

It was after we had just left that we ran into Xander. He crouched atop a branch reaching over the path, his bow at the ready and freshly fletched arrows in the quiver along his back. He leapt in front of Rune, and I sucked in a breath, fearful that he might be about to confess to what he'd done, that his conscience had gotten the better of him. Now was not the time for guilt.

"I'm with you, whatever comes our way," Xander said.

Rune didn't look impressed. "Is that so? Then you can prove it to me after we return."

"I'd rather prove it now."

Rune opened his mouth.

"Let him come," I said, surprising myself. "We need him. You need him."

Marian gave me a furious look but said nothing. Xander appeared grateful. "Please, Rune."

Rune ground his teeth. "We're wasting time."

He brushed past him. Xander, with an appreciative smile thrown my way, quickly fell into line with us.

More minutes like an eternity later, and Hob led us through a nearby pool, the surface so still I could count the individual stars reflected in it.

The tightly knit brambles guarding Mother Mal's home had been grown over with crystal and smashed through like glass.

"Cousin," Vanesi said as all of us stepped over the fallen petals and into the woodland clearing of the Halfway. "Come, join us."

Rune slowed, and I took in the clearing with mounting horror.

Vanesi had managed to bring up half a dozen soldiers from Below, a few of them mounted on crystal beasts. The coils of Kaffa the snake sagged limply around the base of the tree. His head, fanged mouth open wide, lay separate from his body, and Vanesi lounged with her feet rested atop it. The only sign of Xin was a bloom of blood dirtying the clear side of the pool. The air smelled of copper.

Mother Mal and Olette were on Vanesi's left. Mother Mal appeared so hunched and frail that for a moment I couldn't believe I'd thought her anything more than another ancient being of the forest, with no more power than any of us.

I was terrified to see Olette under the rough hands of one of the soldiers. A subtle threat—he could stab her or snap her neck at the slightest fault Vanesi found.

Rune appeared undeterred. "You seem to create a mess wherever you go," he said.

"And you've grown predictable," Vanesi replied. "This is the second time I merely had to wait and you've come running like a rabbit into a snare. It's not even fun anymore, hunting you." Vanesi's expression soured. "All of this stopped being fun a while ago. Now please, bring them some chairs. Sotera is on her way. Might as well make yourselves comfortable."

"Allow me."

In seconds, Rune had knitted chairs of ivy, hemlock, and root before her. "Sit, Val," he said as he took one, crossing his legs with casual ease.

I didn't. I wouldn't make myself more vulnerable than we already were. Mother Mal and Olette were still alive, so I had no intention of running. Better to try to end this here, now, where we had a sliver of a chance.

Vanesi turned back to Mother Mal, ignoring us.

"Surely you know how to do as I asked." Vanesi gestured to her body. Unless I was imagining it, sections of crystal had further crept over what remained of her flesh. "This isn't *me*. This body is not mine. I'm a wildling. You must change me back."

"But Empress Sotera—" one of her soldiers started.

"Gave me command over you," Vanesi snarled. "Hold your tongue or I'll cut it out." Her furious gaze swept back to Mother Mal. She raised her foot and pressed it down onto Kaffa's head. "Do as I ask, or I'll break more of your pets, starting with the girl. We're family, she and I, and have already spent time playing together. She doesn't scream much, unfortunately, but I'm well practiced in finding out how much pain I can inflict on that tiny body without permanently damaging her. Perhaps this time I won't hold back."

Olette was trembling. Mother Mal appeared unconcerned.

"Suffering is temporary. Death is life. I can't do what you ask. I don't possess the ability."

"You have unlimited power. You're a *god*."

"Spoken with the ignorance of a person who has never encountered one. But if you seek so desperately to be free from your mortal shell…"

Mother Mal nodded to the bi-colored pool of life and death. "I'm sure even you can guess which side you need to find the everlasting freedom you seek."

Vanesi looked at it and then at Rune. She gestured for Olette. "Bring me the girl—"

"How did you find out about this place?" I interrupted.

Vanesi appeared delighted. "It was easy. Sotera's spy caught Bendeti's soon after they delivered this location to that disgusting king of fish. I was given the task of extracting that information."

She examined her nails. There were still bits of dried blood beneath, as though she'd kept them filthy as a pleasant reminder. "I'll admit, as much as I loathe this existence, I missed the small pleasures. But even taking what I needed wasn't as enjoyable as it used to be."

"I'm finding your existential crisis incredibly boring," Rune said sardonically. "When is…ah."

He stood, turning with me to face Sotera as she walked into the clearing, alone. Her gaze fell to Rune, and she smiled.

"Had I known we'd be meeting again so soon, I wouldn't have wasted time chasing you. That was a very rude thing you did, warning your stepbrother," she said to me. "I doubt the humans will ever trust me now."

"You'd better not have hurt him," I said.

"What have I told you about keeping others too close, Val? I wasn't trying to be cruel when I taught you that. I was trying to save you from pain. But you refused to listen."

I swallowed the lump in my throat. Joshua was strong. He could have fended her off if Sotera turned against him. I had to believe that.

"Move," Sotera said to Vanesi, gesturing for her to leave the throne-like indentation at the base of the tree. "That spot is for an Empress, a new throne of the Wilds to replace the one I tore apart. With me seated there, it will be a fitting start to the new age."

Vanesi didn't budge.

"I said *move*," Sotera repeated.

Vanesi's body jerked against her will. With unbridled loathing in her eyes, she stood stiffly and flanked Sotera's side. Sotera sat and placed her hands on either arm of the throne. Shards of crystal spread across it and then trailed along the roots until they infected the enormous trunk at her back with veins of lapis blue.

"Now," Sotera said. "Remove your crown, Rune."

She twirled her hand. Half of a thin circlet of crystal, blended with opal, jasper, and sunstone formed in her palm, glittering with malicious brilliance.

It wasn't hard to guess what was supposed to form the circlet's other half.

"Though I failed to get the piece I needed from Bendeti, two thrones are still better than one." Sotera frowned when Rune didn't cave to her demands. "I've had to repeat myself too often today. I told you to take off your crown, Rune."

"I'm afraid not," Rune said pleasantly. "You seem to be under the misconception that you've won."

"And you're under the misconception that you've nothing more to lose." Sotera gestured to Olette. "There are still many, many of those you care about left to hurt, but why don't we start with your blood family?"

I reached out a hand, as though that could stop her. "Don't—"

Sotera closed her fist.

Olette gasped as a spear of crystal burst through her chest. I could only scream wordlessly as her tiny body slumped. Rune looked aghast. Perhaps he'd thought Sotera would merely bluff.

In a daze, I stepped toward Olette. She couldn't be—Sotera hadn't—

There was a flutter of wings, a chorus of growls, a flash of fur. Olette's body broke apart and doves, foxes, minks, elk, a cougar, a wolf, all of them ghost-white, burst into existence where she'd hung. The menagerie of animals circled the clearing once before bleeding into the herd of others like them standing behind Mother Mal.

Sotera wasn't amused. "More wildling tricks. Seems that what should be dead can't stay that way here."

"The beasts will not intrude," Mother Mal said. "This conflict is not up to them. But Olette will be forever safe from you or others. She will forever be free."

"So you say." Sotera frowned, clearly irked. "You misunderstand me, Rune. I don't need your crown to complete my own. You will remove it because you do not deserve it."

She pointed at Mother Mal. "What I need for my own is something far more precious. Give me the seed of the Wilds. If not, I will start finding out just how fragile this place is. And together we'll learn whether gods of the Wilds bleed."

It took me a second to understand what seed Sotera was asking for. The same seed Mother Mal had gifted me? The one that now resided deep within my chest?

Mother Mal sighed. "Much like I told your servant Vanesi, what I give will not bring you what you want."

"Still, I will have it." Sotera's lapis lines of crystal

embedded in the trunk tightened, cutting deep. Golden sap ran like blood down the bark. "Don't continue to try my patience."

"You can't give it to her," I said. I had no idea what sort of power a seed like that possessed, but much like anything else in Sotera's possession, it would likely be disastrous in her hands. "Don't help her!"

"I'm not," Mother Mal said. A flower bud opened on her arm, and she plucked out a single seed. This she handed to Vanesi, who gave it to Sotera.

"This is the last thing I do for you," Vanesi said. "You brought me back to be your puppet and pet, and I've gotten you what you want. You must free me now."

"Must I?" Sotera's smile stretched long. "You have a while yet before the crystal consumes your flesh, and my power over you can last at least that long. No, I think I'll keep you."

Vanesi managed to draw her knife before her body rebelled against her and she froze, limbs trembling. With loathing in her eyes, her fingers uncurled, and the knife point sank into the ground.

"At least let me kill Rune," Vanesi spat. "At least give me that."

Sotera held the seed above her crown. "Like you, he still might be useful to me. But don't worry, with this, my power over him and the Wilds will be complete. You can torture him in a myriad of ways. That will be more satisfying than outright killing him, don't you think?"

Sotera dropped the seed.

It latched onto the half-circlet right away, sprouting green shoots that formed into jeweled berries and lavender blooms dusted with silver.

I shared a look with Xander, whose fingers had tightened around his bow: we couldn't allow Sotera to put the crown on. I tried to catch Rune's eye, but he was transfixed, a hungry look on his face, as the crown finished weaving itself together.

"You've lost your way, Empress of Those Below," Mother Mal said. "You could have put the past aside and had the Wilds as an ally, but instead you played right into their hands. They've won because of you."

Sotera raised the crown. It could have been my imagination, but I swore the air surrounding it rippled with power. "I'm not in the mood to be lectured by a fossil with no concept of what we've endured. Kill her."

One of her soldiers urged their crystal beast toward Mother Mal as Sotera lowered the crown to her head. A branch behind her bent, morphing into enormous hands that blocked the soldier and then swiped at Sotera, who was forced to throw herself out of the throne.

"You will not stop me!" Sotera snarled. She cast crystal darts at Rune, who merely stepped out of their path. Iron-colored stalks rose from the dirt, thorns gleaming like the sharp fangs of Bendeti's sea creatures.

"I believe you have something that belongs to me," Rune said coldly. "Hand it over."

"Help Rune get the crown," I yelled at Xander as I engaged the nearest soldier. He swung his beast around toward me. I slid beneath its swiping claws and plunged my hand against its underside. Moments later it dulled in death, and I had to roll out from beneath as it collapsed. I sank Sliver into the soldier who stumbled off after and let his body fall beside his mount.

Howls and screeches, hisses and screams, filled the clearing. The Wilds themselves were awakening under Rune's command, slowly enclosing Sotera like a coiled snake. She cut down his thorns, but one of Rune's beasts leapt to his side. It opened its mouth, and a swarm of locust shot toward Sotera.

In two vicious swings, she'd halved their number, the husks of hundreds of their bodies adding to the leafy debris covering the forest floor.

The hair along my arms prickled like a sixth sense. I stumbled just out of Vanesi's reach as she emerged from the fray to stab her knife at me.

"Rune's human pet," she spat. "Get out of my way. Sotera has no right to kill him, and you won't rob me of his death."

I remained in place and held up Sliver. "I can free you, permanently. Something I promise Sotera will never do."

Vanesi flung her knife, and I only barely managed to sloppily duck it, the blade grazing my shoulder. Then she was on me. She'd learned some new tricks in her crystal form and had transformed her hand into a weapon all its own, cutting shallow, bloody grooves across my skin wherever I failed to dodge.

I tried to draw myself close enough to steal her magic, but she was wise to that and managed to put space between us every time. One of her kicks bruised my arm. Her foot took out the back of my calf, and I hit the ground hard enough to knock the air from my lungs. Sliver fell out of my hand. Vanesi loomed over me.

"First you, then him," she panted. "Would you believe me if I said I'd have rather stayed dead? That I'd rather not do this?"

"Not at all," I said.

Vanesi's smile was all cruelty. "I guess you're right. Perhaps you know me better than I do."

She brought up her sharpened hand.

Before she could bring it down, I raised my right arm and a second crystal sword pierced from my skin and straight through her gut. The blade easily carved through flesh and bone alike with little more than a soft *snick*, followed by Vanesi's gurgled choking.

I withdrew my second sword, cutting Vanesi deeper in the process, and scrambled up to grab Sliver. What might have been blood, might have been silty water, spurted from her wound.

I knocked her hands aside as she weakly grabbed for me. I wrapped my fingers around what remained of her hair and dragged her, kicking feebly, to the edge of the bi-colored pool. Xin's body floated half-submerged within, her slick skin scored by dozens of spear thrusts.

"Stay dead this time, Vanesi," I said.

Her struggling ceased, her eyes closed, and I swore, right before I plunged her face into the dark side of the pool, she looked at peace.

I made sure not to touch the water as I held her under. I waited until the air bubbles stopped and her weak struggles tapered off. Vanesi's body sank as I let it go and turned to find Xander bleeding on the ground, clutching a gaping wound in his leg. Sotera, similarly bloody, glared at Rune as he held up her crown. He turned it in his hands, as though he'd discovered a particularly interesting insect.

"I expected a lot more from you," he said to her. "Some advice, once-Empress of Those Below: whenever seeking power, make sure you have the strength to protect it."

Sotera spit blood at his feet. "And what would you know about true power, boy king?"

"Maybe nothing. Though I suppose it's time to find out and see if this magic of yours actually works, don't you? Val."

Not taking his eyes off Sotera's crown, Rune removed his own and held it out to me.

"Are you sure about this?" I muttered. "We don't know what that crown will do."

"We know very well what Sotera intended for it to do,"

Rune said. He appeared mesmerized by the glimmering flashes of light deep within the crown's jewels. "With this, I can end Sotera's reign and protect my own."

I reluctantly took his crown. The thorns pricked my fingertips. "What if you aren't strong enough to handle it?"

Rune looked sharply at me. "And if not me, then who else?"

Perhaps your place would be better served on a throne of your own. You would be one of the blades instead of the hilt. Mother Mal's words felt as ridiculous now as they did when she first said them. Rune was the Wild's High King, with immense magic running through his veins. Who was I to doubt? He could do this. He had to.

Rune raised the new circlet over his head, smiling at Sotera.

Sotera smiled back. She made no move to stop him.

I expected a lot more from you.

Rune was strong, but if I was being paranoid, I'd almost guess Sotera had fallen easily on purpose.

Why had she not chased after us?

Why had she not fought harder?

And why, as Rune lowered the crown, did she look *happy*?

"Rune, I think it's a—"

I grabbed for the crown, right as Rune placed it atop his head.

Thorns and crystal slivers sank into his flesh, spraying blood across his brow and speckling droplets on the tips of his hair.

Rune stumbled back. The surrounding beasts screeched in panic. The Wilds frenzied, more out of control than I'd ever seen, as though a great storm was ripping through the trees. Crystal shot up from beneath Rune's feet. A shard pierced his leg and caused him to stumble into me.

"Take it off, Rune," I urged. "Take it off right now!"

I recoiled as I turned him to face me. His eyes were no longer gold-red. Instead, one was lapis-blue, the other black.

Rune opened his mouth, and black, silty water leaked between his teeth. "Val? What have I done?"

Sotera effortlessly got to her feet and brushed grass off her dress. "It was all too easy, letting arrogance be his downfall."

I pointed Sliver at her as she picked up her sword, but she sheathed it and then threw a disgusted look at Rune. "He's no different than the wildlings who trapped us down there, always grasping for more, more, more, without caring who their ambition hurt. The High King of the Wilds could never survive controlling power from both realms. Not even I could. That's why I never intended to actually wear the crown I forged. But I had to make him think it was enough of a threat, make him want it bad enough that he wouldn't question taking it for his own."

"What's it doing to him?" I demanded. "What did you *do*?"

"Something better than outright killing him. He might fight it for a time, but being torn between the magic of the Wilds and the Below will eventually rip his mind in two." A smile stretched across her face. "He'll become nothing but a soulless puppet, free for me to use as I wish. Maybe in the process he'll kill the Wilds and you along with it, Val. And you'll deserve it. Oh, how you'll deserve it."

I lunged at her, but Sotera easily avoided me. In moments, her and her remaining soldiers slipped out of the clearing. My every muscle itched to go after her. She'd created the crown, so maybe killing her would be the key to destroying it.

Rune clutched his head before I could decide. His movements were growing disturbingly weak. Xander dug his fingers into the dirt, trying to drag himself closer as Rune swayed. "Rune—"

"Stay away from him!" I barked.

"If we don't help him..."

"I know." I turned to Mother Mal "You have to do something."

"I cannot," she said. "He made his choice, and now he must deal with the consequences. I cannot interfere, I am merely an observer."

"An *observer* who summoned us, who gave *Sotera* the seed that caused this—You can fix this!" I snarled. "If he dies... If he dies..." I couldn't manage the words. "If he stays like this, he'll destroy the Wilds."

"Death is life. What ends one thing begins another."

I let out something between a curse and a growl and cautiously approached Rune. I put a steadying hand on his shoulder as he tottered even more unsteadily.

Searing pain shot from my elbow to my wrist. I drew my arm back with a cry as a beast of the Wilds—something formed of rot and golden sap, lashed together with spider's silk —screeched at me, its claws thinly coated in my blood.

I held up Sliver as it stalked closer, joined by more creatures—wolves, bears, even elk and other things that shouldn't crave my flesh. All of them had a crazed look in their gold-red eyes. Some were frothing at the mouth, snapping at my hands.

"Call them off, Rune," I said. "It's me!"

"Back up, Val!" Xander had made it to his feet and was urging the remaining wildlings to leave the clearing as the surrounding greenery sought them out. A thick vine tried to tear one of the wildlings in two, but Xander weakly drew his bow and with three arrows expertly pinned it to a far trunk. "Can you make it to us?" he called to me.

Rune had become deathly still. One eye still wept black. High King or not, if I left, I had no doubt the Wilds would consume him.

My stomach lurched painfully at the thought.

"Get everyone out," I told Xander. "I'll be right behind you."

"Val, don't—"

I cut down one of the nearest beasts as it lunged. I stabbed another, and still a third I drew magic from, until it fell lifeless to the ground. I stabbed and sliced a way to Rune, suddenly knowing how I could stop this and hating the idea.

I wasn't sure if Rune could see me, but he turned at my approach. My hand missed his chest as he glided out of reach, the very ground carrying him to safety.

"If you can hear me, Rune, I'm trying to help you," I said.

Each time I reached for him he could somehow anticipate it and slunk farther into the snarl of frenzied Wilds. The beasts were closing in, and soon, not even my magic would save me from the onslaught. I only had one more shot.

I sheathed Sliver and dropped my hands to my sides, giving Rune a clear opening to attack. I had to believe that some part of the Rune I knew was still in there, a part that would never willingly harm me. I had to trust—

I gasped as Rune's knife pierced through my side with a wet squelch, sliding apart muscle and jarring against crystal bone. My blood soaked his sleeve. Warmth covered my shirt.

The pain threatened to make me pass out, but I gripped Rune's wrist as he tried to withdraw the blade. He was close to me. He was vulnerable.

"Trust me," I murmured, more to myself than to him.

I slapped my hand over his heart gem and pulled his magic.

Rune wheezed. He folded forward. The pallor in his skin turned scarily pale. I pulled beyond what I felt was safe, even as Rune sagged to a knee.

As his magic was drawn out, the thorns digging into his brow receded. With my free hand, I ripped the now-loosened crown from his head. Rune struggled against me, reaching for it. The beasts stalked closer.

"Stop, Rune! You have to stop—"

I wheezed as his knee collided with my stomach. Stars filled my vision as he clubbed the side of my head. His nails tore into my skin as he tried to pry the crown from my grasp. He was weaker, yes, but his eyes hadn't changed from their unnatural color. Sotera's crown was still draining him.

I managed to still Rune's arms and legs with crystal, holding him in place. I stood, clutching my bleeding side. "You may hate me for this later, but you'll hate yourself more. And I can't have you dying on me. I just can't."

I held up Rune's crown. I could destroy it, but that could only make things worse, still tied to Rune as it was. Truthfully, I *wanted* the power it promised. Marian had called me selfish, and I could see now she was right. Here in my hands was Sotera's weapon I could use against her, if only I took it for myself.

"If this is a big mistake, tell me now," I said to Mother Mal. Of course she stayed as silent as the useless observer she claimed to be.

I took a deep breath, closed my eyes, and with trembling

hands placed Sotera's crown atop my head. There was needle-like pain as the thorns sank into my flesh, and then...

Power, beautiful, glorious power.

I could feel the life thread of every tree, every leaf, and the heartbeat of each small creature and beast. They weren't individuals but an interconnected, kaleidoscopic web all under my beck and call. The Wilds and all its majesty were nothing but a tool to use for whatever purpose I saw fit.

A laugh exploded from my mouth. The thorns dug deeper into my skin, as though trying to get at the very center of me and root themselves there.

I knelt and dug my fingertips into the dirt. Through the Wilds I could also feel the endless Below, there and waiting for me. It was mine, too. All of it, mine.

"You are resplendent," Mother Mal said. I could see an aura of power surrounding her, but it was dull, unlike the colors cloaking me. "That power suits you."

"I feel like a god," I said.

"A god without purpose, but yes."

Rage, white hot, flickered through me. "I have purpose."

"Oh? And what is it?"

What a stupid question. "My purpose is... Is..."

The Wilds pulled me toward it while magic from Below tried to drag me down. The auras of everything bled together, making my head feel like a hatchet had lodged in my skull. I didn't care. All my life I had sought one thing: power. The power to never be afraid again. To never feel weak.

I sneered down at Rune. It was the fault of Rune, Sotera, Bendeti, the Lords; they were the ones born with power, and because of that, they abused it, striving for whatever they wanted with no regards for others.

"I could make everything better, everything *right*." The

words sounded chalky on my lips. "I can be a better ruler than any of them."

"You certainly could," Mother Mal said. "But you won't. Because, deep down, you're no better than they are."

I flicked out my hand. The surrounding beasts charged Mother Mal, only to divert at the last second like a river flowing around a rock. That same dull magic emanated off her, taunting me.

"I won't cower before you," I said. "I'll prove what I say. The first thing I'll do is kill Sotera. And then Bendeti. This war will end, and the rebuilding begin—"

I crumpled to the ground, my cheek smashing into the dirt inches from Rune's gasping mouth. His eyes had cleared. They had trouble focusing on me. "V-Val?"

I couldn't move. The thorns had furrowed deep inside and wrapped around my heart. As more of them snaked through my veins, a terrible, immobilizing fear rose from within: Mother Mal was right. Now that I had the power to fix everything, I had to become better. I had no excuses. I could do anything, become anyone. The possibilities were endless.

I had railed against my inability to change things for so long that, when finally given the chance to do whatever I wanted, I was overwhelmed by indecision.

Being a god wasn't fun. It was terrifying.

"Help...me," I begged Mother Mal.

"I already have," she said. "But you have to accept it."

Whatever she wanted me to accept, I did so. Anything to free myself from this terrible expectation. I accepted that I couldn't do this, that this power wouldn't fix everything, that if I didn't give it up, it would twist me into something I wasn't, too.

"Please," I gasped.

The thorns inside me stopped growing. The seed Mother

Mal had gifted me uncurled in my chest, took root, and grew. With each passing second, the drug of the crown's power slackened until I could think clearly. Until all I felt was pain and shame.

Mother Mal gave me a toothy smile. "You survived. I'm glad I didn't waste my time."

THIRTY

Rune was on his feet but didn't appear any more lucid than I felt. The wrong color of his eyes had changed back to their usual gold-red, now tinged with rage.

"That was a very clever trick Sotera pulled. I'll have to remember that when I kill her."

It took me far too long to get to my own feet. My joints felt stiff. "Neither of us are doing that right now."

"Nonsense, we just need—" He collapsed to one knee, panting. "A minute."

I reached up and gingerly touched Sotera's crown still atop my head. It had remained tight against my brow, like a leech on a fresh host.

Putting aside the panic that I was forever stuck with it, I forced myself to move. Fiery pain accompanied my every step as I limped over to the bi-colored pool. I refused to look at Xin's body and scooped up a handful of clear water to dribble over where Rune had stabbed me. In seconds, sharp relief took the pain's place as the wound closed.

"You knew this was going to happen," I said to Mother Mal.

"All of it. Sotera. The crown. Olette." Raw, fresh pain made me choke. "You...foresaw it, or planned it. Maybe you're the one who set everything up. That's why you didn't do anything to stop Sotera from killing her."

At the thought of telling Marian what had happened, of telling Luella, I nearly vomited. A gaping sorrow threatened to overwhelm me. I wanted to scream that I'd never meant for any of this; I wanted to rant at Mother Mal that she could have done more, but I was as much to blame as her. I should have known that nowhere was safe, not even amongst a god.

The ghostly-pale creatures that had once been Olette slowly surrounded Mother Mal. She extended a hand to pet the wolf. "You give me too much credit. I merely observed and guided, not influenced."

"You gave me the seed," I snarled.

"It was your choice to take it, just as it was Sotera's choice to come here. Though I might offer many things, ultimately what you do with them is up to you."

"I've been called silver-tongued," Rune said. "And I believed it, until I met you."

"Things have a way of balancing themselves out," Mother Mal went on. "Good, bad, right, wrong, whatever those mean. That is the way of the Wilds, the way of life. It will always turn out the way it means to, no matter how much you dislike the outcome."

The wolf nuzzled Mother Mal's hand. She gently touched the tip of its nose, and it collapsed without a sound, kicking up leaves. I watched in horror as its body decomposed in time lapse. Days condensed into seconds as it bloated; then the skin and fur melted away, followed by the muscles, sinew, and dried blood, leaving only bleached-white bone that vanished to wisps of mist.

Mother Mal released the remainder of the animals that had

once been Olette just the same, until the mist of her spirit circled the base of the tree and dimmed the lapis-blue veins of Sotera's infection. I swore there was tenderness in Mother Mal's gaze as she did all this. I almost believed she was actually sorry.

"Death brings life, and Olette's death will bring more life than most," Mother Mal said. "Her spirit is that of the Wilds. Therefore, the best gift I can give her is that she remains here, forever safe from harm."

"Unless the Wilds are gone," I said. "Thanks to what you've done."

"If that is what you believe. But you're not going to let that happen, are you?"

Still furious, I helped Rune to his feet again. He tried to walk on his own, but only managed to lean heavily on me.

"I end up in this position with you a lot," he muttered. "And yet I can't seem to find it a punishment."

Limping in tandem, we left Mother Mal's woodland clearing behind us. The pale-white trees thinned and filled with color until at last we were stepping through the pool's reflection and into Wilds I knew.

We hadn't made it far before a figure stepped out from behind a nearby tree: Erena, from the disbanded Council of Loam. She looked furious to see us still alive, the leeches on her face thrashing.

"You can't do anything right, not even die." Erena spat at my feet. "You didn't stay away from him like we asked. Did you think we wouldn't *watch* to make sure you followed our command? Now all this pain is your doing."

How did Erena know about what just happened, about Mother Mal and Vanesi? Unless...

Oh.

No.

Erena cackled. "You should have listened. You should have let our bastard High King die."

That was why the assailants had looked surprised that Rune wasn't alone. Why Mother Mal didn't say anything when I blamed her for Olette's death and everything before it. Though Vanesi may have found out how to reach Mother Mal, Erena must have helped her and Sotera both enter the Halfway. And since their arrival fit in with Mother Mal's desired *fate*, she hadn't stopped them.

There are old magics, and there are ways to circumnavigate them.

"Long live the House of Worms," Erena snarled. "And your death, when it comes, will be agonizing."

I tried to throw Rune off and drive Sliver through her gut, but a mixture of leeches and mucus pooled beneath her feet, and she sank into it, vanishing from sight. Heaving, I scanned the remaining patch of soggy ground. Fury and helplessness at my inability to get revenge made my arms shake, or maybe that was the fatigue. I wanted to go after her. I wanted to kill her. But I couldn't. Not right now. We had bigger things to worry about.

"Rune! Val!"

Marian and several other wildlings appeared from the undergrowth nearby, clearly agitated.

Marian limped up to us, face flushed. "Are you—"

"We'll live," Rune said.

Marian looked over our shoulders, clearly expecting someone else. "Is Olette all right? She's probably terrified, and I'll bet that bony monstrosity doesn't know how to comfort her properly. I should—"

"Marian," I snapped, finally managing to shove Erena's escape from my head. "Sotera. Where is she?"

Marian was still looking around me. "Sotera ran the second

she saw us. I told the others to set up a perimeter, so we should know the moment she comes back. Can you please tell me if Olette—"

"Marian," I said, softer this time.

At last Marian looked me in the eye. Her entire body sagged. "No. Please tell me it's not true."

"I'm sorry. It was quick. Mother Mal changed her. She's...in a better place." My tongue soured with the words. "We need to focus on where Sotera is now."

Marian looked as though she'd been forced to swallow something vile. But after years of unimaginable anguish, she recovered quickly, hardening her body, tightening her scowl, as though anger alone could stave off the sensation of her heart being ripped in two once again.

"Pitius saw her moving northeast toward Seattle with what was left of her guards."

"Then we have to stop her," I said.

With great reluctance, I shrugged Rune off onto one of the wildling healers. "Keen found out what she's going to do. I have—"

My world spun. I pitched forward, barely catching myself against a tree. When I looked down, Rune had wrapped an arm around my ribs, easing my fall. In his gaze was something like concern.

"You're too weak," he said.

"Excuse me?"

"You need to rest," he amended. "And when I'm the one saying that, you know it's serious. You'll be next to useless fighting in this state. She'll kill you easily."

Thoughts of Seattle collapsing under Sotera's command flashed through my mind. Damn me for being so frail. Damn him for being right.

"Pitius has to keep an eye on Sotera," I told Marian. "With

Rune weak, that means the Wilds will be weak and she'll more easily be able to move soldiers up from Below. Hopefully, that'll take her some time and she won't feel confident to start any attack until it's done. But the moment she makes an aggressive move, we have to act."

The other wildlings stared. None of them moved.

"Well?" I demanded.

"Yeah, sure," Marian said. She, too, stared at me a little longer; then she pulled another wildling over and gave him some specifics before letting him run off. "We'll know the second she makes a move."

"That was very queenly of you," Rune said as all of us started moving back to camp. He nodded at my head. "It seems you've already grown accustomed to it."

I'd forgotten all about the crown. Now some of the awed, wary looks the others had given me made sense. Xander and a few of the others had seen what had happened in the Halfway, but to the rest, I'd simply reappeared with it and started giving orders.

"This crown doesn't mean anything," I told Marian.

"I'm not sure that's true," she said. "I can feel power coming from it. From you, too."

I'd never felt less powerful in my life, but I was too tired to debate her. I was too tired to think about what wearing it could possibly mean.

I SPENT the next half day restlessly tossing in and out of a dreamless sleep, pricked awake every few hours by the thorns sticking into my brow.

More than once, my eyes had flown open, and I'd lain in a sleep paralyzed stasis, barely able to take a shallow breath.

During these times, it felt like I'd peeled back the skin of the Wilds and saw things as they really were. Each creature and plant was a thin, glimmering thread of life, delicate, yet strong, crisscrossing over me, over the walls, the ceiling, burrowing into the dirt. So many lines that I was sure I'd have gone crazy if I hadn't managed to shut them out.

The third time this happened I discovered these strings were mine to tug on, to manipulate, to follow; though each time I tried, they seemed snagged on something and held fast.

When a wildling came in to tell me the general had arrived with the rest of Rune's army, I gratefully pulled my exhausted self out of bed and went to meet everyone at the next tree over, on an enclosed platform set atop the central bough.

"I know why you summoned us together, my High King," General Forcheck was saying when I entered. "But it still makes me nervous leaving no force guarding the most likely places where the Undersea would come ashore."

"Have you seen any sign that might happen soon?" Rune asked. He looked as though he'd gotten about as much sleep as I had, his shirt ruffled, face drawn. He spared me a glance before returning to the maps.

"No signs," General Forcheck said. "Unusual for our fishy neighbor."

"He's probably waiting for the right opportunity," I said. "He knows there's going to be a fight. He'll let each side wear the other down and move in like a scavenger when the dust has settled."

"I'd say that's an accurate assessment of what I believe," General Forcheck said. "Most of the kings and Lords I've known are cowards that shirk at the thought of true victory through fighting their own battles. Present company excluded."

Rune smirked. "Were it not a necessity, I'd avoid it, too."

"I suppose that's fair. Then, if Sotera is to be your main focus, we'll worry about this one foe for now, and when the time comes, we'll deal with the other."

Rune looked at Marian. "Assemble all the wildlings. I'll speak to them in a moment."

"*Now?*" Marian scoffed. Her eyes were puffy, as though she'd been interrupted from crying or hadn't stopped since we'd returned from the Halfway. "You're too weak, Rune. You *look* too weak. Wait until you feel bette—"

"I'll speak to them now," Rune said. "I'm their High King, and this can't wait. Please," he added.

Marian raised an eyebrow before giving a curt bow and stepping out. Rune's gaze fell on me, before moving to the crown. "There is one more matter that requires some serious attention."

"Ah, yes," General Forcheck said. "You weren't kidding. Dip your head, child."

I allowed her gnarled fingers to turn my chin this way and that as she looked me over. "I've never seen anything like it, a crown crafted from the power of two kingdoms. Does it hurt, Val?"

"Only when I try to sleep," I said, though that wasn't entirely true. Still, I didn't need them more worried, now of all times.

"Is it killing her, like it nearly did me?" Rune said.

"Of course not," I said, but Rune waited as General Forcheck mulled over her answer.

"It would appear not," she said at last. "Though I imagine there are other changes."

Rune cocked an eyebrow. "Such as?"

"Why don't you ask her?"

Both of them looked expectantly at me, and I found my

resolve to stay quiet on the matter withering. "I can...feel things a bit more strongly, both in the Wilds and the Below," I admitted. "Animals, plants, things beneath the earth, all of them. They're like threads. Only, I can't really *do* anything with them."

"You can't do anything with them *yet*," General Forcheck said. "If I had to guess, I imagine there's a point where that stops becoming true."

"That point is me," Rune said. "And Sotera."

"What are you two talking about?" I asked.

Rune seemed to weigh his words. "I control the Wilds, so with me as High King, your power here is diminished. The same with Sotera. Were she to be removed, I imagine you'd suddenly find your connection to the Below infinitely stronger and your command over it stronger still."

"Are you saying I would be ruler of the Below?" My voice came out in a breathy whisper.

General Forcheck cackled and pounded my back, surprisingly strong for an old woman. "Fear not, I don't believe you have to worry about becoming as delightfully malicious as our dear High King."

She had it all wrong. It wasn't my fear of becoming like Rune that was scaring me. It was scaring me how much I *wanted* power like he commanded.

"Simply killing her would not make you Empress," Rune said firmly. "Sotera never consolidated her power into herself or her crown like I did. Even though you have *this* crown, any new ruler would still need to take her throne. Which," Rune gave a wry smile, "I imagine Those Below would have something to say about. Even still, killing her likely *would* make you stronger. Not that it matters. That crown won't stay on your head forever."

I blinked, ripped out of my fantasy of what it would mean

to claim Sotera's title. "We're going to find a way to remove the crown?"

"Before it kills you, yes. And then I'll find a way to control it and destroy her and the Below."

I cocked my head, sure I'd misheard. "You're kidding, right? Rune, wearing it nearly killed you before."

"Because I wasn't ready. I made a mistake, one that won't happen again. Sotera sought to destroy me, but instead, she's handed me the greatest weapon to use against her."

I was confident it wouldn't work like that. Sotera had created something not even Rune could control, no matter how much he believed it. All he'd be doing was making a second, more terrible mistake.

Perhaps your place would be better served on a throne of your own.

Rune's gaze seared into me, seeming to beg me to agree. "It's for the best, Val. If left unchecked, I'm sure it would kill you."

"Yeah, it's for the best," I repeated, almost robotically. Because it was. I had to believe that.

"Then I'll have some of the more learned wildlings look into how to remove it right away," General Forcheck said. She smirked. "The search may have gone faster had we a scholar from the Council of Loam to reference, but alas, we find ourselves lacking both."

Marian poked her head back inside before I could answer that. "I've got the wildlings gathered. Those I could, anyway. I still think you should wait."

"I've noted and disregarded your thoughts," Rune said.

I followed him out as he brushed past her. He braced himself against the wooded railing, arms tense as he surveyed the wildlings spread out on the platforms below. I spied Xander next to Zuri, cradling each other. Zuri's skin seemed more flushed and hydrated than before. Her eyes darted nervously from one wildling to the next.

Xander caught my gaze. *"You have any idea what he's doing?"* he mouthed.

Of course I didn't. I never had a clue when it came to Rune.

"We have a singular enemy." Rune's voice carried, and the wildlings stilled. "Empress Sotera moves to attack Seattle. We will move to stop her. If Sotera succeeds in her conquest, she'll eventually turn on us, and this time we'll have no other enemy to distract her."

Nobody muttered disagreements. Nobody fidgeted.

Rune clenched the railing tighter as he leaned forward. "You will show the forces of Those Below no mercy. You will shatter their every crystal. Break their every spear and blade. Whatever claim Sotera thinks she has on the surface world and on the Wilds ends today."

There were some brief, unsure cheers and shouts of exaltation. A few wildlings raised their swords and bows toward Rune. Rune watched them all impassively, lips pressed into a grim, thin line.

"Before we leave, there is one other matter I need to address. Xander, step forward."

A dull hush fell over the wildlings again.

Xander's throat bobbed as he swallowed. "Me?"

His face drained of color as a long thorn with serrated edges and a polished hilt rose from the ground beside Rune. He drew it. "I said, step forward."

"Rune, don't." I started forward, but Marian stopped me. She wouldn't look me in the eye.

"He has to do this," she muttered.

"Did you tell him?" I demanded, as though I hadn't asked Xander to do the very same. "Did you know?"

"I didn't, I promise," Marian said, though I wasn't sure which question she was answering.

"Xander!" Rune barked. "I won't ask again."

Zuri was pleading with Xander, tears cutting lines through the salt on her face. Xander soothed her. Then he stood and kissed her brow before freeing himself from her desperate grasp. Hand pressed tightly on his still injured leg, he limped across the bridge to stand before Rune.

"I knew what you did," Rune said, speaking low. "Almost from the very beginning, I knew. And still I waited for you to come to your senses. I held out hope that you'd see I only ever wanted what was best for you."

"How did you know?" Xander said.

Rune smiled, but there was no mirth in it. "How could I not? You are—were—like my brother. It was the little changes in your demeanor, and the big ones. I make it a point to know the feelings of all those who fight for me."

"And I'd keep fighting," Xander said. "Until my end, however that was. From *whomever* that was."

Rune caught my eye, as though seeking my advice.

You told me that you couldn't rule the way you once did, not if you wanted things to be different, not if you wanted to be a better High King.

Were you lying?

I wouldn't plead for him to change his mind anymore. Whatever choice he made, it'd be his alone.

"You betrayed me, Xander," Rune said louder. "You worked with the enemy. You tried to steal part of my crown for Sotera, didn't you?"

Xander raised his chin. "I did."

"On your knees, then."

Zuri sobbed harder, barely consoled by Cassius, as Xander

knelt, wincing from his wound. My palms prickled where my fingernails dug in.

"This is what happens to those who betray me," Rune said. He raised the serrated thorn. "I trusted you," he whispered. "I trusted you with *everything*."

"I know," Xander said. "You were why I did this, even knowing from the very start what it might mean."

The thorn trembled in Rune's hand. Xander closed his eyes.

Rune brought down the thorn in a wide, sweeping arc. Once. Twice. There was a collective held breath. I waited to hear the dull *thunk* of a head falling from a neck.

When I could stand to look, I found Xander blinking at the ground, where a small pool of blood dripped from his chin. Two deep gashes intersected across his left cheek, gouged by the tip of Rune's thorn.

Rune stabbed the thorn into the ground, where it was immediately absorbed back into the wood. "I banish you from these Wilds. You leave tonight. If you're found after that, your life is forfeit. That mark on your cheek indicates what you've done. That is the way of traitors," Rune said loudly. "No home. No allies. And may others they meet know what they've done."

Xander sank forward onto his hands, heaving in great lungfuls of air.

"Take Zuri and go," Rune said. "I don't want to see you ever again."

Rune swept back to his room, and only then did the spell he'd cast over everyone break. Zuri ran, weeping, to clutch at Xander's bleeding face. Xander could only stare at where Rune had stood, clearly not anticipating this turn of events. He wasn't the only one.

"Did you talk Rune into sparing Xander's life?" I said to Marian.

Marian scoffed. "You actually think I could change Rune's mind once he's set it? I'm not you."

Then Rune had meant what he'd said. He had ruled with fear, and he had ruled with blood, and neither method had stopped those he cared about from leaving. The tighter he'd held on, the more things slipped away. Now, it seemed, he was trying a different way.

"Are you going to say goodbye to Xander?" I asked.

Marian hugged herself. I suspected it was to keep her hands from shaking rather than the cold. "No. It'll be easier that way. You should, though."

I should. But I wouldn't. If Xander was smart, he'd take up with Keen as they left these Wilds. If Xander was smart, he'd never come back.

General Forcheck ambled over to us. "Perhaps not the best timing, on the eve of battle, but I admire Rune's restraint."

"I need to see him," I said. I felt certain of that. Rune had just lost one of his closest friends and allies. Again. Whether he knew it or not, he needed support.

"If he'll see you," Marian said. "I'll make sure Xander and Zuri get away okay."

Zuri was leading a still-stunned Xander down to the forest floor, the slashes on his cheek partially clotted with damp moss. He met my eyes.

I'm sorry, I mouthed.

He gave a jerky nod, and I turned away, unable to look at him anymore.

I slipped past clusters of fervently whispering wildlings, only slowing when I approached Rune's room. Now that I was actually here, I was left with the bewildering problem of what to say. I wasn't good at condolences, and Rune wouldn't want to hear them.

"I see you still have the bad habit of skulking outside doorways," Rune called.

I stepped inside. He lounged on his bed, head propped on a pillow. He stared at me for a long beat and then lay back, draping an arm over his eyes.

"You have a very loud heartbeat. I used to think it was like a rabbit's, fluttering and scared. Now I know it's like a beast's, warning others away."

I had no idea he'd thought about my heartbeat that much. "Thank you for sparing him."

Rune was silent, his chest slowly rising and falling. I hadn't come here to give him false praise for something he hadn't wanted to do. He clearly wanted space.

"Did you think I was wrong?" Rune said when I turned to leave. "Should I have killed him? Should I have doled out justice for what he'd done, just as you did to Lord Hallas?"

"I won't answer that," I said. "Even if you actually wanted my opinion."

"But I do." He flung his arm off. His glare was back, more intense than before. "You've never been shy to give it before. 'More valuable than glittering jewels or a sharp blade is honest perspective.' Isn't that what General Forcheck said? I expect that perspective from you, always."

I waited for him to go on. Rune sighed, exasperated.

"You have an opinion, and I want to hear it: was I wrong?"

"No." As though approaching an injured wild animal, I cautiously took a seat on the edge of the bed. "You weren't wrong before, and you're not wrong now. It takes more strength to restrain yourself than to punish everything with violence."

"Violence worked in the past."

"Maybe. But it breeds animosity among the survivors. It created what you—"

Rune sat up, arm draped over his knee. I had intentionally sat as far from him as I could, yet I still felt his body heat flushed and close, as though we were in one another's arms.

"Created what I am?" he finished. "And what am I?"

I refused to play along, giving him answers he already knew just so he could hear them coming from my mouth.

"What am I, Val?"

I scowled. "Not as heartless as you pretend to be."

Rune winced as he placed his hand across his chest. "You've proven that on more than one occasion. And yet I find myself coming back again and again."

I stood, bristling with fury. "Stop. You keep playing this game. Both of us do. I'm not what you need, and yet I—"

I wanted to scream in frustration. Somehow this conversation had drifted into territory I was entirely unprepared for. We danced around what we actually wanted to say, two combatants in a duel, wielding words as sharp as blades. "Don't patronize me. I won't pine after you like a lost puppy."

Rune's expression darkened. He beckoned to my crown. "Let me see it. I haven't examined it up close."

I'd said my piece. I should have walked out. Backed up my words with action. We were no good for each other. We didn't fit.

I sat beside him once again.

Rune reached out, paused, as though waiting for my permission. I tilted my head toward him. With a gentle touch, he parted the strands of my hair, brushing away bits of dried blood that had crusted near the base of the thorns.

"I hate it," I admitted. "I can't take it off, and I can't use it." A dry laugh escaped my lips. "I feel so stupid. I wanted to be strong for so long, and now that I have power, it's not what I thought it'd be."

"I understand that more than you know," Rune said.

I was mesmerized by his fingers in my hair, brushing across my temples, trailing down my cheeks.

"Sometimes," he murmured in a tone shockingly intimate, "you have to take power you're ill-suited for in order to survive."

I never thought he'd had doubts about what he'd done, but it sure sounded like it.

"But you won't have to do this," he went on. "Once we remove this crown, it will be my burden."

"I should keep it," I said, surprising myself.

"Trust me when I say you don't want that."

"What if keeping it's the right thing? What if—" *What if doing so protected you?*

Rune wasn't smiling anymore. "Say it. Say that when the time comes, you'll give me the crown and, with it, Sotera's power. If anyone has to suffer, it should be me."

I bit the inside of my cheek until I tasted blood. Of course he believed he should take that burden, just as he'd taken so many other things onto himself—never mind that there were others willing to help him with it.

"Val, please tell me you will let me take on that power."

"I will let you take all the power you can," I forced out.

"Good. It has to be me," he said, though so softly he could have been speaking to himself. "It always has to be me. And then you, and everyone else, will be all right."

The two of us had moved startlingly close. I turned to him, working to clear my throat. I was teetering on a precipice, and in lieu of nearly losing him, the plummeting fall suddenly didn't seem all that scary.

My voice was scratchy, "I think it's best if we—"

I wasn't sure who leaned in first. I certainly didn't bother holding myself back, but unless it was my imagination, I swore Rune instigated it and then I was kissing him, practically smashing my mouth against his. He let out something like a growl, something like a groan, as I opened my lips to further capture his.

I pressed my hand to his chest, bunched his shirt in my fingers, partly to steady myself in this whirlwind of sensations, partly to prevent myself from losing further control and hurting him. For a mouth so often set in a hard line, I'd forgotten how soft it could be. Though it wasn't like I thought about it often.

Liar, my thoughts teased. *You terrible little liar.*

All argument I might have given was wiped clean as Rune pushed me back against the wall at the foot of his bed. The scent of wood and char, like fire after a lightning strike, swelled in my nose. Rune's scent. His arms caged me but offered an open space beneath them. A promise that I could stop this craziness and leave at any time.

I pulled him closer.

I had lost so much. The love of my family. Wildlings I called friends. Olette. And Rune. I'd nearly lost him too many times to count.

I wanted him close. I wanted him as far away from me as possible.

He was the problem. I was the problem. I was the reason everyone I'd ever cared about got hurt.

But I couldn't stop kissing him.

His lips moved down my chin, down my throat, and I was embarrassed when I let out a gasp. Be it pleasure or pain, showing anything so intimate was uncomfortable. Like flipping a prickly creature onto its back and exposing its soft, vulnerable underbelly.

I could feel the tension of resistance as I ran my hands along Rune's muscles, too. As though he was holding himself away from me out of fear. Or barely holding himself back.

I resisted as Rune pressed his chest harder against my hand. "I don't want to hurt you."

"Too late for that," he said.

I pulled farther back, not to get some air, but some sanity. If I could separate from him long enough, then maybe I could see what a terrible thing this was.

He too had drawn back to look at me. The light of the moon through the window covered half his face in shadow. Ink black bled out one eye and down his cheek. The other eye emanated a vibrant crystal blue.

"Rune!"

I squirmed beneath his arms and was on my feet, pulling him up with me until we were face to face, until I blinked and could see that his eyes were gold-red and he was himself, only himself.

"Are you—Are you all right?" I asked.

He looked as though he'd been clubbed in the back of his head. His pupils were blown wide, and it took him a moment to refocus on me.

"I honestly don't know anymore," he said.

I rested a hand on his temple, using my thumb to stroke the skin beneath his eye.

"We can't keep doing this," I murmured.

Rune's lips twisted into a wicked smirk. "You didn't seem too eager for me to stop."

My cheeks heated. "Not *this*. You're pushing yourself too far, and soon you might be too out of reach for anyone to help. Your need for power is going to kill you."

I moved my hand too close to his brow and pricked my finger on his crown. The small pain was a harsh reminder. Rune would never stop. Be it Sotera's crown or someone else's, he would always try to get more until he was dead or until he was beaten.

That left me with only one option.

He watched me as I continued stroking his temple. Then he tilted his head to the window. "Pitius."

"My Lord Rune." Pitius's whispery voice was barely louder than the wind. "I have news."

I slowly drew my hand away from Rune and straightened my shirt, refusing to act as though we'd been doing something illicit. "Sotera?"

"She and a large contingent of soldiers are assembled north of Seattle," Pitius confirmed. "I think she means to attack. Soon."

"Then we'll meet her there," Rune said.

CHAPTER
THIRTY-ONE

The air felt charged as I stepped out of the path Rune summoned and onto the cracked asphalt of the human world. My every nerve buzzed with anxiety. Either Sotera would fall here or Seattle would, and from there, the Wilds.

Rune waited until the few wildlings he'd chosen to come with us had finished crossing before closing the path. "Summon the beasts," he told Raquel. "Have them seek out Sotera and relay her position to General Forcheck."

Raquel made a face at our greenery-deprived surroundings. "I'm not sure how many I'll be able to conjure here, but I'll do my best."

"You will," Rune agreed. "Or we're all dead."

"No pressure or anything," Marian muttered. I'd been surprised when she'd chosen to come along, and more surprised when Rune allowed it. Then again, we were going after the one who'd killed Olette. Though she claimed to be done with us, Marian hadn't forgone the need for vengeance. That I could understand.

Raquel knelt and raked his fingers through the dirt until a

half-dozen sleek, stoat-like beasts waited expectantly for his command, their eyes dully glowing.

"You are my eyes and ears," Raquel said. "Go."

The beasts slipped into the darkness. After receiving her orders from Rune, Pitius vanished after them.

"Wildlings, on me," Rune said, and his motley force assembled to him.

I matched steps with Rune as we started toward Seattle. Though the Wilds had encroached this close, the trees were smaller and sickly. The only sign of human activity other than unoccupied dwellings was an unmaintained highway and an abandoned rail car that had long been fastened in place by vines and roots.

"You have to wait until the final moment to strike against her," General Forcheck had warned us before we'd left. "Save that strength of yours, my High King. Create paths for us to join you only when you're certain. We are wildlings. We'll be at a disadvantage. Don't spoil the little element of surprise we have."

"Sotera will be ready for us," Marian said. "Pitius is good, but Sotera has to expect we'll try to stop her."

I shared a look with Rune, one that felt far too intimate now. "She likely thinks we're dead."

"Hopefully she'll continue thinking so until it's too late," Rune added.

We had surprise, and we had ferocity. That was the extent of our plan, and what a meager and desperate one it was.

We moved until Pitius returned to us.

"There's a human checkpoint up ahead," she said. She swallowed. "From the looks of things, Sotera has already passed through it."

A terrible dread stole over me.

"Show us," Rune said.

Pitius's warning only barely managed to prepare me for the carnage we found. I knew from the times Joshua actually talked to me about such things that the cement of the checkpoint's thick walls was mixed with heart gems and topped with barbed wire. The combination of magic and a physical barricade had always kept the wildlings out. Sotera had simply busted right through.

Inside the walls, we found border guards skewered with crystal spikes. Some had been ripped entirely in two. An overturned jeep spilled bodies. A few had been stabbed through the back, as though they'd been in the midst of crawling away when Sotera reached them. I hoped somebody had managed to send a warning call, but judging by the viciousness of the aftermath, I guessed not.

"Your stepbrother's not here, is he?" Marian asked.

Some of the bodies were so mangled it would be impossible to tell *who* they were. "I don't think so."

But he could have been. Had things turned out just a little different, any number of these poor people could have been him.

We reached the other side of the checkpoint, where a dirt road transitioned to asphalt and merged with the other end of the highway. Surrounding it was rolling hills of thin, long grasses and a few dead trees.

"Sotera's close," Pitius said. "She stopped her forces on a hill just ahead. I couldn't get a closer look. She has guards everywhere, and even I can't go invisible."

That meant this next part would be up to me.

"I'll find out where she is," I told Rune. "Bring in the other wildlings when you can."

He was in the middle of coaxing a dying snarl of grasses to form a path. A moment later, a dozen wildlings came through. Some had beast blood streaked across their faces, lips stained vivid magenta and coal black; they clutched glass-tipped spears, diamond-edged swords, and poisoned arrows notched on polished bows. Their bark and steel and ice armor glistened like their barred teeth. There was no uniformity, no cohesion.

Only now did I truly understand just what we were up against. Not just Sotera and her crystal army—and Bendeti and his Undersea soldiers if we survived her—but the pickings of what Rune had to work with. Despite all their Lords and Houses and kingdoms, wildlings were capricious by nature, solitary in all the ways that made them terribly suited for any sort of army. Rune had done what none had in a long time and brought together the ones he could—those who believed in a better, more united Wilds.

I was scared it still wouldn't be enough.

"General Forcheck might have overestimated my abilities," Rune growled, as the grass he'd used to summon the path withered to ash. "There's almost nothing here I can work with."

"Go, Val," Marian said. "We'll be ready."

With great reservation, I left them and hunted close by until I found the darkest patch of shadows. "Make me unseen, Erebus."

He growled and frigid cold cloaked me seconds later. Staying out of the light, I moved through what few trees remained. When those disappeared, I slipped between the long grass, the shadow my body had become conforming into every shape it passed.

I found Sotera's army atop a small rise surrounded by collapsed human buildings. I didn't need to see the other side of the hill to know that it overlooked an expansive view of Seattle.

And there, in the perfect spot to watch her destructive spectacle, entirely alone, stood Sotera.

I stayed frozen where I crouched, my heart beating a terrible, frantic tempo.

Her forces were close by, sharpening weapons, casting their spells, shouting to one another as they prepared to swarm down amongst the ignorant and unprotected humans.

And here their leader stood apart, unaware I was here, likely thinking me dead. I could kill her, right now. There'd be no need for Rune to struggle to bring others over and put them in danger. I could finish this in one solid stroke of my sword.

Sweat prickled the back of my neck. "A little farther, Erebus," I whispered.

He growled in warning. *Do you know what you're doing?*

"Move quick," I urged. "Stay away from any enchantments."

We slithered around the outside of their camp, past prepping soldiers and chained crystal beasts. I recognized her general Abaki standing amongst the others. He'd been fitted with etched crystal plating I was sure was magicked against bullets. He glanced my way, and I held my breath until he returned to his tent.

I crept up to Sotera's exposed back. She'd knelt, pressing her palm flat against the ground. Sliver made barely a sound as I drew it.

"You're just in time," Sotera said.

She stood. Beneath her feet, veins of blue magic carved the dirt in a pattern like forking lightning. Its light grew brighter the deeper it went. "I was afraid you'd miss your handiwork."

Only you can create those things, Rune had said. *But could Sotera destroy them?*

She couldn't. She needed me. She'd *always* needed me.

"Know that this is your doing," Sotera said.

I took a step toward her, right as the earth rumbled. I was thrown off my feet, and it took more than a few seconds to steady myself. By the time I did, Sotera was nowhere to be seen. In her place was a scene out of my nightmares.

The center of Seattle was the first to fall, sinking into the abyss like a black hole and dragging its buildings and streets along with it. Skyscrapers collapsed. Entire neighborhoods were swallowed within seconds. The Space Needle listed and then snapped in two before plummeting beneath the cracked earth. I was watching a beast bigger than imagination drag its claws across the northwest's last bastion of humanity.

I might have screamed, but my words were eaten up in the following aftershocks. A plume of concrete dust and earth blotted out the stars as it hurtled toward me, and I was forced to cover my face before its tidal wave hit.

THIRTY-TWO

I tasted dust between my teeth, on my tongue. It was the flavor of oil and metal and a rain-dampened street on a warm night. It carried the footprints of millions who'd walked across it. It was everything I'd just seen swallowed up.

My fingers found the dirt and sank into them. I exerted my will, using the paltry power I'd stolen from Sotera to seek out anything still living in the wreckage of the city below.

Screams filled my head. Anguish seeped into my bones. I got the privilege of watching dozens of vibrant threads of life once interconnected dim, one by one.

I yanked my hand back.

I imagined Gracie settling in for the night. Maybe she'd brewed herself some more tea and sat on her balcony to watch the sunset, turning one of the useless gems Rune had gifted her between her fingers. Gracie, who'd trusted me more than anyone else should have. I imagined she'd heard an ear-splitting crack as the world tore apart. And then nothing.

And Peyton... Oh, gods, Peyton.

I uselessly ripped at the crown on my head until I'd properly shredded my fingers. If Sotera still won, if all the power in the world hadn't stopped her from destroying what she wanted, then what was the point of having this?

I sobbed as I clutched at my chest, my tears cutting tracks down the filth coating my face. The pain was a cresting wave with no end. Dead. So many were dead. All because I hadn't been strong enough, hadn't been quick enough, hadn't been good enough.

Only when I had nothing left to cry did I pick myself up. The air was so thick with dust it resembled the hazy quality of a bad camera filter.

Clutching Sliver tight, I stalked through Sotera's camp. I wanted to sink it into someone. Wanted to see them bleed. My rage was an inferno, fed only by what Sotera had done and what I'd failed to stop.

The camp was empty. Within minutes of her destroying the city, every general, soldier, and beast had vacated. Sotera had prepared for that, too. No doubt they were already moving toward what little remained of Seattle to claim it for themselves.

The dusty air shifted at my back. I whirled and stabbed.

Rune sidestepped, though Sliver still came dangerously close to cutting him open.

"We were too late," he said.

"She killed *everyone*." My voice came out as a sob. "I saw— the entire city—it just—"

Rune pulled me into him. I held him so tightly there was no risk of him vanishing, too. His shirt absorbed my tears as I pressed my face into his chest. In his arms, if only for a moment, I could pretend that everything was all right when it was anything but.

"We'll make her pay," he promised.

I nodded into his chest before pushing off him. This wasn't

the time for comfort. Pain needed to be dealt, punishment handed out.

"The edge of the sinkhole isn't too far," one of the wildlings said. "Little over a mile."

With a flick of his hand, Rune directed Pitius to inform Marian and the others about what had happened so we could coordinate our attacks, and we set off.

My breathing quickened as we approached where the asphalt ended, and the gaping abyss began. The collapse resembled a jagged chunk of flesh ripped from the earth, leaving the outside edges ragged. Tiered levels of destruction —filled with the jutting skeletons of houses and townhomes— sharply declined toward the center. Parked vehicles had been unceremoniously flipped. Their alarms screamed ceaselessly into the void.

One of the wildlings leaned over the edge. "I can see Below!"

Down through the tons of rubble, I too saw what might have been a city far below. It could have been the remnants of Seattle, or perhaps it was the Deep now crushed by the destruction. I already knew Sotera had no qualms about hurting her own people in her quest for victory.

I started to lower myself closer to the center, using a collapsed light pole for balance.

Rune held up a hand. "That's strange. Where are the bodies?"

He was right. Not a dust-caked corpse or mangled figure was anywhere nearby. Perhaps they'd fallen to the bottom or been trapped in the buildings-turned-tombs.

Something else was bothering me, too. I knelt, craning my neck to listen.

"What's that sound?"

Over the car alarms, trickle of water from broken pipes,

and falling rock, a roaring bounced off the walls, growing ferociously in volume every second. Terror seized me as I realized what it was.

"Everybody get to higher ground!" We moved as one, leaping atop the tilted roof of what had once been a gas station, right as a gush of water punched through rubble across from us. More water streamed over the edge until there were no less than a dozen waterfalls pouring into the sinkhole. A faint mist thickened the air. It smelled of salt.

Rune scowled at them. "You were right, Val. It seems the Undersea scavengers have arrived."

"We need to find Sotera before Bendeti floods everything," I said. It was difficult to imagine even something as vast as the Undersea filling the Below, but Bendeti would sure try. "Sotera and Bendeti may not be allies anymore, but we can't risk her getting away and aligning with him again. We have to kill her now."

Rune examined the chasm and the millions of gallons of water flooding in every second. "What's done is done. Is that your vengeance talking?"

As if he had the right to question my vengeance. As if he didn't fear this very thing happening to the Wilds. "Does it matter?"

Rune looked grim. "I suppose not."

I pointed to a relatively flat spot about a hundred feet below. If I were an Empress seeking to kill all who survived my first attack, that would be where I'd start. "There."

The sea-slicked rocks and sheer steepness made for treacherous going. I tried to avoid looking inside the crushed buildings we passed. I tried to avoid thinking about how I had a hand in all this.

I lowered myself and caught a blue glimmer among the

cement gray and earthen brown. I kept Sliver at the ready and warily approached.

It was one of Sotera's soldiers, slumped against a wall and very much dead. Judging by the enormous gash sliced from the crystal flesh at the top of his hip, across his midsection, and through his shoulder, it was easy to tell what killed him.

"He must have run into a soldier of the Undersea," Rune said. "Perhaps Bendeti was more prepared to swoop in and claim his prize than we thought."

I knelt beside the body. I dabbed my fingers into the silty black water oozing down his crystal plating and touched them to the tip of my tongue before spitting.

"I don't taste salt, and Bendeti always leaves some trace of it with his attacks. This wasn't him. Maybe there are still humans alive."

Rune looked suspiciously at the body's injuries. "Capable of doing that?"

He had a point. It was unlikely. Unless Joshua had been producing more of his new weapons than we were aware of and those had somehow found their way into the hands of DFA soldiers who just so happened to escape the collapse.

"We found more like that dead one up above," Marian said.

She awkwardly dropped from a nearby ledge, escorted by no fewer than a dozen of Rune's soldiers. "At least six of Sotera's. Somebody's been busy."

Six dead? Even if Sotera hadn't expected any resistance, it would take more than a surprise attack to down that many.

"There's something not quite right," Rune said, voicing my thoughts aloud. "Keep everyone close."

"The sea, Rune," Marian said. "It won't be long before Bendeti calls another wave."

"Then we'd better hurry."

As we moved, slabs of rock groaned as they shifted below us. Enormous shards of crystal had punctured the concrete and spewed every direction. I knew of only one person with the kind of power to pull off an attack of that magnitude, and they were close.

Trusting that the others were right behind, I vaulted down, skidded around clumps of rubble, and landed hard enough to jar my knees atop the flat section of earth we'd seen from above.

Crystal covered everything like a second skin, transforming my surroundings into a wonderland of shimmering, reflective blue. Human soldiers in full tactical gear had been skewered on bundles of spikes. But for every one of their dead, one of Sotera's was dead, too. Shattered crystal bone and spilled red blood mixed. This hadn't been a battle so much as a massacre.

And in the center of it all was Father Dumas.

On one hand, the leader of the worshippers of the Mother Tree wore a metallic glove encircled by a dim light; in the other, he clasped a sword not unlike the kind I'd seen in Rylan's workshop, also glowing with magic. This he'd embedded into Sotera's stomach, and in a single fluid motion withdrew it.

Sotera wobbled in place before she collapsed. Her lifeless eyes stared at the destruction she'd caused, at the grave she'd dug for herself.

"So it is done at last," Father Dumas said.

THIRTY-THREE

"I have to admit, my dear, you got a lot more involved than we ever anticipated."

Father Dumas wiped the blade on the thigh of his pants, smearing a mixture of black and red. He was dressed in military attire and a bulletproof vest, instead of his priestly cloth cap and coat. "When we uncovered what you were all those years ago, I knew you'd be the key, but you've insisted on continuing to play a part long after your contribution was over."

I couldn't stop staring at Sotera, trying to make sense of everything.

Rune raised a hand, primed to direct his wildlings. "Is this someone you know, Val?"

Translation: was this an enemy, and should we kill them?

A long-forgotten memory bubbled to the surface: Sotera had wanted us to kill a human priest. At the time, I'd thought it was their zealot beliefs that made her fear they'd become a larger problem. Never had I imagined the worshippers of the

Mother Tree and their leader had been a very real, very tangible threat to her rule.

"Val?" Rune said sharply. "Who is he to you?"

Memories were reconstructing themselves like the video of a shattering glass played backwards. I was a child and Father Dumas was carving open my arm to reveal the crystal bone beneath.

I was a preteen, and Father Dumas was visiting more often, whispering fervently to Peyton about me whenever they thought I wasn't listening.

I was with Peyton as she dragged my paralyzed body through the Wilds, pleading for me to forgive her for all the lies.

"You've been watching me my entire life," I said to Father Dumas. "You needed me to open up the Below. But why? Why would you want to free Sotera just to kill her?"

"She played her part," Father Dumas said. "Once that was done, she was no longer needed."

Just like you, his words implied. *A disposable pawn.*

"It's funny," Father Dumas said. "Though he disdained Peyton's involvement with us, Joshua saw the plan from the very beginning. He knew the scope."

"What *plan*?" I nearly shouted. "What the hell have you been up to?"

Father Dumas approached the edge of the sinkhole. A sour draft from below rustled the whiskers of his beard. "You didn't really listen to your High King when he spoke about wildling legends, did you? Even in the age of impossibilities, humans, and those raised by humans, strive to explain with the rational before believing in the divine." His eyes turned hungrily on me. "But you've seen it, haven't you? You've felt it Below."

Rune flicked his hand. The other wildlings took up positions around Father Dumas, some aiming arrows at his heart.

Father Dumas didn't look the least bit concerned, and that frightened me. Either he had another plan or he didn't fear death.

"How many times did you hear it while you were Below?" Father Dumas went on. "Did she let you see it? Even before asking for my death, I believe she suspected I had some involvement."

I was tired of these mind games. "I have no idea what you're talking about."

"The tremors, child. Did you feel the tremors? Did you feel the beast of the Below?"

How could I forget? The tremors had plagued the Below since Sotera had taken me there. They'd terrified her, and in the brief snippets of private conversations I'd overheard between her and Bendeti, they'd scared him, too.

"Your part heralded it," Father Dumas said. "Sotera never wanted to take the Wilds just to control it. She wanted to use the Wilds to keep it trapped."

I remembered the palace walls shaking. Those Below screaming. The stricken look on Sotera's face. In a few short words, Father Dumas had reframed my memories; Sotera, not as someone trying to conquer, but as someone trying to escape.

"To keep *what* trapped?" Marian said.

A wildling suddenly pitched from their perch, dead before they hit the ground. The sound of a gunshot followed a half second later, and then everyone was scrambling for cover as more bullets shattered crystal and ricocheted off concrete.

A squad of soldiers wove through the debris at Father Dumas's back. They matched our number, but without the help of the Wilds, we would be at a disadvantage.

"No, don't attack him!" I yelled as another wildling leapt at

Father Dumas. Stupid, stupid, stupid, as though they could finish what Sotera couldn't.

Faster than I expected, Father Dumas countered their strike, driving his blade into the wildling's gut. Their entire body leeched of color as the blade killed their magic.

"Everybody hold!" Rune snarled as Father Dumas flung the wildling off the edge. With another snarl, Rune summoned exposed tree roots to cover us from the soldiers. It would buy us time, but not much.

"I offer you a truce, High King of the Wilds," Father Dumas called. "In a gesture of my goodwill, I've killed the Empress, your greatest enemy. All that's left to contend with is the King of the Undersea, but the Wilds have held up against him this long. Even if he floods your ground and salts your roots, even if he turns your water brackish and sends his serpents to snap up your subjects, I know you'll prevail."

"Pretty words and promises have never worked on me," Rune said. "Now, if you threw yourself off this cliff, that might make me happy."

Father Dumas gave a booming laugh. "How callous. Let's have no more petty fighting between the wildlings and what remains of the humans. You keep to your Wilds, and we'll try to rebuild our world."

Rune's expression smoothed to cruel indifference. "Yes, I'll stay respectfully out of your business, all while you wait for whatever you've done to reach its end. I'll give you some advice others failed to learn: you're no idiot, so don't treat me like one."

Rune walked to the edge of the sinkhole and peered down. "Just what have you freed?"

"A new beginning and a clean slate," Father Dumas said. "The destruction of it will set this world right, once and for all."

"A rebirth and new beginning," Rune muttered. His scowl deepened. "When the wildlings were first created, the Mother Tree's leaves became the clouds and the sky. The sap dripping from where Grislehaut, the god of destruction, chewed became the oceans and the forest.

"What little about our legends I was taught told me that destruction was a part of life. But if left unchecked, even that which brings life will be our ruination."

Father Dumas was smirking, as though Rune finally understood some grand joke. My mind reeled. Rune couldn't honestly believe that Father Dumas had freed an *actual* god.

Yet I'd considered so many things impossible once. And bit by bit, the impossible had chipped away at my reality until nothing but skeptical acceptance remained.

Marian had gone startlingly pale. "Grislehaut isn't... He can't be..."

"As real as the wildlings?" Father Dumas said. "As real as Those Below? As your Mother Mal, woven from the thread of legend?"

"It doesn't matter what you've done," Rune said. "You weren't there for my coronation speech, but I'll give you a taste: With my reign, Grislehaut's destruction will be halted. We wildlings, like you humans, enjoy our metaphors and gaudy wordplay. I never expected for my promise to be taken literally, but you've proven me wrong."

Father Dumas approached the wall of roots separating us. With a single slice of his blade, they withered into ash, leaving only a dead black spot in their place. "I won't wax and wane about histories and rights and wrongs. This," he pointed at the chasm, "is as much your doing as it is mine. But humanity will endure. And from it we'll have a new age."

The soldiers had arrived, forming a line behind him.

"Take my truce, High King," Father Dumas said. "You want what I have to offer, for what little it'll do you in the end."

We couldn't let Father Dumas leave. I didn't know the full extent of what he'd done yet, or how much of this he'd orchestrated, but if he'd managed to subvert Sotera's conquest and free a supposed god, all while operating from the shadows, then who knew what he'd be capable of if he didn't have to hide anymore.

"I accept your truce," Rune said. He gave an insouciant smile. "I didn't become High King by playing fair or engaging in battles I wasn't sure I could win. I'm underhanded and a coward."

"I had you measured perfectly, then." Father Dumas turned to go, gesturing for the soldiers to fall in line behind him.

"You're forgetting something," Rune said. "I'm not the only one who has to accept your truce."

At Father Dumas's confused frown, Rune nodded to me. "You forgot to ask her. See if *she'll* let you leave here alive."

Father Dumas's eyes flicked to the circlet on my brow. He seemed to realize what Rune meant the same moment I did. Sotera was dead. Her block on the crown's power was gone.

Father Dumas's soldiers brought their guns back up as I dropped to the ground and reached for the power of the Below. It was clunky and unwieldy, but all the same, the crystal surrounding us melted like liquid gold, covering the nearest soldier. I hardened it, and his screaming cut off.

The soldier closest to Father Dumas yanked him to safety. The rest were spreading out, firing in bursts to keep the wildlings from pursuing. Again and again, I summoned more crystal—even as my strength rapidly drained—to create protective barriers as best I could. I wouldn't be able to keep this up forever, but while I had the advantage, I needed to use it.

I slid into cover and sank my fingers into the dirt to discern where some of the soldiers were hiding. I twisted my hand and was rewarded by more cries of pain. It didn't matter that they were human, the very beings I wanted to avenge.

They were protecting Father Dumas, and I would tear through anyone to get to him.

"We got this," Marian said. She hurled ice at some of the nearest soldiers, forcing them to duck. "You going to stand there or go after that guy?"

I gripped Sliver tighter and hastened up one of the remaining shafts of crystal to leap to the other side of the barricade I'd created. Rune landed silently beside me. He pointed his glass knife at a swiftly retreating Father Dumas. *"You will stop,"* he said, voice dripping with compulsion.

Father Dumas didn't so much as stagger.

"His weapon is probably blocking your magic entirely," I said.

"If I ever see your human smith again, I'll kill him," Rune said.

I believed him.

We pursued Father Dumas and his remaining pair of soldiers through the wreckage of what used to be streets, quickly catching up with them.

"Stop," Rune commanded the soldiers, and they dropped their weapons, arms falling slack at their sides. "Now..." Rune pointed at Father Dumas, *"Kill—"*

Father Dumas brought his blade around in a flash of silver. The soldiers' heads were cast off the edge, followed moments later by their crumpled bodies.

"I'd heard you had a serpent's tongue, but it's stronger than I realized," Father Dumas said. "I might have to cut it out."

He scooped up one of the dropped guns. I leapt behind a

wall of earth Rune conjured moments before bullets peppered the other side. Father Dumas fired until the gun clicked empty.

"Go," I said to Rune.

We split, both of us converging on Father Dumas.

Too late, I saw the triumphant gleam in his eye as he swung. His blade easily broke Rune's dagger. The heart gem he wore dispelled the magic Rune conjured to defend himself, and with another swing, Father Dumas sank his sword deep into Rune's shoulder.

I barreled into Father Dumas's other side, just missing sliding Sliver between his ribs. He grunted and shifted his weight to bring his armored fist down. My vambrace-covered arm took the worst of the blow, and the pain of a hundred searing cuts radiated through my body as my forearm shattered.

I screamed, and Father Dumas used my staggered momentum to hurl me away. I barely had time to grab a crystal handhold I'd summoned to stop myself from plunging over the edge.

Father Dumas appeared over me, Rune's blood still coating his blade.

"My dear, soon even your magic will be useless against us. But I want you to see. I want you to be there for Grislehaut's rise. Both of you."

Rune had staggered to his feet, but Father Dumas knocked him down again. He cast us a final triumphant look before vanishing amongst the rubble.

I tried to stop my body from swaying as my muscles started to give out. My broken arm hung uselessly at my side. The yawning chasm beneath me beckoned, taunting.

Fall to me, I imagined the beast whispering below. *Fall to me, and I'll be your blissful end.*

My grip failed. I started falling.

Rune caught my wrist. His hand and arm were slick with blood, but he managed to pull me up until I collapsed atop his chest, broken and bleeding.

"I'm such an idiot," I whispered. "I should have known. He was there, from the very beginning. He's *always* been there."

"I didn't realize clairvoyance was part of your skillset." Rune grimaced as he sat up. He used small threads of grass to weave his bleeding wound shut. "I'll live," he said to my concerned look.

Wincing, I wrapped my fingers around my broken forearm and urged it to mend. It felt like filling the cracks of my bone with melted metal, and more than once I let out a pathetic whimper. After a few moments of agony, there was euphoric relief.

"We're out of time," Rune said.

Distant figures were gathering atop the closest waterfall. Some clutched tridents while others were coated in lobster-shell armor. The Undersea had come. I had no doubt Bendeti would relish the chance to catch us weakened.

I stood and offered Rune my hand. "We have to go."

He glared at the soldiers of the Undersea assembling above and then down into the sinkhole. Fury and helplessness raged across his face. At last, he allowed me to help him up. As we limped away, broken, bloody, beaten, the earth rumbled. It sounded like it was laughing.

It sounded like a god awakening.

THIRTY-FOUR

The narrowed streets of the Deep were eerily silent.

With so many of Those Below turning out—young, old, sickly, and healthy alike—there should have been some noise. Murmured disapproval. Disgruntled jeering. If I was feeling particularly hopeful, I could have wished for gasps of awe.

I mostly expected hisses and curses at us, the ones who had killed their beloved Empress and now moved unchallenged toward the palace.

No one made a sound. Fear, it seemed, was as powerful a deterrent as ever.

"Escaping as a prisoner." Rune's mouth twisted in a wry grin. "Returning as a conqueror."

And feeling just as out of place, I wanted to say. I couldn't get my mouth to work. I was sick with the thought of what I still needed to do. In moments, Rune's playful smirk would shift, and I had no doubt he'd treat me as maliciously as his enemies. And I would deserve every bit of his animosity.

A loud snort, and the beast Raquel had summoned for

Marian to ride pulled up beside us. She yanked on its reins and jabbed her cane at the surrounding crowd.

"Back up!" she snarled.

Two of Those Below who'd inched closer to me shrank back. One eyed Sotera's sword I'd strapped to my side; the other whimpered. With a full procession of wildlings at our back, I couldn't imagine they were trying to attack us. In their scared faces, I saw hope: the same hope they'd always had in me, their cherished, even when I'd been Sotera's prisoner.

"It's okay if they follow," I said to Marian.

"I'd rather you two not get stabbed moments after you've won," she said. "They should stay here."

"They need to know. Better they see it firsthand. It'll make things easier."

For them, at least.

With great reluctance, Marian returned to her place behind us. As we passed, Those Below lining the street trickled after and our procession grew. By the time we crossed the final bridge and approached the front of the palace, it had swelled to such an immense size that I wondered if we hadn't emptied the entirety of the Deep.

One of Sotera's generals—Gebre, if I remembered correctly—stood firmly in front of the gate with a dozen guards at his back. He was one of the younger generals, his joints not yet stiffened with a crystal crust. A number of earth-wyrm fangs hung on a silver chain around his neck, and the armor plating of his shoulders were laughably large, rising almost to his ears. He looked like a child who'd dressed in his father's equipment to play fight.

But when he drew his sword, it was as wicked looking as any I'd ever seen. "That's far enough."

"You must not have learned to count," Rune said. "You're greatly outnumbered."

He raised a hand, and I heard the strain of a dozen bows being drawn behind me. The first volley might only wound them. The second would certainly finish the job.

Gebre's hand tightened on his hilt.

"Sir?" one of his guards asked, voice trembling. "Y-your orders?"

If I had any doubt that waltzing into the Below and securing Sotera's throne would be an easy affair, Gebre's resistance proved it. His Empress might be dead, his soldier's loyalty wavering, but I had no doubt that if he had his way, he would fight until he and everyone who followed him fell.

By the time this was done, there might not be any of Those Below left to lead.

Jaw tight, Gebre stepped aside. But as Rune moved past, he lunged. "For the Empress!"

I drew Sotera's sword without thinking. It met brief resistance, followed by a scream. Gebre's arm went flying. He stumbled back, howling in pain, and the wildlings closed in on him.

"Stop!" Rune said. "Let him live. Let everyone see the price for standing against me."

Gebre, panting, pulled himself up, trying to staunch the heavy bleeding. He shoved through his guards, leaving a trail of silty black blood in his wake. "Out of my way!"

"He may become a problem, my High King," General Forcheck said.

"One I'll remedy later," Rune said. "We have more important things to do."

In moments, the throne room was packed with bodies and murmuring voices. General Forcheck, Marian, Cassius, and several other wildlings took positions around the perimeter of the room. I had no doubt Gebre wouldn't be the only one trying to stop us. There would be trouble.

I shifted uneasily. My calves were damp with seawater. The

palace slowly filled with the smell of salt. While crossing the bridge, I'd noticed the crystal fields below had already started to resemble the tide pools along Bendeti's shore.

Sotera's remaining generals watched us sullenly. Abaki was missing, no doubt killed in the ensuing fight with Father Dumas, or he'd fled once his Empress had fallen. Tenia glared at me, hand firmly grasping the metal cudgel at her waist. She looked as though she blamed me entirely for her Empress's death.

"It's over, Val," Rune said, noticing my hand shaking where I rested it on Sotera's sword. "There's no need to worry. In moments, I'll take Sotera's throne, and you'll be free of that crown."

I was nervous, but not for the reasons he thought. "You believe that will work?"

"Of course."

"You there, priest," General Forcheck called into the crowd. "Do you know how to perform a coronation?"

One of Sotera's priests, a sickly thin man scabbed with sunstone, half his jaw frozen in crystal, hobbled forward. "I-I do. However…" His eyes flickered between Rune's brow and then mine. "One of you already has a crown forged of the Below."

"And we wish to transfer that to me," Rune said.

The priest performed a scraping bow. "With all respect, High King Rune…you already have a throne. This… There is no precedent for this. The throne may not accept you. What I mean is, you may die."

"Only if there is any justice in the world," I heard Tenia hiss.

"It will accept me," Rune said. "But let's make a spectacle of it. Preferably before we all have to swim out of here."

In two long strides, Rune ascended the dais. I followed,

positioning myself just behind him as he turned around to those assembled.

"Your Empress is dead," he said. "The Below is mine. Be assured that I am not so cruel as Sotera no doubt made me out to be. We have a common enemy, one who at this very moment seeks to kill you all."

If he was trying to be reassuring, I wasn't sure he was succeeding. But Rune had never been about coddling or pleasant, false promises. What we needed now was action, and one strong enough to carry it out.

My heart pounded so loud I was sure Rune could hear it.

Your heart is more like a beast's, warning others away.

If only it could warn him now. I wanted him to stop me. Whatever choice I was about to make, it was going to be a terrible one.

"Priest," Rune said, motioning for the sickly man to approach.

As the priest hobbled up to the dais, I slid behind Rune. Sotera's throne was deceptively smooth, with bits of glimmering sunstone, obsidian, jewels, and gold frozen within. There were none, but I imagined the seat and arms adorned with spikes, ready to shoot into anyone who dared try to take its former Empress's place.

A zing of power shot through me as I rested a hand on one of the throne's arms. The priest was gaping in my direction, and Rune followed his gaze. He gave me a confused frown.

"What are you doing?"

"What I have to," I said.

I stood just above the seat, feeling the power compel and rebel against me in equal measure. I was on the precipice, ready to plunge in.

Since I'd settled on taking Sotera's throne for myself, I'd gone over how this scene might play out a dozen times. I imagined Rune furiously demanding I back down. I imagined him callously calling me out for my weakness, pitching to all how useless I would be should I take his place.

I wasn't prepared for how hurt he looked, as though he'd have preferred I literally stab him in the back.

"I need to take the throne," I said, throat tight.

"You don't know what you're asking," Rune said.

I know what I have to do.

I have no idea what I'm doing.

I gestured to the cold seat. "Sotera tried to kill you once. This throne might do the same. I can't—I won't—risk you almost dying again."

"You said that you would let me—"

"'I will let you take all the power you can.' That's what I said. And you already have. Any more, and you'll die."

Rune swelled with anger. "I'm to be the ruler of both the above and Below. Without doing that, there cannot be peace. I am supposed to unite the thrones—"

"*We* will unite them," I said. "As allies. That's what Mother Mal meant."

All her insinuations about me taking Sotera's throne had clicked into place after I'd made my choice. For someone who often claimed they didn't interfere, she sure liked giving me plenty of hints.

"And you didn't think to tell me this before, when we were *alone?*" Rune snarled. "When the entire Below wasn't watching you usurp me?"

"I can't usurp what you never had. And I wasn't sure then."

"And you're sure now," he said, sneering.

I couldn't erase the image of Rune dying with Sotera's false crown fastened to his head. The same crown that sat on my brow, the same crown I *had* survived. I didn't want to be here, in the place of my imprisonment, any longer. Every second felt like the walls were closing in, like the floor was collapsing beneath my feet. To be trapped down here as its Empress was akin to a personally crafted hell.

"Yes," I said firmly. "I'm sure."

"*Val*," Rune said, voice thick with magic. "*You don't want this throne—*"

I shook my head, and his compulsion fell away like cobwebs. "Don't you *dare*."

Our audience was beginning to whisper. Tenia watched me shrewdly, perhaps thinking that our distraction was the chance she'd been waiting for. Marian gave me a startled look, her lips a thin line, no doubt wondering just what the heck we were doing.

Rune reached out, trying to pull me to him, but I stepped away, until the backs of my knees were pressed against the edge of the throne. I couldn't bear to be any closer to him, or else all my grand plans might crumble to dust.

Rune's expression was icy. "As you say, if you take this, we will not be enemies, but allies. I am not always kind to my allies."

"You could make an exception for me," I said.

"I could."

But he wouldn't. He hadn't assured his and the wildlings' survival by playing favorites and making exceptions.

"I know what it means," I said. "Maybe you won't have to worry. If the throne's power takes me over, I want you to kill me."

Then, before I could double-guess my choice any longer, I lowered myself into the throne.

Sotera's priest began intoning the words of my ascension, but I didn't hear a single thing. The moment my butt hit the throne, invisible spikes stabbed into my arms, legs, back, and neck. I couldn't move. I couldn't even scream.

The throne room vanished as my vision darkened. I was aware of every prickle of pain in my body as it all funneled into a single point before shooting out in all directions. I was the earth and the Below. I was every rock and crystal, every creature. The threads of light connecting everything overwhelmed me with its brilliance, as, for a hair's length of time, I could feel it in its entirety, the monstrous weight of eons crushing me.

Something alive coiled within. From it radiated black and red veins of hatred. Hatred toward me, Those Below, wildlings, all of life itself. It picked no sides. It simply wanted everything gone.

Grislehaut, my mind supplied, and the threads of light vibrated in agreement.

I drew closer to him. His power was of the beginning of time, a primal force of nature that even I, with the power of the Below, had no chance of quelling. Now I understood why Sotera had been so desperate to escape. Now I knew what Father Dumas had awakened.

Go back to sleep, I urged. *This isn't your world.*

But it will be, Grislehaut answered.

I tried to close him off from the rest of the Below, but it was like trying to shut a door against a tidal wave, and I was hurtled back into my body.

I slumped back into the throne and then tilted forward and collapsed face first onto the stone. Cassius cried out. I heard shuffling feet and the grinding steel and crystal of weapons being drawn. General Forcheck barked orders for the wildlings to close rank.

"E-Empress?" the priest warbled. "Are you all right?"

Empress, I thought sluggishly. *He means me. Get up. I have to get up before things get any worse.*

But my body was slow to listen, and I could only lethargically push myself to my knees.

Then I smelled thunderclouds before a rain and the faint trace of something like bitter herbs.

"Have you regretted your choice yet?" Rune whispered.

I hadn't, but that was likely because my mind was still reeling and I couldn't fully appreciate the damage of what I'd done.

I waited for him to continue berating my stupidity. Instead, he grabbed my arm to help me to my feet.

"No, let me go," I hissed. "You can't help. I can't show weakness."

Rune released me as though I'd burned him. When I looked up, his face had hardened into a cool, cruel mask. The same one I'd first known him to wear when we were still enemies.

"As you wish, *Empress*," he said.

Muscles twinging as though spikes were still being driven into them, I stood. The sea of expressions that met me ranged from awe to enraged. A strange lightness circled my brow. I reached up to adjust the crown that had finally relinquished its grip. I didn't dare remove it.

"Say something," Rune said.

My tongue remained stuck to the roof of my mouth. In all my imaginings, the only thing I *hadn't* imagined was what I'd do if this actually worked.

General Forcheck sank to one knee, bones popping. "Behold, the King of Thorns, behold the Empress of Glass. May there be peace between our kingdoms. Long may they reign."

The other wildlings sank into a bow immediately, cloaks, feathers, and foliage rustling. Like the grating of unoiled machinery, Those Below eventually mimicked them. The last to bow were Sotera's generals. *My* generals now. There was no disguising the hatred in their eyes. Whatever the heights of my newly acquired status, to them it was merely temporary.

"Yes, long may we reign," Rune said.

Black blood dripped from one of his eyes, his other a vibrant glowing blue. Fury radiated off every inch of him.

"Give a command," Rune said, and it was just him again. "You're so good at giving them to me, so it shouldn't be a problem."

After everything that had happened, the strangest part of all was that he was right; I did have a plan. I held a hand beneath a thin trickle of saltwater squeezing through the cracks in the ceiling.

"If Bendeti keeps this up, even the palace will be submerged in a couple days," I said, trying to keep my voice from shaking. I nodded at General Tenia. She looked the most likely to kill me at the first given chance. Best to keep her busy and far away. "Do you have anywhere safe above the rising tide?"

"Since we find ourselves at a truce, then I'm sure the Wilds would be more than accommodating," she said, voice dripping with disdain.

"There are details that need to be discussed first," Rune said. "Until then, you'll all remain Below."

"If that's the case, then we have chambers higher up," General Tenia said. "They're not fit for any long-term living, but Bendeti will have to let up eventually, lest he wants to drain his entire kingdom."

"Start moving everyone there, then," I said. To the next general, or maybe an advisor, one surprisingly young with an arm already rigidly frozen at his side. "You..."

"Estmar, Empress."

"Estmar. I want to know what else Sotera was working on. I'm sure she had other plans in motion."

"I don't think it's best..." He reconsidered, giving another stiff bow. "As the new Empress wills it. I will draw together everything we have to present to you."

"And I'll help," General Forcheck said. She gave a toothy grin. "Just to make sure you don't *accidentally* lose anything."

Estmar looked at me, as though to see if that were my order, and I realized this, like a hundred other choices, from the largest to the smallest, would be mine to make. The thought was enough to shrivel my stomach. "She'll assist you. I also want to see Grislehaut. I know there was a place Sotera sent her guards to check on him."

General Tenia gave a barking laugh. "If you're so eager to meet death, Empress-Slayer, I will gladly show you where to go."

"Stand down," General Forcheck barked as a number of wildlings surrounded her. Rune wore a smile that told me he wanted nothing more than to drive a blade through her throat.

"Let's do it," I said, before wincing at how un-ruler-like that sounded. "All of you are dismissed."

As the audience slowly dispersed to their various tasks, I turned back to the throne, still grappling with what had happened. I could feel people staring, friend and foe alike, their eyes like knives in my back.

"Congratulations," Rune said. "You got the power you so desperately crave. Now that we're allies, we have much to discuss."

I gave a shallow nod, my insides twisted into knots. Why did his words feel so much like a threat?

And then he leaned in, as though to share a secret, and I understood it was because they were. "You're going to regret what you've done," he whispered.

He straightened, giving a playful smile with all teeth, and I couldn't help seeing the wrongness in his eyes again, one bleeding black, one glowing blue.

"Long live Val," he said. "Long live the Empress of Glass."

After the Fall

The sky threatened rain as Erebus's shadow peeled off me, leaving me sequestered alongside one of the few city streets in south Seattle that had survived Sotera's attack. It felt strange to be here, in this perfect snow globe of untouched apartments, office complexes, and a plumbing supply store, when just one street over the entire world had fallen into the abyss.

"Let me know if we're being watched, please," I told Erebus.

He bled into the shadows. To ease my nerves, I fidgeted with Sotera's crown—*my* crown—in my hoodie pocket, pricking my finger every so often on the thorns. Despite taking Sotera's throne and the connection to whatever power she had, the Below's magic was a fickle thing. It didn't always come when called, and here, in what remained of the human world, I was and would always be weaker than I'd like. Wearing it would only draw unwanted attention.

Erebus returned and, with an encouraging growl, settled on my shoulder like a sheet of diaphanous silk. Satisfied, I crossed the street and entered the Thai restaurant. I'd gone here once on my tenth birthday, or at least the anniversary of the day Peyton found me.

The smell of sizzling food and spice mingled in air stifled with warm breath. The place was packed with many who had no home to return to. Still, a small table in the back had a surprising amount of space around it.

I approached and stopped, mouth falling open.

"You were banished," was all I could think to say.

Xander—his gold-red eyes and wildling aura both glamoured—gave me a weak grin. He looked every bit a human, except for the crisscrossed scars across his cheek that he either couldn't, or wouldn't, cover. He fidgeted with a pair of chopsticks, twirling them clumsily between his fingers. "Good to see you, too, Val. These aren't technically Rune's Wilds, so I figured I was safe."

"I'm glad to see you," I said. "Really. It's just…"

"I won't be staying long," Xander promised. "Despite what Rune and everyone thinks of me, despite what I've done, I still wanted to come, to give you a warning."

The second surprise of the day came when I looked at who he sat across from. I'd expected to see Peyton—the shock of her contacting me, alive and well, to meet still hadn't worn off— but the woman giving Xander an untrusting look put me on edge.

"Leah," I said. "You're one of Joshua's soldiers."

She seemed offended that I would dare know her name. "And you're his sister. Shame we didn't get better acquainted, but last we met, you were scampering away with that coward High King, tail between your legs."

"Technically, I'm his stepsister," I said, sidestepping that last comment.

"Not the way Joshua described it."

I should have been comforted by the fact that, despite everything, Joshua spoke about me with such familiarity. All I felt was more confused.

"If this is a trap, I want you to know I won't be coming quietly," I said.

"It's not, Val," Peyton said hurriedly.

After a pause, Leah tightly nodded. I took some solace that she didn't carry any obvious weapons, nor body armor. If she meant to take me in, going so lightly equipped against someone who'd proven dangerous was a serious gambit. A blanket covered the tops of her legs. Behind her was a parked wheelchair.

One of mine, she'll never walk again, Joshua had said. *And each time I visit her, I have to look her in the eye and know that.*

I took a seat beside Xander and cautiously returned Peyton's smile. Her fingers, including the remaining stump of the one Sotera had cut off, twitched. I suspected she wanted to clasp my hands, to pinch my arms to see if I was eating well, to check if I was hurt, if I was still *me.*

I drew my hands back. "Thanks for meeting me. And for not laying a trap. But where's Joshua?"

"I was hoping you knew," Leah said tightly.

I startled, drew back. "Why would I know?"

"Because according to other accounts, he vanished not long after you met with him and Sotera. Your tip about what she was up to…" Leah gave an acknowledging grunt. "Saved thousands, tens of thousands, of lives. Well, you and another. The leader of the Mysts."

"*Keen* talked to you?" I said in disbelief.

"He brought Joshua and a contingent of soldiers to where the columns were and showed him what Sotera was going to do. Along with what you told him, it was enough. We had contingency plans for if we ever needed to evacuate Seattle, but even still, we didn't get everyone out. Some refused to leave. But it did something.

"But after Joshua gave the order to evacuate, he said he had something he had to do. It wasn't orders. I think it was off the books, but he came to tell me before he left. He…"

Leah scrunched the blanket covering her legs. "I begged him to wait, but I couldn't help him, not like I used to. He left, and he hasn't been seen since. He hasn't even reached out to me, even outside of military channels. He would have if he was all right, because I…"

Because you're important to him, I thought. *Because you care about each other more than you could bear to say.*

I wanted to tell her that she *had* to bear it, that when Joshua came back she had to confess it, before it was too late. Maybe I was only talking to myself.

"Maybe he had other orders you weren't aware of," I said. "I get the feeling the Department of Fringe Affairs and the worshippers of the Mother Tree were far more connected than we thought."

"I want you to know, Val," Peyton said tentatively. "I've cut off contact with them and Father Dumas."

"Why not before, after what they did to me?"

The last few nights, my dreams had been a slideshow of long-buried memories, as though taking Sotera's throne had shaken something loose from the back of my mind. One memory in particular stood out: Father Dumas laying my drugged body on a plastic sheet near the Wilds. Of him cutting my arm open down to my crystal bone.

"Why did it take until Father Dumas revealed his grand, cataclysmic plan before you saw them for what they truly were?" I demanded.

"I...don't know how to answer that," Peyton said.

"Forget it. It doesn't matter anymore. Do you know where Father Dumas is now? What he's planning next?"

"I don't. That information wasn't shared with me."

"We're looking for him, too," Leah said. "He may not have been directly responsible, but he's a problem. He's not among the humans fleeing Seattle. Some live here in the south. Some have taken refuge in the Wilds. A lot have, in fact. The city of Spokane is shipping supplies, but there's no telling how long those channels will remain open."

"Rune will protect them, I'm sure," I said.

"Uh-huh. You can promise me that?"

"Unlike what you think, I'm not his master, Leah. The DFA will have to talk to him. But I'll ask."

Leah smirked. "Of course you will. Way I hear it, you two have become quite close."

"Is that a problem?" Xander said, bristling.

"No," Leah said. "I could care less who Val chooses to associate with."

"You shouldn't because we have bigger problems. That's what I came to warn you about. Bendeti's gathering his forces, but the Lords of other Wilds are closing in. They felt the tremors. They may not know the full extent of what happened, but they sense weakness."

"I'm sure my superiors have a way to deal with them and Those Below when the time comes," Leah said. "If Joshua were here... Once he comes back, he'll have a better idea. Until then, that Sotera bitch killed a lot of people. How do we know one of her generals won't try to finish the job?"

"They won't," I said. "They're under control."

"Oh?" Leah cocked an eyebrow. "And you know this how?"

The crown poked into my leg as I shifted. "I just do."

I couldn't tell them what I'd done. Not until it became

impossible to keep it secret. The less of a target I and those around me were, the better.

Xander slid out of his seat and dropped the chopsticks to the table. I stood to hug him. "I'm sorry, really, for what happened," I said.

He gave a sad smile. "It was my choice. Zuri and I are safe, I promise."

"And you'd better stay that way."

I watched him thread through the crowd until he was gone.

"I'm sure we could find the worshippers of the Mother Tree," Peyton said. "I'm sure we could get them to talk, to stop what they're doing."

I was sure that, whatever Father Dumas's plan, stopping wasn't part of it. "We can try. I'll talk with Rune," I told Leah. "See if we can set up a time to meet for an official truce with the DFA. I have a feeling we're both going to need it."

"You can't trust Rune. I'm not being vindictive or petty," Leah said when I frowned. "I know Rune, or at least I know others like him. He won't be content with what he has. Not with these Wilds, not with being allies, not until he has it all. He wants power, that's it. The second things go bad, he'll only look out for himself."

I wanted to disagree. I hated that I couldn't.

"Thanks for the advice," I said. Leah caught my arm as I turned to go.

"I don't care that Joshua loves you," she hissed. "I blame you for whatever happened to him. Even if we have a truce, don't expect us to be friends."

I freed myself from her grasp. "I'm well aware."

"Wait!" Peyton shot out of her seat. "Just...why? Why did you choose them? I know that what I did hurt you and I can never make it up, but this was your home. This is where you belong."

I'd only gone over that question a dozen times, and each answer I came up with felt hollower than the last. The only thing I could think of was, "Sometimes we're meant for something more. *Made* for something more, even if there are parts you don't like about it. People you have to give up. I...love you, Peyton. I don't forgive you, but I'm not your enemy, no matter what you might think."

Tears were streaming down Peyton's cheeks. She rounded the table, arms open wide, and something inside me broke. I sank into her hug. For just a moment, I allowed myself her warm embrace and pretended that everything was all right.

"Don't let them, or anything, destroy you," she whispered.

I nodded into her shoulder before pulling away. "We'll find Joshua," I said. "Trust me."

Leah gave me a begrudging nod of her own before I walked back out into the chilly night. The rain had just started.

I removed the crown from my jacket and turned it over in my hands.

My enemies were closing in, with plans I didn't know. I was a tenuous ruler over a world I'd only wanted to escape from, one that didn't want me. Rune ruled the Wilds—that savage, beautiful place I'd come to love. Rune, who'd made it clear that, after what I'd done, we would be allies, nothing more, and maybe not even that.

Rune, with whom something was terribly wrong.

I placed the crown atop my brow, feeling the thorns gently press against my skin.

Despite everything, I was an Empress. I had the power I always wanted.

I'd never felt so alone.

Scorn their gods. Save the world.
Grab the stunning conclusion to the Savage Wilds series,
Savage Wild Gods.

Get notified about new releases, exclusive ARCs, cover reveals,
giveaways, and more by **joining my author newsletter.**

Please Leave a Review

I can't thank you enough for choosing to read my books! Every single review helps me find new readers and continue doing what I love: writing great stories for you to enjoy. If you get a second, could **you leave a review or star rating?** Thank you so much for your help and support!

Get notified about new releases, exclusive ARCs, cover reveals, giveaways, and more by **joining my author newsletter.**

facebook.com/seannfletcher

bookbub.com/profile/sean-fletcher

amazon.com/author/seanfletcher

instagram.com/seanfletcherauthor

goodreads.com/seanfletcher

x.com/seannfletcher

MORE BOOKS BY SEAN

Savage Wilds Series

Savage Wild Hearts

Savage Wild Souls

Savage Wild Gods

Legacy of Dragon Series

Dragon Born

Dragon Lost

Dragon Unleashed

Dragon Blood

The Heir of Dragons Series:

Dragon's Awakening

Dragon's Curse

Dragon's Bane

Dragon's Fate

Paranormal Outcasts Series:

Elemental Outcast

Elemental Trial

Elemental Queen

The Darkness Within Series:

Called by Darkness

The Cursed One

Enemy of Magic

The Dark Prince

The Mages of New York Trilogy

Mage's Apprentice

Mage's Trial

Mage's End

ACKNOWLEDGMENTS

It takes an author to write a book, but as always it takes a village to make that book readable. For *Savage Wild Souls* I have this village to thank:

To my beta readers, Lana Turner, Marie Reed, Andrea at Hot Tree Editing, and Kristen Frantze.

For talking me through why removing the prologue, as much as I liked it, was the right idea, I can thank Katie Reed.

To James T. Eagan at BookFly designs for the incredible cover.

To Tia Bach for impeccable proofreading.

To my family for making *slightly* less starving artist jokes this time around.

And to my fans, of course, who support me, visit me at festivals and conferences, message me about different books and characters, keep up on my going-ons, and in general give me a target to write for.

About the Author

Sean Fletcher is an award-winning and bestselling fantasy author across multiple age ranges and subgenres, with over thirty books in more than five different series, many of which have hit #1 in their categories. Since writing and pitching his first book at fifteen, he's forged a path through the publishing industry, continuing to hone his craft and expertise at a premier literary agency before becoming a full-time author, speaker, and editor.

When not jotting down highly enjoyable lies, he's often doing something most people find masochistic, like cycling long distances, hiking high mountains, and indulging in more sweets than is medically advisable.

Stalk him on social media or his author newsletter to learn more about his upcoming releases.

Fletcher, Sean
Savage Wild Souls (The Savage Wilds Book 2)
Denton, Texas
1. Young Adult Contemporary/Dark Fantasy

ISBN (hardcover): 978-1-963248-99-9
ISBN (paperback): 9798852163790

First edition published February, 2024